"Wasserman's engrossing second novel is told through the perspective of multiple characters who are all trying to piece together the story of an unknown woman with no idea how she came to lose herself."

—*Bitch Media*

"Wasserman asks big questions about how well we can really know another person, the nature of truth as it relates to memory, and what this all means for how we perceive ourselves. . . . [The novel] ultimately has some great twists and all those questions Wasserman raises make it an excellent book discussion choice."

—*Booklist*

"Shrewd, beguiling . . . This examination of how one man in power can abuse the women closest to him delivers the goods."

—*Publishers Weekly*

"Elizabeth, a forty-eight-year-old widow, is forced to re-examine her marriage when a teenager shows up at her doorstep. The girl is the daughter of 'Wendy Doe,' a woman with a severe form of amnesia whom Elizabeth had studied nearly two decades earlier as a research fellow under a charismatic adviser, her then-married future husband."

—*The Wall Street Journal*

"Ultimately, in addition to the slipperiness of memory and identity, this is a story of love, friendship, and family with an intense beating heart. The way these women find their way back to themselves is through each other."

—*Broad Street Review*

"Wasserman's sophomore novel is a labyrinthine story about memory, truth, and power, told in two timelines."

—BuzzFeed Book Club

"*Mother Daughter Widow Wife* is more than a compelling novel; it's a psychological engagement with the pressing question of what it means to occupy a woman's body in twenty-first-century North America. Wasserman has given us the whole package: a book that makes you both think and feel, with a story driven by the radically mysterious movements of the human heart."

—Lydia Peelle, author of *The Midnight Cool*

"For a novel so steeped in questions of identity, and so engaged in exploring how the roles we inhabit—and are forced to inhabit—inform the construction of self, it's fitting that *Mother Daughter Widow Wife* satisfies on a multitude of seemingly incongruent levels: as riveting page-turner; as psychologically rich and emotionally nuanced portrait of intersecting lives; as intellectually dazzling meditation on memory and trauma. As in the novels of Jennifer Egan, Jonathan Lethem, and Dana Spiotta, these elements are somehow seamlessly fused. I'd venture the reason is Wasserman's prose, which moves at the speed of synapses firing and is spunky and lyrical and beautifully, humanly alive."

—Adam Wilson, author of *Flatscreen*
and *What's Important Is Feeling*

ALSO BY ROBIN WASSERMAN

Girls on Fire

MOTHER DAUGHTER WIDOW WIFE

a Novel

ROBIN WASSERMAN

SCRIBNER

New York London Toronto Sydney New Delhi

Scribner
An Imprint of Simon & Schuster, Inc.
1230 Avenue of the Americas
New York, NY 10020

First Scribner trade paperback edition July 2021

SCRIBNER and design are registered trademarks of The Gale Group, Inc., used under license by Simon & Schuster, Inc., the publisher of this work.

For information about special discounts for bulk purchases, please contact Simon & Schuster Special Sales at 1-866-506-1949 or business@simonandschuster.com.

The Simon & Schuster Speakers Bureau can bring authors to your live event. For more information or to book an event, contact the Simon & Schuster Speakers Bureau at 1-866-248-3049 or visit our website at www.simonspeakers.com.

Interior design by Kyle Kabel

Manufactured in the United States of America

1   3   5   7   9   10   8   6   4   2

Library of Congress Cataloging-in-Publication Data has been applied for.

ISBN 978-1-9821-3949-0
ISBN 978-1-9821-3950-6 (pbk)
ISBN 978-1-9821-3951-3 (ebook)

For Barbara Wasserman

*It was not my body, not a woman's body, it was the body of
us all.
It walked out of the light.*

—Anne Carson, "The Glass Essay"

I

WENDY

This body

This body is white. This body is female. This body bears no recent signs of penetration. This body has never given birth, but may or may not have incubated a fetus. This body offers no means of identification. This body bears the following distinguishing marks: Crescent scar behind left ear. Surgical scar along left calf. Mole on right breast, lower quadrant. No tattoos. Medical history: Healed fracture in each wrist. Three silver fillings. Mild scoliosis. O-positive blood. Cholesterol, average. Blood pressure, average. Nearsighted, mildly.

Emergency room intake records indicate severe dehydration. Bruising to shoulders and back consistent with a fall or a struggle. No physical indication of recent head injury. No evident physiological cause of amnesic state. CAT scan: inconclusive. MRI: inconclusive. Rape kit: inconclusive.

This body is uncoordinated. Its breasts have ghost nipples, pale and undersensitized. Its clitoris is small, but demanding. Its sinuses often hurt. Its eyes sting in the sun. It wants to sleep on its side, wrapped tight around something solid and warm. Its fingers are uncalloused; they do not work for their living. Its nails are ragged, its cuticles bloody. Its teeth are cared for, nutrition maintained. This body is not a temple, but it has been loved. You'd think someone would be looking for it.

LIZZIE

For all the obvious reasons, Lizzie preferred rats. Rats were adaptable and interchangeable, smart and cheap. Rats proffered no opinions, demanded no small talk. You could anesthetize a rat, pierce its skull, lesion its brain. Then euthanize, extract, examine: comprehend. Rats were explicable. This was their whole point. Damage had consequence; behavior had cause. Here was a material link between spirit and flesh. Here, in the humble rat, was obviation of soul and its god. It was, of course, also the case that if your rats inhabited a climate-controlled basement whose climate controls failed, not one of them would think to call 911 before the colony overheated. Rats were replaceable; two years of carefully cultivated genetic lines were not. Lizzie tried not to blame the rats, whose death had nearly capsized the carefully constructed ship of her career—but the rats were not here to defend themselves. It was easy, as she packed for her year in exile, to imagine a rat god visiting hell upon her, not just for the crate of tiny parboiled corpses, but for the indignities she'd visited upon their forefathers, all those rodent generations for whom Lizzie had played both grand inquisitor and executioner. Not that this was hell, she reminded herself. This was Philadelphia.

Lizzie Epstein, home at last. Suburbscape depressingly unchanged: same mediocre Chinese takeout, same ticky-tack split-levels, familiar flutter of rumors regarding a new high-end mall eatery, in this case, the long-awaited Cheesecake Factory. Illusory adult independence given way to shameful squat in her childhood bedroom. She had, after an efficient hygiene layover in the airport bathroom, arrived at orientation straight from her red-eye, granting herself one final day of avoiding her mother. Lizzie Epstein, reporting for duty at the Meadowlark Institute for Memory

Research, cheeks still sun kissed with California glow, ass neatly pencil-skirted, rat-brown hair primly bunned, glasses wire rimmed and not strictly flattering, semisensible mules already blistering her feet. Here was her last, best chance, a wonder-stuffed Willy Wonka factory of world-class memory research, the fellowship packet in her bag a golden ticket. Four graduate students from across the country had been selected to spend a year exploiting the Meadowlark's scientific opportunities and—of more practical pertinence—to spend the next several years of their academic careers coasting on that glory: genius by association. So what if she had never intended to return east, if she had screwed up her research and, as a consequence, the closest thing she'd had in years to a successful relationship? So what if it had brought her here, to the threshold of Benjamin Strauss's Meadowlark Institute, to the chance to work beneath cognitive psychology's latest golden god, to relaunch her research with the help of his infinite resources and reputation, publish something—*anything*—with her name tangentially linked to his, then return west in triumph, her academic destiny manifest?

That at least was the plan she'd hatched after several sleepless nights grieving her rats. By then, the Meadowlark application was due in only three days, its requirements draconian—not just the standard research proposal, faculty recommendations, CV, personal statement, but also work samples, analytic essays on recent developments in the field, peer review of an anonymous preprint, and an extensive questionnaire that seemed part IQ test, part personality test, all invasive. Lizzie knew all this because the body snoring beside her had spent the last three months talking of nothing else; Lucas had his heart set on the fellowship and, as the second-best student in the country's second-best cognitive psychology department, he was convinced he had a shot. Lizzie, generally agreed to be the best student in the program—although they discussed this about as often as they discussed what it would mean for Lucas to move three thousand miles away, i.e., approximately never—had spent several boozy nights brainstorming with him how best to position himself to appeal to Benjamin Strauss's infamously peculiar tastes. She'd proofed his application materials before he dropped them in the mail only a few days before. She understood later the mistake she'd made not telling him about her decision to apply, but at the time, there had seemed no point.

Her dissertation was dead; she had no reason to believe that her slapdash statement—with its overconfident implications about what she could accomplish with the Meadowlark's resources; its overwrought paean to the grand unified theories of the past; its coda disclosing secret ambition to be a Newton, a Darwin, a (forgive the shameless flattery, she wrote) *Strauss*—would work. She also had no reason to assume the boy who claimed to love her would be unable to do so once she won what he had lost, but maybe she'd assumed this anyway, because when it happened, she wasn't surprised.

Not that he broke up with her when the acceptance letter arrived. Lucas was not, or at least refused to be seen as, that kind of guy. Nor was he the kind who would say to her face that it had been to her advantage that she was a woman, that academia was making it impossible to succeed as a white man; but he said it to enough of their friends to ensure it got back to her. They had plenty of sex that summer, though decreasingly so as she signed her sublease and shipped her boxes, serviced her car, curled up alone in bed while he stayed late at the lab, cried. Let's see how things go, he said, whenever she brought up the future, which she also did decreasingly as summer burned on. It was breakup chicken: she swerved first. If that's what you really want, he said, the week before she got on the plane. What she wanted was for him to arrive breathless at the gate, declare his inability to live without her. She would have boarded anyway—she was able to live without him—but still, that's what she wanted.

So Lucas was in California, already—rumor had it—de facto domestic partners with a blond undergrad he'd picked up at a frat party, and Lizzie was here. The Meadowlark Institute: a multidisciplinary mutual embrace of neuroscientists, cognitive psychologists, biologists, neurologists. Every *-ology* with a defensible connection to memory research was represented, or could petition to be. The promotional materials she'd received with her fellowship acceptance leaned, unsurprisingly, on the metaphor of the brain: parallel processing, functional integration—this was demonstrably nature's most efficient method of knowledge production, so why was science so intent on segregation? Why not attack a topic without observing absurd rules of engagement? Science, Strauss wrote, is not a boxing match. It's a street fight. Lizzie didn't know what the intellectual equivalent of brass knuckles would be, but she was prepared to use them.

The central building was a disorienting jumble of colonial brick and space-age fiberglass. Despite faithfully following the receptionist's directions, Lizzie took several wrong turns before finding her way to the cavernous lecture hall where the other three fellows had already arrived. She introduced herself, trying not to make it too obvious that she distrusted strangers on general principle—and these particular strangers on the more specific one that they were, by default, her competition. Only one of them would earn the right to publish with Strauss. The other woman, ponytail yanked so tight it tugged at her eyebrows, made no such effort to disguise hostility. She gave Lizzie a brief nod, then crossed her arms over her sweatshirt's rhinestoned Mickey Mouse, and returned her concentrated gaze to the empty podium at the front of the room. Lizzie didn't need an introduction, she'd done her homework. This was Mariana Cruz, Rhodes scholar with two years at the National Institute of Mental Health and what Lizzie had to admit was an exciting theory about neuroregenerative stem cells. Dmitri Tarken, the AI expert and piano prodigy from MIT who had the kind of taffy-pulled height that looked unnatural and was compulsively bending his spindly fingers backward one by one, offered his name and asked whether she'd seen any sign of Strauss in the hall. Lizzie shook her head. The final fellow was identifiable by process of elimination—a process unnecessary, because Clay Weld III was a type Lizzie knew all too well from college, a prep school boy who'd been slightly too smart and skinny to snag a prom date but hit freshman year high on blue-blooded cockiness, daddy an alum, daddy's daddy an alum, already set for a scotch date with daddy's old roommate the dean. He was hot in an obvious, chiseled-jaw kind of way, although not as hot as he clearly believed. He studied primate sexuality, he told her. You don't know sex, he added, until you've seen those hairy red asses in action.

"Strauss is always late," Mariana said, sounding sullen. "I hear it's his thing."

"Probably fucking his secretary," Clay said. "I hear *that's* his thing."

"That's not respectful," Dmitri said, but Lizzie suspected the disapproval was for her and Mariana's benefit only. The bro look he shot Clay suggested the boys would pick up their speculation later.

They waited. They discussed their projects, or rather, the other three did while Lizzie evaded summarizing her rat massacre and subsequent blank slate. They exchanged gossip about Benjamin Strauss, his research, his habits, his hypothetical affairs, all of them—even Dmitri, once he read the room—trying to disguise their hero worship, pretending they weren't vibrating at a higher frequency just knowing he was in the building. Lizzie was no exception: she'd worshipped Strauss from afar since undergrad. It didn't seem quite real that Strauss himself, the Columbus of neural pathways, codeveloper of the Strauss-Furman measure for flashbulb-memory-imprinting, MacArthur Foundation–certified genius, boy wonder—only in academia could you still be considered a boy wonder at forty-four—was about to stride through the double doors and change their intellectual lives.

The doors opened. The fellows silenced, straightened, held their breath, posed in their best brilliant intellectual posture. But the figure in the doorway was not Strauss, unless Strauss was secretly an elegant older woman with steel wool hair and a silver brooch the shape of a human brain. She stepped up to the podium and informed the fellows that Dr. Strauss would be unable to officially welcome them to the Meadowlark but had sent his regards. The woman was his secretary, she said (Clay nudged Dmitri, who swallowed a snort), and they should consider her at their disposal should any problems arise. "Of course, it would be preferable that none do." This apparently being all the orientation they were going to get, she dismissed them. "You've received your lab assignments in your welcome packets, please report there forthwith."

Clay, Mariana, and Dmitri propelled themselves from the room like runners from a starting gate. Lizzie did not move. She had no lab assignment and was seized with the irrational but persuasive thought that she'd made a terrible mistake, did not belong here after all. The secretary pointed at her. "You. Come with me."

Lizzie paused before a baroque wooden door, the only thing standing between her and her future. She wanted to preserve the moment, the possibility that for once reality would live up to fantasy. Then she knocked.

An irritated voice. "What."

"I'm Lizzie Epstein." The ensuing silence left too much time for her to consider the negligibility of self. "Your assistant sent me." Still nothing. "It's my first day?"

The door opened. "That sounds like an excuse." This was him, the infamous, the legend, the genius, peering down at her—well, not down; something about his bearing gave him the illusion of height—with disappointment at first sight. "Which begs the question of what you've already done wrong."

He stepped past her into the hall and indicated with a crooked finger that Lizzie should follow. He led her backward, toward the lobby, toward the front door, toward the end of her last chance before it had its chance to begin. She tried not to panic. Then they were in the parking lot. A line from an old self-defense class—*never let him take you to a secondary location*—surfaced briefly, absurdly, floated away. She climbed into the car.

"You like Bach?" He didn't wait for an answer before sliding in the CD. Dirgelike strings relieved them of the need for further conversation. She pretended to study the road—studied him. He wasn't as attractive as he was in his official department photo. Also not as young: reading glasses, receding hairline, skin at his neckline starting to crepe. She pictured Strauss examining his reflection in the bathroom mirror, combing fingers through curls to urge them unrulier, a mad genius determined to look the part. Imagine if he were a woman, she thought, with that brusque, aggressively ungroomed Garfunkel halo . . . but she checked this line of thinking abruptly. She was growing tiresome on the subject of double standards. She knew this because Lucas had told her so.

Strauss drove them into the city, deigning to explain only once they'd reached the hospital and found their way to the mental ward that they were here to recruit a subject. It was Lizzie's first trip to a locked ward. It was unlike she'd imagined: no shrieking, straitjacketed theatrics, only the occasional glassy-eyed patient shuffling down the corridor. The closest approximation to Nurse Ratched and her muscled goons was a clutch of pink-suited orderlies, one of them braiding a patient's hair, another blotting an old man's bloody nose. Still, Lizzie stiffened at the whine of the door closing behind them, its electric bolt sliding shut.

Strauss stopped at the door marked 8A. "Try not to get in the way."

Inside, a woman lay propped on pillows, her face turned toward the television, where a bathing-suited bottle blonde pressed presumably fake boobs against the sheen of a new refrigerator, and Bob Barker bared his Chiclets grin. "You again?" the patient said, underwhelmed. Neon dollar signs blinked, a wheel spun, cash fell from the sky.

"Me again."

"He's been here three times this week," the woman told Lizzie. "Doesn't seem to realize I'm no one's guinea pig."

Lizzie wasn't sure how to react to this. The woman gave her a careful look. "Are you?"

"What?"

"A guinea pig."

"I'm . . ." She shook off her nerves. If this was her first test, she intended to pass. "I'm Lizzie Epstein, a research fellow at the Meadowlark Institute. I work under Dr. Strauss." She extended a hand, but it went unshaken.

"You want to tell her?" the woman asked Strauss.

"You seem to have a firm grasp of your own narrative," he said.

"Not that you're taking notes on how I frame it."

"Not that I would ever."

"Because I haven't agreed to let you study me."

"Not that you ever would."

Lizzie was stymied.

"Three weeks ago, a woman was found on a Peter Pan bus with no means of identification, including her own useless brain," the patient said. "The state named her Wendy Doe and diagnosed her with dissociative fugue state. Defined as, quote, sudden, unexpected travel away from home or one's customary place of work, with inability to recall one's past. Unquote. Usually trauma induced. Frequently faked. Though not in this case. Says me." She turned to Strauss, sardonically proud student awaiting her gold star. Lizzie liked her already. "Did I get that just about right?"

"Just about."

"I've been in the paper," Wendy Doe said. "On the news. I've been on Jerry Springer. No one recognizes me. Impressive, huh?"

"I'm sorry," Lizzie said, and was sorry, more than she'd expected. She sometimes felt like life was a series of losses—grandmother, father, and in the less corporeal but still permanent category, all the friends, rooms, cities she'd ever made the mistake of loving just enough to miss when they were gone—and she'd done her best to design a life that would be a bulwark against the inevitable. She allowed nothing to feel essential except that which she could control, but this woman—Lizzie's age, Lizzie's build, Lizzie's coloring—she could easily have been Lizzie. Everything gone, including herself. And no one, apparently, had missed her. There was a long and noble tradition of modeling brain function via study of malfunctioning brains, but this was a tradition Lizzie had never wanted any part of. She preferred to study carefully controlled damage of her own creation. Another reason to opt for rats. It was much harder to look at them and see herself. "That must be difficult. No one's been able to help you remember?"

"Why would I want that?"

"I just assumed—"

"I get my memories back, I snap out of this fugue thing, and I forget any of this ever happened, that's how it works, right?" The patient turned again to Strauss, who nodded.

"Traditionally."

"Why would I be eager to erase myself? Does that seem like something you'd want?" This she directed at Lizzie, who shook her head, though it was impossible for her to imagine wanting to live without a past—impossible to imagine there would be a *her* without it. Maybe that was Wendy Doe's point.

Once back in the car, Strauss asked what she thought.

"Of the case?" Lizzie scrambled to remember what she knew of dissociative fugues. "The patient shows no obvious signs of emotional trauma, but—"

"No, of the subject. She's yours, if you want her. Well, yours and mine, but I'm assuming you don't mind a bit of supervision."

"I do rats," Lizzie said, stalling, panicking.

"Indeed, you did. I know this because I read your application. Do you know what else I read there? A stated desire to, quote, blaze beyond the boundaries of pedestrian scientific inquiry and chart a revolutionary course."

She cringed at the echo of her own absurd ambition.

"Did you mean that?"

Lizzie nodded, because absurd or not, it was also true.

"Do you think you're going to do that by reanimating your rat project?"

"Am I going to do it by assisting you, and studying a woman who could get her memory back any minute, sending us smack into a dead end?"

"You're right," he said. "It's a risk. She could also refuse to be studied—unlike your rats. Or some relative could dig her up. She could turn out to be faking it. Anything's possible."

She flipped through the file, stalling. According to the records, Peter Pan's lost girl had bounced around city facilities for nearly a month. First a hospital, then a mental hospital, a homeless shelter, the mental hospital again, while social services waited for someone to come looking. The Philadelphia PD, the FBI, the reporters at the *Inquirer* and (more dogged when it came to this brand of tawdry) the *Daily News*, all had failed to turn up a viable claimant. Maybe forgetting her life was simple retaliation, Lizzie thought. Maybe life forgot her first.

"Or we could hit the lottery," Strauss said. "Discover something no one else knows. Together."

There was no way to calculate the odds without a firmer grip on the subject's status, and there were two equally viable possibilities: One, Wendy Doe was lying. Remembered everything, walked out of her life for reasons valid or otherwise. Two: Wendy Doe genuinely remembered nothing. She was a walking dream state, and whatever happened to her now, the things she said, the choices she made, would simply evanesce when she woke up. If Wendy Doe was telling the truth, there was no Wendy Doe.

"You know what I saw in your application?"

"What?"

"Someone who wants to be exceptional, but doesn't quite believe she has it in her. Someone too invested in the past, too worried about the future, to take a true risk in the present. Someone who's realized her life is small and wants to change that."

"You read all that in my application?"

"I read all that in the first five minutes of meeting you. I'm a very insightful man. Maybe you've heard." He grinned, boyish, and she couldn't help liking it. "Take the night, think about it. If, in the morning, you still want rats, then rats ye shall have."

"For the record, I'm not here to start a new life," she said. "Just a new research project."

"Hmm." It sounded diagnostic. "Have you ever been in love, Elizabeth?"

"What?"

"Is that an inappropriate question these days?" Wendy Doe's file sat on the dashboard. He rapped a fist against it, twice. "My advice? Find something here that you love to the exclusion of all else. I can see how sincerely you *want* to want this. That's good. Want it for real. That's better."

The house still felt like her father's house. Here was the crooked magnolia in the yard, the only tree halfway suitable for climbing. Here was the mezuzah, chastising her for never acquiring one of her own. Here was a welcome mat, unwelcome touch that her father—for reasons both aesthetic and constitutional—would never have allowed. She had a key, but rang the bell anyway, a reminder she was technically a guest here. She did not have to stay.

Her mother was draped in a lavender caftan and had eyeshadow to match. They exchanged a polite hug. The house smelled ineffably of Epstein.

Lizzie's sister's room was now an office; Lizzie's room was a guest bedroom. Before that, it had been her father's sickroom, where he slept in a rented hospital bed as Lizzie's mother nursed her ex-husband to his end. The bed had been replaced. Lizzie unpacked, then lay on the nubby carpet, looking up at his last view. The ceiling was the same ceiling. She was not there when he died. She was in her dorm, arguing with her roommates about which of them had promised—then forgotten—to pay the phone bill. The line still worked, but the phone did not ring, so Lizzie spent four superfluous hours believing she still had a father. She tossed a Frisbee with the boys who lived upstairs. And her father was dead. She invented an excuse to walk one of those boys, the one who wore suspenders just ridiculous enough to appeal, down into the Widener stacks, trying not to be too obvious discerning how and in whom he planned to spend his Saturday night. And her father was dead. She had Lucky Charms with frozen yogurt for dinner. She walked home with her roommates, arms linked, and she was laughing, and her father was dead.

For their first dinner together at home in four years, Lizzie and her mother ordered steak sandwiches. These arrived cold, and were not as good as Lizzie remembered. The table sat four. Her mother took her father's chair.

"So, how's your Christian Scientist?"

"Mom, Lucas is not—"

"Is he still a scientist?"

She nodded.

"Still a WASP?"

"He's Catholic."

"Well then."

Lizzie reminded herself it was no longer her obligation to defend her boyfriend, now ex. "How's Eugene?" she countered. When Lizzie was a child, Eugene Stein had been a professionally indignant voice on the radio and a family joke. Now he was having presumably frequent sex with Lizzie's mother in Lizzie's father's bedroom.

"Tiresome." But her smile was unmistakably fond. "There's a new producer at the station we thought you might like, especially if you and the Christian Scientist are—"

Lizzie said she'd rather die alone and be eaten by cats, but thanks anyway.

They ate their cold sandwiches, their soggy fries. Her mother asked after Gwen, Lizzie's oldest friend, best friend, only friend left within the city limits. She had seemed like enough from three thousand miles away but—judging from Lizzie's failed efforts to spend this first evening with a friend rather than family—Gwen's new baby, and the logistical constraints she imposed, meant it would not be. Lizzie let her mother believe this first meal at home had been her first choice. Her mother asked about her day at the Meadowlark. Hewing to long-standing policy, Lizzie offered no details of her work. Other subjects more mutually avoided: politics (especially what Lizzie's mother referred to as Lizzie's radicalization). Israel (especially since the advent of Eugene, when her mother had gone what Lucas called "the full Zionist"). Her mother's long-ago affair, her parents' divorce. Her father's illness, her father's death. Her father's will, deeding the house to her mother. Her father, period. Instead they lingered on the plummeting life trajectories of old enemies, the tedium of Lizzie's sister's updates on her four children—remarkable, in Lizzie's opinion, only as living proof that Lizzie's sister had endured at least four encounters with her husband's presumably unfortunate penis. They discussed the physical ailments of elderly relatives. The vicissitudes of the local restaurant scene (two Chinese places closing, one opening, the seafood place supposedly ridden with botulism, the Baskin-Robbins giving way to a TCBY, and of course, the Godot-like Cheesecake Factory, for which the suburban masses steadfastly continued to wait). The president's genitals, and where he might or might not have inserted them.

The last time Lizzie came for a visit, her mother had been dating a therapist and wanted to talk about feelings. Specifically, she wanted to talk about Lizzie's feeling like she had been abandoned by her mother, back when her mother abandoned her. I'm sorry you felt that way, she'd told Lizzie, who *felt* this was not an actual apology.

Now: "I'm selling the house."

"You are not!"

"You're not a child anymore, Lizzie. Don't act like one."

In a seminar on addiction, Lizzie had learned the theory that addicts are often emotionally stunted, frozen at the age they first encountered their substance of choice. She wondered if she was addicted to blaming her mother. "You can't sell his house."

"It's not his house anymore." Lizzie's mother stood at the sink, rinsing the plates far more thoroughly than needed. Even when the meal came from a paper bag, her mother believed in china plates, silver silverware, glass glasses. Civilization was in the details. She turned off the water but stayed where she was, her back to Lizzie, palms on the counter, holding on.

Lizzie was fifteen when her mother fucked, then fell for, the dermatologist who worked down the hall from her orthodontia practice. She left her husband for him and when, reneging on their plans, he elected to keep his wife, Lizzie's mother stayed gone. Within four years, Lizzie's sister had found God, moved to Jerusalem, married a Talmud student, and gotten knocked up with twins. Lizzie's mother had started dating a yoga instructor and learning German. Lizzie's father had died. Then there was only Lizzie left. She thought now about those first few nights, when she'd still assumed her mother would come home, and had still welcomed the thought of it. She thought about Wendy Doe, and the family who might be out there searching for her, the life or lack thereof that the amnesic woman had abandoned. She thought, mostly, about how easily she'd slipped out of her own life in Los Angeles, as easily as, several years before, she'd slipped from the one here; how inessential she'd discovered herself to be. How, if she one day got on a bus and left, there would be no one to feel left behind.

Lizzie's mother told her the house wouldn't go on the market till April, which gave her nearly six months to pack up whatever she wanted of her things, and of her father's. Lizzie wanted to say she wanted none of it. But she wanted everything. She wanted the house and its contents. She wanted a life-sized replica of her past. She wanted every sock and tie her father had worn, every meal they'd cooked together, every show they'd watched, every time he'd put his arms around her and made life, for that moment, tolerable. She wanted her stuffed animals, she wanted her yellow blanket, she wanted her Wonder Woman PJs, she wanted her things and her belief that things could save her. She wanted so much more than this life she'd made for herself could hold.

ALICE

When Alice finally left, she took the bus, and she did so because when her mother left, *she* took the bus—this was the one thing Alice knew for sure. It was also the one thing to convince Alice that her mother had lost her mind. Travel by bus implied no other option, and Alice's mother was recourse rich: driver's license, Honda SUV, credit limit expansive enough to cover a plane or train ticket to wherever she wanted to go, not to mention a perfectly nice life in a perfectly nice three-bedroom, two-bath, below-market split-level that should have precluded her desire to go anywhere. Her mother, or at least the person her mother had spent a lifetime persuasively pretending to be, would never have boarded a midnight bus bound for a city that held nothing for her but bad memories. And yet she had, so Alice did, splurged on a taxi from her dorm room to the bus terminal. Chicago's central train station, only a few blocks away, was a Beaux Arts wonder, its architecture admonition: *nowhere is better than here.* The bus station, a utilitarian warehouse of crumbling brick and dingy tile, was more an invitation to flee. Alice fled. Boarded a bus to Indiana, where she transferred to the line that would carry her to Pittsburgh, transferred again, veered east, was startled awake at dawn to discover pinking farmland smearing past the window and her seatmate draping his coat across her lap, tucking her in.

"My wife gave me a divorce for Christmas," he said, mouth too close. The bus was all sweat and snoring, no one to see. Alice shrugged off the coat, inched away, imagined bedbugs burrowing into her denim. She had to pee. She could not pee. It was too easy to envision herself hovering over a clogged toilet behind a broken lock, the man's face leering from the doorway. His grubby hand over her mouth. His fingers slipping down and down, his nails scrabbling at her belt, her zipper, her polka-dotted panties. This was Pavlovian, her mother's fault. These were precisely the circumstances her mother had trained her to avoid. Dirty places with dirty men who wanted to do dirty things, and would, if you were careless enough to let them. Alice hunched her back to the man, kissed forehead to window, counted fences and cows and minutes, waited out his attention and her panic, blamed her mother, whose fault it was that she'd boarded this bus in the first place, whose insistence on the necessity of preparation had somehow prepared Alice for little more than being afraid.

Alice's mother was the kind of woman who carried antiseptic wipes on her person at all times and discreetly wiped down silverware when her waiter wasn't looking. She believed life rewarded caution; the reckless would suffer. She believed in the assignment of blame. Alice's father insisted her mother was more delicate than she appeared, but this defied belief. Everything about her mother was ironclad, not least her self-imposed regulations. She did not abdicate duty; she did not venture. She did not tolerate or transgress or risk—would not, could not, until one day, she did.

Here is how Alice lost her mother. The night of graduation, she intended to finally fuck her boyfriend. This was not how he put it, of course. Daniel wasn't the fucking type. Neither, as was evident to everyone other than her mother, was Alice. They were good kids, everyone said so. She read to the blind, edited the student activities section of the yearbook; he cochaired the honor society, played lacrosse, raised money for disaster relief. While it was true he sometimes sucked at her nipples in his parents' basement and she had perfected the requisite pacing and grip to make him groan, their desire always remained responsibly bridled. The pack of condoms secreted inside Alice's old tennis shoe had been purchased less for precaution than principle. It was her mother's refusal to believe this, her mother's hysterical insistence on her catastrophic deflowering, that left Alice determined to prove her right.

Graduation night. They let themselves into the garage apartment Daniel had borrowed from his cousin's best friend and found a flavored-for-her-pleasure condom taped to a helium balloon. The balloon said

Congratulations, and Daniel said, "My cousin is such an asshole" and also "quack-quack," because their relationship had bloomed from a fifth-grade crush that was itself incited by his impressive Donald Duck impression, and this was now their way of saying *I love you*. This was the kind of couple they were, and even in the presence of Daniel's abruptly unveiled genitals, this was perhaps inescapable.

She wanted to be the daughter who channeled rebellion into recklessness, threw her lover down on the bed in a haze of passion and spite. Desire would overpower pregnancy paranoia and the images of decaying STD-stricken skin that her mother's PowerPoint presentation had embedded in her brain. But Daniel was gentle, Daniel was tentative, Daniel was, ultimately, not equipped to be the faceless avatar of testosterone-fueled destruction that her mother imagined him to be, but simply Daniel, who quacked his love for her, who wanted to be sure she was ready, and if he was Daniel then she could be no one but Alice, who was not.

She imagined later that if instead of spending the night in Daniel's disappointed arms she had ceded her virginity as planned and snuck home before dawn, she might have caught her mother mid–disappearing act. She even wondered afterward if catching her mother wouldn't have been necessary—if the pop of hymen might have pinged some maternal radar, alerted her mother to pressing need. Made her stay. Instead, Alice let a deflated Daniel spoon her to sleep, and when she got home in the morning, her mother was gone.

The first true thing she knew about her mother was the leaving. Her mother getting on a bus, her mother carried away.

The last true thing she knew was the bridge fifty miles from their house, the dirt niche by the foot of it where they found her mother's neatly folded coat and both her shoes.

Everyone seemed very certain they could extrapolate what happened next. Alice didn't argue.

Let them drag the river. Let them scour security footage. Let them believe in a body. Alice believed in the leaving. She didn't need a body, drowned or dry, to know she'd been left.

*   *   *

July, no mother. August, no mother. She doesn't break up with Daniel, though sometimes she wants to. He doesn't break up with her, because who would break up with the girl whose mother is gone? They have arguments sometimes about why she doesn't trust him enough to cry. He doesn't believe her when she says she doesn't cry at all. He remains tragically unfucked.

She is alone.

She lies to her father and lets him believe she thinks her mother is dead. She lies to her friends, who are really Daniel's friends, when they invite her along, once it becomes clear they don't want her along. They want to lounge along Boulder Lake and worry about their tans, their future roommates, their fake IDs, their soon-to-be long-distance loves, their ever-insufficient supply of beer. She reminds herself this was always meant to be a summer of leaving.

She is alone she is alone she is alone.

September, still no mother. She leaves anyway, ships everything that matters to Chicago. Trades mountains for midland, welcomes flat, alien ground, towers and smog crowding out sky, nothing to remind her of absence. Thinks that here things will be different—but her mother is still gone. Her prospective new friends all want to know: What do your parents do and how did you spend your summer vacation?

It was a while ago, she learns to say. It's fine. These strangers need a lot of reassurance.

She goes to class. Her mother is gone. She learns about economic collapse and environmental catastrophe. Her mother is gone. She learns about Aristotelian metaphysics and studies his prime mover: that which moves without being moved. The first cause responsible for all subsequent effect. The one hard truth from which all else follows. She stops going to class. She subsists on Twix and ramen, loses weight, loses sleep, loses the thread that binds her. She buys a ticket. She gets on the bus.

ELIZABETH

The girl appeared on a Tuesday, which was inconvenient, because Tuesday was my day for dissolution. Not that every day wasn't a dissolution, not that my whole life hadn't become dissolute, not that fragments of life and self weren't disintegrating; like sands through the hourglass, so are the days of my life. But on Tuesdays—because, allow the poor widow her maudlin whim, Tuesday was the day he'd died—I let myself stop pretending otherwise. Six days of the week, I did not drink to excess, I did not weep in public. I did not consume unwise quantities of white bread and red meat. I did not leave the house in my pajamas or decline to shower. If I also did not do yoga or take my multivitamin, if I did not clean out his closet or answer the phone when his daughter called, I was still, in the opinion of all politely concerned parties, making an effort. I was forcing said sand through said hourglass, rather than dumping it on the ground and grinding it beneath my bare toes, as I'd fantasized about doing with his ashes. The grit of him, caking my fleshy creases. Sanding self away. These were the dissolute thoughts of dissolution I did not indulge, and every day passed, and every day was another day he'd been dead.

Nights were long. Sleep elusive. In the beginning, we slept like babies, he liked to say. Turning and turning in a widening gyre, always together: big spoon, little spoon, little spoon, big. Every night its own nursery rhyme. Sleep, without him, when I managed it: solitary and poor, nasty, brutish, short. I woke at dawn. So did the wife across the street, and I liked watching her walk her stroller up and down the dew. Nearly my age, unfathomably. The husband wore a suit. Left for work early, came home late. She missed him, I could tell. The wife had brought a casserole to the shivah, uninvited. Black sweater stretched tight across ninth-month belly, unseemly. There but for the grace of Mirena and perimenopause, I thought, when she waddled to the freezer. Wondered what I would have done if left behind with a piece of him that was not him. If I could have loved it in his place.

I was forty-eight, and I was a widow. A woman who'd let my husband die on me. Widows were prim or stern, all of them old, or at least older than me, Grimm witches or Woolfian madams. Every room was my own. I wanted none of them.

Tuesdays I spent in sweats, screening calls, watching soaps, soaking comfort from the cycles of suffering and redemption. No happiness went unpunished, no heart unscathed. Most deaths proved as easily nullified as the marriages that preceded them. That Tuesday, I watched a woman weep bedside, waiting for her lover's coma to end, not knowing, as I did, that when he woke it would be with a new face and emptied memory. This was the risk of life inside a soap: the possibility you could wake up to find yourself someone else. Lovers' faces became unrecognizable, children aged a decade overnight; and yet, the circle of life closed in on itself with claustrophobic comfort. Every daughter became a mother, every mistress a wife—every wife a widow.

The doorbell rang. I ignored it. The bell rang again, and I had apparently become a woman too tired not to do as she was asked. Behind the door stood a bedraggled girl, a copy of *Augustine* in her hand. She shoved the book in my face. "Is this you?"

The back cover was dominated by the large black-and-white author photo, face a decade younger than mine, frown carefully calibrated to suggest interrogative empathy, a well-mixed cocktail of softness and rigor, airbrushing and eyeglasses, all to convey the right message, *this may be bullshit, but I am not.* It was me, but only on the technicality that I had once been someone else, someone younger, someone married, someone eager to take direction, frown with my mouth, smile with my eyes. "It's somewhat me," I said.

I diagnosed youth. College, maybe, or—something in the too-firm set of jaw, the fingers tucking themselves into their sleeve then resolutely poking back out again like a compulsion—even younger. Zitted nose, greasy hair, ragged nails, weak chin, but young enough that none of it interfered with beauty. The pink of cheeks. The smoothness of skin. The perkiness of breast. Girls like this never looked tired. When they looked sad, as this one did, it was a fuck-me sadness, a wound that conjured want. I knew about the desirability of damaged young women; I'd made a life of it. Her wrists were thin, her hair limp, the color of discarded Wonder Bread. She looked like she was a runaway, or at least like she wanted to be. A few years younger than Benjamin's daughter, less practiced in wounded hostility, but giving it her best effort.

Benjamin's Nina had run away once, age eight, cruelly sentenced to summer vacation with her estranged father and his newish wife, mind marinated in who knew what vitriol, courtesy of wife number one. She endured two weeks with us, then slung Pikachu pack over shoulder and waltzed out the front door while we slept. She'd only made it as far as the neighbor's backyard, but it had been enough to curtail the custody visits until a year later they tapered off for good. I'd promised Benjamin that when she crashed into adolescence, her mother would become the enemy and we would provide inevitable refuge, that next time she ran away, she'd run straight to him. There was no next time. Even when Nina came to the city for college, under protest, she wasn't, in any true sense of the word, his. She was never, in any sense of the word, mine. We filled our lives with other people's daughters. Benjamin's students, bright, ambitious echoes of a girl I used to be. My readers, whom Benjamin always found cause to disdain. Your Augustine girls, he called them, the ones who slunk into readings and conferences with bandaged wrists, Auschwitzian bodies swimming in slip dresses, damage blinking like a neon sign, *vacancy*, someone, anyone, fill me up. I had written the history of a damaged girl, a girl made famous not by her pain but by the story her doctor told about it. I had, the jacket copy boasted, "enabled an object of curiosity to seize subject-hood, reclaimed her narrative from the men who wanted to explain her to herself, triumphantly recentering her as protagonist of her own story." They had stories, too, my Augustine girls. Pain manifested with infinite variety: an eating disorder. A dead boyfriend. A dead father. A disease, real or imagined. Anxiety, overwhelming. Sorrow, bottomless. Rage against the machine. The girl would set my book before me, whisper her name, then, in a gush, tell me how Augustine and I had taught her to reclaim herself. *Until now, until her*, she would say, *I felt so alone*.

Desperate for attention, Benjamin said. *Posers*. I reminded him we were all posing. He'd made a life's work of stories the mind tells itself,

I reminded him, and should know that the body could tell stories, too. He would call me too soft, too easy, too young; I would call him an ogre. Somewhere in there, argument would become foreplay, then fingers mouth tongue flesh heart until we were both somehow fucking the Augustine girls—their youth, their damage, their need.

The book was ten years old, though. Most of the girls had grown up. "I always appreciate hearing from readers, but showing up at my house isn't—"

"I'm looking for your husband, actually."

"He's dead." I resented, on general principle, anyone who made me say it.

"No, I know. I mean, I found out, when I looked him up. That's why I came to you. I'm trying to . . . I'm looking for my mother, I guess?"

"Well, she's not here."

"No, I mean, I'm looking for her in the past. Like, trying to figure out who she was, really. I thought if I met you—well, if I met your husband. But then he died."

I also resented having to hear anyone else say it.

"I'm sorry," she said. "I shouldn't have come. You seem busy, and I don't want to bother you, so . . ."

"I am busy, and you are bothering me, so tell me why." I said it sharply. I waited. Girls her age had obedience baked into their bones. Too many voices saying too many times: *behave, submit.* You had to work to unlearn it, and maybe I was a traitor to my gender, but her strength of will was not my concern. She did as she was told.

"My mother was a patient at his institute." It sounded less like submission than challenge. Good.

"We didn't have patients," I said. Habit. "Only subjects. We were very clear about that."

"It was just for a few months, in 1999? They found her on a bus, in a fugue state. They called her Wendy Doe."

I tried to keep my face expressionless. Failed, apparently.

"You remember!" Relief made her seem even younger.

"I remember." My first and last research subject. The year that ended my career, began my life. It wasn't in the category of things possible to forget. "Did she send you here?" I hoped for; I hoped against.

"She's . . ." The girl wanted to cry, that was obvious. But she refused to, and I liked her for it. "Can we start again?" She stuck out her hand, and I shook it. "I'm Alice. Karen Clark's—Wendy Doe's—daughter. A few months ago, my mother went missing. Just walked out, disappeared. And that's when my father told me . . ."

"It happened before."

She nodded. "No one's even looking for her anymore. The police, even my father, they think she's . . . you know."

I did know. All those years ago, a woman could erase herself with relative ease. It was a different century now, a future of facial recognition and streaming surveillance. To erase yourself from that picture would require something more permanent than a bus ticket and a new name. "I'm so sorry," I said. "But if you're thinking she came back here—"

The girl, Alice, shook her head. "I'm just trying to understand. Who she was. Why she might have . . ." She paused, and when she continued, her voice was steadier. "I want to know what it was like for her here. What she was like, when she thought she was someone else. I need to know *something*."

"How old are you?"

"I'm not some teen runaway," she said. "I'm eighteen, I can do what I want."

"I do remember your mother," I told her. "It was a lifetime ago, but I remember her very well."

A lifetime ago, and here was the girl, her entire life the proof. A lifetime ago, before there was an Elizabeth Strauss, before there was an us, when there was only a Strauss and a Lizzie, when it still hurt to study the lines of his neck, to imagine the impossible, taking his hand. I loved him most, but Lizzie loved him best. How could we be the same person when this girl's whole life lay between us? A lifetime ago I was somebody else. Wendy Doe was nobody, a fairy tale one neuron told another. But Benjamin was still Benjamin. Benjamin was a constant, axiomatic. I wanted the girl gone, but maybe it would be easier, with her here, to remember, to return to him. I wanted that, too.

I invited her to stay for dinner, and didn't consciously plan that after dinner I'd insist she stay the night, but when the cartons were tossed and the dishes done, it seemed only polite. It was less intention than reflex.

She was a tether to the past—you can't throw a drowning woman a rope and not expect her to cling.

Benjamin's law: you are the story you tell of your life, and every story has its want. I wanted. In the dark. In the bone and the marrow. It was, that day, nearly one year into the after, and my whole life was a wanting. The story I tell of my life: I was alone, once. Then I was alone again.

I wanted to go back.

LIZZIE

Day one. A windowless room. One table, two chairs. The standard battery of tests: Wechsler Adult Intelligence Scale, Wechsler Memory Scale, California Verbal Learning Test, Test of Everyday Attention, Stroop test (Kaplan variant), Posttraumatic Diagnostic Scale, Personality Assessment Inventory, Depression Anxiety Stress Scale, Beck Depression Inventory-2, Dissociation Questionnaire, Thurstone Word Fluency Test, Digit Span Forward and Backward memory tests, Rey Auditory Verbal Learning Test, Rey-Osterrieth complex figure test.

Day two, same. Day three, same.

Strauss believed in knowledge by colonization, understanding a subject by spreading across every inch of its territory until it was wholly possessed. And so Lizzie measured and processed and tallied: average through above average results for all but the obvious subpar performance in episodic memory. Elevated indicators of trauma and depression. Semantic memory intact; areas of specialized knowledge included biology, gardening, medical terminology, food preparation. All what one would expect from a neurologically intact woman of mildly above-average intelligence who either had or was faking a dissociative fugue. The subject had been MRI'd, CAT- and PET-scanned at the intake hospital, but those doctors had been searching only for obvious dysfunction, cause rather than correlation or consequence. The Meadowlark was as concerned with function as with its failure, so Lizzie dutifully ferried the subject to the scanning wing. Wendy lay inside clanking machines, blinked up at a scattershot of images, let associations roam free, while, safe behind glass, Lizzie watched the techs watch the screens, map swaths of gray matter flashing fluorescent as neurons went to work. This part of the Meadowlark was known as the North Pole; brains here lit up like Christmas trees.

Lizzie had signed on to the fugue project because the reward of working side by side with a world-renowned genius had seemed to outweigh any risk and—though she would have preferred this were not a factor—because Wendy Doe had rooted herself in Lizzie's brain. Not just the intellectual puzzle of her, which would have been acceptable, but the human fact of her, the woman untethered from life and self, a tragic figure that some part of Lizzie couldn't help imagining herself swooping in to save. She didn't know why Wendy had signed on, but given her disinterest in her own condition and any possible resolution of it, Lizzie suspected that upon discharge from the state hospital, there'd been nowhere better to go. The Meadowlark was Wendy's last resort, and she was treating it—and Lizzie—accordingly.

Lizzie asked Wendy exhaustive questions about the past, but the woman never slipped from her story of no story. Lizzie showed Wendy pictures, played her music, offered her smells, recorded her responses. These figures would establish a cognitive baseline; subsequent tests at regular intervals would track its evolution over time. The tests were dull, the data crucial, though so far the only data point that compelled Lizzie was Wendy's resolute lack of interest in her own past. Lizzie kept prodding her to speculate about who she might have been, what she might have been fleeing from or to, imagining that free association might guide her toward something true, but Wendy resolutely did not want to guess, did not want to imagine, did not want to know.

They had just finished a third variant of IQ test when Strauss peeked in. "Don't want to interrupt, I just thought I'd see how it's going."

Lizzie's posture straightened, and she could feel a false smile stretch across her face. "Great!" Wendy's smile looked more genuine, and her echoed "Great!" almost sounded sincere.

"That's my girl," Strauss said to Lizzie, which should have galled her. She wanted to impress him—for practical reasons, but she could also feel it pulsing in her, the congenital need for approval. Her mother used to call her a born teacher's pet—bewildered tone implying some kind of switched-at-birth scenario. Her father always countered that there was nothing wrong with currying favor from the people you respected—and it was true that those teachers who lost Lizzie's respect never had cause to doubt her disdain—but Lizzie knew he simply loved her too much to see the flaw. Her mother had nailed it. Her mother's disappearing act, which left Lizzie in ever more dire need of loco parentis approval, had turned impulse into pathology. It was not her favorite trait, but it had gotten her into Harvard, into her PhD program, most likely into the Meadowlark, and if it could get her out with Benjamin Strauss's full-throated approval, then she would swallow the toadying shame of it, and when he stepped out again, leaving Wendy in "Elizabeth's capable hands," she would not berate herself for blushing.

When the door closed, Wendy collapsed forward theatrically, head in hands. "What a fucking joke."

"I know these tests seem dull, but the answers could be illuminating—"

"Not when you're asking all the wrong questions."

It was the first indication Wendy had given of her own curiosity.

"What would be the right question?"

"Can we just take a break for a while?" Wendy stood, looking like a kid asking for a bathroom pass, equal parts impatient and pleading.

"Of course. But—just tell me, what should we be asking?"

"For one thing, you could ask me what it feels like not to remember."

"What does it feel like?"

Wendy was already at the door. "It feels like nothing. And don't ask me how you study that."

Three hours into a miserable, waking night, Lizzie gave up on sleep. Navigated the small room by feel, cursed as a shadow's sharp edge attacked her thigh, but cursed quietly, as if someone were there to hear. The institute in the dark: too quiet. Probably haunted. Tonight, Lizzie would be its ghost. Each fellow was required to spend one night per week babysitting the ward. Not that it was a ward, exactly, because these were neither patients nor inmates, but voluntary subjects. Twenty miles away, in a swank high-rise apartment, Lizzie's best friend since kindergarten was staring glassy-eyed at a Russian novel and nursing her no longer quite newborn, which Lizzie knew because this was what Gwen did every night. She was too tired to entertain company, she told Lizzie, who hadn't realized she counted as *company* when it came to Gwen. Thus was Lizzie's only prospect of a social life foreclosed, and after a week of chasing Gwen and avoiding her mother, she found herself pathetically grateful for the excuse to spend a night at work. Not that there was work to do: the Meadowlark employed security to enforce order, nurses to monitor health. Lizzie need only observe.

Three of the Meadowlark's residential subjects required full-time care: a woman with late-stage Alzheimer's, a man whose Korsakoff syndrome had advanced far enough to erode all but the most basic functions, and the intriguing Anderson, whose withered hippocampus could form no new memories. Anterograde amnesia: he lived in an eternal present, his life measured out in four-minute intervals, each erasing the one that came before. He played a piano, which Strauss had given him, day and night. Then there was Wendy Doe, as capable of taking care of herself as she was without material means to do so: no money, no social security card, no ID, no chance of legal employment or government subsidy. Not ill enough to be permanently housed by the state, not well enough to house herself—the kind of liminal existence Strauss's institute was made for. Strauss gave her a bed, an allowance, supervised liberties, in exchange for her willing participation in the research. *Our* research, he'd suggested Lizzie make a habit of saying, as if a pronoun could fool Wendy into believing she was studying herself.

The fellows' bedroom was spare. The bed felt like a board. Lizzie hadn't yet regained the knack of sleeping alone, even though for nearly thirty years, alone had been her bed and body's natural state. The body remembered what it wanted to remember. Hers, a traitor, wanted to remember Lucas. Lizzie ventured down the dark hall in pajamas and bare feet. Somewhere, softly, a piano ascended a scale, chased itself back down again. The Meadowlark was an asterisk, wings spoking radially from a central hub. By day, it vibrated with its own self-importance. Rats ran mazes; chimps signed; coders coded; talk therapists talked patients through memory palaces; damaged brains and their owners lay down and held still. A steady stream of outpatient subjects flowed through: the man who remembered every minute of every day since birth. The man who remembered things that had never happened. The woman with continual, overpowering déjà vécu, the conviction that everything she experienced was already a memory. Lizzie empathized. She often felt like she was remembering her life even as it happened.

Nighttime returned the institute to its former self. The Meadowlark Asylum for Women was founded in 1853 as the city's proud leap into modern psychiatric care, shuttered in 1982 by state edict after a Pulitzer-winning exposé detailed facilities spattered with blood and feces, patients unwashed, unmedicated, assaulted, strapped down, starved half to death. The acreage had been left to rot for nearly a decade before Strauss secured the funding to make his brainchild manifest. House of horrors turned state-of-the-art factory for knowledge production, shiny and humane. It was only a building; it could not remember. But if it could, Lizzie thought. Epileptics and schizophrenics and late-stage syphilitics, alcoholics and children and prostitutes and women too poor to have anywhere else to go. Dissatisfied housewives dunked in ice baths, frontal lobes ice-picked into obedience. Wives returned to husbands, docile and pliant. Or buried in the backwoods, forgotten.

Lizzie didn't believe in ghosts.

She found a kettle in the staff kitchen and boiled some water. Tea seemed the kind of thing insomniacs were meant to drink. She was still waiting for the tea to cool when Wendy Doe appeared, in a white doily of a nightgown that made her look like a Victorian invalid. Lizzie was wearing Lucas's boxers and Cal sweatshirt; for their softness, she told herself, not his lingering scent.

"Sorry," Wendy said. "I saw the light."

"Do you need something?" Lizzie asked.

"Just couldn't sleep."

Lizzie poured more tea, unsure how to make small talk with a subject, especially a subject with no life, past or present, outside these walls. She wasn't about to offer up her own life for conversational content.

"Seen any ghosts yet?" Wendy asked. "I mean, this place has to be haunted, right?"

Lizzie felt like it was her official duty to pretend she hadn't just been thinking the same thing. "I think we're safe."

"Have you been to that museum thing yet?" Wendy asked. Lizzie shook her head. Strauss had set aside a corridor for relics from the Meadowlark's earlier iteration. Most of the staff avoided it. "Let's just say, if you ever need an emergency lobotomy, you'll know where to find an ice pick."

Lizzie shuddered. She preferred not to think about the women who'd lived here before.

"I kind of like the thought of it," Wendy said. "The idea that they're watching me. The women who used to live here. Like, someone's got my back, you know?"

"If you say so."

Wendy grinned. "Be careful, they've got their eye on you, too."

Lizzie stood, excused herself to go back to her room, make a dent in her pile of reading. She had years' worth of fugue research to catch up on—since starting her doomed dissertation project she'd ignored most new work published on human memory, at least that not published by Benjamin Strauss.

"You really must love this stuff, huh?" Wendy said.

"Why?"

"Doesn't seem like there could be much money in it, sitting around asking me questions. And you seem like someone who could have been anything. Or at least a lawyer."

"Thanks? I think?"

"So why this?"

Usually, when asked, Lizzie told people she studied memory because of her grandmother, who'd died of Alzheimer's. This was a usefully truth-adjacent lie she'd invented in college. The more embarrassing truth: it wasn't her grandmother's disease, it was her grandmother's soap.

Once upon a time, the Epstein family was whole: one mother, one father, two daughters. Becca was older by five years, irritatingly golden in hair and touch. Becca had playdates, sports teams, tennis lessons, play rehearsals, friends and talent and ambition. Lizzie, friendless, uncoordinated, left ever further behind, was content to be the one who had their grandmother. They ate microwaved cinnamon buns, drank hot chocolate, watched her grandmother's stories. Lizzie watched, first, because her grandmother watched, and because here, occasionally, were adults in a feverish sexual disarray that both repulsed and intrigued. Here, eventually, was where Lizzie discovered the monstrousness of love, long before her mother enacted it. Here, ultimately, was where Lizzie found a world more comprehensible than her own, a reality that bent to the exigencies of narrative desire. The soap world was karmically rigid—secrets inevitably revealed, wrongs avenged, innocence redeemed—but physically malleable. Wives became entirely different women, an announcer would inform the audience of the substitution, and life proceeded accordingly. Almost everyone came back from the dead.

Her grandmother was a widow. Everyone's grandmother seemed to wind up a widow. Lizzie's mother told her once, "That's the thing about men, always leaving, one way or another." Later Lizzie would wonder whether this had been a warning from mother to daughter that this particular woman intended to leave first. Lizzie's mother left abruptly. Lizzie's grandmother left gradually, drifted away from herself in bits and pieces, names and nouns. But even when she could no longer recognize her own granddaughter, she still recognized the women on TV, asked after them as if their comas and kidnappings were real. Once Lizzie's father got sick, Lizzie had given up trying to brace the wall between fact and fiction. Reality offered little but loss—why not let her grandmother believe as she liked. She didn't need to know that Lizzie's mother had come home to care for her dying ex-husband, that Lizzie's sister had fled to Israel, abandoned them all in favor of God. Instead, Lizzie would sit by her grandmother's bed, hold her palsied hand, tell her that Yasmine's affair had come to light and Eleanor was about to figure out she'd married her kidnapper, that Jasper had woken from his coma but couldn't remember whose bullet had put him there. She never told her grandmother she was majoring in psychology, specializing in memory, subspecializing in figments, false memories indistinguishable from real ones, because she needed to understand why Yasmine and Eleanor and Jasper had been remembered, while Lizzie was forgotten.

Talking to Wendy Doe was a little like talking to no one, but that was still too much honesty to risk. Nor was Lizzie in the mood for the easy lie. "If you think about life as a war against loss, then memory is the only real weapon we have," Lizzie finally said. "So how could I study anything else?"

"If you think about life as a war against loss, you're kind of setting yourself up for defeat, no?"

"I didn't make the rules."

"I must scare the shit out of you." Wendy sounded proud. "Thank you for the lack of bullshit in that answer."

"How do you know it wasn't bullshit?"

Wendy paused, like this was a good and difficult question. "Maybe it's easier to see through everyone else's shit when you don't have any left of your own."

"What you said before, about how it feels not to remember—how it feels like nothing? Tell me more," Lizzie said. "Please. I want to understand."

There was silence. They sipped their tea. Wendy stared hard at the surface of hers, as if trying to memorize its particular color and sheen. Lizzie tried to imagine building a life moment by moment. There might be an impulse, she thought, to binge on the present, shovel memories, no matter how mundane, into the gaping void.

"Have you ever forgotten anything you desperately want to remember?" Wendy asked.

Lizzie thought about her father's smell, the weight of her father's arms when he hugged her, the sound of his voice when he yelled at her, when he thanked her, when he told her he loved her—all the things she could no longer summon. Her memory of him was like a photo album, finite and fading, the images too flat, the gaps between them impossibly wide. "Yes."

"It doesn't feel like that," Wendy said. "It doesn't feel like a puzzle. And it doesn't feel like a missing leg or something. It doesn't feel like anything's missing."

"That's why you don't want your memory back?"

"You don't get it: I don't not want it back, and I don't want it back. There is no it. You can't miss what never happened."

"But just because you don't remember it, doesn't mean it didn't happen. The it here is your whole life."

Wendy shrugged. "You asked how it feels. That's how it feels. Look—do you have a kid?"

"No."

"You want one?"

"I'm not sure how that's relevant."

"Do you miss him?"

"Him who?"

"Your future baby," Wendy said. "This helpless, adorable creature who you love more than you've ever loved anything. You would die for him."

"Are you saying you think you have a child?"

"No, I'm saying, *do you miss him?*"

"Of course not. There is no him yet."

"Exactly."

When she went back to her room, Lizzie made a list: every moment she could remember from the last two weeks. She managed a few lines of conversation, a drugstore trip for toothpaste, the sense that she'd been mildly sad, the invitation from Gwen that had not come. Almost everything that happens is forgotten. Decades swallowed. Maybe, Lizzie thought, the mystery isn't why we forget some things and not others. Maybe the mystery is why we ever remember.

Lizzie's favorite soap convention was the *retcon*. This was fan lingo for retroactive continuity, an Orwellian revision of past events. The narrative gods recklessly reshaped the past to suit their present needs: *We have always had a third child. We have always had these mysterious scars and the violent backstory that produced them. We have always been at war with Eastasia.* She did not miss the child she hadn't yet had, or any other nonexistent presence from her imagined future. But the logic doesn't hold, she might have told Wendy, were she a person inclined toward personal confession. It was possible to miss a thing you'd never had, a remnant from some alternate and preferable version of the past. Sometimes Lizzie felt like she was missing an entire life. All the people she should not have lost. All the things she was meant to possess: Love. Success. A home. A purpose. A sister who was not absent, a father who was not dead. She would have happily remembered a different life, and almost could. Other Lizzie, better Lizzie, felt like a name dancing on the tip of her tongue, a life she could take back, if she could only remember living it.

WENDY

How to be a test subject

For a CT scan, drink contrast solution and wait sixty to ninety minutes for it to circulate through the bloodstream, make the brain glow. Feel the fluid warm your veins, make you want to pee. Do not pee. Step behind curtain, strip. Gown. The room is too cold. The gown is too thin. Enter a bright white room. Lie down on the padded table. Let technician arrange your body, brace your head in place. Let him fasten a thick strap across your chest. Try to breathe. Watch him disappear from view. Watch the ceiling slide one way as the table slides another, through a large, flashing tube. Try to breathe. Unless the voice in the intercom tells you not to breathe. Do as it says. In this room, it is the voice of your god.

For an EEG test, let the cap be fitted snugly over your head. The cap is covered with small metal probes, each attached to a wire. Try to believe they will not electrocute you. Sit very still as a green gel is injected into each probe. Smile politely when you are told this machine will channel the music of your brain waves, the amplitudes and frequencies. The EEG technician fancies himself a poet. He says, now let's listen to the song of yourself. But first, maintain a resting state for eight minutes. *To rest*, in this context, means sit up straight. Stare fixedly at the image of a small purple cross. Wait for the voice to give you permission to stop, for the real test to begin.

Before an fMRI, remove all jewelry. Any metal in an fMRI could superheat and burn your skin. If you have a metal implant in your body, the machine's magnetic field could yank it out of place, tear a swath of destruction through muscle and tendon and flesh. You don't know if you have any metal inside you. Trust the doctors who claim you do not. Remove all clothing. Gown up. Lie down. Let the technician place a plastic shell over your head and face, a joystick in your hand. This is how you will communicate, while keeping perfectly still. Whatever you do, *keep perfectly still.* Let padded headphones be fitted over your ears. Lie still as the table slides you into a coffinlike tube. Try to listen to the commands playing through your headphones. Focus on the mirror, suspended over your eyes, angled toward a screen. See what they want you to see. Faces you don't know, with expressions you try to recognize. Press one button for happy, one button for sad. Don't move. Don't scratch. Don't fall asleep. Don't panic. Don't imagine what will happen if they leave you here.

Before a PET scan, fast for six hours. Raise arm, allow cannula to be inserted. Watch radioactive dye flow from syringe to cannula, from cannula to your veins. Wait for your organs and tissue to absorb radioactive material. Take off your clothes, again. Your gown is still too thin. Lie down. Behind glass, your scientists watch your brain at work. Wonder what they see, and if they can see what you think of them.

LIZZIE

Their first one-on-one update meeting had barely begun and Strauss was already bored. No one who knew Lizzie would have called her a good observer of social cues, but this diagnosis didn't demand much acuity. Strauss was making a dumb show of distraction, his pencil playing a jazz riff against the rim of his glasses, his eyes volleying between Lizzie's face and a sunlit view of the Meadowlark woods. As Lizzie relayed the results of Wendy's latest brain scans, she caught him checking his watch three times.

"I can come back," she said on the third, wishing she'd sounded less apologetic and more aggrieved. "Or just leave you with the notes?"

"I'm hungry." Strauss stood. "You hungry?"

"Uh, sure?"

"Should I take that interrogatory tone as the lack of conviction characteristic to your generation, or a more idiosyncratic inability to gauge your own physical desires?"

"You can take it as my uncertainty that my hunger is relevant, given the foodlike stuff they serve in the cafeteria?"

"Who said anything about the cafeteria?"

Yes, she was riffing. Yes, her central uncertainty had stemmed from the suspicion she was being dismissed. Yes, everything she said to him came with a terminal question mark, because everything she said was, at base, a variant of the same question. *Am I, Lizzie Epstein, dutiful novitiate in this cathedral to pure science, judged meritorious by you, its god? Am I boring you? Am I impressing you? Am I revealing the deep truth of self and its unworthiness, am I destroying my future with this sentence, or this next one, am I proving that I am special? Am I special? Am I sufficient? Am I pleasing you? How can I please you more?* And yes, she knew that as a student, a scientist, a woman, she was not supposed to care, and to whatever degree she did care, it was supposed to be for pragmatic purposes, the necessity to impress power. It was not supposed to be because she had fallen prey to the myth of the Great Man of Science, or because seeing Strauss close up had only inflated the myth it should have punctured, or because—his respect seeming an improbable goal—she longed for his approval. *Supposed to* aside: there it was. Lizzie was an inept observer of others but prided herself on a supreme ability to gauge her own desires, and she admitted, if only to herself, she desired this.

But it was also true that the cafeteria, state of the art or not, was disgusting, and far too reminiscent of cafeterias past. Junior high, summer camp, retirement home, hospital, all fetid with the same stink—stale refrigerator, soggy french fries. Often, the other fellows ate with the postdocs and junior researchers who staffed their project labs, which left Lizzie scanning the room for safe harbor, some empty corner of a table where she could pick at limp salad and sip weak coffee with a modicum of dignity before fleeing. She'd mastered this skill in eighth grade, the speed eating, the gaze performatively intent on absorbing reading material, but had never hoped to hone it into adulthood. The days the other fellows ate together were worse. Mariana spewed thinly veiled commentary on Lizzie's lack of a solo project; Dmitri dripped jealousy about her proximity to Strauss; Clay simply hit on her, but lazily, as if he couldn't resist the opportunity for practice but wanted to ensure she knew it was nothing else. Worse than this were the evident ways they peacocked for each other, pretending at modesty regarding their own work and innocent intellectual curiosity about one another's, all of them probing for weakness, jockeying for superiority, driven by the Darwinian will to eliminate and survive that had earned them their slot to begin with—and it was clear not one of them considered Lizzie a worthy threat. Why would they? Her project was nearly a joke, and it was only nearly hers. She chose not to care. But she'd taken to eating a granola bar and a bag of potato chips alone in her closet-sized cubicle and calling it a day.

Strauss led Lizzie to the Meadowlark's "hall of memory," his shrine to the institute's earlier incarnation. It was as unsettling as Wendy's description had led her to believe. Framed photos of asylum inmates marched down both walls—nineteenth-century patients outfitted as farmhands, twentieth-century women in ice baths and induced comas, all interspersed with oil portraits of the Meadowlark's medical directors. The hall dead-ended in an exhibition of what Strauss presumably saw as his spiritual forebears: long-dead Europeans framed over glass display cases harboring the tools of their trade. Strauss had collected ice picks and straitjackets and electroshock probes, a century and a half of failed miracles. A display in the center paid tribute to the lobotomy technique, which, according to the plaque, had been debuted at the Meadowlark before spreading across the state. Strauss settled onto a long wooden bench near the ice picks. She sat beside him, trying to be casual about leaving an appropriate distance between her thigh and his.

"So? What do you think of my little tribute to historical memory? I'm told most of the staff finds it unsettling. I hope it doesn't put you off your lunch." He'd ordered Chinese food from a dive down the street, cold Szechuan noodles and chicken lo mein for them to share. She preferred pork, but he assured her the chicken was not to be missed.

"It's interesting." She felt like she needed to seize the moment, convince him he was right to treat her like a hypothetical equal. Groping for something anodyne but not moronic to say, she feigned interest in the nearest painting, a medieval orgy of lunatics in a boat.

"The *Ship of Fools*," Strauss said. "Hieronymus Bosch. Doesn't hold a candle to the original, of course. You've been to the Louvre?"

Lizzie snorted.

He laughed. "Here's where you say, '*If you want me to go to Paris, triple my stipend.*'"

"Would that work?"

"God no."

He opened the takeout containers. Steam rose, along with a rich, greasy smell that made her stomach gurgle, she hoped not loud enough for him to hear.

"You want me to run you through my proposal for the next set of tests?" she asked, flipping through her notes one oily fingerprint at a time.

"I don't like to work while I eat. It's called a lunch break for a reason—let's break, shall we?"

"Oh."

"If that's all right with you?"

There was nothing wrong with a fellow and her adviser having lunch together in a semiprivate locale, and no reason said lunch couldn't stray from professional to personal. Lizzie knew this. She also knew enough about academic optics to hesitate. It was one thing to be seen as a teacher's pet; another to be seen as a teacher's plaything. She knew what happened to those girls, the ones who let themselves notice the body attached to the mind, the unexpectedly muscular forearms, the stubble gracing sharp jawline, the fingers, thick but nimble, long, strong. It wasn't even necessary to notice such things, it was enough for other people to assume you had. Once, in her first semester of grad school, her adviser had reached across his desk to brush a hypothetical strand of hair from her face and said, "If you act like you're beautiful, other people will believe it." Since then he'd been her most tireless supporter. She was never sure whether she was supposed to feel like she owed him something, or the reverse.

"Of course it's okay," she told Strauss. It was just lunch.

"Good. Now. Question for you. What's the first thing you remember?"

"From what?"

"From life. First memories. A little pet project. I collect them from everyone I meet."

He had a rascal's smile, a crooked canine that made his face less intimidating when revealed. There was a tiny shaving scratch at the curve of his chin, a redness on the bridge of his nose where his glasses had rubbed too tight. She wanted to give him a good answer, a memory that was true.

"My mother, crying at the kitchen table. I don't think she knew I was there."

"Do you remember why she was crying? Or how it made you feel?"

"Scared."

Strauss scribbled something in a narrow black journal. "Did she cry a lot?"

Lizzie answered as a scientist. "You mean, because if the episode was an outlier, it would contribute to the likelihood that this memory would imprint?"

"I mean did she cry a lot. That seems like it would have been hard." He closed the notebook, slurped down a large mouthful of noodles, mumbled around it. "Promise me you'll never tell my wife you saw me eat this."

"She's antinoodle?"

"Antisalt, anti-MSG, antiflavor. I think I'd prefer death to another lean turkey sandwich."

"I suspect your wife might feel differently."

"I suspect you'd be surprised."

He stopped, like he'd said something unexpected, or maybe he was simply aping the expression on her face. "A joke," he said. "And she's not *making* me the sandwiches, incidentally. Simply shaming me into making them myself. If I really loved my daughter, et cetera." Then, "In case you were wondering, I do. Not so incidentally."

It was hard to picture, the great Benjamin Strauss fishing LEGOs out of the carpet, washing sippy cups, and scraping spaghetti sauce off the wall; Strauss applauding as a tutu'd little girl spun a pirouette and curtsied. Or would Strauss be the kind of father who'd forbid his daughter the froth of pink and pirouettes? More likely, Lizzie decided, the kind oblivious to its existence, because he had to work.

"You were saying," he said. "Your mother."

"I most definitely was not."

"Hmm."

"You ever consider switching to clinical? You've got a great Freudian *hmm*."

He clapped a hand to his chest. "Slings and arrows to the heart!" But he looked delighted. She had delighted him. "You would have made an excellent Dora. Very satisfying evasions."

"Okay, so what's your first memory?"

"My father, in his armchair, listening to Bach. I would have been maybe four or five? Old enough to have noticed he was a bastard. Young enough not to see why."

It was part of the Strauss mythology: father a Holocaust survivor, son dedicating his life to the problem of traumatic memory, in loving tribute to the man who'd never escaped it.

"In this memory, he was smiling," Strauss said. He was not. "That was the extremity, if one is required. I remember hiding somewhere, low—under a table, maybe? Thinking if I moved, if I made a sound, I would ruin it. The last of his happiness gone, and it would be my fault."

Lizzie watched his hand, felt an insane impulse to hold it, give comfort, warmth.

"The thing about memory, of course"—his fingers sanded the edge of the journal—"was I really worrying about that then, or do I only think so now? Or has the retrieval of that sliver, every time I conjure it up over the years, warped the image so much that there's nothing left of the original? Am I simply remembering something I used to remember, a distorted copy of a distorted copy?" He shrugged off whatever mood had descended. "The only child's burden, I guess. No one left to ask, no one left to remember with."

She liked this version of him, shrunk down to human scale. She liked him small; she liked him vulnerable. She did not like that she liked this.

"After that day, I never saw him listening to that record without tears. Did I miss them the first time? Did I just later imagine the smile, pick the version of the past I preferred? And *that's* the thing, isn't it. No way of knowing."

"I think about that a lot, having no one to check your memories against. Having siblings doesn't save you from ending up alone. Everyone ends up there eventually, right? Alone with whatever memories matter most?"

"Jesus, that's depressing." He laughed. "I knew I liked you." He liked her; this had not occurred to her.

Strauss checked his watch. She checked it, too, more stealthily: expensive.

"I have a meeting. Well, more of a schmoozing. Walk with me?"

They strolled, lingering along the earliest of the historical displays.

"Most people talk about the science of the past as if it was barbaric, but these were wonders, in their day." Strauss gestured to the faces of the dead scientists, framed smugly beside the evidence of their landmark achievements. Pinel and Tuke, fathers of the modern mental asylum. James and Freud, ur-fathers of modern psychology. Charcot, father of hysteria, and beside his portrait, the spiritual daughter, Augustine, teenage hysteric draped in ethereal white, face contorted in what looked like orgiastic joy. Egas Moniz, father of the lobotomy, for which he'd received a Nobel Prize. Walter Freeman, surgeon and salesman, who'd peddled the technique across America, framed beside his winning slogan, Lobotomy Brings Them Home. "In their time, these men were all miracle workers," Strauss said.

"Well. They were all men, at least."

He laughed at this, as if she was trying to be adorable, and made it so.

"Everything we do is wrong," he said. "That's why all this is here: to remind us. The goal is to be a little less wrong, every year, every day. That's the miracle." Then he said he had to go, to the schmoozing for which he was now late. Then he was gone.

The next day he appeared in her office doorway, two foil-wrapped steak sandwiches in hand, eyebrows raised. "Hungry?" And yes, she was.

Lizzie was sincerely trying not to notice Gwen's nipple, but Gwen's nipple was making this impossible. And it wasn't just the nipple, swollen, red, crusty. It was the ballooning flesh it festooned. It was the feral lips fish-mouthing its moist tip, rooting, hungry. Lizzie was trying to tell Gwen about work, about what it was like being back in Philadelphia, about Wendy Doe, whom Lizzie was doing her best not to like, partly because it seemed detrimental to her scientific objectivity, but mostly because it seemed ill-advised to get attached to someone with the existential version of a terminal condition. Gwen bitched about her mother-in-law. Lizzie politely inquired after Andy, whom she was still doing her best to like. She politely did not inquire after Gwen's novel, which was presumably still unfinished. The baby sucked, swallowed. Everything felt like small talk. Lizzie told Gwen about the strange quality of her conversations with Benjamin Strauss, the sense of say-anything freedom that usually required late nights, alcohol, absolute dark. Gwen maneuvered baby on boob, pretending to listen.

When the baby was born, and Lizzie was still living three thousand miles away, Gwen had dutifully detailed every shitlike feeling: contractions, of course, but also the panicked boredom, the vaginal tearing, the literal *shitting* on the delivery table. ("I was married two years before I even let myself shit while Andy was in the next room!" Gwen had said. "Huh," Lizzie said.) It hurt to pee, Gwen had complained, too bad because she now peed all the time. It hurt to shit, which was similarly easier than ever. ("Suffice to say I'm never going for a run again," Gwen said, "but if I do, I'm wearing a diaper.") Gwen wasn't Lizzie's first friend to have a baby, but she was Lizzie's first best friend to have a baby, the first both willing and determined to tell her everything. ("When it's your turn, you're going to know so much more than I did," Gwen had said, and Lizzie didn't say that the more Gwen told her, the less Lizzie wanted her turn, which in retrospect had marked the beginning of this new phase of their friendship, the phase of Lizzie not saying things.)

Lizzie loved her best friend too much to want her unhappy. Lizzie was glad for her best friend that she'd stopped calling at 3 a.m., crying softly as her baby suckled, wondering in a whisper if she'd made a mistake. She was glad that Gwen was happy, that Gwen loved baby Charlotte, loved motherhood, loved that she could squirt milk from her nipples and suck mucus from her baby's nostrils. Gwen loved the pattern of freckles on Charlotte's little baby ass and the spastic fisting of Charlotte's little baby hands, and of course Gwen loved her baby smell and the way she looked when she slept in her baby bassinet, and the way her baby face lit up when she smiled, now that she smiled, and Lizzie, babied out, was doing her best. She was happy for her best friend. She very much wanted to be happy.

Lizzie and Gwen had bought a joint ad in their high school yearbook, advertising their superior brand of friendship: a large black-and-white photo of their younger selves dressed for Halloween as Bo and Luke Duke, with a caption reading In This Together. *This* was their identical wrist casts after the Roller Skating Incident of 1979. Their three-day suspension after Jennifer Weinberg had pulled her eyes to slits, told Gwen she smelled like wonton soup, and that her mother said Gwen's mother probably wanted to kill herself when she had a daughter, and Lizzie smacked her in the face with a floor hockey stick. *This* was the bat mitzvah circuit, the SATs, Lizzie's mother leaving and Lizzie's father dying, Gwen's mother losing her job and Gwen's sister losing an eye, college applications, loves requited and un-, virginities disposed of, Gwen's dreams of a Pulitzer and Lizzie's plans for a Nobel, the abortion, the date rape, the togetherness of their *this* unabated by time or distance, indivisible, except that now, whatever Gwen was in, Lizzie was not. All through the whirlwind romance, the fairy-tale wedding, the purchase of the swanky Old City co-op, the pregnancy, the birth, Lizzie had prepared for an envy that never materialized; she hadn't thought to steel herself against this, the feeling that she'd been replaced—not by Andy, per se, and not by Charlotte, per se, but by GwenAndyCharlotte, an unbreachable unit. The feeling that Gwen, who'd befriended her on the first day of kindergarten, who had shoplifted Lizzie's first tampons, whose zucchini-based demonstration had coached Lizzie through her first blow job, was leaving her behind.

"So you want to fuck your boss," Gwen said as she switched the baby to the other breast. Maybe she'd been listening after all.

"I'm in it for his brain," Lizzie said. "No other part of his anatomy."

Gwen made a noise suggestive of disbelief.

"It's like with Mr. Vickner," Lizzie said, invoking the eighth-grade history teacher with whom they'd both been mildly obsessed. "It's not like either of us wanted to fuck him."

Gwen's smile suggested she was remembering the day she'd gotten overheated, passed out, woke to find herself on the tiled floor, Mr. Vickner peering down at her with concern. He'd rested his palm on her forehead, she'd bragged to Lizzie later. The most, or at least most thrilling, physical contact either of them had yet managed with the opposite sex. "Speak for yourself."

Lizzie felt herself relaxing, for what might have been the first time since she'd touched down in Philadelphia. There was no need to perform herself for Gwen, no point in trying to choose words carefully when Gwen understood what lay beneath them. All those miles that had separated them, the motherhood that did now—neither could erase their shared history, Lizzie reminded herself. They were family, and the baby didn't have to change that, any more than the husband did.

"Seriously, though," she said. "You know I would never."

"Obviously I know. You would never."

Lizzie would never. Not just for professional reasons and not just for ethical ones, but because her life was the result of her mother fucking someone else's husband, because she had witnessed her father deal, daily, with the fact of some other man fucking his wife.

"But there's nothing wrong with wanting to," Gwen said. "Or entertaining a poor, undersexed mother with details of your hot-for-teacher fantasy come to life."

"You and Andy still aren't . . . ?"

"It's not like I don't want to. In theory. But when the moment is upon us, I just . . ." She shrugged. "It's hard to explain."

Lizzie took her free hand, the one not holding the baby in place, and squeezed.

"I missed you," Gwen said. "Never leave me again."

"Just to be clear, I'm taking that as an invitation to move in."

"Done."

"I'm sure Andy will be thrilled," Lizzie said.

"Fuck Andy."

Lizzie grinned. "He wishes."

"Fuck you, too," Gwen said, and then they were laughing, like they used to, like there was no one on the planet but the two of them, and Lizzie thought maybe this could be enough.

WENDY

How he looks at me

Like I'm a car that won't start, and if he opens the hood, examines every valve and piston, he'll find the problem.

Like I'm an insect pinned in place, and if he angles the magnifying glass just right, he'll watch me burn.

Like I'm a piece of furniture, without will or consequence.

Like I'm a mosquito bite, begging, *scratch me, please*. Like I'm a mountain, and he wants to climb me. Like I'm a dog, and—it's a miracle!—I can speak.

How he looked at me when we met: like I was human.

Everyone before him had treated me as a set of problems to be handled. A *thing*, broken. Everyone before him would say, Now I'm going to check your blood pressure or now I'm going to take an X-ray or now I'm going to insert the speculum, now you're going to feel the pinch. No one asking my permission, only narrating my future on my behalf.

There was something about the way he said my name, as if it was a name rather than a label. It made me feel newly real, and I thought, am I the kind of woman who needs someone else's permission to believe in my own existence?

I had by then been this woman, in this body, for a month. Hospital first. Mental hospital, worse. Then women's shelter, two nights, then the third night when I couldn't stop crying. These tears were happening to me. I was not making them happen. I was calm—but only in a secret inner corner no one else could see. The body made its noisy fuss and was carted back to the hospital, a pill forced down its throat, and soon the body was as calm as I was, and we both fell asleep. When we woke up, the body was strapped down. It screamed.

Time floated. I swallowed more pills. The pills made a fog. Sometimes I talked to myself, to see if my voice would sound as far away as everything else.

His voice didn't slice through the fog so much as dissipate it. He painted two pictures for me. First, the Wendy Doe who stayed in the hospital. Not for long, he said. The bed cost money, the oversalted soup cost money, the state could find cheaper ways to house me, and would—back to the shelter, then, or maybe the street. "You're not a prisoner," he said. "They can't keep you, and trust me, they don't want to." This Wendy Doe had no means of legal employment and no claim to unemployment or disability or any other official payout from the state, because in the state's eyes, Wendy Doe did not exist.

In the second picture, he said, I would have a room of my own. A bed, food, an allowance, freedom to do as I liked, for as long as I liked. I only needed to agree to let myself be studied. He said we would be collaborators. "Spelunkers," he said. "Exploring the mysteries of your mind." He called me a fascinating case. He said he monitored the news for possible subjects, but I was the first in months he'd deemed worthy of further study. I asked if he thought he could help me remember. He asked if I wanted him to.

"No." I liked that he seemed unsurprised.

"Good," he said. "Frankly, you're of no use to us once you get your memories back."

I liked that, too.

I wanted to be a spelunker of my own mind. Maybe I was the kind of woman with a thirst for knowledge, I thought. Or maybe I was the kind of woman who would shape myself into what this man wanted me to be.

"Let's achieve greatness together," he said. Maybe it was a lie, him looking at me like I was a person, but I don't think so. I think I was real to him then, for the last time. A real person is someone who can choose, even if she's choosing to give her choices away. A real person can say no or she can say yes.

I said yes.

LIZZIE

It wasn't all paperwork. Wendy Doe had no source of income but the largesse of Strauss, who was happy enough to extend it as long as Lizzie governed its use. Absolute freedom to come and go as she liked, but if she would like to go anywhere requiring a vehicle, Lizzie was her ride. It left Lizzie feeling part chaperone, part lady-in-waiting, part probation officer, and left Wendy feeling resentment she didn't bother to disguise. It also meant Lizzie could spend an afternoon at the mall or the movies on the institute's dime, and count it as work. Today's mission: new clothes, enough to replace the shapeless, missized hand-me-downs Wendy had accumulated in her month bouncing between state institutions. Maybe she would feel less like a mental patient, Wendy said, if she had some better jeans.

"I feel like I'm in a very downscale *Pretty Woman*," Lizzie said from her corner of the dressing room as Wendy extricated herself from a strappy pleather tank top and buttoned herself into a conservative chambray shirt. "Or any rom-com ever, I guess." They'd been in the department store for two hours, as Wendy sampled one sartorial self after another: punk, goth, grunge, girly, high fashion, tomboy, comfortable and un-, glaring, with each costume change, at her reflection, as if daring it to weigh in—to indicate that Wendy had finally hit on a stylistic manifestation of her abandoned essential self. Now Wendy ripped off the button-down, pulled on a sweater the color of a sunset.

She spun slowly in front of the mirror. "This would look better on you."

"I was just thinking that."

"So buy it."

Lizzie shook her head. The stipend she got from the Meadowlark wasn't insignificant, especially given that she was currently living rent-free, but the complications of said rent-free lodgings weren't insignificant, either. Lizzie was hoarding every dollar she made for an eventual sublet and the freedom from maternal oversight it would ensure.

"Then how about we let the Meadowlark buy it for you?" Wendy suggested.

Lizzie eyed the price tag, winced, and told Wendy the clothing allowance she'd been given was for Wendy alone.

"Have you ever met a rule you didn't blindly follow?" Wendy asked.

"I don't blindly follow anything."

"Uh-huh." Wendy exchanged a grin with her reflection, then put on the coat they'd bought earlier that day and began buttoning it over the sweater.

"What are you doing?" Lizzie whispered.

"What does it look like I'm doing?"

"I'm sure there are *cameras* in here."

Wendy shrugged. "What can they do, arrest me? You think jail would be that much different from the institute?"

"Yeah. Actually, I do."

Wendy looked at her carefully, then laughed. "Oh, I get it."

"What?"

"You *want* me to. It's the closest you can get to scratching the itch. Pleasuring your inner delinquent."

"Bullshit." But Lizzie remembered an afternoon with Gwen, half her lifetime ago, an aging drugstore attendant, an overpriced lipstick, a half-hearted effort to dissuade, and Gwen's diagnosis as she pressed the stolen lipstick into Lizzie's palm, Lizzie's fingers closing over the cool plastic, Lizzie's pulse, quickened. Gwen's theory that Lizzie needed this, the safety of moral superiority sprinkled with the rewards of vice. Fifteen years had passed. Gwen had transformed herself into a wife, a mother—was it possible that Lizzie was still exactly, pathetically the same?

Wendy stepped out of the dressing room. "You coming? Or you telling?" She walked casually to the exit, then through it, and when no sirens attended her departure, Lizzie followed.

Wendy had been at the Meadowlark for three weeks, mired in her fugue for seven, and there was still no indication as to where—or who—

she'd been before that. Wendy made it clear she resolutely didn't care. Lizzie, on the other hand, was consumed by speculation. The better she got to know Wendy—if you could be said to know a person whose personality was about as stable as a weather system—the more she wondered. Who was this woman before? Did she seem like someone's mother, someone's wife, someone's teacher, someone's killer? Was this woman she was now, or was in the process of becoming, consistent with that past self, at odds with it, or something in between? And who was looking for her—was it out of love or hate, was it desperate or despairing, had they given up, and if not, where were they, and if there was no they, then why?

These were not questions Wendy had any interest in. She didn't give a shit, she said, about the woman she'd been, the one who'd abandoned her body to Wendy's occupancy like a reckless homeowner leaving the door wide open on her way out. In the absence of personal history, Wendy had developed an interest—a fixation, Strauss called it—in the Meadowlark's history, specifically the female patients who had come before. She took long walks in the graveyard at the edge of the Meadowlark woods, and when Lizzie joined her, Wendy narrated imagined lives for the women buried there. Lizzie had asked why she was so willing to speculate about these strangers' pasts but never her own, but Wendy said it wasn't their pasts that interested her. It was the eternal present they'd lived within the asylum walls, cut off from whoever they'd been or might have become, spending decades, some of them, tended to by demons internal and external. Endlessly treated, never cured. "You're not a mental patient," Lizzie reminded her. "This is no longer an asylum. You're not one of them." She said it to comfort. Wendy didn't want comfort, at least not from Lizzie; she took it from the women, she said, from the bodies in the ground and the ghosts in the walls. In this place, she said, in this eternal present, she never felt alone.

It was the kind of crisp fall day that demanded apple orchards and hayrides, sun glinting off gloriously dying leaves, and they lingered in the Meadowlark parking lot, nowhere to go and in no hurry to go inside. Wendy wriggled out of the stolen sweater, offered it to Lizzie—unless, she teased, Lizzie was afraid of receiving stolen property—and Lizzie took it. The wool was impossibly soft.

"You love it," Wendy said.

"I love it."

Wendy looked to the sky with exaggerated alarm.

"What?"

"Just waiting to see if you get struck by lightning for admitting it. There's always got to be a consequence, right?"

"Fuck off," Lizzie said, as she would to an actual friend, and when Wendy pulled out a pack of cigarettes—probably also stolen, Lizzie realized—she didn't stop the subject from lighting up.

"You think he's attractive?" Wendy said. "Dr. Strauss?"

"I never thought about it. Why?"

"Just free associating, your favorite. I've been trying to figure it out, but I can't tell—he looks too much like himself, you know?"

Lizzie did know.

"There's something about him, though," Wendy said. "Like he's a little more . . . I don't know, *awake* than most people?"

Lizzie knew that, too. "I'm not sure you should be smoking."

"By the time the body gets lung cancer, I'll be long gone, so . . ." Wendy took a long drag, coughed, tried again. Offered it to Lizzie, who shook her head. "You keep telling me I'm someone's imaginary friend, and one day I'm going to vaporize. So why not try everything? Risk anything? What do I care what happens to the body?"

Lizzie had once briefly toyed with the idea of studying developmental psychology—she'd never much liked children, but she did love the idea of them as natural-born physicists, the theory that babies began life as miniature Aristotelians and only by trial and error discovered Galilean inertia and Newtonian motion, every toddler a live-action Wile E. Coyote, running off the cliff and learning gravity on the way down. It occurred to her now to imagine a moral philosophy taking shape in the same way, baby Hobbeses and little Lockes bumping into sin and consequence. Wendy had experienced neither yet; she had begun this life with literally nothing left to lose. Why not expect her to do anything, risk anything, at least until she'd acquired something of value, then been forced to suffer its absence?

"Everyone's life is temporary in the long run," Lizzie said. "By your logic, anybody has permission to do anything."

"Now you're hearing me." Wendy stubbed out the cigarette, tucked the pack into her pocket, suggested, with only a slight ironic twist on the operative word, that they go *home*.

"What if we're studying the wrong thing?" Lizzie asked Strauss that night when he wandered into her office. He did that a lot—he liked to work late, liked the shadowy quiet in the wake of the day's bustle, often left to put his daughter to bed then came back to the Meadowlark, concentrated best, he said, in the moonlight dark. She said she did, too, and that had once been true but no longer was, because now, when the building emptied and sun abandoned sky, she could only ever half focus on the page in front of her, the other half of her attuned to the hallway, waiting for the sound of his footsteps. He liked to stroll his corridors, he said. He liked to lean in her doorway—not that there was much other option, as the office was barely big enough to fit desk, chair, and Lizzie. Sometimes he stopped in to check on her latest results; sometimes he raced in with promising results of his own, or, her favorite times, with a question for her, a need to bounce around an idea—as if Lizzie was a peer who could sufficiently bounce it back. Some nights he would invite her to walk with him, and they would talk.

They talked about his father, who'd died when he was a teenager, without offering any indication that Strauss had satisfied him or ever would. Isaac Strauss was a Viennese Jew, born into an empire and shaped by its wreckage. Supposed to be a great man, Strauss said, a physicist or a philosopher—then he blinked, and the world ended. Blinked again, and he was shaved and starved and marched away from his wife and sons, left for dead in a ditch, one more blink and there he was with a job as a bookkeeper, a new wife who spoke Russian, an American son who spoke only English, and a row house in, talk about mortal insults, *Germantown*. And he was told to be grateful, Strauss said, to think, there but for the grace of fucking God, so what kind of father could I expect him to be? They talked about his marriage and its evolution, the extraordinary turned ordinary by time and habit and—much as Strauss hated to admit it but, always the empiricist, could not deny—child rearing, his wife turned into his daughter's mother and Strauss, loving them both, feeling if not left behind, then left alone. He wanted to be a good father, he said, and a good husband, and a good man; he wanted to be a great scientist; he worried, he said, that these were not reconcilable goals.

She told him about LA, and what she missed. About Lucas, and what she didn't. Strauss said it sounded like he wasn't smart enough for Lizzie, and resented her for figuring this out. Strauss gave her the name of the Bach piece his father had loved, and that weekend she rooted through Tower Records until she found it. Strauss showed her a picture of his four-year-old, and admitted he was afraid of what damage might be wrought; he knew too much about the developing brain, too much about fatherhood and its flaws.

She had discovered the institute was less Strauss's brainchild than a physical manifestation of his neural map: he did not think like normal people, in straight lines and demarcated zones. He wandered in strange loops from quantum physics to music to geopolitics to the nature of the soul to, inevitably and always, the mind and its memory, which for him was not one subject but all subjects. He had a perfect ear for pitch, but could not remember the sound of his father's voice; he wanted to know why. He wanted to know everything, like she did, but laughed when she said so. He believed, he said, in the quixotic pleasures of the asymptote. If he wanted a solvable mystery, he'd be a physicist. She asked him what the point was, asking questions to which one didn't expect an answer. Maybe *you* should be a physicist, he said.

There was the night he burst in, buzzing with pleasure at some promising result, then caught a hint of something on her face, and asked her what was wrong. Nothing was wrong; nothing, at least, was the sum of what she intended anyone to know was wrong. She told him, nothing, and he asked if people generally believed her when she said so. People generally did. That sounds lonely, he said, and because he was right, because he was paying attention, she admitted it was her father's birthday, the first she'd spent in his house since he'd died. He sat on her desk, flipped open a research journal. He said this was how he preferred to pass the night.

She woke up some mornings thinking of him. If he would come that night, and what she would say. This night, though, she only wanted to talk about work; she was bursting with it. She'd spent the hours since her shopping trip blasting through every recent journal article she could find on autonoetic consciousness—the capacity to imagine a self consistent over time, the conviction, or illusion, that there was such a thing, a cohesive consciousness rather than an ever-evolving constellation of experience and impulse. It was a foundational element of autobiographical memory, but there was little said about the reverse, the question of how autobiographical memory, that beaded string of experience and impulse, informed or—Lizzie's nascent theory—formed the self. This was what she suggested, hesitantly, to Strauss. That studying Wendy's nonexistent memories, or the mechanism that had purged them, was a dead end—that the untapped resource here was the nearly blank slate of the subject's unformed ego.

He was intrigued. She cited the hippocampal role in decision generation, name-checked Kahneman and Tversky, and Strauss, with gathering enthusiasm, threw in Damasio's work on emotion and selfhood, and she said exactly, she wanted to do for memory what Damasio had done for feeling, recenter it as a keystone of consciousness. It was a perfect project for the Meadowlark's integrative philosophy, he said, Wendy Doe as the nexus of a multidisciplinary attack on the construction of the conception of self. Stage one in the revolution, she said, and they were off, the ideas flying between them—brain image studies, dips into artificial intelligence, neurobiology, computational psych, a dab of philosophy and religious studies, all an eventual outgrowth of the primary project, one woman's self-creation, the emergence of something from nothing in violation of natural law. It felt like a fever, both of them burning with the same flame. It felt like creation, ideas accreting like matter, like they were gods of an intellectual universe, bouncing a sun between them, its mass and luminosity swelling with each volley. She had never felt less self-conscious in his presence, more like her stripped-down self, the person she was when alone, only better.

"Yes," he said. "Perfect. Run with it."

"Me?"

"Yeah. You. The genius who came up with it."

Was she blushing? She was, fuck, blushing.

"Elizabeth, this was always a side project for me, another way into the questions of consolidation, trauma, erasure—but for you? Nail this, and it could be your life's work. At the very least, we'll get a paper out of it, and you can be sure I'll stick my name on there, I'm not a fool. But yours will go first. Take the lead. You can do it."

"Of course I can do it." This was the only possible answer, and if he thought it was true, maybe it was. When had she become someone who needed his permission to believe that?

"I knew you were special," he said. He was standing very close to her, but then, the size of the office demanded it. "Every fellow here is special, I make sure of that. But you've got . . . something else."

"What?"

The shadows were doing strange things to his face. She should stop focusing on the lines of his neck, the curve of his ear, she thought. She would have to tell Wendy in the morning that yes, it turned out he was attractive.

"You don't just see data points in isolation, or as evidence supporting a theory—you see them as plot points in a story. You want to find some cohesive explanation. A theory of everything, am I right?"

"You're right." Lizzie didn't believe in a god or a divinely ordained moral order, but she did believe, fervently, in the existence of an answer, the ultimate knowability of universes both inner and outer.

"You know how I feel about the delicious impossibility of ever knowing everything, but the impulse to try? The ambition? That's exceptional. That's what you needed to recognize in yourself. Now that you have? Now that you're ready to start asking the big questions? Let's see how much you can know." He rested a warm hand on her head, as if in benediction, then left.

Lizzie breathed. The rush of adrenaline receded. She felt limp. She felt bare. She turned out the light, wanted to sit in the dark, silently recite the conversation back to herself—and to sit with the consequence, the thing she had recognized that she couldn't now *un*-know. She and Gwen often debated the true definition of love: Gwen wanted to be wholly cared for. Lizzie wanted to be wholly seen. That's not love, Gwen argued. That's something else, something probably not even possible, and it was true none of Lizzie's relationships had ever measured up. People saw what you let them see. They saw what they wanted to. She held on to it, though, her secret fantasy, a man who would see a truth so essential she'd never glimpsed it herself. Gwen always said she asked too much, and Lizzie thought she was probably right. But now, Strauss. Strauss's gaze, aimed straight at her, narrating her to herself. She tried, halfheartedly, to believe she was simply feeling the aftereffects of intellectual communion, that this effervescence was strictly aboveboard, above neck. But her mind was not what she felt stirring, and not where she felt heat when she thought about his voice saying the word *exceptional*. He was married. He was old. He was her teacher and her employer. He was the most remarkable man she had ever met, and he thought she, too, was remarkable. She was in trouble.

WENDY

How I live now

A room of my own: one twin bed, one dresser, one stainless steel sink, one small bathroom and shower. No tub. No mirror, at first, but one has been supplied at my request. The face, to me, seems both familiar and strange. Lizzie says everyone feels that way.

The door has a combination lock, but no one locks me in. Three doors down, a man who remembers everything that once happened to him but nothing of what happens next has been locked inside for years. For his safety, Lizzie told me. I watched Dr. Strauss enter the combination, and now I can visit him as I want, safe or not.

Everything is new here, shiny and expensive. Everything but the walls, the floors, which are old, and still remember what they used to be. When Dr. Strauss was a child, he says, the Meadowlark was an asylum, and the asylum was a boogeyman used to frighten children into behaving. I make him tell me stories of the women who were here before I was, the voltage and knives that blunted their brains. This building is a body that remembers itself, which I may be the only one to recognize, because mine is a body that does not.

At night sometimes he knocks on my door.

He brings me to his office, and we sit side by side in the lamplight. He tells me about the women. He tells me about his wife, whom he is afraid he no longer loves. There are nights he turns out the light and puts on his music, and we let the chords shake us. He lets me see pieces of him no one else sees. It's only because he thinks being with me is the same as being alone.

He told me the story of the girl in white, the girl who looks like a tormented ghost, photographed and framed over his desk. He says her body is the most famous of bodies, that she was never one of the Meadowlark women but all of the Meadowlark women are, in a way, her daughters. He said she saved herself, ran away. He said her name was Augustine. He asked why I was so curious, and I lied that something about her felt familiar, that it would make me happy to have her close, and it was that easy. He gave her to me. If I'd admitted that I hated to see her there, trapped on his wall, that I wanted to help her run away again, he wouldn't have; I knew him well enough to know that. I watch her now while I'm trying not to fall asleep, and she watches me when I fail. I dream about her daughters, the Meadowlark women. I imagine them locked inside these same walls, dreaming their way toward me.

WENDY

This book

This is for you. Me. Whoever we are. This is the memory of me, once you remember yourself. This is the tang of lemon gelato, licked off a wooden stick, sweetly splintery against tongue; this is the elephant devouring the moon that the clouds paint across the November sky; these are the morning glories and beardtongues and dayflowers and turtleheads and scarlet beebalm of the woods behind the Meadowlark, and this is Dr. Strauss's voice enumerating each species, this is his one hand warm on mine as he helps me over a fallen tree and his other hand stroking bark or plucking a berry, this is sweet juice staining lips, breath of sky and pine; this is the taste of smoke, roll of cigarette between fingers, shrill of Lizzie's worry, tobacco staining borrowed lungs.

Don't you want to know who you were, everyone asks me. Who I was. People imagine a different kind of forgetting. A forgetting that's like a puzzle to be solved. Where are my keys, who's that girl, whatshisname. Or they imagine a forgetting that's like a death. I remember I used to love her, but not how, not why; I remember my hands on her body, but not the softness of her flesh. They hear mental block and they think *wall*. They think footholds or rope ladder or cannonball, they think *what's on the other side*. They think a boundary implies a crossing. There are no footholds. There is no other side. Dr. Strauss says this feeling is a symptom of the fugue. I remind him I am a symptom of the fugue. What kind of symptom wants to find its own cure?

This will be your body again someday. I intend to leave evidence of myself behind. Pictures of me are also pictures of you. So I have found other ways.

ALICE

Alice had done her due diligence on the widow and her dead husband. She'd slogged through some of the husband's academic papers, skimmed articles about his astonishing promise as a young scientist and what seemed to be, reading between the lines, his eventual decline as an aging bureaucrat. She'd found both of them on YouTube, the husband shilling for his institute, the wife chatting awkwardly about her book. She'd studied photos of Elizabeth and Benjamin Strauss posed awkwardly at various gala fund-raisers. She'd found nothing either of them had said or written that had anything to do with fugue states in general or Alice's mother in particular, but she'd read *Augustine*, the story of a lost girl held hostage in a house of science. She'd read about the genius men who reduced Augustine to a pathology, their very own psychiatric freak show. She'd read the widow's deliberations on whether these men had discovered symptoms that conformed to their predictions or generated them, their desire for a well-behaved disease spurring Augustine's mind to invent one.

In the press interviews, Elizabeth Strauss was stiff, overly made up, prone to fake laughter and the occasional inopportune giggle. The Elizabeth Strauss of the book was different, not just an intellectual searchlight roving across history and science in search of one girl's truth—as the flap copy put it—but an author trying to bribe her way into sealed archives, trespassing on private property, writing while tipsy with wine and despair, her own story leaking onto the one she was trying to tell. There was an edge of sadness to it, and Alice had liked this the best. Finding Benjamin Strauss's obituary had been a blow at first, but toward the end, the article had noted that the great scientist's wife had once been an academic herself, that she had arrived at the institute in 1999 for a fellowship, and stayed for a happily ever after. This was the year of Alice's mother's original disappearance—slim hope, but enough to propel Alice across the country to the widow's front door, and through it.

The widow's sadness, in person, was less poetically amorphous than husband-directed, and reminded Alice too much of her father missing his wife. She was about the same age as Alice's mother, but dressed like a college student, ratty jeans and tangled bun, which made her look older and younger at once. Alice's mother lived in crisp silk shirts, pleated slacks, skirts with tasteful hemlines, sensible heels—looked distinctly momlike, a woman to be trusted with bake sale proceeds or a Girl Scout troop blazing trail through woods. While her mother was all potential energy and disaster preparedness, the widow seemed spent. This aged her, too.

Alice hadn't planned to stay here, uninvited guest in a stranger's house. She had made a reservation at a hostel, had a date with Taco Bell and a lice-infested bunk bed, had girded herself for another night of guarding bag and body against the incursion of strangers, but she was too tired to resist the temptation of free food and, following, a clean bed with a thick pillow and a door that locked. There was a piece of her mother in this house—the mother she'd never known, the mother who'd vanished from the world before Alice entered it—lodged in Elizabeth's memories, and Alice was in no hurry to let either of them out of her sight. The widow—*call me Elizabeth*, she'd said, and though Alice had been drilled from birth in the necessities of honorifics, Mr. and Ms. and Dr. and ma'am, she tried—ordered them greasy Thai food, and Alice told the story she'd gotten too good at telling. Her mother's disappearance, her father's confession, the calling off of the search.

"They think she jumped off a bridge," Alice told the widow. "But there's no body."

"Then what makes them think she jumped?"

It was strange to see a reflection of her own grief on a stranger's face. Alice told her about the shoes left by the bridge, didn't explain how this was the detail that made suicide seem least viable. It was too obvious. If her mother had wanted to fake her own death, this was exactly how she would have done it.

"You think she might have come to Philadelphia?"

Alice shook her head. This was something she had not allowed herself to think. She was too practical to allow that particular fantasy. "I thought if I knew more about what it was like for her here—or, what she was like? Maybe it would help."

It was the rest of the sentence Alice had been unable to complete for herself, whether more information would help her explain where her mother had gone, or why, or how she had gone anywhere and left her daughter behind. Whether the story of her mother's time in Philadelphia would help Alice decide who her mother had been without her memory, and whether that person was more real than the woman Alice had thought she'd known. Whether she was here for help finding answers, or simply, as her father had suggested once he'd given up talking her out of the trip, for closure, whatever that meant. *If it helps you accept that she's not coming back*, he'd said. *If it helps you grieve.*

She refused to grieve a woman she did not believe was dead. She did not need help with that.

Elizabeth, like everyone else, said she was so, so sorry. Alice had learned to nod politely and accept the apology, but now there was the temptation to ask: *sorry for what?*

"How much do you remember about her?" Alice asked.

"A lot. We were friends, I guess you could say. Your mother was a remarkable woman."

"That's true, but . . ."

"What?"

"I read about fugue states. People inventing, like, whole different personalities? Acting like they're someone else? Do you think that happened with her?"

"I never got the chance to know her as Karen Clark," the widow said, but maybe Alice could draw her own conclusions. There were files, she said. Not just test results, but extensive notes about Wendy Doe's personality, her desires and fears. There were audio recordings. Alice wasn't ready to hear a stranger speaking with her mother's voice. Or maybe it was the familiar she wasn't ready for. Not yet.

"There's no hurry," the widow said. "We can do it in the morning." Instead, they retreated to safe territory, traded trivia about Alice's college classes, about the widow's writing process, about—though only glancingly, because this way lay danger—the history of the Meadow-lark, about this suburb and the concept of suburbs and the de- and reurbanization of America and at this point, bleary and on the brink, Alice nearly face-planted into her pad Thai, and the widow put her to bed. Another reason to stay that Alice preferred not to acknowledge: the comfort of care. To be back in the hands of a grown-up, to be offered a stack of freshly laundered towels, to be told to speak up if anything else was needed, the implicit promise that need would be met. By 9 p.m., she was tucked into crisp sheets, and after her sleepless night on the bus and her sleepless months in Chicago, something in her, some inner muscle that had been clenched since she left home, responded to the scent of fabric softener and released.

She jolted awake sometime after midnight, unable to remember her dream. In the dark, a stranger's furniture casting strange shadows, too jittery to fall back asleep, it suddenly seemed insane she was here, impossible to know what to do next. The decision to leave school had been impulsive, but there was a difference between decision and action. New Alice was capable of impulse, incapable of shedding so much of herself that she didn't prepare carefully before following it. She had been taught to believe that preparation was the best means of avoiding disaster. This was her mother's lesson, and while her mother had failed to prepare her for the disaster she'd dumped in Alice's lap, Alice had learned it too well. She'd applied for an emergency compassionate leave of absence, ensured her scholarship would remain if she returned by January. She'd done her research on the Meadowlark Institute, the Strausses, the unsatisfying theories of how and why a mind could suddenly eject its memories. She had been fine, she had been in control, as long as she kept moving toward her goal, checking things off her to-do list. Now, here, all things done, all motion ceased, she was without a plan.

She slipped out of the guest bedroom, quietly as she could, poked around the house using her phone as a flashlight, looking for evidence of . . . she didn't know what, but found only irritating vacation pictures, rich middle-aged tourists doing rich middle-aged tourist things. She found stacks of record albums, all pretentiously classical. Walls of books on the brain, the past, the great minds of so-called civilization. Dusty mahogany, silk-screened art, a framed letter handwritten by Freud. Everything in Alice's house was linoleum, wall-to-wall carpeting, and flowered wallpaper, except her room, which was still stenciled to look like a zoo.

She paused outside the widow's bedroom, recognizing the voices filtering into the hall. The widow was awake, too—and watching, of all things, her mother's soap. Alice was tempted to flee. She was tempted to open the door and, as she'd done so many times with her mother, tuck herself cozy beneath the blanket, watch the women on-screen weep and fight and love, watch life go on. Her mother had loved complaining about the show as much as she loved watching it, needled by the way its women were interchangeable, husbands swapping wives, actresses swapping roles. Alice suspected that for her mother, who rationalized every system and abided by every rule, this was the soap's greatest pleasure, a safe space within which to rage against the machine. And Alice couldn't disagree, but it had always comforted her, the daily constancy, the implication that all women were in some sense the same woman, behavior differentiated only by their position on a rotating cycle of fundamental drives: lust, duty, vengeance. The women on the show lived in real time, enduring one day and then another and another. Alice grew up; the women grew old. Happy endings ended, tragic ones, too. Days passed, and Alice kept going, and so did they, and even standing in a stranger's house, ear pressed to door, listening to the women who'd been fighting the same fight and loving the same man since before she was born, Alice felt a little less alone.

Mothers leave. Alice knew this, had seen it on TV and had once caught Madison Chee crying in the skating rink bathroom because, contra Mr. Chee's desperate hopes, fifteen hundred dollars in facility rental, private group lessons, gourmet cupcakes, and designer skates couldn't make up for the fact that Mrs. Chee had taken half the communal assets to Albuquerque where she was learning to blow, among other things, glass from a sculptor named Samuel. Alice didn't think her mother had a Samuel in her, figuratively or literally. But she preferred not to know what anyone else thought, or to watch them wonder what she thought, and so, for the first few days of her mother's disappearance, she'd refused to leave the house. She didn't want to talk to her friends, so she did not. They sent her worried texts, funny Snapchats, and Daniel left a Tupperware of his mother's brownies on the doorstep, which seemed mildly insensitive, considering. Alice ate them anyway.

To be young, she decided, is to believe love dissolves the boundaries of self. Yours is mine and mine is ours. This was what she'd told herself about Natalie and Emma and Daniel, what she'd imagined might be true for the whole of them, the loose group of friends, enemies, and nonentities with whom she'd endured seventeen years of educational efforts, even Brian Fletcher, who'd once picked his nose and smeared the results on her forehead, even Marcus Boone, the one non-Daniel boy she'd kissed, who had found her alone in a storage closet beside the junior high art room, pushed her against the wall, stuck his tongue in her mouth and his hand up her skirt, then let go, never mentioned it again, never knew she'd spent the rest of the day inside the closet, not sure if she should cry. She had believed they were all one—that to whatever degree they knew themselves, they knew each other. That if she loved the people she loved hard enough, she could guard against ever being alone. After her mother left, Alice knew the truth. There was Alice, and there was everyone else. This could not belong to them, and if this didn't, nothing else could.

Nights, Alice lay awake. Thought, slow and deliberate, the words: *Your mother is gone.* She could never quite make herself believe it. On the fifth day of *your mother is gone*, she and her father drove to Alice's grandparents' house. Each gave her a stiff hug. As always, Alice tried not to stare at the photos of Ethan, who would have been her uncle if he'd lived, and whom she knew only as the angelic blond boy of the portraits and the monster who'd haunted her childhood nightmares. No one talked about him. Alice wondered whether the same would happen to her mother: a few creepy photos added to the wall, then case closed, forever. Except that Ethan was dead, and her mother was coming back. Five days in, she was still certain of this.

"Honey, can you go downstairs and visit with Aunt Debra a bit, while the grown-ups talk?" her father said. She searched herself for the expected resentment, found only submission. To be a child, sent away while problems were dispatched: if only.

"So, Mom's missing," Alice told her aunt.

Debra made some noises that might have been Alice's name or might have been her mother's. Saliva drizzled from the slack side of her mouth.

Her eyes were the same green as Alice's. Uncle Ethan had died at ten; Aunt Debra had made it to eighteen before disaster struck. Alice grew up assuming her family was cursed.

"I'm not worried," she said.

Debra stared.

"I mean, obviously, I'm worried. But it's not like she got kidnapped or something. She just walked out. But she'll come back. She wouldn't actually *leave*. For good, I mean. So you don't have to worry or anything."

The wall behind Debra's bed was decorated with the postcards she'd sent her big sister during her year delinquenting across the country—the Golden Gate Bridge, the Alamo, the Statue of Liberty, some diner in the middle of a desert, a baby lynx dangling from a tree in Yellowstone National Park. It had always seemed cruel to Alice, trapping Debra here with the reminder of how desperately she'd wanted to get away.

The older Alice got, the more insistently her mother wielded Debra's story as cautionary tale. This was what happened when you dropped out of high school, when you slept with a Phish groupie and let him drive you away, when you got dumped in a strange city and instead of crawling home, moved into a squat with a bunch of wannabe artists, when you took drugs from whoever offered them and you OD'd on the floor of some South Street warehouse like a junkie. This was what happened when you behaved irresponsibly, broke the rules, even *one* rule, because sometimes one was all it took—you fell down a deep, dark well of self-destruction and ultimately, you broke your parents' hearts. Alice's mother testified with the authority of an eyewitness: she'd gone to Philadelphia, that first time, to bring her baby sister home. Had done so, but only after witnessing the overdose, riding with Debra in the ambulance, sitting beside her every day in the hospital and then for the long drive in the specially equipped ambulette her parents had hired, with their remaining crumbs of retirement savings, to bring their baby girl home for good.

When Alice was younger and Debra was stronger, the basement had been their shared sanctuary. Debra would play dolls, finger paint, call upstairs when the apple juice ran low. It felt sometimes like they'd started out the same age, one growing up and one growing down.

"They're not telling me something, and I'm not even sure I want to know what."

Debra smelled like expired milk and Alice wanted to scream.

"I'm probably not even supposed to be telling you this. But you have no fucking idea what I'm saying, do you."

Picking up on her tone, Debra started to tremble.

"Calm down, Aunt Debra, it's okay. Please."

She wanted, wanted, wanted to scream.

When she was younger, she'd hated Debra a little for being the one her mother loved best. Later, she'd hated her mother for turning Debra into a future that Alice was meant to fear. The lesson landed: She never looked at a joint or a pill without seeing Debra and abstaining. She never looked at Debra without seeing herself.

"Okay. Good. See? I'm chill. You're chill."

These days, Debra wore a diaper, and Alice could smell now that she'd used it.

Alice wanted to be the kind of person who could love her. But even more Alice wanted a real aunt, who would tell her bitchy family gossip, slip her condoms and nonjudgmental advice, say, *Your mother is coming home*, then take Alice in her arms until it came true.

They drove home from her grandparents' house in silence.

"I'm sorry," she said finally.

"For what?" He put a hand on hers, squeezed lightly, did not take his eyes off the road, which made it easier to pretend that when he smiled and said they would be okay, together, whatever happened, he actually believed it and she did, too.

Alice took after her mother, everyone said so. Their shared height, sharp angles, dishwater brown hair with a slightly greasy sheen could all be ascribed to genetic lottery, but everything else was conscious choice. Her mother, however prim and retiring she endeavored to be, was a presence. She had standards, impossible to meet. Alice resented this as much as she respected it, measured every decision against her mother's principles—acted sometimes to comply and sometimes to rebel, but never considered acting without her mother's approval as a metric. She loved her mother, but the ways she lived that love were complicated, and shifted by the day. Sometimes she thought the complication was what gave it value. Alice loved her father, of course she did, but there was nothing complicated about it, or him. In their family's ongoing war of great powers, he was less Switzerland than Luxembourg, a nonentity.

Alice's mother was a committed believer: in cleanliness, in order, in rules, in etiquette, in rigorous honesty. Alice was committed to gaining her mother's respect, even as she chafed, ever more vocally, against the way of life her mother had ordained. Her father sometimes seemed committed only to checking species off his birding wish list, tuning out wife and daughter, the better to focus on his search for a calliope hummingbird or a Gunnison sage grouse. Her mother found birding incomprehensibly dull, so the year Alice turned twelve and had woken to the pleasure of irritating her mother, she'd pretend to adopt her father's calling as her own. He'd been so grateful for her company in the woods that she never had the heart to revoke the enthusiasm. It wasn't so bad, following him through the trees. She liked the silence, the obligatory dissolution. Every other context demanded Alice construct a presentable version of herself, a face to meet the faces that you meet, as that irritating poem had it. In the woods, padding carefully behind her father's silent steps, listening for the crackle of twigs, gaze fixed at the sky, there was the opposite demand: to be not-Alice, not-anyone, only a transparent eyeball, observing without interference. She wondered sometimes if her father's attachment to his birds sprang from the same source, but never would have asked. It was like the woods, between them. Quiet, easy, no need for a face.

They were not equipped for this, the kind of silence weighed down by the necessity to break it. On Alice's tenth birthday, when she'd officially lived as long as her uncle Ethan, her grandmother showed her a scrapbook of Ethan's finger paintings, attendance certificates, report cards. The glue holding it together had long since evaporated, and as Alice turned the pages, one memory after another fell off, drifted to the floor. That's how she felt now, with her father, the glue between them all dried up.

They made dinner together, still without speaking. She sensed he was stalling. She thought maybe she wanted him to.

"Alice." They sat across from each other at the kitchen table. He para-diddled his fingers against the edge of his plate. "Alice, I have to tell you."

She wanted to say, *Whatever it is, don't.*

"Alice."

She hated the sound of her name almost as much as its derivation. It was an insipid book, and diving down holes in pursuit of rabbits ran counter to everything she'd been taught. What kind of parents named their daughter after a girl they would raise her not to be?

"The thing about your mother is that she's done this before," he said.

The thing about her mother is, once upon a time, she lost her mind. Couldn't remember who she was. Ran away to a city that had only ever brought her misery, lived under another name for six months—then woke up to find her memories returned, as abruptly as they'd departed. She remembered nothing of what had happened during the months she'd been gone. It was as if she'd gone to sleep one night and woke up half a year later, as if none of it had ever happened.

So we decided to pretend she had, he told her. To pretend it never happened.

This was all before you were born, he told her. There was no reason to tell you.

Except that no one knew why the memory loss had happened in the first place. And if you didn't know why something had happened, there was no way to prevent it from happening again.

Except that her mother had prepared Alice for every possibility except the possibility she would one day forget Alice's existence.

Except that her mother demanded absolute honesty and claimed that this was what she offered in return; except that Alice had molded herself to her mother's specifications, and now it turned out her mother might be a person she didn't know—must be, because the mother that Alice knew would never have walked out the door.

It was easy enough to find online records of her mother's past, once she knew to look. The Internet gave her the city, the names of the Meadowlark Institute and the doctor, but that was all. It was already more than her father wanted her to know, and he asked her to stop asking questions. He'd never asked any himself, he said.

"It's got nothing to do with this," he said. He'd believed it was possible, in those first few days, that the fugue had descended again. But the nineties were dead, and with them the likelihood an amnesiac woman could just disappear. This was the age of surveillance cameras and facial recognition technology, smartphones and DNA databases. When the police closed their case, Alice's father had bought a tombstone, installed it over an empty grave.

"Drop it," he kept telling her. "Why dredge up unhappy memories?" He was angry. He was always angry now, always trying to pretend otherwise, and someone who didn't know him well might have been persuaded, as anger only deepened her father's silence. His emotional lake, always ripple-free, had turned to glass. Mirrored glass, Alice thought. Impenetrable. She reminded herself often that he wasn't angry at her. Alice's father said she wasn't allowed to think her mother didn't love her, nor was she allowed to imagine her mother had ever been a someone else. He said Alice was allowed to be mad at him as much as she wanted, but not at her mother. Never at her mother. You only think you're mad, he told her. You're grieving. We're grieving.

She was, unlike him, not mad. She was not grieving. She'd studied up on fugues enough to know that a person who had one could be expected to have more. Her mother was someone other than who Alice had thought, but she was not dead.

Alice suggested deferring college for the semester. She said she couldn't leave him all alone. He told her he wouldn't let her throw away her future for him, that this was the choice Alice's mother had made for Debra, and look where that got all of them. He watched her pack, drove her to the airport, hugged her goodbye, and on the plane she tried not to wonder if what he felt, driving home to a silent house, no obligation to perform his emotions or monitor hers, was relief.

Relief was supposed to be her turf. Freshman year: freedom. She was no longer hostage to her mother's rules. She could drink and smoke and fuck as she liked, no one to root through her underwear drawer for contraband, no one to read her diary and annotate, in unabashed red pen, the parts disapproved of. But drinking and smoking and fucking would have felt like an admission that her mother was gone. And whoever her mother had been, Alice was still the daughter her mother had raised her to be. So when her roommates got a guy who worked in the dining hall to make them fake IDs, she declined. When game night shifted from Trivial Pursuit to strip Twister, she pled homework and retreated. On a sweltering September night, she did not join the group skinny-dipping expedition, and when the boy in her chemistry lab who'd invited her, a water polo player with exactly the body that implied, suggested a rain check for just the two of them, she said a polite *no, thank you,* and switched to a different lab period. Not because of Daniel, whose imagination would have balked at the prospect of imperfect loyalty in his perfect girlfriend, but because of her mother, who would not approve.

When her philosophy professor described the theory of the panopticon, the surveilled man become *principle of his own subjection,* she understood. And, slouched over her tiny desk, blinking against the fluorescents as the professor droned and the class napped, she understood this, too, for the first time: no one was watching.

She was her mother's daughter. Even once the decision was made, she deliberated: not just how to go, but where. She rejected the fantasy that she could play Nancy Drew and ferret out her mother; she refused to impose herself, unwanted, on her father's life; she determined, finally, to go back to the beginning, to track down the woman who had never existed, to meet the people who'd known her, to understand who she was, what she had wanted, what had happened to her then, whether what had happened to her then had dictated what had happened to Alice all these years later.

It wasn't running away. Her mother was the one who ran away. Alice was running toward. *Fugue,* she had learned, came from the Latin *fuga,* which sometimes meant *flight,* sometimes meant *the act of fleeing.* That was what psychological fugueurs did, they fled. It turned out the musical *fugue* had the same root. Melodies took flight, chased one another, the second voice hopelessly behind the first, never surrendering to the futility of catching up. Fine, then: Alice would be a fugueur, like her mother, but essentially different. Her mother ran. Alice would chase.

WENDY

You

You were a wife. You were careful not to make him angry. You made him angry anyway. You made him do it. You apologized. You tried harder. You made him do it again. You hid your bruises. You lied. You had enough. You left everything behind including yourself. Or maybe you went too far, you fought back. There was shouting and blood. You let yourself be consumed.

Or maybe.

You were a mother, but you didn't want to be. You wanted it dead before it was born. Now it was here, crying, biting, needing you with a need that had no bottom. You imagined how easy it would be to make the crying stop. Leaving your baby would be unforgivable, but you left anyway, or you stayed, and did something unforgivable. You made yourself disappear. No one left to forgive.

Or you escaped from a cult. Or you escaped from a bomb blast. Or you escaped from a mugger, from a basement, from a car trunk, from a dumpster, from a plane crash, from a prison, from a suburb, from a terrorist, from a crime scene, from a burning building, from a dead end.

Or you were fine. Privileged, even. Nothing to complain about. You were the worried well. You were exhausted. You were afraid of being selfish, or you were selfish. You were tired of being yourself. You wanted to be someone else, anyone else, so you walked out. You kept walking. You made yourself forget.

Stay forgotten.

ALICE

Alice preferred her Cheerios drowned in milk. Especially once she'd eaten enough of them that the bowl was more milk than cereal, and the remaining Os were left bobbing helplessly in a dairy sea. "Do you think it was another fugue?" she asked Elizabeth. "Like, something set her off and it happened again?"

The widow frowned, then apologized, which seemed to be her default stance. There was no way of knowing, she said.

"Yeah. I figured." There was one lone Cheerio stranded at sea; Alice dunked it, then mashed it against the bottom of her bowl. She had been awake most of the night and spent too much of it online, scanning a government database of missing people—the National Missing and Unidentified Persons System. She'd discovered NamUS over the summer after googling "how do I find a missing person." Many of the resulting sites paired cheerful illustrations with suggestions like "inquire at nearby hospitals and morgues." Every site ultimately funneled her to NamUS. Alice had made an entry for her mother, but had little faith it would generate any leads. Instead, she spent her time scanning the database's list of "unclaimed persons." Most were elderly or mentally ill, but if Alice's mother washed up somewhere without her memory, she would eventually land on this shore. The database had a third section, "unidentified bodies": skeletal remains found in the Montana woods, bleached bones found in the Arizona desert, unsettlingly vague "partial limbs" recovered from a dumpster in New Jersey. Before the database, she'd almost enjoyed imagining her mother's alternate lives—a mountainside in Nepal, an Indonesian beach, a bustling village in India. Now her vision was crowded with bones. The site offered free forensic odontology and fingerprinting, which meant if she ever stumbled over a skeleton, Alice could determine whether it belonged to her. The site also offered the services of an investigator, but the woman Alice talked to had only been interested in playing social worker, pointing her toward local groups that might help her accept her mother's supposed suicide. This was a service for which she had no need. According to NamUS, six hundred thousand people went missing every year; four thousand unidentified bodies were recovered. Alice wanted to know where were the rest?

"You're in a much better position to gauge your mother's emotional state in the days before she . . . left," the widow said. "What do you think happened?"

Alice thought plenty, of course.

She thought the timing, her graduation night, could not be coincidental. The symbolism was too obvious: graduation meant childhood was over, that Alice would really be gone. Alice thought maybe her mother was so bereft by this, so terrified by her venturing into the world as Debra had, at precisely this age, that she'd broken. Alice thought alternately that maybe her mother had hated being a mother and that graduation marked the end of her sentence, prison gates swinging open. Alice thought that her mother had loved her either too much or not enough. She knew this was an only child's fallacy, the belief that everything her mother did was about her, but this was a delusion her mother had nurtured. *My happiness is contingent on your behavior*, she always said, and Alice thought: happy mothers do not disappear.

Alice's mother was a science teacher, and she'd taught Alice that the universe was rule-governed and thus comprehensible. You could understand anything if you had enough data points. So in August, while her father was out browsing tombstones, she'd ransacked their room for data. She found no suicide note or secret diary, only evidence of a woman she barely knew: a stockpile of Ativan and Zoloft. There was a two-year-old plane ticket for a flight to California never taken. A police report from a recent mugging. No one had reported it to Alice.

When her father got home, she set the evidence before him. He was unperturbed. The antianxiety meds were nothing new, he told her. The mugging, he said, was a nonevent, purse snatched in mall parking lot, no injuries, no trauma. He hugged her. This is not our fault, he wanted her to understand. We could not have known, and so we do not bear the blame. Alice didn't stop asking questions, but she stopped asking him.

"I know a fugue usually happens as a response to some kind of trauma," Alice said.

"You've done your research."

"I couldn't figure out whether it was, like, immediate trauma, like something bad happens and you lose your memory, or if it could be something that happened a long time before."

"I'm not sure there's a straightforward answer to that," the widow said. "It seems to differ, person to person. In your mother's case, we were never able to pinpoint the timing of onset, which made it even more difficult to determine causality."

The scientific jargon seemed to carry the widow back to a former self, one who was more confident and less weighed down. Even her posture had straightened.

"I thought she woke up on a bus, that's what my dad said."

"Yes, but according to the information she gave us once she regained her memory, that was nearly two weeks after she left home. Where was she before that? Fugue states can have phases—it's possible she fugued from the start, and only woke to what was happening on that bus. Or it's possible she left your father voluntarily and something happened afterward."

This had never occurred to Alice, that her mother had left, the first time, on purpose. Her father had said he just woke up one morning to find her side of the bed empty; he'd given no inclination that she might have wanted to leave, that they'd been fighting or unhappy. But Alice no longer trusted her father not to leave something out.

"Did she ever talk to you about it?" the widow asked. "Did she have any theories about why it might have happened, or any memories of her time here?"

"No." Alice was too embarrassed to explain that this was because her mother had kept the episode a secret for her entire life. "My dad says that once she came back, they just tried to make everything as normal as possible, pretend like it never happened. And once they had me, I guess they had other things to keep them occupied."

Those first few months she was back, it was like a second honeymoon, he'd told Alice, and when the test stick turned pink, their fresh start was assured. Alice had tried to focus on the romance over the implied gruesome details, the frenzied lust of a husband for the wife who he'd thought was gone forever, the desperation of a wife to make up for forgetting her husband.

"It sounds like she was happy," the widow said. "I've really hoped that she was happy."

Alice's mother was too guarded against disaster to ever quite embrace happiness, but she seemed to have forged her life to suit her precise specifications, and that seemed close enough. "I thought she was."

Alice looked down, letting her hair fall over her face long enough to blink back the tears. The widow cleared her throat. "A different tack, maybe. Philadelphia—do you have any idea why she might have come here, of all places? We'd thought at the time that might offer a clue."

That one was simple, almost embarrassingly transparent, and Alice told her what she knew of the saga of Debra, which wasn't much. She knew, and told the widow, how Karen and Debra had grown up under the shadow of their dead big brother, that Karen was seven when he went into the hospital to get his appendix removed and never came home. Debra was only three, and didn't remember life before. So Debra grew up knowing only that her parents were shattered and her home miserable; Karen grew up knowing things could go wrong at any moment, and that it was her job to ensure they did not. To protect her baby sister: this was her mission. Alice knew, and told the widow, how when Debra ran away, Karen was tasked with retrieving her, and instead found her sister seizing and frothing on a dirty floor, choking on vomit, losing, with every second the ambulance didn't arrive, another piece of herself.

The widow had forgotten she was supposed to look sad. Instead, she looked the way Daniel had when he first saw Alice's bare breasts: baffled by the untrammeled access to a knowledge that until then had been denied him.

"That was way before the fugue thing, though," Alice said. "She hadn't even met my dad yet. The way he talks, she spent, like, four years taking care of Debra full time." Every day, all day, in that basement, feeding her sister with a spoon, wiping her sister's drool and her sister's ass, facing her own failure. Karen asked to take a vacation and her parents threw her out of the house, her father told her once, after an ugly Thanksgiving dinner jarred loose his normal circumspection. Thank god for it, he said, because she finally moved into her own place, got a life, quiet as it was. Otherwise I would never have met her, we would never have had you. "You think that could be why she came here? That if it happened again, she'd come back?" Alice reminded herself she was not here to look for her mother.

"I don't know, Alice. I'm sorry."

Wendy Doe's case file came with pictures. Alice stared at her mother looking utterly unlike her mother. She'd seen pictures of Karen Clark at that age—the photo albums at home were full of Karen Clark pregnant, Karen Clark nervously cradling a tiny Alice in her arms—but this woman was like her mother's identical twin. Same face, different everything else. In one of them, her mother leaned toward the camera, plunging V-neck inviting a peek, grin wide and untroubled, arms stretched like she wanted to embrace the world.

The widow described her as careless and carefree.

"It's hard to explain," the widow said. "Well, maybe this: we were walking through the woods once, one of those spectacularly clear winter days, so deep into the trees that it felt like the world could end and we'd never know. For most people a day like that just blends into all the other good days. But for her? Everything counted. Everything was new. She picked up a pinecone and said, '*This is the first time I've ever touched one of these.*' She said, '*Imagine if you could do that, something truly* new, *every day.*' That's what she was like. I think we all envied it a little."

"Was it real?" Alice asked, trying to imagine this and failing completely. "Was that the person she really was, deep down, or some fantasy person she secretly wanted to be?"

"That's actually what I was trying to study, in part."

"And?"

"And I didn't get very far."

There was a small stack of cassette tapes and an ancient tape recorder for which the widow finally dug up two AA batteries. They included conversations between Elizabeth Strauss and Wendy Doe. Alice chose a tape at random and popped it in.

"I can leave you alone for this, if you want," the widow suggested.

Alice did not want to be alone. She pressed Play.

"I don't know why I do it," her mother's voice said. Alice made a noise, unwittingly, something a little like a whimper. The widow seemed not to hear.

"I like hearing their stories. Maybe I want to know what that would feel like, having a story of my own."

"You just walk into an AA meeting and pretend you belong there?" That voice was recognizably Elizabeth, something about it almost more familiar than Alice's mother's voice. It was the tension in it, Alice thought, the effortfulness of stringing together the words. This woman was thinking before she spoke, worrying about what she was going to say. The other woman, the stranger, was not. *"No one questions you?"*

A laugh. *"You worry too much. Who's more anonymous than me?"* Alice's mother was defined by her fears, and the fortresses she built to protect against them. It was another way Alice had taken after her; she'd not been given much of a choice. Who would she be, Alice wondered, if she'd been raised by this woman instead? Because this woman sounded fearless. *"Anyway, it's just AA meetings. NA, Al-Anon, whatever I can find. They're all trying to give up the same things, in the end."*

"What?"

"Bad memories. It's funny, isn't it? That they think they can forget by remembering. As if giving their story to someone else means they've given it away for good."

Alice stopped the tape. "She seriously used to crash AA meetings?" she asked. The widow's first instinct had been right—Alice couldn't listen to these while someone was watching. It took enough energy to endure her mother's voice; she had none left to spare for keeping the emotion out of her own. "That's fucked up."

"I think she found it comforting. But also . . ." Elizabeth laughed, almost fondly. "Your mother, back then, enjoyed doing things she wasn't supposed to do. It made sense at the time."

It made no sense to Alice. Which meant, if she wanted to understand this other mother, it was a place to start.

A church basement, a semicircle of folding chairs, a rainbow coalition of suffering. She'd picked an evening meeting near Penn, figuring it would draw mostly college students, but almost everyone was old or older: businessmen in suits, nurses in scrubs, an ancient man in a wheelchair, a gym teacher self-identified by her lanyard whistle. The only one around Alice's age was a straggly haired emo with black nail polish and a leather choker, the kind of guy she would have expected to need an AA meeting but not actually attend one.

She did not belong here. And, having come all the way here, having forced herself into the building, down the stairs, right up to the threshold, she could not bring herself to go inside. She hovered in the doorway, half in, half out. The anonymous alcoholics milled about, waiting for whatever invisible signal meant the meeting would start. The emo guy caught her eye, headed for her. Alice froze.

"It's okay," he said gently. "We don't bite."

"I'm—I—bathroom," she spit out, and fled.

Into the twilight dark, past the huddled shapes on the sidewalk—*bodies*, bodies on the sidewalk, she thought, trying to feel each one of them, failing—up the stairs to the train platform, only two minutes to spare, ticket creased and sweaty in hot palm. Furious with herself. What was the point of coming this far if she wasn't willing to go any further? It was the same question she'd asked herself the night of graduation, the question Daniel had been too polite to voice.

The train did not come. A muffled announcement failed to illuminate. She was alone on a dark platform in a strange city. The train did not come. She was afraid. She was, on some level, always afraid. Her mother had made sure of that—and done so under false pretenses, because somewhere inside her mother was a woman who wasn't afraid at all. The train did not come. A man appeared, approached, rapidly, and Alice almost screamed, thinking her mother had been right, danger was at the gates and all it took was one bad decision to let it in, that when she was found naked and bloody on the tracks, she would have no one to blame but herself. Then she recognized him from the meeting, emo guy. A bulky, ostentatiously old-fashioned camera dangled from the leather strap across his chest. Emo-hipster, she thought, and not kindly.

"I know you," he said.

"No you don't."

"Well, obviously. Anonymous."

"Did you follow me here?"

He laughed, as if the idea of this was ridiculous. "The meeting let out early—someone set off the fire alarm. It wasn't you, was it?"

"No!"

He laughed again. He had a mildly appealing laugh. "Kidding." He was, close up, mildly cute.

They waited together in silence. No train. "You left in a hurry," he said.

"I did."

"You want to talk about it?"

"I do not."

He shrugged. "I'm guessing you also don't want to tell me your name?"

"I'm nobody."

"Amazing coincidence, I'm nobody, too." When he realized he was laughing alone, he stopped. "Not an English major, huh?"

"Not an anything major."

"Bullshit. You have Penn written all over you."

"Ballpoint. Not Ivy."

He snapped a photo of her, without warning or permission. Twisted the lens, snapped another. Alice resisted the urge to snatch it from his hands, and instead asked what he thought he was doing.

"It's how I see," he said.

"Who asked you to look?"

They waited nearly an hour. No train. He said, "Fucking SEPTA. Want to give up, get a drink?"

She looked at him sharply.

He said, "Joke." Then leaned in too close. "Want to know a secret, though? I'm a little stoned. Don't tell."

Alice raised two fingers. "Scout's honor."

"Guessing you were never a Boy Scout." He took her fingers, raised a third. His hands were warm. "So, was that your first meeting?"

Alice nodded.

"If you don't want to tell me why you left . . . do you want to tell me why you came?"

She discovered that she did, at least a little. "I guess I thought I could be a different kind of person."

"Than what?"

"Than the kind of person I've always been." It was true, if not the way he would take it. "Stupid, I know. That's not how anything works."

"It actually kind of is. You know how you change yourself into a different person?"

"How?"

"This is gonna sound cheesy, but." He blushed. "What they say in there, it's true. You change by making one decision you wouldn't have made before. You walk into the meeting. Even going to the meeting and leaving before it starts. It's something. One decision at a time. You are what you choose, right? All you have to do is choose different."

"You're right. That sounded very cheesy."

His smile was lopsided. She liked it.

"Look, clearly the train isn't going to show. I'm getting a taxi," he said. "You want a ride, Anonymous?"

"To where?"

"My place, I guess, since that's where I'm going? Joke. Again. Or not. Your call."

Her mother had raised her to be smarter than this. Never get into a car with a strange man. Certainly don't accompany that strange man back to his "place," which, if you were foolish enough to do so, would presumably be the place your body was found. Alice Clark was not the kind of girl who made foolish decisions. Karen Clark had made sure of it. But in this city, Karen Clark had been someone else. Maybe, for this one night, this one decision, Alice could be, too.

It had to be someone else who let him yank her out of the taxi without paying, darted with him around a corner, behind a hedge, where they listened to the cab driver's cursing and the silence left in his squealing tires' wake. It could not have been Alice Clark who allowed herself to be guided into a small apartment over some garage in a suburb somewhat shittier than the widow's. He had Penn written all over him, too, but it turned out he was a barista at some vegan coffee shop serving soy drinks to students, trying to make art from a collection of decrepit film cameras and a bathtub-cum-darkroom, living rent-free over his parents' garage. He was a twenty-four-year-old high school dropout—fall-out, he said, plunge-out, take-a-flying-leap-over-the-cliff-out. He had been sober for a year if you didn't count the pot, which he didn't. He was serious about his sobriety, as he was about little else. The pot took the edge off. And the edge was sharp.

He called her A. She told him she was twenty-two, and he believed it, or said he did. There was an old bottle of Absolut in his kitchen that he said he only kept to remind himself that things can always get worse, and she said she believed him, then she unscrewed the cap and took a large swallow. He said, you're going to be very bad for me, then he said, just one fucking taste, and kissed her, tongue probing deep enough that she knew his need was neither feigned nor for her, so she took another swill and let him kiss her again, and he didn't know anything about her, believed she was someone else, which made it feel, in the best way, like she wasn't even there. She was a girl no one was watching; she was invisible and could do as she pleased, or even simpler, as he did.

She let him shuffle this other girl toward the bed. She let him slide his hands up her back. He could have been anyone. She could have been anyone. She willed herself: be anyone.

Be anyone else.

He did not ask if she was ready, he did not ask if she was sure. He tore open a condom, rolled it onto his dick, and she waited, awkward, unsure what she was meant to be doing with her lips, her hands, whom she was meant to be pleasuring and how, then remembered this accumulation of hands and pits and neck and dick was not her concern, as she was plainly not his, and when he wedged himself inside her, and she gasped, the burn of it, the sigh of it, the *finally* of it, crossing a line that would never need be crossed again, it was like she was alone. She could endure inside the moment. The pain. The sweat. The weight of body on body. The relief of it, to be crushed beneath. When it was over, she was almost surprised to find him still there, because he seemed so incidental to the experience. It felt almost as if she'd lost her virginity to herself.

He woke up when she started crying.

"Fuck," he said. "Did I do something? Did you not—fuck."

"It's not you."

He put his arms around her, and they breathed together. This would hurt Daniel worse than the sex, she thought.

"You can tell me."

He lived with his parents. She had tongued his nipples and he had burped into her unwaxed pubes. She was never going to see him again. "I'm not an alcoholic," she said.

She couldn't see his face in the dark, but she felt his body tense. "So you're a liar," he said, his lips moving against her neck. He whispered, "Little lying bitch," tongue flickering at her flesh on each *L*, then laughed and said he was kidding. Unless she had infiltrated the meeting simply to gawk at the freaks, in which case he was not kidding, so which was it, he said, fraud or fuckup? There was a right answer and a wrong answer, Alice understood, and she was naked in this stranger's bed. She gave him an answer he would want. She had made her one mistake. She would lie to him persuasively, then never see him again, consider herself lucky to have escaped the night alive.

She was from the desert, she told him. She had hitched across the country, because why not. It was unexpectedly pleasurable to lie. He already thought she was the kind of girl who drank, who slept with random men then wept in their arms; he believed her. She said it was pills she liked too much, not booze, that she'd gone to the AA meeting hoping to score, and she said it like that, *booze, score,* thinking this was the way this kind of girl would talk. "Don't worry, I'm definitely fucked up," she told him.

"You?" He touched her nose, then his own. "Me. You have no fucking idea."

She wanted to leave, but didn't know the etiquette for this. So she let him spoon her, tried to relax, or to seem relaxed enough that he would believe it. His sheets smelled like old pizza and her own familiar funk.

"You still don't know my name," he said, then whispered, "Rumpel-stiltskin," but she pretended she was already asleep.

WENDY

Hello, my name is Wendy

My name is Wendy and I'm an alcoholic. My name is Wendy and I'm an addict. My name is Wendy and I can't help myself.

Church basement. School basement. Community center basement. Metal chairs. Weak coffee. Good doughnuts. No IDs. Every one of us a Doe. Like a family.

It was an accident, the first time, a room in the library. I am allowed to go wherever I want, but with no car, no ID, no money, this is an illusion of freedom. I can only go to the places I can walk to, the places where, even if I have no purpose there, they are obligated to take me in. The library is small and smells of mold, but they will answer any question, and never ask me to leave. One day I noticed a door, one I hadn't seen before. I opened it, saw a roomful of women. One of the women asked what I was looking for. I told her the truth, that I had no idea. You've come to the right place, she said. Sit. I only saw the sign on the way out, Alcoholics Anonymous, and I thought, I could be an alcoholic. I could be anything.

I am anonymous. Where else do I belong?

They say tell your story and be healed. We say hello, my name is, and once upon a time, I did, I chose, I leapt, I'm still falling.

Please, help me up.

They drank to feel less alone. They drank to feel less pain. They drank to forget. They cannot forget. They come to these basements. They tell these stories. And together, we all remember.

Hello, my name is Wendy, and I don't remember.

IV

ELIZABETH

The nineteenth-century hysterics of the Salpêtrière could be hypnotized into happiness—or at least a simulacrum thereof—and what was hysteria if not the body's capacity to enact a feeling it had no cause to feel? What hysteria was: whatever the men who helmed Paris's largest women's hospital—that "Versailles of suffering," that "Pandemonium of human infirmities," that "grand asylum of human misery" (so sayeth said men)—deemed it should be. It was sometimes a convenient label for inconvenient women: prostitutes; criminals; freethinkers; girls who didn't want to sleep with their fathers, brothers, bosses; wives who no longer wanted to sleep with their husbands. It was a disease, embodied and suffered; female bodies acting out unspoken pain, seizing and twitching and convulsing; symptoms with no apparent cause. It was, etymologically, a *wandering womb*—you could say, the female body struggling to escape itself. It was, under the late nineteenth-century reign of Jean-Martin Charcot, lord and master of the Salpêtrière and all it contained, the major disease of the modern moment. Its master diagnostician, elucidator, savior was Charcot; its face was Augustine. He translated her body into story, and narrated it for the world. I told it again, my way.

Louise Augustine Gleizes: born 1861. Attacked by an older friend's husband when she was ten years old (*attacked* likely being discreet euphemism for what man did to girl). Sent to a convent school where nuns bound her wrists to keep her from masturbating, then exorcised her when this failed to work. Returned home only to be raped—no euphemisms this time—by her mother's employer. A man who, it turned out, was having an affair with her mother, an affair that might have produced Augustine's brother. It was speculated that mother offered daughter to her lover as a bribe, or perhaps a gift. The incident provoked Augustine's first hysterical attack, which was treated with bloodletting. I imagine her commitment to the mental hospital in 1875 came as a reprieve.

Augustine at fourteen, officially stricken, a model patient, photographed in her agonies and ecstasies, soon to become the most famous of the hysterics, inspiration for artists and poets and sad young girls. Charcot made her his star patient, the belle of the ball—sometimes literally, waltzing with the Parisian elite at the hospital's *bal des folles*. He studied her, photographed her, exhibited her, electroshocked her, cured and employed her, then readmitted her after a relapse. He treated her like a valued guest for as long as she played nicely; locked her in a basement cell at the first sign of rebellion, offering her one daily hour outside, chained to a stone bench in the sun. Louise Gleizes endured the Salpêtrière for three years, then disguised herself as a man, fled the complex, and escaped history for good. The Augustine photos are forever. The image they chose for my book cover was the one I'd seen first, the one Benjamin had taken from his office and offered to Wendy Doe. Augustine sitting up in bed, arms outstretched and face radiant, turned up as if to her God. *Attitudes passionelles: Extase.*

Wendy got obsessed with her first. She seized on the timing, the French hysteria epidemic coinciding with an epidemic of fugues. Something about nineteenth-century France drove people out of their minds: Women fled inward, trapped inside misbehaving bodies and the asylums that housed them. Men simply fled. Slipped loose the surly bonds of past and progeny, wiped their own memories, and went on walkabout.

Here's how you hypnotize a hysterical girl: use the steady vibrations of a large tuning fork to mesmerize hysterically susceptible girls into a cataleptic state. Here's what the hypnotized girl will do: anything you want. Possibilities include smile, frown, kiss, grope, slap, undress, enact semiscripted melodramas like the ever-popular *mariage à trois*, in which a girl would be hypnotized into believing the left side of her body was married to one man while the right side was married to another. Mutual fondling would then commence.

Here's why you do it: For science, at first, presumably. For an audience then, to gain respect or funding and, the great doctor Charcot being only human, to show off. Then for fun, because it was fun. They didn't even try to pretend otherwise.

The skin of some hysterics was so sensitive that a finger lightly traced across flesh would raise an angry red line. So doctors drew pictures on the girls' skin, signed their names. *This belongs to me.* This is a game we played during our sabbatical year in Paris. I would write secret messages on Benjamin's skin. He would explore my body for hysterogenic zones, map my body the way Charcot mapped his girls, press here to trigger a hysteric attack. Make me feel something, I would say to Benjamin, and his fingers would probe and press. A passionate attitude. An ecstasy. Sometimes he made me feel and sometimes he didn't, but I knew how to pretend.

The books all said to pour your grief into your work. Make something beautiful. Every day, I swiped my oxymoronic permanent visitor pass at the university library, nodded politely to the mild girl at the desk—it was technically a series of ever-changing mild girls and occasional boys, but they registered in my memory as a single face—took the elevator to the fourth floor where the carrel I'd occupied on and off for the last decade was reliably empty. I'd chosen a spot in the far corner of the folklore and mythology section, behind a collection of dusty journals as forgotten as the gods and monsters they recorded. Someone must have sat there sometimes, whether in the hours after I gave up for the day or the decades before I'd claimed my spot. The splintered wood was bedecked with petroglyphs: initials, hearts, dicks. I toyed sometimes with the fantasy of abandoning my own work in favor of an anthropological investigation of the collegiate mind, via its etched and Sharpie'd designs. Somewhere in this library, I mused, was a Rosetta stone of adolescent hormones.

This was where I poured my daily grief: distraction, daydream. When Benjamin died, I'd been a year into work on a book about Anna Göldi, the last woman executed as a witch. It would have been my first wholly non-Augustine project, proof to myself and the world that I was not the pop historian equivalent of Dexy's Midnight Runners. Then Benjamin was gone, and my attention span—and ambition, appetite, ability to imagine progress into a future brighter than the present, all necessary components of fooling oneself into writing a book—departed with him. If I'd been an accountant, I thought, or a lawyer, or—better yet—a manual laborer, able to mark time with the mechanics of hoisting or shoving, digging or plowing, maybe I could have poured my grief into my work. If I'd had a boss, or—better yet—a drill sergeant, I could have shut down my brain and allowed my body to heed command. These were fantasies that, even in the depths of self-absorbed despair, I knew better than to admit out loud. My life was meant to be the fantasy—no employer, no office, no time clock. Accountable to no one but myself. I was supposed to be grateful.

The line I'd parroted in countless interviews: *History, like writing, is an exercise in decision making.* If, as the discipline of psychology had drilled into me in my former life, no two eyewitnesses would ever tell exactly the same story of a crime, what hope was there for an objectively accurate narrative of a past none of us had personally witnessed? My job: To sift, select, selectively ignore. Decide what counted as evidence and what did not; decide how to deploy the evidence to compel belief in the story I'd decided to tell. Except I was no longer in shape to make decisions. I had enough trouble choosing what to eat for dinner—many nights I gave up and fell asleep without.

I couldn't think unless I was thinking about him. So when a small academic publisher queried my agent about whether Benjamin Strauss's biographer wife might want to write a biography of her dead husband, I mustered the will to decide on an answer. I decided not to say no. The days needed purpose, and the only purpose that made sense was remembering him, however I could. Two birds, one stone. Now my work was my grief, my grief was my work, and I had no one to blame but myself.

I came to the library every day. I read through his early papers, the ones he'd published before I met him, and this was almost manageable. The closer I got to the year we met, the slower I read—and this was only the beginning. The book demanded a personal touch, not just the resurrection of our marriage, but a deep dive into his research notes, his archives, his emails. Writing the story of a life required a wholesale violation of privacy that made it impossible to pretend away his death. Every day was an accumulation of small reminders that Benjamin was gone. Reading his emails, prying open the lid of whatever secrets he'd had left, would be admission he was never coming back. So I manufactured delays. That day, I was due at the Meadowlark, where Mariana Cruz, his longtime second-in-command, now acting replacement, had deigned to grant me an interview. I hated returning to that building and its ghosts, almost as much as I hated Mariana and the thought that there was anything she could tell me about my husband that I didn't already know, but it was a more palatable opportunity than reading any more deeply into his past.

A cup of coffee landed in front of me, almond milk, a spoonful of sugar, exactly the way I preferred. Leaning against the carrel and looking, as he always did, unduly proud of himself for the successful delivery of contraband, was MIT-educated and Ivy-tenured, double doctorate in physics and history, Guggenheim-, NEA-, and Pfizer Prize–winning professor Sam Shah, also known as the closest thing I had to a work friend. "Get anything done this morning?"

When I confirmed failure, he did not judge. I'd been working on *Augustine* for two years—by which point my amateur research skills had driven me into enough brick walls I was nearing admission of defeat—when Sam had claimed a carrel on the opposite side of the library. I was thirty-three, newly a wife, he was twenty-seven, a baby historian low on the tenure ladder but scrambling up with monkey speed, as willing to tutor me on nineteenth-century political philosophy as he was to spill strategies for sucking up to Parisian archival bureaucrats. After the book came out, in all its pop-history, hybrid-historico-memoir glory, he was the only member of his department to treat me—when the occasional capitulation to undergraduate will forced them to suffer my presence—like a colleague rather than a hack. He was the only man I knew who was as smart as Benjamin, but unlike Benjamin, he'd somehow been persuaded I was his intellectual equal. His thick glasses were the wrong shape for his face; his beard was a magnet for crumbs. I liked him. Not, as we used to say when we were kids, *like* liked him. Not anyone ever again, maybe, definitely not Sam, now. We were friends, and after Benjamin, it was the only kind of friendship I could tolerate, one that had nothing to do with Benjamin, and so one that had escaped the distortion effect of his absence. The women I knew were all wives, and I was something other now. I was pity object; I was nightmare future; I was *widow*. With Sam, our relative marital statuses had never been relevant, nor had any other region of emotional topography. We talked about his latest projects (the intersection of nineteenth-century degeneration theories with developing theories of heat; the steam engine as locus for economic, physical, and scientific concepts of work) and my ever-expanding list of possibilities for future ones (Dora, witches, lobotomies, Zelda Fitzgerald, vibrators, even, for one ill-advised research season, the nineteenth-century craze for clitoridectomies). We talked about the birth of modernity and the arrow of time and why we remember the past and not the future. We talked about whatever we thought, and nothing we felt.

I admitted I was distracted, and not for the usual reason. I told him about the unexpected guest, in the broadest of terms, the daughter of a research subject Benjamin and I had studied together. "My last research subject, actually, before I left the field."

Unlike most people, Sam had never asked why I stopped experimenting and started writing; he was a physicist who'd done the same. To him it must have seemed a natural course.

"Do you miss it?"

I shook my head. "It feels almost like a different life. Like I'm a different person now and I'm just remembering things that happened to someone else."

Sam had an excellent professorial *hmm*, almost as rich with unspoken analysis as Benjamin's. "Would it comfort you to know that physics leaves open the possibility? That maybe you are?"

"What, because our cells all get replaced every seven years? You know that turns out to be bullshit, right? Your heart and lung and skin cells might be interchangeable, but neurons don't get replaced. We are who we are."

Sam laughed. "Leave it to you to bring everything back to the brain. I'm talking basic physics. Unquestioned assumptions. Example: we assume you and I are two separate organisms rather than one. Why? Because we assume discontinuity across spatial states."

"I'm here and you're there."

"Exactly, and so I'm me, you're you. This table, a separate object between us."

"Okay . . ."

"Okay. And we know space and time to be fundamentally connected, each defining the other. A space-time continuum, as Einstein and Zemeckis would have it. So why assume discontinuity across spatial states but *continuity* across time? Why assume the Elizabeth of the present and the Elizabeth of the past are one rather than two? Or infinitely many?"

Benjamin called him my pet historian, and treated the friendship with the same indulgent condescension that, before publication, he'd treated my new "hobby." It wasn't his fault: I'd kept my work on the book away from him for as long as I could. I wanted, in those first few years, something that was mine. I didn't want him to know how hard I was trying, in case—as seemed almost inevitable back then—I didn't succeed. When I unexpectedly did, when suddenly there was a book, a sale, a career, it must have seemed to him like a happy accident, birthed without effort or intent, like a baby slip-sliding out of a prom queen who, until amniotic fluid seeped through silk, had failed to notice she was pregnant.

"I know there's a me and a you because we have distinct consciousnesses," I said. "And continuity of self across time may be an artifact of consciousness or its precondition, but either way, for the record, I bring everything back to the brain because that's where everything goes."

Sam grudgingly acknowledged the role of consciousness, but argued this, too, was based on unexamined assumptions, dependent on an unfounded faith in the collapse of quantum indeterminacy, and we debated the many minds theory, hidden variables, multiverses, and materialism until the coffee went cold and I'd managed to forget I was anything but pure consciousness myself.

Any duration is divisible into past and future. The present occupies no space. So said the other Augustine, correctly. All good things must, et cetera, so coffee with Sam gave way to the Meadowlark, to Mariana. Every time I went back, more had changed. Mariana had occupied Benjamin's office. She'd replaced his dark wood and leather furniture with modular space-age pieces, all synthetics and glass. The walls were pale blue; the oil paintings had been replaced by blown-up photographs of Golgi silver stains. His couch was gone. His armchair, his antique desk, his Moroccan rug: gone. There were no remaining surfaces that would have welcomed a body in heat, only sharp edges, slick plastic, too much light. It felt like the waiting room of a dermatology office. A physical erasure, as if he'd never been, as if this room had never witnessed our bodies in fusion, as if *we* had never been. I hated her, this woman who'd spent more minutes with my husband than I had. I wanted to tag every place I'd fucked him, every spot of floor bearing trace sweat and flesh.

We air-kissed.

"Let's get down to it," she said. "Busy day." Mariana had rescheduled the interview three times. She never would have come right out and told me she didn't think I should write the book. She simply slow-walked files, begged legal liabilities, and expressed an unprecedented concern for my welfare, taking on a project like this in the midst of my "difficulties."

"Of course. The job must be overwhelming."

"Nothing I can't handle."

She smiled, I smiled. Mariana had devoted her professional life to burnishing Benjamin's reputation and carrying out his whims, and sold herself to the board as the ideal purveyor of his continuing legacy. A book like this would be catnip for donors, a free fund-raising tool she should have been begging me to write. But I'd known Mariana for nearly twenty years. She didn't beg.

"Maybe you can walk me through how the institute has changed over the course of your tenure here," I said.

"We're taking some exciting steps toward synergy and team-based research. Until recently the Meadowlark has functioned with a bit of a rock-star mentality, but I truly believe that cooperation, rather than competition—"

"I didn't mean your tenure as *acting* director." I put the inflection where it belonged. "It seems best for everyone involved that the book doesn't go into the institute's decline."

"Has it escaped your notice that I'm doing you a favor here?"

"You're doing yourself a favor," I said. "This book will be good for all of us."

"You keep telling yourself that, Lizzie."

Mariana was the only one at the Meadowlark who still called me that. It was a dog whistle, her covert reminder that I was still the same mangy stray who'd nosed up to the boss and nuzzled his hand till I got a treat. It said: I knew you when, and you turned out even worse than expected. The institute was her life, and she'd never stopped judging me for leaving it, and my "real" career, behind for a man. She thought I was one of *those women*, and in her presence, I felt like one.

I knew her when, too. The industrious worker in the Mickey Mouse sweatshirt whom Benjamin had diagnosed early on as lacking a necessary spark. I could have told her that he knew from the start she had no capacity for greatness, would never do significant work. She would simply be useful, he predicted, and she was.

"Why don't we start with your first years here, and go from there."

We slogged through the rest of the interview without incident, probably because I let my recorder do the listening for me. After twenty minutes, she made clear my time was up.

"I hope we'll be seeing you again soon," she said, insincerely enough that I couldn't help telling her I'd be back later that week. It was such a pleasure to disappoint. "The daughter of a former subject wants to take a look around. I'm assuming that won't be a problem?"

It was as delicate as it was infuriating to have to secure permission to enter the building I had, until recently, considered an extension of my home.

"Which subject?" Mariana asked. "And why didn't she come straight to me?"

"Because it was my subject. Remember Wendy Doe?"

Mariana shook her head, her meaning clear—not *no, she did not remember*, but *no way in hell.* "What could that woman's daughter possibly want with you after all this time?"

"Her mother's . . . gone." The circumstances were none of Mariana's business. "The daughter's curious. I'm trying to help."

"Jesus, Lizzie. What's she looking for? An excuse to sue us?"

"Of course not."

"This woman's daughter comes poking around, and you think she's just, what, *curious*? Do I have to remind you the board is about to make its decision? Are you trying to give them a reason to pass me over?"

"Don't be ridiculous."

"Lizzie, the board is just looking for an excuse—I'm asking you as a personal favor, please don't give them one."

"I'm not your enemy, Mariana. When it comes to this place? I'm effectively no one." As she couldn't help reminding me.

"Just tread carefully."

"Always."

We stood, gave each other the obligatory drive-by cheek kiss.

"I miss him, too, you know." She meant she missed him better. She meant she got the best of him, this place his favorite child, this work his favorite wife.

"I know."

ALICE

The Meadowlark wasn't what Alice expected. She'd scanned its glossy website, but that was all sound bites and press releases, photos of shiny new brain-scanning machines. She'd assumed that in person, the institute would carry more scars from its past. The building had once housed an insane asylum—at least technically, the widow had explained, its concrete foundation and some of its architectural bones still left over from the bad old days of straitjackets and padded walls, and, yes, the widow admitted when pressed, there were still straitjackets and padded walls somewhere within the facility, but only for precautionary purposes. Still, Alice pictured her mother strapped to some stained gurney with probes stickered to her skull, burly nurse looming over with a wolfish grin. She'd always thought of herself as someone without an imagination, but like many of her beliefs, this one had recently given way.

She hadn't expected the infamous Meadowlark Institute to be so sub-urban, sandwiched between a gas station and a strip mall, just down the road from a discount shoe warehouse. The widow explained that 150 years before, this had all been farmland, considered a safe enough distance from civilization to house the nuts. The earliest patients had milked cows, fed chickens, hoed weeds, supposedly sweating out their madness a little more with each hard day's work. Alice asked if this was why they called them funny farms. The widow didn't know. From the outside, the building looked quaint, harmless. On the inside, it was every bit the state-of-the-art mecca for brain science its website had promised. Alice tried to focus: her mother had once lived here. Her mind refused to settle.

For months, she'd been obsessing about her mother's time here—and now here she finally was, her mother all she should have been thinking about, but her traitorous mind had shifted gears. She was thinking about the night before. Reliving it. She was following the widow through the building where her mother had taken refuge, and all she could think about was the blood she'd blotted away when she woke up sometime before dawn and remembered she was supposed to have peed after. The rusty streaks on the sheets they'd both pretended not to notice. The silent SEPTA ride into the city, so he could go to work and she could train back out to the widow's suburb. The relief of having survived her poor choices; the terror of consequence.

Here was the room that had belonged to her mother. It was unthinkably small. She tried to focus: her mother, here, alone, nobody. She lay down on the bed. Her mother, younger than her mother had ever been.

Her mind, though, was too full of a stranger's hands, the strange wet of a stranger's tongue in her ear. Her mind was too full of disease. Secretions. Minuscule openings through which disease could ooze. The tender, raw spot inside her left cheek where she'd gnawed the tissue white, where something of him could have gotten inside her.

She thought, forcibly: *my mother was here.*

She focused on the body. This is the ceiling my mother saw when she tried to sleep; this is the air my mother breathed when she tried to remember.

When Alice's mother disappeared, she had been teaching her online students the unit on the octopus, which was her favorite. Alice always knew when she reached that lesson, because dinner became a forum for "fascinating" factoids about the geniuses of the sea. They think with their bodies, her mother would say, every year, as if for the first time. Each arm thinks for itself. If we weren't so obsessed with the brain, she would say, then maybe we would see it was true of us, too, that we are as much our legs, our kidneys and fingers and heart. Alice wished now she had paid better attention, because it must have signified. Was her mother clinging to the hope of continuity between herself and Wendy Doe, that some trace of that other self was still embedded in her cells? Or did it comfort her to believe body and mind were inseparable, that if she rooted herself in flesh, distributed herself through circulatory and respiratory systems, through muscle and skin and bone, then next time, if there was a next time, she couldn't be so easily dislodged from her carnal home?

"There's no lock on this side of the door," Alice said.

"No."

"There's a lock on the outside, though."

"Well."

"Did you lock her in?"

"We never wanted her to feel like a prisoner here."

Alice imagined herself closed inside this room for one night, for two, and wondered how many nights it would take to internalize the lock, to spend the rest of her life looking for escape.

The widow stopped at the last door on the corridor but did not open it. "You shouldn't expect too much."

"You already said that." Behind this door was the one person left at the Meadowlark who had been close to her mother. But he'd lived here for twenty-five years because he could not form new memories. He lived in an eternal present, and supposedly whatever he knew of Alice's mother was lost in his irretrievable past. Alice wanted to meet him anyway.

"I just don't want you to be disappointed."

This door was locked. The widow punched in a combination, and they stepped inside. The subject, Anderson Miles, was seated at a piano, which was the strangest thing Alice had seen yet. He looked to be in his early sixties, bald with mottled skin and the sick gray of someone the sun had forgotten. He was staring at the piano keys, blank.

"Hello," the widow said. "Would you like some company?"

This won them a smile of yellowing teeth. It occurred to Alice that if your life restarted every seven minutes, it would never seem incumbent to brush. "Everyone's always welcome here."

"I'm Lizzie."

Alice glanced at the widow, surprised. She didn't seem like much of a Lizzie.

"This is Alice. I think you knew her mother."

"Nice to meet you, Alice. Does your mother look anything like you?"

Something like hope, fluttering. "Maybe? A little? Why, do I look familiar?"

"Oh, no. And I'd remember a face like yours, I'm certain of it."

"Oh."

"What was her name?"

Alice hesitated. "Wendy." She'd started thinking of Wendy Doe the way the widow did—as if she were a real person rather than a symptom. "She lived here with you."

"No, I don't think so."

Alice described her mother, and Anderson thought about it, his effort evident. She waited.

"Visitors!" he said after a moment. It was as if his expression had been smoothed out by an eraser. "How lovely."

The widow had explained that hippocampal damage prevented new memories from rooting themselves into Anderson's brain. Anything that had happened since he was thirty-two years old—including his doctors repeatedly explaining his condition, including his wife saying one last goodbye, including his mother dying—had, for him, not happened at all.

Alice tried again, introducing herself, describing her mother. Anderson shook his head. "I don't think so, no woman's ever lived here with me."

"No, not *here*, not *with you*—" They went through another round, and another, more *I don't think so*, more *that doesn't sound familiar*, more *I don't remember*, more *there was no woman*. It was frustrating at first, then enraging, that her mother's existence could so easily be erased, but gradually Alice began to find the repetition soothing. It made sense that her mother would have taken comfort with this man, with whom you could make as many mistakes as you liked, trust in the inevitable baptism of erasure. It made sense that a woman prone to vicious forgetting might want to be forgotten.

As Elizabeth picked up the conversation, Alice let her mind wander— to the past she imagined for her mother, and the pasts she imagined coming before her, barefoot women in filthy nightgowns screaming at the walls. She indulged briefly her panic about the night before, decided to acquire a pregnancy test, just in case. She worried about her father, alone with his dutiful grief, and she worried about Daniel, who was wasting his time worrying about her. Then she let her mind stray to forbidden territory, wish fulfillment. Imagined her mother drawn back to this city, back to this place. Imagined her mother, memories and self buried deep in her damaged brain, wandering into this strange building and setting eyes on Alice. Love, recovery, reunion.

The fantasy broke open with the sound of the piano. Anderson played beautifully, fingers flying across keys, head bobbing with the flourish of a concert pianist. The shock wasn't that he could play well, but that he was playing Bach's "Unfinished Fugue."

Time stopped.

This was her mother's music. These were the chords of her childhood, of letting a Dorito go soggy in her mouth to avoid a crunch, because Mommy was anxious and only listening to Bach's strange loops could soothe. These were the collapsing melodies her mother had taught her to follow. These were the notes she had picked out on the keyboard with her stubby young fingers, her mother clapping with the metronome, cheering her on.

Her mother had been here. It was real, suddenly. Karen Clark, Wendy Doe, whoever she thought she was—she'd been here, with this man and his piano. The music ended midbar. Anderson gaped at his hands like he'd just discovered them. He started at the sight of Alice. "Oh, hello! What a pleasure."

"The playing sustains him," the widow said quietly. "When he focuses on the music, he can make it to eight minutes, sometimes nine. But it always ends." Her face was shiny with tears. That was Alice's pain. It was Alice who should have been able to cry.

She could not cry. This was her mother's favorite piece, and it could not be coincidence. This was a melody of the Meadowlark—and it was confirmation that Alice had been right. Whatever happened to her mother here had left its mark. The music was proof. Something in her mother must have remembered.

ELIZABETH

I read about it first in the *Times*, which for Benjamin was a disqualifying factor. Newspapers didn't break science, he would say. These days they barely break news. Still, we read the *Times* in bed on Sunday mornings, because this was the vision he'd had of marriage. Before the divorce, when he was still comparing his wife to me, rather than vice versa, he admitted that this was what he'd missed most: the quiet rustle of Sunday mornings. It's all cereal and finger paint now, he would say, nibbling my ear, and don't get me started on fucking cartoons. That wasn't even the worst of it: on their daughter's third birthday, his wife had proposed an idea. Take the daughter to church. Take my fucking daughter, my dead father's only grandchild, to fucking church, Benjamin said. As if my father survived the attempted extermination of his people only to see me deliver my Jewish seed to Jesus, talk about a devious missionary program—and when I say *missionary*, he would say, meanly, I mean it in all possible connotations. I wish I could say I hated when he spoke like this about his wife.

Thus we spent each Sunday of our finger-paint-free matrimony swapping sections with ink-stained fingers. That day's paper unveiled a newly coined neurological disorder, *aphantasia*, the inability to close one's eyes and conjure up a visual image. Benjamin was underwhelmed by the research, but then, the more his habitat shifted from lab to cocktail party, the less he wanted the reminder that somewhere out there, lesser brains than his were producing better work. I told him that the research was beside the point, the point was that until encountering this article, it had never occurred to me this conjuring was magic anyone could do. Nine years of training in cognitive psychology, a seventeen-year marriage to a world expert in the workings of the mind, and it had never penetrated that the "mind's eye" was anything but a useful metaphor. What if what you see as red is not what I see as red—no one who'd ever gotten stoned had escaped that revelation, but in all that late-night dorm-room philosophizing, it had never occurred to me that all those pretentiously stoned assholes could close their eyes and literally *see* red. Among the infinitude I could not evoke in my mind's blind eye: A sphere. A sunset. My childhood house. My father's face. A fire-breathing dragon. The photograph from our wedding day, just behind me on the nightstand. Benjamin loved it; we spent the rest of the day experimenting. Can you see this? Can you see that? When you say *see*, how do you mean it? How do you draw, how do you write, how do you dream? How do you fantasize yourself into orgasm? How do you miss me when I'm gone? It was a time warp of a day, both of us slipping joyously back into our younger selves. Then we had takeout for dinner, then we had predictable sex, then he took his various medications and I tried sporadically to sleep, and the next day was the same as any other, and I didn't think about it again.

It only occurred to me once he was gone. *Aphantasia*, an inability to conjure what one wished. Other people could wish whatever faces they wanted to see again. The wife across the street, if her husband left her, if her baby turned blue, she could close her eyes, will their faces to mind, pretend them back to her. Everyone I knew, everyone I passed on the street, the teeming mass of humanity, could accomplish a miracle. When I closed my eyes, willed my brain, *Benjamin, Benjamin, Benjamin*, he never appeared.

I came home from the Meadowlark to find a message from Nina on the answering machine, and resisted the impulse to ignore it. "I got the transfer," she said when I called back. "Thank you." Every call I made to Nina felt like the call I'd made that morning, the call to say *your father is dead*.

Each month I deposited money into her account, as Benjamin had before. And each month she called to say a begrudging thanks and make perfunctory inquiries into my physical and emotional welfare. I told her I was glad she called. She said she was glad to hear from me. We were both, as always, very polite. We left it that we would have dinner together sometime. Talk more, and more in depth, someday. This was where our relationship thrived: an ambiguous future that would never come.

After I'd showered off the stink of the past, or at least lathered it over with lavender bath gel and half a tablet from the emergency Xanax stash, I suggested to Alice that we order a pizza. She wasn't my child, so there seemed no reason not to share the wine. She picked all the pepperonis off her slice, stacking them in a neat, greasy tower. "I read your book."

"Should I ask what you thought?"

"I liked it. But, I guess I was wondering—what happened?"

"To who?"

"To you. You were a psychologist, right? Like hard-core? You worked at this institute, you studied my mom, and now you're, like, a writer? What happened?"

I told her the official version. That well after the end of my fellowship and his marriage, Benjamin and I had started, tenuously, appropriately, dating. That I'd joined him in Paris on his sabbatical, where I'd fallen in love with both Benjamin and Augustine, accidentally begun a book, accidentally begun a marriage. It was true, if not the whole truth. Alice didn't need to hear the ways that her mother's case had tainted the field for me, the ways that loving Benjamin eventually foreclosed the ambitions that had brought us together. Once Benjamin and I went public, a job offer or even a recommendation would have been suspect. Not that it hadn't been done before; it was ignoble tradition, marrying your professor, leveraging love into career advancement. But I wasn't willing. I couldn't work for him and I refused to leave him. So I'd expanded my horizons—that was how I liked to think of it. Loving him had made my world bigger. I'd found something new to love.

"So how come you never wrote another one?" she said.

"I'm working on a project as we speak. Nonfiction is slow."

"I mean, yeah, but it's been, like, a decade. And it's not like you have kids or anything, so . . ."

It was true, I didn't have, like, anything. It was technically not true that I'd never written another one. My name was on the cover of the coffee table edition of Augustine photos they'd brought out a couple of years after publication. There were interviews and essays, requests to write a review or a foreword, the introduction to the anniversary edition, the year wasted consulting on a PBS documentary that never aired. There was Benjamin, his fund-raising functions, his travel schedule, his distaste for any archival research that would put too much distance between us. There was the project I'd set aside in favor of the book about him. There was the book about him, which I could not bring myself to want to write.

"Did you ever want them? Kids?" she asked.

"We had Nina," I said, as I'd been saying in response to this question for almost two decades. "Benjamin's daughter." I had assumed, at the beginning, that we would. My mother had warned me: his child would be my child, and the idea had both terrified and enticed. I thought I'd found a loophole, motherhood without mother or daughter. It became clear, by legal dictate and Nina's desire, that I would be no kind of mother at all. It took longer to understand this was how Benjamin preferred it.

"You never wanted kids of your own?"

It wasn't accurate to say I never wanted to, any more than it would be to say I wanted not to. I wanted Benjamin; Benjamin wanted no more children; I stopped asking myself whether I wanted at all. "No."

"Do you regret it, now that he's . . . ?"

"Why, because then there'd be some evidence of my marriage?"

I must have said it more sharply than I'd intended, because her answer sounded like an apology. "I just thought it might be less lonely?"

I had a career, I told her. I had friends. A house to care for, books to read, health to maintain.

I didn't tell Alice how little it all added up to. How much time there was to fill. Women my age were supposed to crave more time for themselves. This was an evergreen topic of lunch conversation and the infinite email chains of schedule juggling required to get us there in the first place. Women my age were leaning in, having it all or accepting they could not. They were waging small rebellions in the form of aromatherapy and candlelight yoga, Facebooked *self-care* whose prime purpose seemed to be the advertisement of how much time they spent caring for everyone else. I was meant to be performatively overwhelmed, defined by obligation to others. Instead, I was untethered, obligated to no one but myself. I liked to tell myself that this was triumph over the patriarchy, but mostly it seemed evidence that I was useless. No one would be inconvenienced if I disappeared from my own life.

"I'm alone," I told Alice. "Not lonely. You might be too young to know the difference."

"You think my dad's lonely?"

"Maybe," I said. "Probably. It's all so fresh."

"Yeah."

I was reminded the wound was fresh for her, too, no matter how hard she was trying to pretend otherwise. "Does he know you're here?"

She nodded. "It's our family rule, total honesty." A wry smile then. "Until recently, I guess."

"What does he think about it? You coming here, asking all these questions."

"Hates it." She laughed. "You'd think I told him I was going to Syria or something. I don't get what he's so worried about. And I really don't get why *he's* not just as curious. Like, how do you spend all these years not wanting to know what happened? Especially now? I don't get it."

"Maybe he's afraid of what he might find out."

"Like what?"

"Like anything that doesn't line up with the person he remembers. When someone's gone, that's all you have left."

"You say *gone* like you mean dead. It's just as likely she's missing. Right?"

I couldn't tell whether she really believed it. I tried to, for both of them: a new Wendy, off the grid, a hammock in Bali or a beach in Mexico or a cardboard box in a dark alley, making a different life. "But your father doesn't believe that, right? He thinks he's grieving his wife."

Her shoulders slumped, almost imperceptibly.

"If you think someone's not coming back, you don't want to find something out about them that you can't un-know."

After dinner I shut myself in our bedroom, put on Bach's *The Art of Fugue*, closed my eyes, let sound carry me backward in time in a way that no visual cue ever could. If aphantasia was a kind of mental blindness, I wondered if the analogy held, and other mental senses were consequentially heightened. I could summon the Bach melodies in my head at will, and almost persuade myself I was listening with Benjamin; I could almost, when I concentrated, conjure his arms around me, our hearts beating metronomically with the notes. Actual listening was harder on the heart.

Benjamin said the fugue was like the self: fugal subjects inverting, subverting, transforming over time, but always, somehow, ineffably and fundamentally the same. He said the fugue was like the mind, rigid rules imposed on finite elements spawning an infinity of combinatorial possibility, a generative complexity from which arose thought, beauty, human consciousness. He said the fugue was a junction of reason and unreason, enlightenment rationalism fused with renaissance mysticism, a liminal space where finite met infinite. He said Bach used music to encode the divine—like our neurons, Benjamin said, our axons and dendrites, our neurotransmitters, every mind its own creator. He did not say that the music made him a child again, helped him remember how to love his father, for whom Bach had been the only tolerable talisman of a lost history. He did not, as a general and ungently imposed rule, say much of anything about his father or what had happened after his father's suicide, Sacher torte, schnitzel, and cold Viennese gentility replaced with kugel and borscht and the aggressive Russian warmth of his mother's extended family determined to smother the fatherless boy. He did not say that Bach was beyond his mother's grasp, but I could tell he thought it, and never advanced my own theory, that the music was as much about trying to understand his mother as it was trying to recapitulate his father—that the idea of life as an infinite permutation of finite rule, faith encoded in law and law the pathway to faith, was embodied by his mother's Judaism, all those rituals and prayers and kashrut silverware, everything he'd fled from into the arms of his self-described shiksa first wife. Even early on, I knew better than to say any of that.

I liked the canons better, music that turned in on itself with a finite trajectory. Melodies that played again and against until you couldn't help but claim them as your own. The brain's assembly of neural music processing centers is called the corticofugal network; we're programmed to read repetition as love. Music as pattern recognition. Melody as the comfort of an old lover's shirt. You could argue the pleasure of music has little to do with the music itself. The brain takes its pleasure from remembering. Even a bad memory, after enough time has passed, feels like home.

*   *   *

I couldn't sleep. I found Alice on the living room couch watching my soap on my TV.

"You watch this?" I settled beside her without asking. It was my house. "I thought no one under the age of forty watched these anymore. Or no one, period."

She shrugged. "I've seen it."

At the commercial break, she declined to fast-forward the ads, instead asking if I'd been watching the show for a long time.

"My whole life, pretty much."

"Did it always suck this much?"

"Not the way I remember it." What I remembered: giving my Barbies riding lessons on toy horses while my grandmother guzzled tea and yelled at the screen. The bliss of winter vacations, blanketed beside Gwen, laying bets on how long it would take Jasper to kiss Olivia. Late nights in LA, Gwen up with the new baby, nursing, watching the week's recorded episodes and describing the action to me, the phone and me huddled in my soon-to-be ex's closet, whispering, hungry for updates because Lucas, predictably, refused to own a TV. Then later, after I'd moved back to Philly, Gwen still nursing, forever nursing, me playing hooky from the Meadowlark to keep company with her boredom, the two of us playing at kids on Christmas break, scarfing Doritos and Tastykakes, Gwen passed out and drooling on the carpet, baby Charlotte done same on my chest, tiny fingers sleep-clutching at my nipples like she could sense their fallow potential, her soft skin, soft breath, soft weight, the feeling, in that room, like Charlotte was part of Gwen and so also part of me. I remembered watching with Wendy.

The show came back on. A desiccated Jasper was trying to sweet-talk his on-again, off-again wife, Olivia (second, fourth, and fifth marriages), into forgiving him for kidnapping their child twenty-five years before. Jasper had given the baby up for a black market adoption, told then mistress Olivia it had died at birth, let the secret fester ever since—until now. I should tell Alice, I thought, that I watched the show with her mother.

"My best friend and I have been waiting half our lives for this secret to come out," I said instead. It was still how I thought of Gwen, even now: best friend. Embarrassing, maybe, that this far into adulthood I still clung to a child's concept of friendship—or maybe just embarrassing that I'd never made a new one.

"Satisfying?"

I'd only said it because I needed something to say, but realized: "Deeply."

"You can go call her and celebrate, or whatever. I don't mind."

"Thanks for your permission." It came out sharper than intended. "Sorry. I just . . . we're not exactly on speaking terms."

"Big fight?"

"Something like that."

Once a cheater, Gwen had warned me for the last time, but by far not the first, when I asked her to witness the wedding. An intimate nonevent, I told her, city hall, just the two of us and our two witnesses. She reminded me I'd always been the girl who wanted the fairy-tale dress, flowers in my hair, was a sucker maybe not for the wedding-industrial complex, but wholeheartedly for the juvenile trappings of love. I'd also wanted a father to walk me down the aisle, give me away, dance with me to Ray Charles or the Everly Brothers, but I didn't explain this to her, because I was tired of explaining things to her. She reminded me I hated Philadelphia, and even more hated the suburbs, but here I was planning to move into another woman's house, mausoleum of her dead marriage. A man who marries a mistress creates a job opening, she said, then pretended it was a joke. You're giving up your career for him, she said, not a joke. Look how well that worked out for his wife. *Ex*-wife, I said. I said a lot of things. As did she. I disinvited her from the wedding. Benjamin and I got married alone, witnessed by two strangers recruited from the courthouse lobby. I missed Gwen, until the memory of missing her overtook the memory of having her. Then there was nothing left to miss.

Alice paused the show. "So whose fault was it? Like, which one of you has to apologize?"

"It's more complicated than that."

"Huh." Amazing how much judgment you could infuse into that sound.

Maybe Wendy Doe was dead after all, I thought, her spirit empowered to visit this girl's presence on me. See how it feels, I imagined her saying, to have a witness. To be an object studied objectively, without mercy.

"My mom watched this show, too," Alice said into the silence. "That's why I do. Weird coincidence, huh."

"It's a popular show."

"Or she remembered watching it with you. She did, right?"

I nodded, caught. Seen.

"Maybe she remembered everything, and just pretended not to."

"Eighteen years is a long time to lie."

"Yeah. It is."

Just before dawn, I gave myself permission to check on Gwen's Facebook page. This was a temptation I'd been indulging more and more since the funeral, which was the first time I'd seen her in more than a decade. She'd skipped my wedding, but showed up for the funeral. It felt like she was there to gloat. Per her prediction, the marriage hadn't lasted.

To be clear: I knew why she was there. She'd come to express sympathy and care and maybe even apology or forgiveness, depending on which she believed was merited—and I knew this because I would have done the same. Knowing did not alter the feeling. I felt, on seeing her, too much rage and too much remembering, and that was a day I endured only by doing my best to feel nothing at all. So I kept my distance, and she kept hers. Afterward, she'd sent a card. Generic, a swan on the front, Hallmark conjuration of sadness. Inside, beneath the printed "sorry for your loss," she'd written: *I wish I knew what to say. Love, Gwen.* I'd been unable to decipher its hidden meaning, whether this was her version of reaching out or an admission that she couldn't be bothered. Maybe we were, in her mind, childhood friends who'd drifted apart in the natural way of things. It felt juvenile, stalking her on social media, obsessing over our past—the kind of thing people with children, with living husbands, wouldn't have the spare time to do.

Her Facebook page was all good fortune. The baby was in college. I'd held her while she sucked from a bottle; I'd dangled a rubber frog over her face while Gwen bathed her in the sink; I'd scrubbed her vomit off my shoulder, her shit off my jeans; I'd missed her entire life. She had her father's stupid smile, but the rest of her face was all Gwen. Her prom dress was several inches too short.

Gwen looked shockingly old. I considered sending her a message, but did not. Her latest post announced her recent return from a romantic anniversary trip to the Bahamas. The pictures: Gwen and Andy dancing in the surf, Gwen and Andy swimming with a pig. Gwen and Andy, mugging for a poorly focused selfie, the caption *20 years and still going strong*. I logged out.

V

ALICE

In the dream, there is always a moment of denial. Hands creep across swollen stomach, fondle stretched flesh, press newly penile nub of belly button, sense deep within an alien churn. She says, no, no, I can't be, but undeniably, yes, now, she is. She feels colonized. She feels ruined. Always, she thinks, *How did I forget that I did not want this?* She wakes needing to pee. This ritual discovery of disaster averted is her only unqualified happiness, now that her mother is gone.

The week after she lost her virginity, Alice took three pregnancy tests, just in case. When they all came up negative, she considered texting the sperm dispenser, who had entered his number into her phone as *Emergency Services*. She did not.

To alleviate the guilt of temptation, she called Daniel. She missed Daniel. He asked if she was still glad she came. He hadn't wanted her to—like her father, he'd urged Alice to accept, move on, heal. Daniel believed in smart choices, healthy caution, and this was part of what she'd loved about him. He was worried she might ruin her scholarship, her year, her future.

"You know your mom would want you to take care of yourself right now," he said.

She told him she had no idea what her mother would want, and that was the whole point.

"I just don't see why it has to matter so much, that she kept a secret from before you were born."

"Because it does." Because it wasn't a secret, it was a time bomb. Because Alice's mother had been someone else without her memory, that was becoming obvious. Wendy Doe was a stranger, and that made Karen

129

Clark part stranger. And because Alice took after her mother, everyone said so. If her mother's psyche had a hidden fault line, who was to say that Alice didn't have the same fracture?

"Can we not have this same argument again?" she said.

"Fine."

"How'd your history test go?" she said.

"It was physics. And it was shitty. I think I failed."

"You always think that," she said. "Then you always ace it."

"Oh good, I guess I don't have to worry." There was a slight edge to his voice. But he wasn't mad. Daniel never got mad. Add it to the list of qualities she'd thought she loved. "How's your dad?"

"Honestly? I have no idea."

Her father always told Alice he was fine, described days at the office and dinners with friends, but it was hard to believe him, especially in this house, every room suffused with the widow's longing.

There was a long silence.

"Alice, when are you coming back?"

"I don't know. I have to stay here until I find some answers."

"And what if there aren't any? What if there's nothing there to find?"

"I'm not ready to consider that as an option," she said.

"Yeah, but what if? You just stay forever?"

"I said—"

"You can't run away, Alice. Eventually you're going to have to face the fact that—"

"I said I didn't want to talk about this."

"Fine."

"Good."

"Anyway. I should go," he said.

"Yeah. Okay."

But he didn't go. He was waiting, hoping she would say it first. She was the one who'd said it first, the very first time, and she was the one who'd started saying it routinely, because the echo was reassuring.

He gave up waiting. "I love you."

She was the one who'd stopped saying it at all, after her mother left. He'd brought this up only once. They were watching *The Simpsons*, as they were always watching *The Simpsons* that summer, because it made him happy and she no longer had the energy to. Upstairs, his father would be baking bread or stirring soup; his mother would be editing copy for the next morning's broadcast, his little brothers wrestling with such fierce, thumping joy it made the ceiling shake. Daniel's family was a stop-action movie of Kodak moments. His parents were always kissing each other. They hugged everyone, even Alice, who was too polite to refuse. They were all easy with the world—as if to *be yourself* required not conscious and continuous self-construction, hesitation, readjustment, but simply giving way to the gravity of existence. That night, he sat with his feet on his mother's coffee table; she lay with her head in his lap, eyes closed, waiting for another day to end. Daniel asked why she never said she loved him anymore, and she said, please don't ask me to feel something. Two weeks later they left for their respective campuses. He thought she was afraid, that to feel anything was to risk feeling everything. That wasn't it. She simply didn't: feel. That was gone.

She wanted to say it now—could almost make herself want *him*, want to tell him that she'd let a stranger inside her, that she was sorry and not, that she'd done it because of loving him and in spite of it and for reasons having nothing to do with him and for no reason at all, that she hadn't thought of him while the stranger was on her, in her, wet and heavy and gasping, but she thought of him when she was alone, that she pretended her hands were his hands, that last night, writhing on the widow's ugly sheets, she had mashed her face in the pillow and groaned his name. It was like a break in the clouds, a shaft of gray light—then the wind shifted, the sky closed again, and she said goodbye and hung up.

The widow had given her a stack of tape recordings of interviews with her mother. Alice listened to them only in private, lights off, shades closed, her mother's unmotherlike voice alone with her in the dark.

"*Of course it's occurred to me,*" Wendy Doe said on the tape. "*Imagine you woke up in a public place, your back and shoulders covered in bruises. Imagine you had no fucking idea where they came from, no idea who you were, no idea of anything. Wouldn't you assume something terrible had happened? You think I needed you people to tell me this was probably caused by trauma? What else is there?*"

"*It doesn't bother you, not knowing?*" That was the young Elizabeth, whom Wendy Doe called Lizzie.

"*What makes you think it doesn't bother me?*"

"*You seem very adamantly not to want to know.*"

"*I don't see what one thing has to do with the other. Does it bother me to know something might have happened to me, or to this body, before it belonged to me? Of course it fucking bothers me. Do I want to remember what it was? Would you?*"

A pause. "*Definitely.*"

Laughter. "*You know where the word* trauma *comes from?*"

"*Do you?*" Young Elizabeth was kind of patronizing, Alice thought.

"*Dr. Strauss told me.* Trauma *is ancient Greek, for* wound. *So you tell me. If I stabbed you right now, that would be a trauma, right?*"

"*Okay, sure.*"

"*Would you rather feel the pain, get stitched up, wait for it to heal, keep the scar forever? Or would you rather just snap your fingers and have it disappear like it never happened?*" Wendy Doe said.

"*I guess I'd rather have the scar—I think the worst things that have ever happened to me make me who I am.*"

Another laugh, a bitter one. "*Maybe that's because nothing bad has ever happened to you.*"

"*I think we're done for the day.*" A crackling silence followed. Alice turned off the tape.

Just before leaving for college, Alice had read an interview with the actress who played her favorite character on her mother's soap. She was almost exactly Alice's age, and had been on the show since she was a child. Alice had grown up with her, watched her parents die flamboyantly and—thanks to a few miraculous returns from the grave—repeatedly (helicopter crash, stabbing, earthquake, building collapse, stabbing again). Alice had watched the girl defeat cancer, fend off a gang rape, survive a gunshot that left her wheelchair-bound from spring sweeps through Christmas, had watched her love and lose and lose again. In the interview, the actress revealed the toll enacting this trauma had taken on her body, which only knew what it had done, not why. Her body, she said, remembered the tears and the screams and the battery and the longing; it bore the full weight of an imagined life. Forgetting something, Alice thought, didn't erase it.

The idea of trauma had occurred to Alice, too, of course. The causal link between trauma and memory loss seemed to be the only thing everyone agreed on. Alice had forced herself to think through what might have happened to her mother, and when. *Bruises all over her back*—Alice hadn't known that part. The things that could happen to a woman on a bus, or on the street, or—Alice hated herself for even indulging this option, if only to dismiss it—in her own home. They were infinite, but didn't they all boil down to the same thing? Brutality done to the body, brutally enough that the mind fled. Karen Clark was a strong woman. If something had broken her, it must have been something even stronger.

You're just like your mother: This was the steady refrain of Alice's life. She'd resented this, for all the obvious reasons, but was also pleased by it. But she could not have been much like this version of her mother, because Alice couldn't imagine not wanting to know. Was this what her mother had expected Alice would find a way to do now, let her wound go numb until she forgot it—and her mother—ever existed? Alice had nothing in common with a person who could do that.

Elizabeth knocked on the door. Alice liked this about her, that the widow didn't assume ownership implied access. Alice invited her in.

"My stepdaughter's in the neighborhood and just invited me to a last-minute dinner. I was wondering if you'd like to join us?"

It felt like a pity invite, and Alice wondered whether she'd been listening from outside the door.

"Unlimited garlic breadsticks," the widow added.

"I guess it has been a long time since I've had a family dinner. Even if it is with someone else's family."

The widow laughed, its bitter edge sounding more like Wendy Doe.

"What did I say?" Alice asked.

"Something you definitely shouldn't say in front of Nina."

"What?"

"That she and I are a family."

Table for three at the Macaroni Grill. The daughter, Nina, arrived late, sweaty from biking to the restaurant, in cargo pants and a T-shirt that read Have You Punched a Nazi Today? Nina was the kind of girl Alice's mother would have deemed *an undesirable influence*, her catch-all term for the blunter *slovenly, slutty, irresponsible, unsafe*. Silver studs climbed her left ear from lobe to tip, a chain link tattoo cuffed her bicep, and blue streaks threaded her spiky black hair. Their mall-banged cheerleader waitress didn't even pretend not to stare.

The widow seemed terrified of her stepdaughter—flinched from Nina's arrival hug, then overcompensated by squeezing her for too long, complimenting her spiky hair with a tentative pat, as if appreciating a well-groomed but formerly feral pit bull. Alice now understood her presence here was not imposition but favor. Stepmother and daughter needed a buffer.

Nina asked the widow about her book: a nonstarter. The widow asked Nina about her internship and law school prospects: the former unpaid, the latter on hold. This left a single safe route: both turned to Alice, asked after college major, future plans, childhood in the Rockies, small talk skirting family and past. They ate their bottomless bowls of pasta, dipped garlic breadsticks in garlic oil.

"I remember your mother, you know," Nina said as the widow picked up the check.

"You couldn't possibly," the widow said. "You were too young."

"And yet. Dad would bring her on these picnics we had sometimes, by that old graveyard behind the main building. I remember, because she taught me how to make etchings from the gravestones."

"I did that with her, too," Alice said. "Cemetery etchings."

Nina asked Alice what she'd thought of the Meadowlark, and Alice tried to be diplomatic, leaning hard on the impressive technology, avoiding mention of imagined straitjackets and angry ghosts. "Your father must have been really impressive," she said.

Nina rolled her eyes. "If you say so. You ask me, that place is totally creepy. Horror movie material. Though maybe I'm biased, given that it's also the place my father cheated on my mother and murdered my childhood. No offense, Elizabeth."

The widow glanced at Alice, clearly chagrined, as if she'd expected Alice to actually buy the story that grad student and professor had hooked up only after the demise of the latter's marriage.

"Your father tried very hard to repair his marriage," the widow told Nina. "He and your mother had a lot of problems, and the way things ended up, it wasn't—"

"Please don't. You shouldn't have to defend him to me."

"No, I shouldn't, because he was a good man."

"We all know what he was," Nina said. "I knew back then, and I was in *kindergarten*. You think you were the first mistress he got to babysit for me?"

The widow's face drained like an unclogged sink. It occurred to Alice: that *was* what she'd thought.

"I wish you wouldn't say things like that. You didn't know him like—"

"Like you did?" Nina said. "I'd think you might be in a good position to know how much a man like that keeps from his wife."

Elizabeth stood abruptly and excused herself to the bathroom, mumbling something about meeting them outside the restaurant, then she was gone.

"Fuck," Nina said. "Why do I do that?"

Alice followed her into the night. They waited on the curb, minutes passed, the widow did not appear.

"You think she's okay in there?" Alice asked.

"I don't know."

"Do you think one of us should, like, go check on her?"

Nina laughed. "You don't know her very well yet, do you?"

They waited.

"So how's the house?" Nina said.

"Okay, I guess? It's nice." Alice wondered what Nina thought of a stranger staying in what had once been her childhood bedroom.

"I keep hoping she'll sell it. I can't even imagine how fucking depressing it must be for her."

It almost sounded like actual concern. "You two don't seem very . . . close."

"She thinks I hate her."

"Do you?"

"It's complicated. Whatever. She's got this idea that I need to think my dad was some kind of saint, or, I don't know, maybe she thinks he *was* some kind of saint."

"What was he?"

Nina shrugged. "According to my mother? A toxic man-whore. You ask Elizabeth and—well, you see how that one goes."

"What if I ask you?"

"My father was . . ." Nina looked away. "I don't know. She's right about that at least. I never really got to know him. It seemed like maybe, after I graduated, things were going to be different, but then . . ."

"I'm sorry," Alice said, then winced. "Actually, forget that. I hate when people say that."

"Totally. It's like, what are you apologizing for, you didn't kill him."

It felt comfortable talking to Nina about this, like they were in the same club, and Alice resisted it: there was no club. She didn't believe in psychic crap, auras, vibrations in the ether, but still, wouldn't some part of her know if her mother was dead?

"You really remember my mother?"

"I only remember the cemetery thing. She was just another adult to me, you know? I wasn't paying attention. I am sorry about that."

Alice hated it, the idea of her other mother mothering this other child.

"Why do you care so much anyway?" Nina asked.

"About what she was like when she was here?"

"Yeah, it was so long ago, and she was having, like, some kind of mental episode, right? Why does it matter?"

This was the same question she'd begged Daniel to stop asking, but Nina was a stranger. Honesty seemed easier.

"If it didn't matter, why would everyone lie about it for so long?" Telling that kind of lie, sustaining it for Alice's whole life, contradicted everything she'd thought she knew about her mother. "The more I find out, the more it seems like she was this totally different person. And it's like, is that who she really was deep down? Or is that who she gave herself permission to turn into when she escaped everybody she ever knew?"

"You almost sound jealous."

"I feel like she designed me to these precise specifications," Alice said. "She made me *exactly* the daughter she wanted me to be—and now I find out she got to turn herself into this whole other person? It's hard to explain, but it feels . . ."

"Unfair?"

"Maybe."

"Look, I'm going to take off before Elizabeth shows up, it's probably easier that way—but can I tell you something you might not want to hear?"

Alice indicated her permission.

"You asked what kind of man I thought my father was? The real answer is I never looked too hard. That's his shit, and my mother's. I decided it wasn't going to be mine. You're allowed to do that, you know? You don't have to be who your parents 'designed' you to be. You get to be anyone."

"Easy to say, but it's not like I can just wake up and decide to be a different person."

"Why not?"

Alice was still considering the question when the widow finally emerged, unsurprised that Nina was gone. Her makeup had all washed away. Alice imagined her crying in the bathroom, splashing cold water on her cheeks, preparing her face to face the world, and as they drove back to the house, Alice wondered who Elizabeth would be if she could be someone else.

That night, as she was falling asleep, Alice texted Emergency Services. It's not an emergency, she clarified, but if he would like to see her again, she would be amenable.

He would like to see her, he wrote. Alice proposed a picnic.

ELIZABETH

Benjamin liked to say that every great romance was allowed one sentimental cliché. Ours was Paris. Our city of light and love, our made-palatable-for-the-public origin story, our foundational narrative from which all rationalization and raison d'être derived—and the dirty truth is, I hated it. From *le jour premier*, even. It was gray, drizzling, we were drizzling with sweat, the apartment was six elevator-less flights up, less of a bargain than it had seemed from the ground. Our suitcases were heavy. Our flight was a red-eye. We were cranky, filthy, hot. The apartment smelled like someone else. Benjamin's back ached. Because of the plane, he said, and the suitcases. Because you're old, I thought, and so is your body. My heart ached. Because I made my choice and now I have no job no home no friends no exit, I thought. Only this and only you. Every day, I thought, this is a mistake. I thought, *Paris, je te deteste. Mon amour, je te deteste.* The pillows were flat. The bed was soft. The sun never set. Benjamin never noticed. Benjamin refused gloom, and why not, Benjamin was free. No more job, at least for the year. No more wife, forever. No unmowed lawn, no unschmoozed donors. No more fucking his mistress in secret. Benjamin was a conquistador, free to seize what he wanted, which was wine, cheese, work, me, work again, more. He was on Rumspringa. He was so fucking happy. He was hiding a ring in his dopp kit. I didn't know.

Paris shuts down in August. He promised everything would change come September, and it did. In September, we stood midday in the mouth of a bar, in a gang of slack-jawed strangers, in nausea and disbelief, in the wrong language, in the wrong country, in extremis, watching the world end on live TV.

Even at home, Benjamin pointed out, we would have been watching on TV, just as later we would watch the war. Our air would not have smelled of fuel and flesh; our skies would have remained clear. Distance was distance, he said; it made no difference how far. He also said, when I cried at night or refused to attend a dinner at the Eiffel Tower, because now I recognized a target when I saw one, you don't understand. These things happen. You're still so young. I would think, but never say, you're so fucking old.

He worked. He was on fire with work. I did not work, had no work. Had given up fire for him. Not for me, he always insisted, that's not what I wanted. But what he wanted was me, with him. In Philadelphia, when he was in Philadelphia. In Paris, when he was in Paris. And in these places, there was no work for me to do.

He worked; I walked. As I walked, I recited to myself the two lines of poetry I'd memorized in AP French, all that remained. *Il pleure dans mon coeur / comme il pleut sur la ville.* It rains in my heart like it rains on the city. This did not seem melodramatic that September. Across the ocean, it was raining people. Across another ocean—or maybe a continent, I wasn't exactly sure, was the thing, and even when I checked the map I forgot within days—it was raining bombs. In Paris, it rained rain. Benjamin made us new expat friends, who declaimed about terrorism over wine and steak tartare. Stiff upper lip, they said. Keep calm and carry on. *The thing about Americans*, even the Americans would say, having proven themselves superior by getting out.

I walked. Paris was dirty. Hot, at first, then a damp, soul-deflating cold. Paris was a cliché of itself. The men did smell and smoke and grope. The women did pedal home with basketed baguette and stiletto-wrapped feet. There was an unholy quantity of cheese.

When I tell the story of Paris, I say September 11 broke my heart, then Benjamin and Augustine knit it back together. Truth: Paris broke my heart and Benjamin did, too, because both were old and broken down, both had baited me with a fairy tale and switched it up with constipation. Augustine knit me back together with myself. She had nothing to do with Benjamin and that, though I could never say so, was the point.

"You ever think about her?" I'd asked him once, a few months after Wendy Doe remembered herself and left us, when we were still fucking in his office after hours, door locked, lights off, guilt lighting our way.

He did not, he said. She was a subject that didn't pan out, a dead end. There was nothing left to think about. This was not entirely dissimilar from the terminal ease with which he'd archived his first marriage.

"It disturbs me that you think of her like that," I said.

"It disturbs me that you don't."

We tried not to talk about her again. Maybe that was why I didn't tell him about Augustine from the start. Because she was Wendy's before she was mine.

Augustine. Wendy's Augustine, my secret, my small piece of home. Benjamin had laboratory space in the Salpêtrière, which, two centuries after Pinel and Charcot, was still warehousing misery. This was Paris, where everything was recycled. What had been a workshop for flawed knowledge manufactured on the bodies of broken women was now a modern hospital complex the size of a small town. Gurneys and white coats, but also courtyards, cafés, libraries, plaques. When I tired of Paris proper, I made the city of Salpêtrière my own. I sat where Augustine had sat, and tried to imagine her, imagined Wendy imagining her. A body inhabited by a woman, narrated by a man.

I asked the Salpêtrière for access to their archive, and because I belonged to Benjamin, they agreed. With my pidgin French and pocket dictionary, with Charcot's own bookshelves watching over me, I began.

I'm going to tell her story, I told him eventually, tentatively. Four months after I'd started, once I was sure. I told him over dinner at our favorite café, the one at the base of Mouffetard. By that point, we had a favorite café, along with a favorite *boulangerie* and *fromagerie* and *pharmacie* and an inside joke about the counter guy at our local *tabac* with his polished handlebar mustache, and ongoing arguments about the best flavor of Berthillon, the sunniest, most scenic spot in which to lick it along the Seine. It was April in Paris, and Paris was somehow becoming home.

"Like a novel?" he asked, indulging.

"No."

"Like a biography?"

"I don't know."

He laughed. "Next you can write a history of lab rats."

We walked home along the road with a Baudelaire poem inscribed on a long stone wall. I took his hand. I'd told myself I was keeping Augustine a secret until I was sure. But also, I knew there was a chance that he would make me feel like she was worthless—that so, by extension, was I. He had. And maybe this is love: I still took his hand.

I always told the story that I had abandoned science because I wanted to be a writer, but this elided the reason I wanted. It was in Paris that I understood science belonged to him. It was his world, which meant if I didn't find something that belonged to me outside his domain, then his world would be the entirety of mine. Augustine made it safe to give the rest of myself to him. So I took his hand, and I took him home, which by April smelled like lavender and Parmesan and us.

After the dinner with Nina, I took Benjamin's laptop into my bedroom, which had once been our bedroom. I locked the door. Then I finally opened his in-box. I didn't do this because of what Nina had said about there being other women before me, not entirely. Benjamin had sworn I was the first, but he'd sworn that twenty years ago, before we'd made any promises to each other. If Nina was right, then so what. So what, he'd told a lie to a version of me he barely knew, so I wouldn't take him for a cliché. So what, he'd made a cliché of me. I'd live.

It wasn't that. Or not just that. It was the suggestion that I didn't—not then, but now—know him as well as I'd thought. I knew which brand of toothpaste he liked best; I knew the sound of his breathing when he was pretending to sleep; I knew he preferred booth to table, window to aisle, oat milk to cow's; I knew the weight of him and the taste of him; I knew everything I'd learned over all those thousands of days and nights, but if I knew him so well, what did I have to fear from his emails? Nothing, I decided. So I opened one.

Elizabeth is flaneuring, he kept telling the people we met in Paris. *Mon amour, le flaneur*, sic. He said it like he was proud of me, which is how I knew he wasn't.

In the beginning, I paid attention. Searched for offerings: Did you know the Hebrew name of God is inscribed on the towers of St. Sulpice? Have you seen the homeless man dressed as a pirate on the corner of

Odeon and St. Germain? I found him a wall inscribed with a poem Baudelaire could have written just for him. *J'ai plus de souvenirs que si j'avais mille ans . . .* I memorized the best lines for him, recited it like a proud child. *C'est une pyramide, un immense caveau / Qui contient plus de morts que la fosse commune. / Je suis un cimetière abhorré de la lune.* I have enough memories for a thousand years, my brain is a pyramid, a mass grave of the dead—he liked that. I liked, *I am a cemetery abhorred by the moon.*

I brought him beignets and hazelnut pralines. A lush leather-bound edition of the *Iconographie Photographique de la Salpêtrière.* An overpriced wooden train for Nina that he said was too young for her, and anyway too heavy to bring home. And anyway, he didn't have to say she doesn't know you exist, and once she does, she will hate you, the way her mother hates you, and this is the closest you will get to motherhood. When he flew back to the States to spend Hanukkah with his daughter, there was no one to pay attention for, so I walked only to walk. I walked for motion, for the escape from thinking about spending Christmas alone, which I was not supposed to care about, since, as he pointed out, it wasn't even our holiday. Hanukkah was for children. He'd secured permission to visit only on the condition I stay away. Nothing was stopping me from going home to my own family, he pointed out, like that wasn't him. Like I could afford it. Like three months after September 11, I wasn't still afraid to fly. You're not a child, he said. She is.

I stopped pretending I was walking to or walking for. I walked so I wouldn't have to stay still. I read Virginia Woolf on the haunting of winter streets, slippage into the solitude of city dark until *we are no longer quite ourselves,* until *we shed the self our friends know us by and become part of that vast republican army of anonymous trampers.* I tramped. I shed. I walked toward away. This is how I remember it, at least. The movement. The drift. Tireless legs, taut calves, pain-free, ever-enduring feet. I was so young, and felt so old, like all my decisions had been made. On Christmas, he called. Transatlantic, expensive, so I should know he cared. He whispered, *je t'aime,* and I wondered who was listening.

He'd archived every email; he was a memory hoarder. And I knew which names to look for, of course. His best and brightest students were always, somehow, young women. He was known for this, the great champion of the female brain. There were those I'd gotten to know, worshipful girls we'd taken to dinner or hired to housesit while we were away, girls who'd ventured into the wilds of academia, slayed the tenure beast, sent us occasional Christmas cards featuring the children they'd finally dared to have. These didn't interest me. It was the girls I'd only met once or twice, in passing, girls he'd gushed over for a time—their promise, their possibility, their extraordinary potential—girls who'd ultimately disappointed him. Switched fields, dropped out, burned out, failed, in myriad ways, to live up to exceptional expectation. The brain, as ever, was a miracle of contradiction. I'd filed away the names, which meant I must have known, but somehow, I had allowed myself not to know.

I already miss you, he wrote.

If this project slams into a dead end, it will still have been worth it, because it brought you into my life, he wrote.

I've never met a mind like yours, he wrote. *It makes me feel alive.*

There were no incriminating photos, no love letters, no explicit references to physical contact or romantic rendezvous. That would have been more tolerable, maybe, than the intimacies he'd allowed himself. Confessions, moods, anxieties I'd assumed he shared only with me—and worse, those he hadn't. Moments that had struck him funny; strange dreams that had startled him awake. Worries about the past; complaints about the wife. Those were, of course, the most incriminating. The most familiar. I recognized the tone he took to bemoan his marriage, half guilty, half wounded, poor Benjamin held hostage to a life partner who made him feel increasingly alone. I'd heard it before. How else would I have given myself permission to fall in love?

But I'm telling it wrong. Paris in the springtime was everything the song promised; love was everything every song had ever promised. Paris was lying naked in a shaft of sun feeding each other Nutella-smeared baguettes; Paris was a precarious perch on the hillside beneath the Sacré-Coeur, grass whispering against bare feet; Paris was wine-sodden dinners and rose bouquets bought off wandering women, street violinists bowing Beatles songs on foggy bridges, tangerine gelato and truffled cheese and raspberry kir, sunsets over the Seine, sunsets over the Luxembourg Gardens, sunsets over the Pompidou, sunsets over the Eiffel Tower, an ungodly quantity of sunsets, each more undeniably romantic than the last. Paris was the commutation of terror—fear that Benjamin would abandon me seamlessly replaced by the fear he would be killed in some gruesome fashion, here on the cusp of our happily ever after. I imagined ever more baroque calamities, Benjamin crushed by the doors of a Metro, Benjamin blown sky high by a sewer explosion, Benjamin concussed by the gigantic Foucault's pendulum he loved to stand beneath. Benjamin killed in a rain of fire, airplanes or bombs or whatever else might plausibly fall from the sky. I had never let myself love anyone so much. I had always been enough for myself, I had made certain of that. I had filled up all available space. Benjamin colonized me as if I'd been uninhabited, and by the time we left Paris, it felt as if I had. *The cradle rocks above an abyss*, Nabokov wrote in the memoir of memory I'd read that year, or at least pretended to, still trying to convince Benjamin I was the woman he imagined me to be, *and common sense tells us that our existence is but a brief crack of light between two eternities of darkness.* That would be our life together, that crack of light. *Although the two are identical twins, man, as a rule, views the prenatal abyss with more calm than the one he is heading for.* In Paris, I understood: the person I'd been before him, the one who could be whole without him, had no doubt existed, but she was a mystery to the person I'd become. Someone who, without him, could only be broken.

Before he loved me—or at least before it occurred to me he could—he told me all about her. *The wife.*

Her intellectual spark had gone out. Her curiosity about the world had warped inward, toward the baby, the home, the self and its sartorial accoutrements. She wanted to own him and his choices, tether him to the mundane. All the things she'd loved most about him—his expansiveness, his drive toward intellectual conquest, his insatiable need for *more*—now threatened her. She was content to endure: motherhood, marriage, life. She insisted he be the same.

I'm not interested in ENDURING, he wrote. *I want more.*

*   *   *

Benjamin had his own story about Paris. He had his vedette gliding over the Seine, ring lodged in palm as Bastille Day fireworks burst overhead. I let him tell the story often enough that he assumed it belonged to both of us. What belonged to both of us: the ride to the airport, my hand trembling in his, my bags stuffed with chocolate, wine, the first three chapters of what would become a book, an extra Xanax in case fear erupted into panic once I forced myself onto the plane. The diamond on my finger. In the airport security line, they made us take off our shoes. As the plane lifted off, I imagined the crash, the obituary, his obituary of course, with a dead fiancée footnote, and the resulting indignation got me through to cruising altitude. Then there were only the eight hours of flight time to endure, and the customs tribunal, and the baggage carousel, and the taxi line, and the hour in rush hour traffic, and the return to the suburbs and the rest of our lives.

Benjamin would remind me that memories self-reinforce, that each retrieval of a memory further blurs the edges of reality. The way you tell yourself the story changes the story. That discovery might have been his legacy, if the NYU team hadn't beaten him to it. Instead, it was a cautionary tale for us both. For him: never let yourself be distracted from what really matters, lest you spend the rest of your life wondering exactly how narrowly you'd missed your Nobel. For me: remember that the past happened the way you wished, and eventually you'll believe that it did.

ALICE

She told him she didn't need to know his name. He overruled her. Now she knew his name was Zach. She called him Z; he still called her Anonymous. They picnicked between mossy gravestones, forgotten plots carpeted with weeds. The old state mental institution was now shiny private property. He liked that. They met at midnight, as seemed appropriate for a cemetery picnic. She brought pizza and a blanket. He brought condoms and a bag of chips.

She had not yet been to her mother's grave.

She tried not thinking about her mother, shrinking the universe to a party of two. Boy, girl; food, sex; dirt, stars. Maybe that was how she would punish her mother for leaving, for erasing herself, once and again. Alice would find a way to erase everything her mother had impressed on her, every prudent scrap of fear and loathing. Maybe this was already under way, or how else could she be meeting a strange man in the woods and saying, as the pizza got cold, oh god, yes, please. It was less painful this time, somewhat.

"At least you didn't cry," he said, not meanly.

He tasted saltier than Daniel and his crotch smelled like a department store. He called her beautiful—several times during and once after—and she wondered whom he saw when he looked at her. She was still zipping and buttoning when he aimed his camera lens at her. No, she told him, and closed herself safely into her sweatshirt. Not going to happen.

"Why not? You're beautiful. And with the moonlight on your skin—"

She indicated her clothing-swathed body. "No skin. You keep aiming that thing at me and there won't ever be again."

He offered her the camera. "You want? I'm not shy—" His jeans were still unbuttoned, easily tugged down, as he demonstrated. She waved him off.

"No one wants a picture of that."

He grinned. "Not the feedback I've gotten in the past." But he put the camera down, and she relaxed. Let him nip at her nose, play his fingers across her nipples, and down, and down. "What's with you and getting your picture taken?"

"Nothing. What's with you and taking them?"

"I like seeing people's stories—you find the one moment that cracks open the door, and you can imagine a whole life."

He told her about the photography class he'd taken in high school, the one class he never showed up to drunk, the teacher who'd given him his first camera, and—not unconnected to his arousal to the art, he acknowledged, but not strictly causal, either—an occasional blow job in the school darkroom. He told her that the way he felt with a camera in his hands was the way he felt with vodka in his bloodstream, or the closest he was going to get, that he could almost escape from his own head, use the lens to flee into someone else's story, and, envious, Alice let his words slide into noise. She thought about the weight of him, heavier than she was used to. She thought about how Daniel touched her body like he knew he wasn't supposed to. When Zach wanted her to turn over, he turned her over, and just like that she'd tasted dirt and he was hoisting her up by the stomach, onto hands and knees, thrusting. It didn't feel like she was his subject to command—more like his object, to do with as he pleased. It wasn't that she liked this better, it was that he recused her from having to *like* at all. There was a moment, his hand on her breast, guiding her upright, straddling him, his other hand stroking the liminal zone where his body offered itself to hers, that she went rigid with a sensation entirely unlike the pleasure she'd learned to visit on herself, entirely unlike pleasure at all, and she forgot to feel ashamed.

Z and A ate cold, gummy pizza. Alice told him a story of a girl she might have been, if she'd been the daughter of Wendy Doe. She grew up with a single mother, she said. An addict: pills and drugs, also men. Then Alice told him her mother was dead.

Z told her he had his first hangover in seventh grade. That drinking made him feel less lonely. He told her that when he was a kid, he'd been afraid of cemeteries.

"How'd you even know about this place anyway?"

"My mom brought me here once when I was a kid," she said. "Back when it was still haunted."

The cemetery wasn't much of one. Alice skimmed her phone's flashlight along the crooked stones. They looked centuries old, weedy and weather-beaten. The dates belied the decay: 1947, 1942, 1959—all of them women, all of them young.

As a child, Alice had ridden her bike through the local cemetery almost without seeing it. By high school, the cemetery had taken on a different resonance. A cemetery at night rewarded trespass. To party boldly with the dead proved age and youth all at once. It was the safest kind of rebellion—trespass against people who couldn't fight back. Alice thought about graves differently now. Maybe there were two kinds of people in the world, she thought, the kind who laughed at ghosts, and the kind who thought about coffins, and who was inside them, and who was not.

Some of the women had first names, but no last names. Some just had descriptions: *loving daughter, loving mother*. One read, *loved and missed*, which seemed twice unlikely.

"It's kind of sad," Zach said, aiming his lens at a grave. "Rotting away all these years, no one even remembering they're here."

"Everyone dies like they lived, right?"

She could tell he thought that was profound.

"So how do you?" he said.

"What?"

"You know. Live."

"Dangerously."

He didn't laugh. "How did she die? Your mom?"

"She killed herself." It was the first lie she thought of.

"Shit."

It is a lie, she reminded herself.

"You must hate her."

"That's kind of a fucked-up thing to say, don't you think?"

"But you must *really* fucking hate her."

"She hung herself. From the ceiling fan. I found the body. I guess it didn't occur to her that would fuck me up for life. That I would never stop seeing her body just turning and turning."

"Wait, the ceiling fan was *on*? Why would she—?"

"She could have done it when I was a kid. But she waited. You think I'm supposed to be grateful?"

He pressed his palm to hers, measuring their fingers against each other. "I never told anyone in those meetings why I started drinking. Or, why I started drinking too much, I guess." He studied their fingertips, which were almost the same length. "You want to know?"

"Fuck no." She kissed him to shut him up, as she'd seen on TV.

Mission accomplished, she thought, as they unzipped what they'd just zipped, tangled together what they'd just pulled apart; she'd turned herself into someone else. Because the Alice she'd been would not be here. That Alice would have been too prudent and too loyal, would have felt like Daniel's love gave him claim to her body, would have built of that love a wall to keep trespassers out. That Alice would not betray someone she loved. There were two kinds of people in the world, she thought, and Alice could not be the kind who did that. So this girl, naked and moaning in this boy's arms, she must have become someone else.

VI

IV

WENDY

The things I learn at night

I am the shadow who haunts the shadows. I listen for ghosts. I choose to be the kind of person who believes in ghosts. It makes sense to me, that the dead would agitate against being forgotten.

I prefer not to sleep.

On the second floor, I found the office where Lizzie stores her notes. At night, I read what she says about me. She doubts I am a whole person. She believes I have a "semiconstructed self." She says my emotional reactions are "contingent and post-hoc." I am "presenting" a self but do not yet consist of one.

She also prefers not to sleep, at least here. I see her lurking in the spaces that belong to him. I see her kiss her forehead to his office door.

She doesn't know how often he sleeps in that office. Sometimes, at night, he and I walk the darkness together. He asks me what I think of her, whether she's smart, whether she's attractive. I tell him I've seen the picture of his wife, and she's no more attractive than that.

"It's easy to be moralistic when you've never been in love," he says.

"How do you know I've never?"

"Not the woman you were before. I'm talking about *you*. Virginal in every sense of the word."

At night he doesn't talk like a scientist.

I ask if he thinks I'm attractive, and if so, more or less than Lizzie.

"Feeling a little competitive, are we?"

"What if I told you I was in love with you? Stockholm syndrome."

"You're not a prisoner. I'm not your kidnapper."

"But what if?" The building is shut down; we're alone. I point out that no one could stop him from doing anything he wanted. He asks if this is an invitation.

"I'm wondering what you would do, if you had permission."

"What makes you think I need permission?" He smiles to show it's a joke. He takes my hand. He touches my face, and says, like it's a gift, "For the record, I think you're beautiful. If I were a less ethical person, we might be having a different conversation."

I'm so used to it here, men moving my body where they want it to go, that by the time it occurs to me I don't want to be touched, not in the dark and not by him, he's already let go.

LIZZIE

She needed Strauss to believe that nothing had changed. Nothing, she told herself, had changed. Except. She woke up with the thought of him, whether she would see him that day, whether they would be alone, whether this would be a day he would descend with lunch or for a moonlit walk through empty corridors. She thought about what she could wear that he might like, though he had given no indication he liked anything; she applied makeup with care, wore shoes that accentuated her calves, tried and failed to master the curling iron Gwen had given her years before. She scoured journal articles; she brainstormed future experiments; she shadowed Wendy, recorded, took notes, imagined tunneling into the mysteries of consciousness. She did all of this because she was genuinely curious, diligent, ambitious, because it was her job and her calling, but also because she wanted to impress. She felt like a cat slaughtering birds and mice, dropping them at her owner's feet, waiting for praise. She waited eagerly for opportunities to praise him. She discovered with horror her longing to be an audience, the ease with which she gave herself over to awe. Only as she was falling asleep did she allow herself to fully indulge fantasy. She'd never been able to conjure the faces of hypothetical lovers, but her other senses were more pliable, eager to satisfy any longing. Her hands in his hair. His mouth at her ear. His whispered confession, that he fantasized about her, too, that he could not have her, but wanted her nonetheless. She avoided the other fellows more than she had before, because conversation with them inevitably found its way to him, and she couldn't be sure of controlling her face, her voice, her posture, any of the myriad autonomic signals that might give her away. Relief from thinking about him or trying not to think about him came only from the physical reality of him, and this saved her from humiliation, from behavior of which he might have taken note, because to be with him meant she could relax back into herself. Her body was a muscle that unclenched only in his presence.

Embarrassed, she did not tell Gwen. She did not tell Wendy, either, but she was tempted.

"New plan," she'd said the day after she and Strauss agreed on the new direction. "I'm taking your advice. We're going to stop focusing on what you don't have, study what you do."

"And what do I have?"

"That's the question, right?"

Wendy laughed, Lizzie laughed, and the sound leveled them. This would be partnership, subject and object entangled, fates aligned.

"You," Lizzie said. "We'll study *you*, whoever's left now that the past is gone. Which we can't study with tests." Laboratory hypotheticals carried no stakes, induced no consequences. An amnesiac could reason herself out of a maze just as well as a rat—the key question, the new question, was whether she would bother. Whether she preferred prison to freedom, effort to stasis, what future she desired in the absence of a past. "Are you in?"

"So you're going to, what, observe me? In my natural habitat?"

"In whatever habitat you want."

"No more tests—"

"Fewer tests," Lizzie clarified.

"And more trips to the mall."

"With fewer crimes and misdemeanors, preferably."

"So if I ignore the fact that you're recording everything I say and using it to figure out whether I'm an actual person or not, it'll just be the two of us hanging out, like we're friends?"

"Do you want a friend?"

Wendy considered this, shrugged. "How would I know?"

Lizzie made a mental note. The forging of relationships without the experience of an emotional bond; the desire, or lack thereof, for connection, in the absence of love or loss. If you had never had a father to lose, a mother to fall short, if you had never wanted someone you could not have, would you want nothing or everything?

"Do I have a choice?" Wendy asked.

*   *   *

This was how she filled the time without him: she shadowed Wendy Doe. They went to the movies; they watched TV. Wendy explored the grounds, traced the names on graves, made snow angels; Lizzie took notes. Wendy talked with Anderson; Lizzie took notes. Wendy tried an exercise class, tried a cooking class, tried sushi; Lizzie took notes. Wendy took up smoking, as a habit; Lizzie took her to task, lectured her on her responsibility to the body and its safety, then acquiesced, lit one of her own, took notes.

In November, Strauss gave a colloquium for the fellows and postdocs, a glimpse into the project he'd not yet made public but that he hoped would be the centerpiece of his career. She knew this because he had asked her to read the paper before he delivered it; he had wanted her opinion on his words, his work. He was nervous, and he had confessed this to her. Watching him at the podium, confident and charming, she felt like she knew a secret.

"William James tells us, '*Memory requires more than mere dating of a fact in the past. It must be dated in my past. In other words, I must think that I directly experienced the occurrence.*' My challenge for good old Will, for all of you: Must I? Says who? Imagine," he said, and looked down at the paper so rarely it seemed less like he was reading than that he was inventing possibilities on the fly. "Imagine if you could experience your worst memories as if they happened to someone else. Imagine the freedom—from sorrow, from trauma, from pain—if we could divorce memory from emotion, drain the past of its power to shadow the present."

The fellows, seated beside her, were rapt. Even Lizzie, who'd heard the rehearsal, who knew what was coming, felt slightly spellbound as Strauss shifted gears from his current research to blue sky, stratosphere. He was convinced, he said, that memory consolidation—the process of the brain turning experience into long-term memory, encoding the detail and emotions that would be remembered, streamlining away that which would be forgotten—persisted over time. That memories were altered and reconsolidated with each retrieval. In other words, a memory could be changed by the remembering of it. Imagine, Strauss said, that this alteration could be controlled. Imagine the future, a modulation of amygdaloid participation, the severing of memory from self, that we could remember a better past than we'd lived, or remember our pain as if it had been suffered by a stranger, a story once heard that could do no harm.

After the applause, Lizzie lingered, hoping Strauss might catch her eye, beckon her over, and he did. He wanted to introduce her to someone, he said. The elegant blonde standing beside him with ballerina posture and a body to match extended her hand. "My wife," Strauss said to Lizzie. "My protégée," to the wife. A tiny child peered sullenly from behind the woman's legs.

"And the little munchkin here is Nina," the wife said. The girl whined something about wanting munchkins, preferably chocolate. No one acknowledged it. "So you're the one he can't stop talking about." The wife's pearl-pink lips pulled back to reveal perfect teeth. She had 90 percent of a PhD in cognitive neuroscience, Lizzie knew. She also had hair like Barbie. Long, lithe limbs that she extended with grace. Obviously, but understatedly, expensive clothing—curve-hugging cashmere that invited touch. Strauss talked about his wife sometimes, but always in the context of the domestic—errands she nagged him to run, food she nagged him to eat, supplies she nagged him to buy for the child. Lizzie had pictured a mother, like her mother, someone nebulously older and much further down the road toward frump. A woman who, in an imagined side-by-side comparison, would be older than Lizzie, saggier, baggier, less fun and more work, a woman who—though she knew very well it was beneath her to think this way and added it to the list of ways she'd become unrecognizable to herself—would make Lizzie feel young, superior, even, unprecedentedly, sexy. This woman simply made Lizzie feel like a child. No one who wanted a woman like this could ever want a Lizzie.

The wife was going on about all the wonderful things Strauss had said about her, how much promise she showed, how bright her future could be, how delightful it was to work by her side, and Lizzie smiled, resisted the urge to curtsy, waited until she was back in her office to cry. He talked about her to his wife. He had no reason not to. There was no mutual longing, no forbidden temptation. There was nothing between them that had gone beyond the bounds of appropriate. And this was the way she wanted it. She wanted him to be a man who would never cheat on his wife with a student, who would be so far from tempted the thought had never occurred. This was the double bind: wanting Lizzie would disqualify him as a man worth having Lizzie. Her fantasies were only fantasies, her crush harmless. Healthy even, she told herself—long-awaited evidence she was capable of heedless wanting, the depth of need her actual relationships had never managed to plumb. Maybe she had unlocked some wellspring of feeling that would eventually be channeled toward a more appropriate target. In the meantime, though, it was hard not to feel delusional, and pathetic, and alone.

The next day at lunch, she was shy with him. He was standoffish, too. She assumed she'd given herself away. He stood to leave. Rubbed his hands through his curls. "I don't think I can stand one more meal inside these walls," he said. "Tomorrow I might go out." She told herself this, too, was fine, and she shrugged, so he would know it. It was time to recalibrate, remember she was here to learn. Learning did not necessitate shared Szechuan noodles. She should not have been relieved when he added that—if she wanted to—she should come along.

He drove. The last time she'd been in his car he was a stranger. She had not thought much then about the closed ecosystem, the intimacy of shared breath. There was a Dr. Seuss book in the back seat, a Cheerio embedded in the floor mat. They listened to Bach. He explained musical fugues to her. Think of the fugue's subject like a memory, he suggested. The ultimate question of the fugue, he said, is the ultimate question, period. How much can something change before it becomes something else.

She made various noises to indicate she understood.

He said, "You know what Aldous Huxley said about Bach, of course. '*The only music that holds up under mescaline.*'"

She wore her sleeveless black sweater with the mock turtleneck and soft black pants, the uniform that made her feel closest to the woman she imagined herself to be. Then they pulled in to the lot of the Silverado Diner, where she had last been, only ever been, with her father, and she felt like a daughter who'd climbed into the wrong man's car.

He noticed her quiet, did not ask. She ate pancakes here, in her previous life. Today she ordered a tuna melt, fries, anything to be a different person. She didn't want to hear Strauss tell the story of how this had been his favorite diner when he was a child, that his mother took him to this suburb just over the city line as if it were a field trip to the zoo, see these strangers who live so much better than we do, with their maple syrup and their slabs of cake, someday this will be you. She'd heard this story before. This was her father's story. She recognized the waitress.

Strauss admitted that he had hit a wall with the consolidation research, unable to verify his early results, and the New York team was gaining. She pretended to listen. Strauss admitted then that he'd gotten no sleep the night before, having spent it fighting with his wife. She listened. His wife wanted him to spend less time at work, he said. She didn't understand that science was less a job than a calling, that she would love him less, because he would *be* less, if he gave himself over to her any more. "I probably shouldn't be telling you this," he said, and she agreed, probably not.

They didn't speak on the ride back. They listened to Bach again. The next day, he did not appear for lunch, but the day after that, he did. They didn't reference the diner. He didn't propose a second outing. Everything stayed the same.

She liked to sit in their corridor at night, in the dark. She liked the stillness.

Officially, she was claiming more overnights so she could spend more time with Wendy, who rarely slept. They rendezvoused in the TV room, decaf spiked with whiskey, watched the episodes that Lizzie faithfully taped every afternoon on her mother's VCR. She'd been saving them up to watch with Gwen, but Gwen claimed to have no time anymore. This seemed believable, as Gwen also had no time for sleep, showers, or returning Lizzie's phone calls. It also seemed, in Lizzie's pettiest heart of hearts, like bullshit. Gwen had the same amount of time as ever, one hour after another for twenty-four in a row, enough time to do what mattered. It was simply the order of mattering that had changed. So Lizzie watched the show with Wendy instead. Wendy, who had no family, was happy to claim these conniving, willfully forgetful women as her own.

"Have you ever been in love like that?" Wendy asked after an evil twin had locked the good one in a basement, driven mad by losing her husband to her twin's ravishing virtue. You were supposed to root against her wicked ways, this was clear, but also clear was the depth of her wanting, the heedless plummet. This was soap logic: she who wants most shall have. This was soap law: she who has will eventually lose. The villain would ultimately regain her heart's desire, and love would turn her virtuous, while loss would curdle the good twin's heart and set her on a path of vengeance. The only way out of the cycle was to love with a little more heed, but by the rules of these women's world, careful, contingent love was no love at all.

"It doesn't seem like the smartest idea, does it? Giving yourself wholly over to something you can't depend on."

"But what can you depend on?"

"Exactly." Love, the soap kind of love, necessitated a belief that life, without the object of said love, was unsustainable. It wasn't that Lizzie didn't *want* to love like that, but it was hard to imagine the chain of logic that would persuade her to allow it. She could never let herself rely so thoroughly on someone until she knew they were a permanent fixture, and how could you ever know that? She didn't need a degree in psychology to understand why it was easier for her to pour emotion into an unavailable man. Those feelings felt real; the pain of longing denied felt unbearable. But deep down, she knew this was fantasy, no closer to love than the melodrama on-screen, and just as safe.

"What about you?" she asked. "Do you want that? Love?"

Wendy thought about it; she took questions seriously, like someone who'd only been asked a limited amount. "No. No, I don't think I do."

"Do you actively not want it? Or do you just not actively *want* it?"

"The former. I think."

"Romantic love? Or any love?"

"It's not that it sounds unpleasant. It's more I don't see the point. This idea of being obligated to someone else. Of needing someone else. I just . . . don't."

Lizzie tried to contain her giddiness. This was praxis: Wendy didn't need anyone because Wendy had never had anyone; loneliness had to be learned.

"I figured it was the same for you," Wendy said.

"What? Why?"

Again, she took a long time to answer. "You just don't seem like you need . . ."

"What?"

"Anybody." She gave Lizzie a funny look. "Stop making that face, it's a compliment."

WENDY

Object permanence

This is what will happen, according to Dr. Strauss. Something will shift, and in the shifting, the memories will fall out. Think of this life as a dream. What will happen is: you will wake up.

When the memories return, the woman who remembers them will be someone else. Someone who fails to remember me. So then: death, basically. The body will continue without me. The body doesn't care who's in charge.

Dr. Strauss reminds me to be cautious with the body, as it might belong to someone else, a husband, a boyfriend, and I tell him I'd like to think I'm the kind of woman who doesn't belong to anyone but herself.

When I repeat this to Lizzie, she asks why a woman who belonged only to herself would take such drastic measures to escape.

Dr. Strauss says I should think of myself as a subletter, with an ethical obligation to the owner. I say possession is nine-tenths of the law and no one can begrudge me scratching my initials into the wall. Wendy Doe was here.

Dr. Strauss thinks he has an ethical obligation to the owner, too. Every home needs its caretaker.

Tonight I broke a glass bottle in the sink and rinsed the edge with rubbing alcohol. I raked it across the inside of my thigh. I held my breath against the pain. The cut bled nicely. I have faith it will scar. Sometimes, when I look in the mirror, I imagine dragging jagged glass across the face. Imagine: you could never look at yourself without seeing me.

LIZZIE

Wendy wanted to visit a fortune-teller. Everyone else had a story of where they came from, she said. Let the psychic tell her a story of where she's going. Psychics were bullshit, Lizzie said, and the only story she'd get would be whatever story she wanted to hear. A test, then, Wendy proposed. Let's see if the fortune-teller can tell I don't have one.

Lizzie had resolved: *no more wanting what she could not have.* She had always been a little unsettled by how readily she could shut down her own feelings, no matter how extreme, elect not to indulge. It seemed to indicate some lack—of depth, of commitment, of amygdaloid engagement, she wasn't sure—but now she summoned it as her superpower. She had let some combination of Strauss, Wendy, the simultaneous strangeness and familiarity of present circumstances wake up a sliver of self that had been better left asleep. She would now return it to bed. She would, in other words, focus on her career, her education, her research subject, her future. All emotional dead ends would be officially closed off. This, Wendy, was her only viable future.

Lizzie took her future to South Street, where the psychics were legion. South Street, where the hippies meet, so the song said. South Street, where the cool girls of Lizzie's youth, the girls who hotboxed their way through high school, who dated boys with hemp necklaces and hacky sacks, acquired provisions for their mysteriously effortless adolescence. She and Gwen had made their own dutiful treks, but South Street would not yield its secrets to the likes of Lizzie. Tacky tourist shops, yes, their shelves lined with glass pipes the use for which Lizzie, naive beyond her years, had not fathomed; a Wiccan outpost that smelled like her mother's underwear drawer; a dusty record store that only made them feel less like the girls they aspired to be. Once Gwen bought a love potion; once Lizzie bought a leather cuff she never dared wear in public; each time they returned home defeated and deflated by reality. They were, in the end, girls who belonged at the Gap.

Lizzie had picked the psychic out of the phone book. Ever the organizer. They parked a few blocks away. Wendy looked queasy.

"You okay?"

"I don't know. You didn't tell me this was where we were going."

"Do you know this neighborhood? Are you feeling like you've been here before?"

Wendy shook her head. "I just . . . don't like the feel of it."

"You want to go back?"

"Fuck it."

The psychic's suite was up a narrow staircase. It doubled as her apartment, the living room curtained off by shimmering beads, and smelled like the fried chicken joint downstairs. Madame Harriet, in a purple caftan and several ruby rings as large as her swollen knuckles, faced her customers across a weathered wood table. A pale purple runner sliced down the center: macramé, of course. There was no crystal ball. Lizzie had encountered a fortune-teller only once before, a college girl at a carnival booth, who'd told Lizzie she was destined to marry rich. Madame Harriet took Wendy's hand and thanked the spirits in advance for their willingness to contribute. When Lizzie made manifest her "negative energy," Madame Harriet suggested she either open her mind or wait outside. They held hands. They breathed evenly, together, Lizzie through her mouth because Madame Harriet smelled so thickly of lavender.

The tarot cards told Madame Harriet that a great change was imminent in Wendy's life, one that might present itself as opportunity or disaster, depending. Depending on what, Lizzie wanted to know, but her want was denied. Next, palm reading: Madame Harriet diagnosed Wendy's lifeline as long. There would be health difficulties, she warned, but these would be overcome, resulting in greater strength. "A hard road, but a worthy one." After this, Madame Harriet excused herself to take a call on her cell phone, a flashy incongruity that she could somehow afford while Lizzie—gainfully, nonfraudulently employed—could not.

"You hate this." Wendy seemed delighted by her discomfort.

"You're not actually buying this shit, are you?"

"I'm not buying this—but the possibility of it? Sure, why not?"

Even as a child, encouraged to believe in magic, Lizzie had not. No fairies, no gremlins, no monsters under the bed. God, on the other hand, she had allowed. It had seemed all too plausible, the idea of an ultimate consciousness judging her worst desires, and even in her atheistic adulthood, she sometimes caught herself in frantic mental revision: I take it back, I would never consider cheating, I do not blame him for living, I do not wish her dead, I've committed no sin in my heart. This exhausted her capacity for faith.

Madame Harriet returned with an offer to do a past-lives reading on Wendy for only twenty dollars more. Wendy thanked her politely but said she already had enough lives for one person.

"And you, skeptic?" The psychic took Lizzie's hand, squeezing too tight for Lizzie to squirm away. "Half off for a second reading."

"I'd pay not to have a reading." It was rude; Lizzie could live with being rude.

Madame Harriet walked them to the door, but before they could escape, she snatched Lizzie's shoulder. "You lost someone, someone important."

"Who hasn't?"

"A woman . . ." She scanned Lizzie's face, not even subtle in the search for tells. "No, I'm sensing, a man."

Lizzie pried away the woman's grip. This required more flesh-to-flesh contact than she would have liked. She was forced to squeeze the psychic's fingers, and they squeezed back. "You've shut yourself off from wonder," the psychic said, as if claiming this tragedy as her own. "He's always with you," she added. "And he doesn't approve."

Downstairs, outside, sucking air, heart doing an Irish step dance in her chest, Lizzie fumed, teared, breathed. Let the brick wall hold her up. "Bitch." She breathed.

It was not a normal reaction. She knew this.

"Bitch." Wendy leaned beside Lizzie. They watched a woman wheel her shopping cart through the gutter. A scrap of dog rode high on a mountain of bottles and rags. "She was fucking with you."

"Obviously."

She did not believe in life after death. She did not believe her father was in a cartoon heaven, or hiding under her bed with the nonexistent monsters and fairies. But after he died, she had made the effort. She looked for him—in skies, in trees, in flame. She spoke to him, and examined herself for faith that someone was listening. She tried to will him into her dreams. He was nowhere; he was gone. There was no spirit, no God, but it was still so easy to believe that someone was watching and did not approve.

From across the street, flickering neon delivered unto them its command: Beer Here. Wendy suggested they obey.

"It's practically morning."

"We're both adults. We're thirsty."

The too-high sun beamed bright and judgmental. She should hustle Wendy into the car and back to the Meadowlark. There were notes to transcribe. Another dense Haslovitch and Chen study to shamble through. She needed fresh highlighters. She needed to start on grant proposals for next year. It had been forever since she'd been inside a bar—since LA, she realized, since she had a life, philosophical debates and department gossip soaking in cheap pitchers of PBR, sorry stipends siphoned off for a basket of wings, Lucas's hand under the table, creeping, warm and needy on her thigh, feuds and futures temporarily truced in favor of a beery fog, the cellar dark of the pub a plausible denial of daylight, of palm trees and ocean breeze and squandered productivity, the longing for someone else to postpone reality, to say, again, just one more round. She was so tired.

Wendy seized her hand, turned her palm over, and scratched it, viciously. Lizzie squeaked in protest, yanked herself free, and checked to see if Wendy had drawn blood. "What the hell?"

"You're afraid of doing anything that might hurt," Wendy said. "But was that so bad?"

"You're insane."

"Pain is just one more thing to remember."

"Fuck it," Lizzie said, the throb already fading. "Let's go in."

When Lizzie drank, Lizzie talked.

Lizzie talking: This fucking city. This fucking, fucking city. Everything dirty. Everything broken. Can't get from here to there because you'd have to go through *there*, and god knows you probably wouldn't survive *that*. So stick to the suburbs, sure, good, safe, sterile, hide in your little boxes behind your aluminum siding with your cul-de-sacs and your strip malls and feel good about yourself that you don't see color, everyone's the same, which is easy when everyone you know is the same. My father is buried in this city, but I don't know where. Don't know where the cemetery is. Which cemetery it is. Don't know how to find the grave. Too embarrassed to ask. Have never gone to visit, never put stones on stone, that's what you do if you're good, a good Jew, a good daughter.

Wendy had a bourbon. Lizzie had a bourbon. Wendy had a second. Lizzie had a second. Both had tequila with a beer chaser. Wendy got quieter, Lizzie louder.

Lizzie told Wendy about Saint Augustine, whose CliffsNotes she had crammed after Strauss made her feel like an idiot for her ignorance. I am not an idiot, Lizzie told Wendy, or if I am, it's not because I don't know some fucking Christian philosopher's Christian philosophy, and it's probably anti-Semitic to say so. But anyway, Augustine, the saint. Lizzie had read about his *Confessions*, then tried to read the actual *Confessions*, because she was not an idiot, got bored, skipped to the good parts, the part about memory and time travel and God. The saint, Lizzie told Wendy, thinks we remember everything when we're born. When we're born, we remember God. Life is a forgetting. Our mortal purpose is to remember back to what we've forgotten. You get it? Lizzie said. The saint says we're all like you, we're all fractions of ourselves, we're all emptier than when we began. The saint says the past is as much a dream as the future, and only the present is real. But the present happens too fast for us to notice. Did you know all that?

I did not know that, Wendy said.

Lizzie felt very smart. This, too, tended to happen when she drank.

The first time I got drunk, she told Wendy, I was sixteen, drama camp with Gwen, because Gwen was actually talented and wherever Gwen wanted to go was where I wanted to be. Wendy asked who Gwen was.

Gwen was my best friend, Lizzie said, is my best friend, is supposed to be my best friend, who even knows what tense to use anymore? I'm not thinking about her, Lizzie said, because I promise you she's not thinking about me. Gwen doesn't matter, Lizzie said. I'm talking about wine coolers. Lots and lots of wine coolers. I puked. But before that, I thought, why didn't anyone tell me? I thought it was magic, that you could just *be* without worrying how you were going to be. It was like being alone when you weren't alone. And if you wanted to touch someone, you could touch someone.

If you want to touch someone, Wendy said, you should touch someone.

There were only three other customers, beefy guys in baseball caps huddled by the TV. The Eagles fumbled, the men shouted. The whole bar smelled like hoagie. This bar, Lizzie told Wendy, is so Philly.

Is this what you thought it would be like to have a friend? Lizzie asked Wendy, and Wendy said, is that what you are?

Lizzie said, I'm embarrassing myself, aren't I, and Wendy laughed and said she liked Lizzie better this way.

Which one would you fuck, Wendy whispered, pointing at the Eagles men.

Lizzie raised her Rolling Rock and said, I'd rather fuck the bottle.

Wendy said, we both know who you'd rather fuck. Lizzie said, I don't know what you're talking about, Wendy said, whatever. Then said, he wants you, too, I can tell.

Lizzie sealed her lips with her fingers, told herself not to say anything, but her lips moved, and she said that she wouldn't want to be with the kind of man who would cheat on his wife. Wendy said that was every kind of man, and when Lizzie asked how the hell she could know that, considering, Wendy allowed she could not.

There was too much she had never done, Wendy said. She'd never, for example, picked up a man in a bar. Lizzie laughed and said as far as you know you've never picked up a man anywhere. Wendy gave her the finger, then crossed the bar. She stood between the men and their screen. Lizzie thought, I should go over there, but it seemed like effort, and then Wendy was putting her hands on beefy shoulders, lips on lips. She'd picked the one with the most hair, hair sprouting from beneath the cap and hair busy on his upper lip, but also hair matting his chest above the collar of his shirt, hair on his neck where Wendy's fingers massaged saggy flesh. And then Wendy laughed and strolled back to Lizzie as if nothing had happened.

Lizzie had never done this.

Did you like that, Lizzie asked her, and Wendy said, no. But how could I know until I tried. She took a swig of Lizzie's beer, because her own bottle was empty and her need to rinse out the taste, she said, was dire.

Lizzie laughed. Someone put Pat Benatar on the jukebox, which sounded right.

They could not drive back to the Meadowlark. They would have to take a taxi, but Lizzie had spent her emergency taxi money on beer. Wendy had no money, was at Lizzie's mercy. Bought and paid for, Wendy said, so what will you do with me now.

Lizzie could not call Gwen, because Gwen was at a baby birthday party with her baby and all her new baby-breeding friends. She could not call her mother, obviously. She had no one to call.

Wendy said it was not a problem, they would call Strauss. Even though it was a Saturday and Strauss was home, because Wendy had Strauss's home number. For emergencies, she said, and later Lizzie thought about that, a lot, but now Lizzie punched the number into the pay phone by the bathroom, a dark cubby stinking of shit and blood, and when a woman answered, she said as carefully as she could, hello, is this Mrs. Strauss, stopped herself just in time from saying, can your husband come out and play?

By the time the taxi pulled up to the Meadowlark, Lizzie was feeling slightly more sober. Wendy had fallen asleep on her shoulder.

Strauss was waiting on the curb. She'd never noticed it before, his ursine affect, but noticed now. Nervous system registered *hairy* and *large* and *growling*, read threat, amygdala triggered hypothalamus, activated pituitary and adrenal glands, heart rate increased, pupils dilated, face flushed. Mouth went dry. Hands trembled. He said many angry things. Wendy slept in the back seat.

When Lizzie drank, things seemed like a good idea that were not a good idea. She had the idea that if she and Strauss were in a soap, this fight would escalate until he swept her into his arms and kissed her, because sometimes love tasted like hate. She had the idea that maybe Wendy was right, that maybe he did want her, that it was possible he could want her. That she wanted, so much.

The human brain operates on a delay. It takes one and a half seconds to process what the body experiences. Consequence: there is no such thing as living in the moment.

Lizzie had puzzled over this line from the *Confessions* more than any other: *Any duration is divisible into past and future: the present occupies no space.* And yet Augustine also said past and future were only figments. Consequence: there is no now, there are no thens. There is only memory and imagination, no differential of reality wedged between. This made no sense to her, except that she had imagined kissing him, and then, a second and a half later, she had kissed him. The decision already made. She remembered her body making it, remembered hands reaching, skin stubbly, lips hot, eyes wide. She blamed her body. Her brain too slow to stop it.

Strauss said no.

Strauss shoved her away. Paid the driver. Shook Wendy awake, but gently. He was gentle with Wendy. Took her by the hand, helped her out of the car. He was not angry with Wendy. She was a nonperson; she bore no blame. He would not look at Lizzie. Informed her they would not speak of this again. When Strauss ushered Wendy inside, Wendy was the only one who looked back. Then the door closed between them, and Lizzie was alone.

Alone, jealous of Wendy's will, her mind over her body; Wendy Doe, master of escape. Lizzie willed her own brain: *forget.* The kiss; the day; the grief, guilt, loneliness, hope, failure, self. Burn it away, let me start again. Her brain did not accommodate.

Lizzie on the curb, throbbing head in hands, waiting for Strauss to return, but Strauss did not return. Lizzie, stumbling alone and unsteady to the SEPTA station, swaying on the platform, dozing on the train, stumbling, again, cold, tired, sick, shamed, toward home that was not a home, where she hid under the same blanket that kept her childhood safe, closed her eyes against the spinning world, woke at dawn, staggered to the toilet, dropped to her knees, remembered.

WENDY

Augustine

Her body was a lie. Her body told stories—of seizure, of passivity, of pain, of collapse. The body played at damage, but the body was fine. The body spoke because that was the only way to make someone listen.

Dr. Strauss says that in a different time, I would be a hysteric. Internal distress manifesting as external symptom. He says women then had nowhere to go, so they fled into themselves. He says in a different time, I might have held on to my self but lost control of my body, watched it tic and seize and faint. The mind that wants to break will find a way, disconnect itself from a reality it rejects.

He urges me not to pity the woman in white whose photograph now hangs over my bed, that the hospital was her refuge, and she its star. She had more power on the inside than she did out, he says, coddled by the men who knew her necessary to their own advancement. Why then would she run away, I asked once, and he said people do irrational things. Lucky for the advancement of psychology, he said, and laughed.

The book he gave me is not about her, but about the scientists who invented her. That's where I found her other pictures. Augustine, in a white hospital gown, captured in each stage of her hysterical fit. Augustine sitting up in bed, palms together: *Amorous Supplication*. Augustine lying down, swathed in white cotton, arms crossed corpselike, eyes closed, satisfied smile: *Eroticism*. There was *Menace*, there was *Mockery*. There was the Augustine I knew best: *Ecstasy*. The book quoted one of her doctors: *The female hysteric represents an extraordinarily complicated type, of a completely particular and excessively versatile nature, remarkable for her spirit of duplicity, lying, and simulation. With an* essential perverse nature, *the hysteric seeks to fool those around her, in the same way that she has impulses that push her to steal, to falsely accuse, to set things on fire.*

An essential perverse nature: we are all liars, by definition.

LIZZIE

Strauss was nice about it, the next day—*nice* being the perfect, anodyne descriptor of his echt professional mien when he summoned her into his office, offered her the chair across from his imposing desk, said vaguely that everyone made mistakes. It was often easy to misinterpret things, he said, and as long as these mistakes went unrepeated, they could continue on as they had been. Lizzie nodded, chastened, slipped out without further discussion. An unrepeatable mistake, and now there were no more private lunches, no more late-night strolls, and when Lizzie arrived in his office for their weekly Wendy Doe update meeting, the first time she would be alone with him since the "mistake," she found Mariana there, notebook open, posture ramrod, smiling as if it were totally normal for Strauss to have asked her to sit in. Always good to have a fresh brain on the case, he said. A week ago, Lizzie would have taken this as a sign of illicit desire—the idea that they might need a chaperone, that they should strive to maintain appearances—but she knew better now. He thought *she* needed a chaperone, while he needed a guard dog.

She wasn't going to tell Gwen, but then she told Gwen.

"It's official," Gwen said. "We hate him."

"We don't hate him." Lizzie hugged a throw pillow to her chest. She wasn't sure when Gwen had become a person who knew how to select appropriate throw pillows, but it was useful for those conversations that required padding.

"You don't hate him because you're lost in some kind of pheromonal brain fog. Thus the royal-we will hate him for the both of us."

This was the reason Lizzie had planned to keep the incident to herself. She knew Gwen would find a way to make the situation Strauss's fault, and once Gwen deemed someone an enemy of the people, there was no going back. Which wouldn't matter, Lizzie allowed herself to acknowledge, if some secret part of her didn't nurture the hope that Strauss would remain a relevant factor in her future, the kind of factor you didn't want your best friend to dislike.

Stupid, Lizzie reminded herself. *Pathetic. Humiliating.* It didn't help.

"I'm the one who kissed him," Lizzie said. "I'm the inappropriate idiot. I'm the crazy one. He's the one acting like a normal person. Or not even, because a normal person would probably fire me."

Gwen set the baby in her lap, very gently, just long enough to launch a throw pillow at Lizzie's head. "This is what I'm talking about! How is this *your* fault? Fuck this guy."

Lizzie sighed. "One more time, in single syllables. I. Kissed. Him."

"Only because he's been completely inappropriate with you from day one. All your little midnight 'talks'? All that shit about how his poor wife doesn't understand him? It's like he gave you an engraved invitation to fuck him, and then when you try to accept, he has the nerve to make you think you're crazy?"

"Forget it," Lizzie said. "You don't get it. You're—" She waved toward the baby, the color-coordinated embroidered throw pillows, the Hallmark life they embodied.

"Okay, maybe. So explain it. What is it with this guy?"

"It's not him," Lizzie said. "Or, I don't know, it's not *just* him. I know I can't have him—I don't even want to, he's fucking married."

Gwen laughed. "Like that's ever stopped any man in the history of time."

"He's always telling me I have the capacity to be extraordinary," she said. "And when I'm with him, when I'm *seen* by him, it's like I can actually believe it. He makes me feel like I can be someone new. Does that make sense?"

Gwen at least pretended to consider the question, then: "No. You already are extraordinary. I don't like that he's got you thinking you need some big transformation—into what? Whoever he wants you to be?"

"Into someone who takes some risks, maybe? I guess, since I met him, I've been thinking . . ." It was the last thing she wanted to admit to Gwen, of all people, but Lizzie reminded herself that Gwen, of all people, was the person she was supposed to admit everything to. "Maybe the reason I don't have anything is because I never let myself reach for anything?"

"How do you not have anything? You have this huge fancy fellowship, for one."

"Yeah—because I pretended to be a completely different person in the application. The kind of person who actually has the nerve to say what she wants and go for it." Lizzie didn't know how to explain it to Gwen, who always had whatever she wanted, or at least accommodated herself to wanting only what she could have. Who was someone else's most important person; who could go to sleep each night held by someone who believed she was special. The math they could never discuss: Gwen's addition of husband and baby had been a subtraction for Lizzie. She wanted to be someone's priority, too. She knew this was childish. She knew equally that it was ridiculous to imagine getting this from a man who had a wife and child. But it didn't change the fact that she wanted. "I'm not saying I should have kissed him, okay? That was a mistake, but is that the kind of idiot mistake you've ever known me to make?"

"No, that's my point."

"And that's *my* point," Lizzie said. "Being who I am isn't working. Is it such a bad idea to try being someone else?"

Lizzie's mother's boyfriend's assistant producer had a stringy goatee and a girl's name. He also had a faintly horsey smell. Or maybe that was just the odor called *woodsy*, which she had only ever before encountered in Body Shop samplers. Jody liked camping. He liked cities, but found suburbs constrictive. They'd competed in the same high school debate league.

This is good, she told herself. You can work with this.

She had promised Gwen she would at least try.

The bar was Jody's choice, a tasteful one. Its wine menu was twelve pages long. Each bottle came with a recommended cheese pairing. She'd let him order for both of them. She worried this was false advertising, but Gwen had told her once that first dates were all about soft edges, implied accommodation. No one wants to fuck the captain of the debate team, Gwen told her in high school. Gwen was the president of the honor society, and no one wanted to fuck her, either.

"Eugene's been talking you up forever," Jody said. "I admit, I'm kind of surprised you turned out to be so . . ."

Lizzie waited.

"Un-Eugene-like?"

Lizzie gave him the laugh. "Same."

When he reached for the bottle to top off their glasses, his hand brushed hers, lingered. She told herself to let it.

"What's it like working for him?"

"How well do you know him?"

"I try very hard not to know anyone who gets to see my mother naked."

He laughed. He liked her, she could tell.

"Working for him is like working for a mildly bright toddler."

This time, when Lizzie laughed for him, she forced herself to touch his knee.

The relevant statistics: Jody had a degree in communications from Penn and had started in the TV world before shifting to radio, an industry he loved all the more for its terminal condition. He dreamed of NPR, which she pretended she also enjoyed. He was not and had never been married. He rooted for the Eagles, but mildly. His favorite author was Murakami. He read Chomsky. He was two years out of a failed engagement, he was one year older than Lizzie, he was neither her employer nor married, and so wholly appropriate.

What are you holding out for, Gwen would have said. It's like you want to be alone.

She told him about her research and he said *autonoetic consciousness* sounded dirty. Then he suggested they stop talking about work. "Let's talk about something interesting."

She told herself not to judge him for it.

On the third glass, after she told him how much she missed freeways, sculptured cement slicing sky, she found his hand on her thigh.

"You're adorable," he said.

She shrugged.

"I really need to kiss you," he said.

She was embarrassed for him, the need that seemed so obviously misplaced.

"No one's stopping you," she said, and this was true, so he leaned across the table and kissed her. It was wet. He palmed her head, pressed her closer. Her brain took notes. Note how he rubs his hand down your calf, note how his tongue tastes of honey and jam. Note how his face Picassos when you open your eyes.

Lizzie pulled away. "It's maybe a little too well lit for this?"

"My apartment's only a few blocks away. Much better lighting."

She knew, once they were outside and he hooked an arm around her shoulders, that she should not have agreed, but to renege now demanded a breach in etiquette that felt beyond her. How did one say, *I thought I could make myself want you, but I see now I was wrong*?

She told herself to take it as a learning experience. She had never gone back to a man's apartment on a first date. She had never stripped for anyone she barely knew and didn't want. If she wanted to be a grown-up, a single woman in the grown-up single-woman dating world, maybe this was a necessary stage, the undiscriminating one.

And Jody could be a boyfriend, she thought. She could go over to his apartment after work. They could cook spaghetti together, watch reality TV. He could join her at dinners with her mother, and she would be someone's partner rather than someone's child. She didn't need a true love, just a boyfriend. Technically she didn't even need a boyfriend. She needed a reminder of what she was supposed to want.

It didn't matter anyway, because Jody was taking off her shirt and kissing her nipples and she was too embarrassed by his need and her lack to do anything but let him. Maybe he didn't notice her stiffen as his hands traveled down. Maybe he couldn't tell how dry she was, though she was. Sandpaper. Desert. Maybe he couldn't tell from the look on her face how much it hurt. He wasn't looking at her face.

This is good for me, she thought.

She allowed herself the duration of the taxi ride for tears. She had made this happen, so it wasn't fair to feel like it had happened to her. In the morning, she would narrate it for Gwen as entertaining anecdote, emphasis on stupid girl's name and stupider goatee. They would laugh. The taxi rolled to another stop, honked the horn. There was more traffic than there should have been. It felt like a gift. Lizzie opened the window and let in the night.

VII

WENDY

Post-trauma

The best anonymous group is the PTSD group that meets Monday nights, in the basement of a church. A stained glass Jesus watches from the wall, his abs distractingly well defined. There is always a plate of doughnuts by the coffee. The members of this group are addicted to their own pasts. They cannot stop remembering. They dream. They hear voices in silence. They imagine their trauma into their post-. They panic. They weep. They hurt.

One Monday night, Dr. Strauss was waiting for me when the meeting closed. He followed me to the church, he said. My religious turn had piqued his curiosity. This, he said, makes more sense.

I told him that I liked to hear their stories. I tried to understand what it was like, a haunting by the past. I told him I never said anything about myself that wasn't true.

"You know, it's likely you did suffer a trauma," he said.

I told him knowing yourself to be erased, knowing the return of yourself will erase you again, was trauma enough.

He said, "I have something you should see."

His meetings are the same, but different. Instead of a basement, an institute conference room. Instead of doughnuts, Oreos. There are twelve subjects on the first Tuesday night, and all of them nod when Dr. Strauss asks if I can join. He tells them I'm one of them, and no one asks either of us to prove it.

He doesn't participate in the meeting. He sits in a corner and takes notes. They share with each other, trading memories that never happened.

One of them is a college boy, blond and milk fed, looks like he should be playing lacrosse, getting frat drunk. He remembers vividly what his preschool teachers did to him. He remembers goat masks and blood drinking. He remembers the please-touch-me game, a ring of children in the woods. He remembers large hands guiding his small ones, touch here, touch how. He remembers lying in a ditch, three women looming over him like trees. A rain of dirt and hands. He dreams about these women. He writes them letters he will never send. He writes that he's sorry, and tears blur the ink, and he throws them away. He says he knows it didn't happen. He cannot make himself stop remembering that it did. He balls fists, he reddens with shame. He cries. "Why the fuck can't I make myself stop?"

Afterward, I ask Dr. Strauss why he wanted me to hear these stories, and he says he wanted me to understand my power. My superpower, he called it. "Your capacity to forget is the hand that shapes you—I wanted you to see how warped, how powerless the rest of us can be, shaped by incapacity. Unable to do anything but remember."

LIZZIE

Once a week, Lizzie accompanied Wendy to get a physical. It seemed somewhat pointless, as there was nothing medically wrong with Wendy, as weeks of measurements and blood testing continued to confirm, but all data was good data. Wendy never resisted, only complained. "I think I hate doctors," she said that morning.

"Old or new?" This was their shorthand for whether an impulse felt like a remnant of the body's former self or a new construction, derived from experience.

"Both."

Lizzie made a note.

They crossed into the neuropsych wing, where the young medical interns had better things to do and made sure everyone knew it. They rotated shifts through the Meadowlark Institute on a perplexing system, and Lizzie never remembered their names. Behind their backs, she and Wendy called them all Doogie Howser. Wendy was already gowned up, waiting for this week's Doogie to fasten the blood pressure cuff, when someone knocked.

"May I?" Strauss's voice.

The Doogie looked at Lizzie, Lizzie looked at Wendy, Wendy shrugged, The Doogie opened the door.

"I thought I might observe. If you don't mind, Wendy?"

Wendy did not mind.

This was unprecedented. Lizzie tried to breathe normally and told herself not to make anything of it. There was no reason to assume Strauss was here to see *her*, that he'd grown tired of keeping his distance, and was making an excuse to be near her, if only in a safe space, with ample witnesses. She could hope, but she could not let herself assume.

Strauss took a seat beside Lizzie. It was the closest they'd been physically in nearly a week. They watched the exam. She had never been so conscious of the watching.

This Doogie was older than the others, bearded with a silver stud in his left ear. He had Wendy settle herself on the exam table. He slipped a hand inside her gown, pressed stethoscope to skin, and it must have been cold, because she flinched. No one made conversation.

"Deep breath," he said. Wendy gave him one.

He peered into her ears, up her nose, down her throat. He shined light at her pupils. Then Wendy lay down, before being asked, and fixed her eyes on the ceiling. The Doogie opened her gown. Palpated her abdomen. Palpated one breast, then the other.

Lizzie also hated doctors. She resented slipping her feet into something called *stirrups*, and the expectation to smile and answer questions about her weekend while rigid metallic instruments were inserted. Then the pinch of the pap. She hated doctors as she had hated her grandmother's doctors and her father's doctors. Doctors told you what was wrong with you and why it couldn't be fixed. Doctors told you when it was time to give up. Doctors told you *I can't tell you what to do here*. Doctors imposed responsibility but would not take it. They told you that maybe, probably, statistically, but really, who could say for sure.

"Her blood pressure's a little elevated," the Doogie said as Wendy ducked behind a curtain to reclothe herself. "Nothing to worry about."

There was nothing physically wrong with her. This continued, week after week, to be true. Lizzie wondered now, if the scans had turned up a tumor squatting on the hippocampus, whether Wendy would have refused its removal. A tumor holding the body hostage, and why not. Would it be any easier to give yourself up if you knew you were simply an excisable lump of mutated cells?

"Did you ever think about how there's no word for it?" Wendy had asked once. "*Memory*—we have a noun for the thing you remember. But there's no noun for the things you forget."

Lizzie suggested this was because an absence was not actually a thing.

"Except I am," Wendy said. "You people never let me forget that."

After the appointment, Wendy retreated to her room. Which left Lizzie alone with Strauss, at least for the duration of the walk to his office. She searched for something to say that would make him linger, make him stop looking at her the way he did now, wary. For one month after her father's death, Lizzie had given herself over to a counselor's haphazard weekly care, and he had asked insistently, *How does it feel?* Lizzie would say, *I think*, and he would stop her. *Don't think. Feel.* Listen to your body. Locate the pain, lungs belly groin heart. *My pain is amorphous and omnipresent*, she'd thought. Her pain was divine. After the fourth session, she'd decided she could not risk feeling anything more, and never went back. Now, when Strauss was this close to her, she felt. A tightness across her chest. A stricture, a fluttering. She pictured wings rubber-banded together, twitching against elastic, jonesing for flight.

"My mother wants to invite you over for dinner," she said, which was both true and a joke. The joke fell flat.

"Why would she want to do that?"

"It's possible I've been avoiding her and blaming work. She claims she wants to meet the man responsible."

"You seem dubious."

At least they were talking again, she thought.

"She just wants an excuse to meet you. You're a man, and a semi-famous one."

"You're not a parent," he said, and the part of her that felt like a child wanted to spit in his face. His bushy brows quirked. "*Semi*-famous?"

At least he was smiling. Then, disaster.

"What night did she suggest?"

"What?"

"For dinner."

"No, I didn't mean you should actually take her up on it."

"Then why did you bring it up?"

This was an excellent question, and Lizzie preferred not to look too hard at the answer.

"So you don't want me to?" Strauss said.

"You *want* to?" Lizzie said.

"You let me know what night would be good. I don't think I should pass up the chance to meet the woman responsible for Elizabeth Epstein."

"She's not responsible for me."

What were they doing, the two of them? Lizzie did not understand.

"Everyone makes mistakes," he said. "We move on."

He left her alone to wonder who had made the mistake, and why the feeling in her body was now limp relief.

Wendy wasn't in her room. Lizzie found her in Anderson's room instead. It was increasingly these days the most likely place. He was at the piano, Wendy on the bed. Lizzie settled beside her. Anderson was squinting at a spread of sheet music, picking his way slowly and discordantly through the notes.

"It's Bach," Wendy said. "Or it's supposed to be. 'Unfinished Fugue.'"

"Appropriate," Lizzie whispered.

Wendy responded in her regular voice. "He doesn't mind people talking while he plays. He likes it, don't you, Anderson?"

"Why not?" he said.

Anderson unsettled her. Talking to him made Lizzie feel erased.

The music stopped. Anderson's fingers hovered over the keys. He looked up, started in surprise at the sight of two strange women sitting on his bed. "Hello."

"Do you know Bach's 'Unfinished Fugue'?" Wendy asked. "Could you play us that?"

"I don't know it, I'm sorry."

"Isn't that the sheet music for it right there?"

"Oh! It is, yes. I could give it a try, if you'd like."

The childlike trust in strangers, the eagerness to please, these were symptoms of his hippocampal damage. But it made sense to Lizzie: Why not be joyous, if you believed you were only a few minutes away from the rest of your life?

He began again, picking through the notes as if he'd never seen them before. The theory was that repetition would embed the fingering in his implicit memory—that he could remember even without knowing he remembered.

"It's an unfinished fugue," Wendy said quietly.

"So I gathered."

"No, it's actually unfinished. They used to think Bach just died in the middle of writing it. But Dr. Strauss thinks he left it unfinished on purpose, as a statement of the impossibility of completeness."

"When did he tell you that?"

"We come here sometimes, to listen. He loves Bach."

"I know this."

"Dr. Strauss says it's a miscarriage of justice to the ears and to poor, dead Bach, the way he's murdering the music like this. But he also says it's like watching a slow-motion miracle."

"I didn't know you and Dr. Strauss spent so much time together." Lizzie was careful to modulate her voice to clarify just how little she cared.

"Well . . ."

The music stopped, again. Anderson flinched at their presence, again. Wendy asked him to play. It was no better.

"I didn't tell you because I knew what you'd think," Wendy said. "But I started going to his group sessions."

"The recovered memory thing?" It was one of Strauss's pet projects, a longitudinal study on the victims of the recovered memory craze.

"Yeah. They think I'm one of them."

"Why?" She meant, why would Strauss let her lie and intrude on what was implicitly understood to be a protected space, but also why Wendy would bother. And why both of them would keep it from Lizzie. She didn't like this, the idea of them having secrets from her, with each other.

Wendy admitted this was not her first trespass. She had hit AA, NA, survivor groups, PTSD support groups. "You wouldn't believe how many there are, once you start looking."

"But *why*?"

"I like their stories." She blushed. "Dr. Strauss said I should come to his group because that's one where I actually belong, sort of. They all remember something that didn't happen. I remember a nothing that didn't happen. So."

"You said you knew what I'd think."

"Yeah."

"So what do I think?"

"That I'm a liar."

She was, in fact, thinking Wendy must be a good liar, better than Lizzie had lately given her credit for.

"And you think it's wrong," Wendy said.

"Apparently Dr. Strauss disagrees."

"You're a better person than he is. Or—no, that's not quite it."

The fugue looped on and on.

"You care more about being a better person. That's it. You care about people thinking you're better."

"That's not the same thing."

"I saw him kiss you," Wendy said.

The music stopped. Anderson noticed them all over again.

"Can we not talk about this right now?"

"Who cares if he hears?" Wendy said. "If he doesn't remember, it didn't happen, right? Anderson, Lizzie and Dr. Strauss were necking on a street corner, isn't that shocking?"

"Would you *stop*?"

Anderson furrowed. "Do I know a Dr. Strauss?"

"He gave you this nice piano. Also, he's married. What do you think of that?"

Lizzie stood up, unsteady, unsure how to regain control.

"So, are you sleeping together?"

"Of course not!"

"It is a very nice piano." Anderson ran his hands along the maple wood. "Do you think I could play it?"

"Please," Lizzie said. "Loudly."

"Okay, you haven't slept with him, but you want to."

Admitting it would be an unfolding, limbs forced fetal for too long finally set free.

"There's nothing wrong with wanting," Wendy said.

"You have an MRI appointment. We should go."

Wendy thanked Anderson for the performance, but he'd already crossed the next threshold, no longer remembered it. "Did I play well?"

"Magnificently." Wendy cupped his face and kissed him, tongue visibly sliding past her lips, then his.

Anderson was half man, half coping mechanism. The latter must have decided that if a strange woman was kissing him, she had good reason to, because he pulled her closer, sighed.

"What the hell are you doing?" Lizzie said belatedly.

Wendy let go. "What?"

"You can't do that to him."

"He won't even remember."

"That's the fucking point."

"He shouldn't be allowed to have what he wants?"

"He can't *know* what he wants."

"Says you. You think if his body can learn the piano, it can't learn this?"

"Oh, hello!" Anderson said, noticing them again.

"He can't tell on me, obviously," Wendy said. "And you won't." She sounded very sure.

Lizzie decided she would not tell. She would not worry about being passive-aggressively blackmailed by her own research subject. She would not stalk Strauss, finding more feeble reasons to position herself where she would be seen. She would not feel his approach on some animal level, forgetting in his presence what her body was supposed to do, every motion requiring conscious thought—hand reaches for pencil fingers wrap and tighten hand lifts pencil places pencil in bag face frowns legs lift and fall and carry away. She would not stare at the empty space where the Augustine photograph had hung before Strauss moved it into her subject's room and wonder what other special favors the subject had asked for and received. She would not feel jealous of her subject. She would not trade shifts to sleep more nights at the Meadowlark because she wanted to possess his building in its dark, to sleep in its grip. She would not return to their corridor in the middle of the night because she woke up wet from a dream of what she might find there. She would not linger before the photographs of inmates past because she liked to imagine herself sliding into an ice bath, cold fire burning out unwanted desires. She would not imagine a version of herself gone wild, gown torn, feet bare, a self swaddled in straitjacket and dragged down dingy corridor, strapped to metal slab. She would not imagine Strauss's palm on her forehead to quiet her screams. Him her keeper, her the kept. She would not feel her heart quicken and something clench at the thought of this other Strauss unwrapping her other self like a candy bar, extricating her limbs from straitjacket, her body from gown, securing leather restraints around bare wrists and ankles and waist and neck, asking if she wanted him to take away her pain, not that it mattered anymore what she wanted, if she wanted. She would not imagine him forcing her rigid jaw open, jamming a wooden dowel between her teeth, and she would not gasp at the thought of him tightening the restraints until they bit flesh, drew blood, and she could not move or speak or scream, but could feel his hands on her and the hot breath of his whispered promise, that this would make her feel better, but first it would hurt. She would not. She was not that kind of woman. She refused to be.

WENDY

Conversations with Anderson

Do you mind if I come in?

    You're welcome. Everyone's welcome here.

    You look familiar. Do we know each other?

    I don't think so. In fact, I'm certain not. I would remember a face like yours.

    How is my face?

    Lovely. The face of someone kind.

    I don't think so.

I thought it would be good practice, watching myself be forgotten. I thought, if I could experience it in real time and see that it was painless, I could be less afraid. Less angry.

Hello, can I come in?

    Welcome, everyone's welcome here.

    Have we met before?

    I don't think so. In fact, I'm sure not. I would remember your face, I'm sure of that.

    What is it, about my face?

    It's . . . it seems very sad. Except your eyes. They're—oh!

    Did that hurt?

Yes. It hurt very much.

Remember that.

Dr. Strauss told me that some infinities are greater than others. There is an infinity of even numbers, but the infinity of all whole numbers is twice as large. If the opposite of infinity is nothingness, then maybe some nothings are greater than others, too. Which is to say, I have no power in this place. Anderson has no power in this place. But between the two of us, I still have more than him.

Hello, would you like some company?

Always. Welcome.

Have we met before, do you think?

Have we? I'm sure I'd remember your face.

Does it seem sad to you?

Why? Are you sad?

I am nothing, Anderson. I'm somebody's bad dream. How could I be sad about that?

You don't feel like a dream to me.

How do I make you feel, Anderson? Right now.

Warm. Safe. How do I make you feel?

Like a person.

Lizzie thinks I'm fearless, free to do what I want, because I live without consequence. She misunderstands. I can act like nothing matters, because I know what does and does not. What matters is that I am allowed to stay here, because here is the only place I have to go. Which means what matters is satisfying Dr. Strauss. I'm free only within these parameters: do what is necessary to maintain his interest, do nothing that would alienate it. Everything I do has consequence. Except here, with Anderson. After seven minutes, whatever happens here never happened at all.

*   *   *

I'm not sure you should do that.

It feels good, doesn't it?

Yes, but. Well. I.

Maybe you deserve to feel good. Maybe you've done something to deserve it.

What could I have done?

You don't remember?

Things are a little foggy sometimes.

So you should trust me. Do you trust me?

I don't even know you. Which is why I'm not sure you should be . . . *oh.*

Let's pretend I do know you, just for now. That we deserve to make ourselves happy. Would that be all right?

. . . yes.

LIZZIE

The worst part of dinner was not her mother's dress, funereal black with a hooker hemline. Nor was it the anecdotes of awkward adolescence, bolstered by the supporting evidence—crimped hair, bedazzled denim, roller disco diva dance, bat mitzvah crinoline—of photographic record. Nor was it even the fact of the dinner itself, her mother simpering, Lizzie glowering, Strauss in her father's chair, picking gamely at his treif chop. The worst part was the discovery that Strauss and Lizzie's mother had grown up in the same pocket of Germantown, and the subsequent fusillade of shared memories. He was more than a decade younger, but still. Their synagogue youth groups co-organized dances; their high schools rivaled each other in football and chess. They had both, on a dare, scarfed enough White Castle to puke. Strauss remembered Lizzie's uncle from a JCC fund-raiser. His broken arm had been casted by the same orthopedist who treated Lizzie's mother's broken ankle; both had, at one time or another, hopped the fence at the Philmont Country Club. Strauss bought his rugelach from the bakery where Lizzie's grandmother did the books and Lizzie's mother spent summer vacations behind the counter.

"I would have remembered you," Strauss said. "I was very precocious back then—dedicated crushes on every pretty girl in the Northeast by the time I was eight."

"You're assuming I was a pretty girl."

"Indeed."

They clinked glasses. They toasted, "To Jewish geography!" They laughed together.

This is disgusting, Lizzie thought. *She is disgusting.*

I am disgusting.

Lizzie's mother, who had never evinced interest in Lizzie's research, now slavered for details of their guest's work. He explained his theory that every culture had its own signature ideal of remembrance, its own term for grasping helplessly at the past—the French *nostalgia*, the Portuguese *saudade*, and then along comes us, he said, grimly determined to bring down the mood. *Zachor*: never forget. Camps, deportations, death, pain. Destruction of the temple; enslavement of the Israelites; famine in the desert; exiles and inquisitions, ghettos and uprisings, death, death, death. And always with the imperative never forget, as if *forgetting* pain has ever been the problem. Let our enemies zachor, he said, this is a moral imperative, but the victims of pain, the victims of suffering and persecution? This is my moral imperative, he said: to help them forget.

Lizzie's mother gazed, dazzled. "You didn't tell me he was so fascinating."

"How's Eugene?" Lizzie said, apropos of nothing but her steadily rising gorge.

"Eugene's a putz."

"Boyfriend?" Strauss asked.

"He'd like to think so." She winked.

In return, perhaps, for Lizzie's evocation of her mother's drive-time lothario, her mother asked whether—now that she was moving in such rarified intellectual circles—she still insisted on watching that misogynistic drivel, then asked Strauss whether Lizzie had revealed her most secret and sexist of guilty pleasures. Despite surely knowing said pleasure was secret for a reason, especially from the man so aggressively *hochkultur* that he not only didn't own a television but didn't even realize this was supposed to be cause for smugness.

"It's for research purposes," Lizzie said. Her mother issued an ungainly snort.

"What misogynistic drivel are we discussing?" Strauss asked, and Lizzie's mother outlined the soap in her preferred terms, a retrograde vision of fifties domesticity, its wide array of female archetypes extending from wife to mother to homewrecker to wife. She was forgetting heiress and perfumer, Lizzie thought, but declined to say.

"My sense of the cultural landscape is that drivel is equal opportunity, but it's only culture designed for women that's loudly and universally derided as such," Strauss said. "Maybe our Lizzie is watching it as a subversive feminist act."

The idea that Strauss imagined her a subversive was almost enough to make up for the *our*.

"It's fascinating to watch the scramble—especially among the pretentious, and mea culpa on that—when the lines between high and low culture get redrawn, don't you think?"

"Fascinating," her mother agreed thinly, and Lizzie couldn't help but think that whatever game they were playing here, she'd just scored a point.

After dinner, more pictures: neon shirts, plastic glasses, side ponytail, rainbow leg warmers, cherry lip gloss. You could almost smell the hair spray, the raspberry-scented cream with which Lizzie had shaved her stubbornly hairless legs. There was a display of grandchildren—and an obligatory round of compliment and demurral regarding whether Lizzie's mother was old enough to sire any. Lizzie was surprised to realize her mother knew not just the kids' names, but their likes and dislikes, their latest achievements, and each memorable incident of saying the darndest things. This was genuine affection; this was pride and pleasure. Her grad school friends, even the unmarried ones, were constantly needled by their parents about the likelihood of imminent offspring—but not Lizzie, whose mother had always purported to be wearied by the concept of grandchildren and the consequent bragging. It now occurred to Lizzie that her mother's reticence on the subject might be for Lizzie's benefit. Maybe she let her daughter believe she didn't need more grandchildren because she assumed Lizzie would never be in a position to supply any.

Strauss's phone was stocked with pictures of his own, preschool portraits of his daughter, a ringleted blond toddler with a toothpaste smile. "My wife is an apostate WASP. I'm afraid it shows."

"She's lovely," Lizzie's mother said.

"With no help from my brackish side of the gene pool."

Lizzie's mother assured him that any child would be lucky to inherit his dashing DNA, his genius genes; what a prize for a wife, what a wonder for a daughter. Lizzie stuffed down a third slice of cake. She had, via her own bad judgment, manifested this night. Her mother, fed up with the complaints leading up to the evening, had the same question for Lizzie that Strauss had posed: why tell him about the invitation, if she was so horrified by the idea of him accepting it?

Some part of her had wanted this. Maybe as a test, proof she could feel appropriately about him, that she could will her emotions into a more permissible shape. Or maybe because hellish proximity to him was better than none at all. When hell abated, Lizzie gave Strauss a ride to the SEPTA station. He preferred trains over cars, because the train offered time to work. Lizzie had taken his cue, and now skimmed journals on her daily commute. They pulled in to the deserted parking lot and he peered out with distaste.

"This is how you get home? Then you walk back to the house? Late? Alone?"

"It's the suburbs. I'm not too worried about getting mugged."

"Maybe I'm worried. Didn't I just promise your mother I would look out for you?"

Lizzie closed her eyes, let her head drop heavily against the backrest, swore.

"Elizabeth?"

"Why do you keep calling me that?"

"Not to be reductive, but it's your name."

"No one calls me that."

"Lizzie is a girl's name. You're not a girl."

"Right. I forgot. You know me better than I do."

"You're angry at me."

"That would be unprofessional." Her head hurt. She wanted to open the window, breathe something that didn't belong to him.

"Can I ask you something?" he said. "How old were you when your parents separated?"

"I thought you didn't believe in psychoanalysis."

"That's not why—"

"Fourteen. And they didn't separate. *She* separated from us. We stayed in the same place, she left."

"That must have been hard on you."

"Not as hard as it was on him."

"Your father. What was he like?"

This was her least favorite question. He was like air and stone and brick and water, he was the materials of life, too much everything to describe any one thing, and so, always, she fumbled, felt inadequate, because the details—black hair, crossword puzzles, cat allergy, dentist jokes, barbecue tongs—added up to so much less than the whole, and any attempts to distill the whole were feeble, generic, made her feel traitorous and him forgotten. The overpowering memory of wanting him back was leaching away her memories of him, his distinct *him*-ness. He was a tree. He was a laugh. He was a hug, the safety of arms that would always open for her, hold her steady, hold her tight, but she did not talk about this.

"He was good. He didn't deserve any of it."

"You've never forgiven her." Strauss looked out the window at the deserted tracks, the flashing signal lights. A train thundered into the station. Lizzie answered under cover of its roar, *yes, never.* They stayed in the car. The train loaded, pulled away.

"My daughter is perfect," he said. "There's nothing broken in her yet."

He was calling her broken, and she should have resented this. She wanted to be wanted for her strength. She had always thought, at least, that this was what she wanted. But now, breathing beside him, she wanted only to stop feeling like she was hanging on to life with a slipping grip—she wanted someone to recognize the strain in her smile, give her permission to fall.

"I was so young when I met my wife, you know. We were only half people, half possibility. I thought she was brilliant, beautiful—she thought I had the possibility to be someone entirely other than what I turned out to be. And now . . . she thinks of me as someone she has to endure life with. I'm not interested in *enduring*."

Lizzie did not want to know about his beautiful wife or his unbroken daughter. "Why are you telling me this?"

"That's the question."

He would not face her.

"I thought if I subjected myself to this ridiculous dinner, it would remind me."

"Of what?"

"That you're my student. That you're absurdly young."

She could stop this from happening, or she could let it happen. She did not want to want this. She cupped her hand around the gearshift, wanting something firm, something real. Then his hand was on hers. That, too, was firm, real.

"I wanted to be a better man than this."

This kiss was different. She was fumbling, urgent, but he was slow, steady. He pressed her trembling fingers to his cheeks until they stilled. She smoothed her hands across his stubble, as she'd waited to do for so long. She closed her eyes and breathed with him. She slipped her hands beneath his shirt, sought warm skin.

"Not like this." He pulled away. "Not like criminals, in a parked car."

They drove to the Meadowlark and locked themselves in his office. "I wanted you the first time I saw you here," he said.

"Please don't say that."

"Elizabeth." It was no good here, both of them standing up, parking lot fluorescents casting seedy glow through the curtains. Here he was both Strauss and Dr. Benjamin Strauss, she was Lizzie Epstein who still felt like a girl but also this stranger, this Elizabeth, whose existence he'd willed into being, and it was Elizabeth who let him back her against the wall, kiss her neck, kiss her throat. She was wearing a saggy beige bra. She had shaved nothing. He was peeling away and peeling away until she stood in her striped cotton panties. His shirt remained buttoned, his pants buckled, and she realized she was supposed to be taking action of her own, enacting desire. It was cold. She was cold. He eased himself down to his knees. Kissed her stomach. Kissed the narrow lace band of her underpants, sliding them down. She shivered. Crossed her arms over her breasts. He stopped. She had never seen him from above. His hair was thinning.

He looked up. "Is this okay?"

It was not okay, him all the way down there, her up here, alone, exposed. She wanted his arms around her. She wanted his face pressed against hers so she could remember that she did want, so she could feel less alone and not more so, but she did not know how to say this. She dropped to her knees and met him there. She unbuttoned his shirt so she could feel his skin against hers. She imagined their hearts sending secret Morse code messages to each other. SOS.

"Save our ship," she said, kissing him again, and let herself believe, if just for this night, that he would.

WENDY

A prayer

Lizzie wants to know if I believe in God. There's a theory, she says, that the capacity for belief is cognitively innate. Our brains are designed for gods the same way they're designed for language. She wonders if this varies from person to person, if there's a cognitive setting for faith. It could be lodged in the genome; it could be invented, like the rest of me. The question, she says, is whether we need a god, or simply want one.

Here's what I believe in: you.

Aren't you my creator? Isn't it inscribed somewhere in your genes, brain, hippocampus, soul exactly how long I have to live and where I'll go when I die?

I won't ask you not to come back. Just try to remember me when you do. Please.

VIII

LIZZIE

So she is the other woman, the mistress, the thing on the side. The homewrecker. The whore. She is the serpent, she is the succubus. She is the vector, his secret and his sin. It's hard to get a handle on her, this new self. Since her mother's affair, Lizzie has built her foundation of self on the certainty that she is not the kind of woman who. Now she has. So she has either fundamentally misunderstood herself and her capabilities or she has misunderstood the act of which she now finds herself repeatedly capable.

The second time they meet in her house when her mother is out and fuck on her mother's paisley sheets.

The third time they close themselves into an unused subject room. Flattened between his body and the wall, palming plaster, she can't move and does not want to. It's too bad the bed no longer comes with restraints, she says after, joking and not, and he says maybe something could be arranged, he knows a guy.

The fourth time is their first in the morning, sunlit bodies all moles and flab, rosacea blush of his cheeks and swollen nose, ACL scar on his knee, slightly scoliotic curve of his spine.

After that, it would be easier to pretend she stops counting.

They meet in the dark. He makes furtive midnight calls, she lies in bed, lights off, lets her fingers follow. His wife is used to him working nights. He insists on actually working nights. Willing to cheat on his wife but not his research, she thinks, but does not say. They contrive excuses to sneak away. He never has enough time. She has the opposite problem. She learns his body, its rhythms and desires, the soft strokes that will make him moan.

She learns to read the pace of his breath, the tension in his hands, knows what he wants, when he wants more, and she can say, when he is inside her, that she needs him there, that she loves the feel of him, the slide and thrust. This is permissible. He reads her, too, with fingers and tongue, and what starts well gets better, easier. He never says *need*, only *want*. They don't talk the way they used to. They talk like this, bodies in conversation, give and take and give. She has never wanted someone so much, and sometimes she loses herself as she has never been able to, gives way to brute sensation, stops worrying about pleasing him or seeming pleased herself and simply sighs and feels. Sometimes, mind-bogglingly, sex is sex, even with him, pleasant but mundane, and he feels the same as any other body in the dark.

She still can't believe she has permission to want him. Wanting is all she will let herself feel. She tells herself she can control this, parse it out, can accept having this much of him, for however much time he allows. She will want his body, and his presence, and nothing more. This will be their fugue, and she will not ask for his future, she will not ask for his heart, she will not ask anything but what she has miraculously been offered. She tries. They order Chinese food. They eat Ben & Jerry's out of the pint. He smears ice cream on her so he can lick it off. He gives her a list of his Philly favorites: favorite cheesesteak, favorite water ice, favorite pretzel, favorite ziti; sends her on missions from which she is to report back. He wants her to love the city as he loves the city. He leaves Butterscotch Krimpets in her mail slot, because these were her favorite after-school snack. He calls her Elizabeth, and it feels like their secret.

There is the day he deposits his daughter into her care, says please, it's an emergency. The only emergency, Gwen points out later, is that he has both a daughter and a job to do. Lizzie has a job, too. Lucky thing her boss gave her the day off.

Gwen does not approve. She would never judge, she says. She's not talking as a married woman, a wife with a young child who knows all the ways a husband is vulnerable, she insists. She's simply worried. None of this is in character for the Lizzie she knows. The Lizzie she knows is not this kind of woman. You're compromising yourself, Gwen says. I've never been more myself, Lizzie says, and after that she tries to say less.

She only told Gwen about the affair in the first place because not telling her would have indicated she was ashamed.

She's never done anything so shameful she had to keep it secret—and maybe, Lizzie thinks now, this is another one of her problems, a recipe for an unmemorable life.

You're too smart for this, Gwen tells Lizzie. How can you think this will end well?

Lizzie doesn't want to think about it ending.

Then what do you think will happen, Gwen wants to know. What are you *doing*?

Lizzie has no idea. What Lizzie understands of cheating, she understands from soaps, where cheating is inevitable and comes in two distinct flavors. There's destructive adultery, vulnerable men preyed on by sloe-eyed succubi, fallen victim to secret vendettas—woman-on-woman violence, husbands collateral damage to wifely war. Then there's adultery of the heart, on which every great soap romance is built. Love-as-higher-law, cheaters excused by the purity of passion. Neither archetype suits; Lizzie rebels against the constraints of archetype. She does not know what either of them are doing. She knows that when she's with him, when his arms are around her, she is too happy to ask these questions. The feverish, restless, ceaseless questioning that has driven her life finally stills. Her brain quiets. Her body gives way to its present, to him. Whatever it is she's doing, how could she stop?

Wendy knows. She can tell Wendy knows.

One day Wendy says, "Do you think I could fall in love when I'm like this?"

"What do you think?"

"I think love is knowing someone. If I don't know myself, how could anyone love me?"

"Hmm."

"But I also think, maybe, there's so little of me to know that I'd be easy to love. There's not so much of me to see."

"So you're asking if someone could fall in love with you, then. Not if you could fall in love."

"Is there a difference?" Wendy laughs. Sometimes Lizzie forgets they're not actually friends.

*   *   *

All the men she's loved before. Tried to love. Failed.

Lucas, maybe. She liked thinking he might be smarter than her, liked less that he seemed so sure of it himself. She liked the focus that fell over him when he got to work, as if he were trying to alchemize flesh into pure thought. He was the first to say I love you, but he said he *thought* he loved her, which seemed not quite the same thing. She thought she loved him, too, which meant sometimes she thought the opposite. Then they left each other, and they both survived, so what kind of love was that?

Before Lucas, Adam. Taller than she would have liked, with limp mustard hair. The first man who did not seem like a boy, with not just a job but a career, the kind men had on TV, managing accounts, angling for promotions. He worked in naming. The best name, he said, sounds like one you already know and have simply forgotten. He'd named: a toothpaste, a cookie, an insect repellant, a line of stainless steel cookware. He named what she felt for him: love. It became a game between them. You know you love me, maybe I do, maybe I don't. When she summoned the nerve to dump him, he said thank you.

Before Adam, Caleb. She was a sophomore, he a senior. Her first older man. He was handing out heart-shaped cookies at the Valentine's Day blood drive. She fainted and woke up to find her cold hand in his. He was an artist, her first and only. Painted in the nude. Painted her once, literally, red streaks down her legs like blood, blue ringing her nipples. It tickled. It was the most unlike herself she had ever been, but her father was dead, and she wanted to be anyone else. They only kissed, and only rarely. It was too embarrassing to admit, even to herself, that her need for him was the need against which she measured all others.

Then it's New Year's Eve and Lizzie is at a party surrounded by scientists and benefactors in 1999 novelty sunglasses, and she's squeezed into a dress she saved from her mother's scrap heap, a crinkled velvet left over from a college formal, outdated even when she bought it, but she still felt a little like Cinderella until she arrived at Strauss's door, where she is greeted, again with impeccable politesse, by the wife.

What she now knows about the wife, from Strauss: smart, not brilliant maybe, but able to keep up. Planned to be a neuroscientist but ended up teaching biology at a suburban public high school. Did not intend to get pregnant when she did, or ever. Fell in love with the baby, quit for the baby, changed by the baby. Husband and wife had been equally ambivalent about procreation. Motherhood, once enacted, became the only dream the wife had ever known, and the wife judged her husband for his lack of similar myopia, his inclination toward anything but the paternal. The wife wants to send their daughter to private school so she will have the right advantages and not mix with the wrong people. The wife is no longer the wife he married. It's easy to forget, in his telling, that she's still so beautiful.

Madeline Strauss introduces her to the moneymen she's chatting with as "Benjamin's protégée," a phrase Lizzie has come to hate. The possessive apostrophe, which she resents not resenting the way she should; the compliment of the noun, in which she no longer has faith. She knows now that he wanted her from first sight, which makes all praise retroactively suspect. Lizzie has confessed this to him, and Strauss has dismissed it. He would not want her, he says, in absence of her mind. Would not call her special if it wasn't true. But it's Strauss who's impressed upon her the need for objectivity, and she can no longer trust his.

"She's pretty," Wendy whispers. Wendy is, at Strauss's suggestion, her New Year's Eve date. "Don't you think she's pretty?" Pretty is beside the point. The point is that the wife can throw a careless arm around Strauss, can kiss frosting from the corner of his lips, is flesh and blood and silk and his.

Lizzie tilts glasses of champagne down her throat, one after the other after the other. The only thing Strauss says to her all night is, *maybe you should slow down.*

Just before midnight, she gives in to temptation and drifts up the spiral stairs, peeks behind closed doors until she finds their bedroom. Their bed. Beneath her, the floor gives a champagne wobble. She sits down, hard. Does not lie down on the bed, her head on the wife's pillow. Does not want the view of the ceiling the wife has when he's on top of her. Does not want to know what they see out the window when they wake up together, lazy and lounging as the sky turns pink.

Downstairs, a countdown. Time is running out, then runs out, then Prince is instructing the crowd to party like it's 1999, because now it is, and Lizzie knows that Strauss and his wife are kissing, because this is how you greet a new year, if you can, to prove to yourself that you're not alone.

It's 1999, the year of the end of the world, and she tells him she can't do this anymore. She won't do this again. By the end of the conversation, she is doing it again. He swears she is the only one, and this seems to matter, though Lizzie is unsure if or why it should. She does not accept that her actions should be defined by his heart—that if he loves her, she is a tragic, romantic heroine, that if he simply lusts, if she is a link in a chain of lust, then sex is *just* sex, her body just a body. She does not accept that she should be categorized like a Shakespearean play, end defining the means—as if adultery resulting in marriage is inherently nobler than adultery that simply expires. She does not accept that she is a type, a tool, a *hole*—if he deems it so. She is neither helpless in the face of love nor ruthless in her weaponization of lust. She is this kind of woman: the kind who wants. If it is just sex, just desire, just one body in need of another, then let it be just.

Sometimes, though, she's less convinced. Sometimes she thinks he is every husband who's ever fucked a woman who's not his wife; she is every woman who's ever said I don't care if he leaves her, and longs for him to leave her. She wants this to be different, but sometimes secretly suspects Meg Ryan is right, Tolstoy is right, nothing is ever different. She dreams of the day he discovers he cannot live without her, even if it means enacting a Russian tragedy. When the pull of the dream grows too strong, she promises herself she'll stay away. When the pull of his body grows too strong, she boomerangs back. He's a married man. She's the other woman. Note, she thinks, the articles. A married man could be any of them; the other woman is particular, the active agent, the one to blame.

What are we doing, she asks, always, but always after.

Elizabeth—he says it like a sigh.

Lizzie hears it like a promise, because there is no Elizabeth without him. Then he says can we not ask that, not now?

He says "we," as if they are one person, and that one person is him.

IX

XI

WENDY

What they do when they think no one's watching

She's lying to herself, pretending she's not in love with him. I wonder how I can tell, if it's because I've been in love with a married man. If my husband was cheating on me. Maybe I caught him red-handed and bare-assed, and fled. Though I would prefer to think I was not the kind of woman who would be broken by a man.

I listen to them in his office sometimes, my ear pressed to the door. I like the way she sounds when she forgets herself. It's a noise between a whimper and a laugh, and her *please* lives in the same gap, a wounded joy. They are my soap opera now. He creeps up behind her while she administers my tests, watches me watch him subtly stroking her neck. He's hard on her in public, she's lost her golden girl glow; he wants everyone to know he sees her flaws, and she wants everyone to know it, too, so no one imagines the truth. She never stops watching him, or watching for him when he's gone. When I catch her crying, she pretends she isn't, and I pretend to believe her. If she asked, I could tell her I'm pleased she's finally allowed herself to want. I could tell her it would be better if she wanted someone else.

I can tell she's lonely. I could tell her I remember that, the feeling of being lonely with someone else. That sometimes, before I fall asleep, I can remember how it felt to lie beside someone who doesn't love you enough to stay awake. I don't tell her this, though, because she would only want to know how I remember, and whether the memory is tethered to person or place, and what this kind of memory feels like compared to the memory of whether I want pepperoni on my slice or how many stars are on the American flag. It wouldn't occur to her that I could help. I'm a subject, and subjects don't do, we're done to. I see the way he looks at her. If she asked, I could tell her: she's a subject, too.

LIZZIE

At work, Lizzie told herself, nothing would change. She refused to benefit professionally from her personal choices—and she refused to be penalized. She would neither leverage sex for ambition nor trade it. This, at least, was the plan. Unfortunately, the plan didn't take into account how much of her cognition would be consumed by thoughts of Strauss, how distracting it would be to have him either present or absent, both their own kind of exquisite pain. Whether she was in her office or the imaging lab or across from Wendy, she was mentally with him. Rehearsing the trail of his fingers down her stomach the night before or the pressure of his hands on her hips as he guided her onto him, held her rhythm steady, showed her where he wanted her to be. This was not to her professional advantage. Nor was Strauss's increasing reluctance to be alone with her during business hours, to praise her in public, to indicate, in any way, to any possible viewer, that she meant more than she should have, or anything at all.

"What did you do to Strauss?" Clay asked. "Kill his cat or something?" They were at the musty dive bar the fellows haunted after work. With new incentive to stop standing out, Lizzie had forced herself to join them.

"What makes you think I did something to him?"

"Because he used to treat you like the lady of the manor and now he's treating you like . . ."

"Like a dead raccoon that's started to smell," Mariana said.

"What did you do, seriously? Fuck up his results?"

"Fuck up his fund-raising?" Dmitri said.

"Refuse to fuck him, more like." That was, inevitably, Clay.

"I didn't do anything. Nor did I refuse to do anything."

"The fall of the favorite," Dmitri said knowingly. "Standard courtly dynamics. Cf Galileo."

"Am I the only one who has no idea what he's talking about?" Clay said.

"Just the only one so eager to admit it," Dmitri said. "Which is why he treats *you* like a dead raccoon, for the record."

She was struck by the ease between them. They poked one another's weak spots, but not so hard it would hurt. Lizzie wasn't one of them, and now she couldn't be. A second beer and she might get sloppy. No beer and she felt like clawing off her own skin. Her life had begun to feel like a performance, one she could drop only when she was with him, which made being with him the only time that felt real. It was necessary but impossible to remember that being with him was the least real thing. This sticky table, this cheap beer, this was real life. She was sometimes very lonely. Even lying with him in the nest of blankets they sometimes made for themselves in his office, Lizzie trying not to feel like they were in a dog bed, two animals rutting on the ground, even with Strauss's lips nuzzling her neck in his sleep, she was swamped by loneliness.

That morning they'd stolen an entire two hours together, necking in an empty movie theater like horny high schoolers—*necking*, that was his rusty word. He'd asked, as Mel Gibson raced the city with a gun and a rage hard-on, whether she wanted to go back to LA, if she missed it. What she missed: hiking along the Palisades trail under a full moon. Smoking on the balcony, blowing puffs into the avocado tree blossoms. The chitter and rustle of her rat lab, the sighing of fluorescents, shiny blade of scalpel, quiet rhythm of slice and scrape and plate and slice and scrape and plate. Slurping soba noodles, arguing about quantum mechanical models of cognition and Kantian reasoning and free will and wishing Lucas would shut up already about his pigeon brains. Lucas, daring her to forget driving home, daring her to walk the deserted sidewalks, walk west and west, see how far they could get. Lucas slipping his hand in hers as the ocean stretched endless before them. Lucas at dawn, sun rising on what still felt like the wrong side of the world—rising on what felt like the beginning of some new self, a Lizzie who plunged, fully clothed, into a moonlit ocean and dozed damp on its shore. She missed an LA that no longer existed for her; she could not go back. She told Strauss she hoped to stay through a second year, if she could. Her research was too promising, her connection with the subject too well developed to abandon. She didn't phrase it as a question, saving him the need to answer.

"Galileo's crime was being the teacher's pet, favorite courtier in the Medici court," Dmitri said now. "Which meant every other courtier was gunning for him. Guy should have kept his head down. He had no one to blame but himself for getting it cut off."

"Why do you even know this?"

"Uh, because I *read*?"

"Oh, Stephen King's writing about dead astronomers now?" Clay said.

"I was no one's favorite," Lizzie said.

"*Are* no one's favorite," Mariana said. Strauss was taking Mariana with him to the upcoming Chesapeake Conference, a UK gathering of world-class cognition experts that occurred only once every five years. It would be her debutante ball: a copresentation with Strauss, endless schmoozing with hypothetical future employers. Strauss's flight home from the conference routed through Chicago. Lizzie, whom he couldn't have chosen without arousing suspicion—they both agreed on this—would fly out to meet him at a hotel near O'Hare.

Gwen kept asking, *is this enough for you?*

But nothing was ever enough for Lizzie. Gwen was the one who always said that.

"You didn't do anything wrong," Dmitri said. "I hear he does this every year—picks someone, gets bored, moves on."

He was trying to be nice. Lizzie made herself smile, and let him pay for her second beer.

Strauss told her that work was his only respite from missing her. She resented the privilege. Work was where she missed him most. The Mead-owlark Institute was Strauss embodied, his will made flesh and concrete. He ran his hands along its walls as if it were a body, as if it were *her* body, and it seemed to her the building was her truest rival. She thought she'd been obsessed with him before, but this felt different. This felt physical, her body shaping itself to his, her nervous system readying itself, like prey sensing a predator, for his withdrawal. She had never intended to need someone like this, and with need came the terror of what she would do if—but *if* was the wrong word for inevitable, for something baked into the terms of engagement, the word was *when*—he took himself away. If she weren't so certain of this, his absences would be easier to endure. But because she was, because she understood that his presence in her life was weather, not climate, every absence felt like a foreshadowing of the final one.

Gwen's baby was old enough now to enjoy playing peekaboo, or at least to giggle at the appropriate intervals. Lizzie marveled at Charlotte's shock each time hands fell away and restored the face behind them to the world. There was a theory of developmental psychology that infants are not born understanding object permanence—that the brain's default assumption is that an object, once removed from sight, ceases to exist. Hence the peekaboo cycle of terror and relief, every adult an alternately vengeful and merciful god, dematerializing then restoring the objects their children loved most. Lizzie felt like she'd retrogressed, could not maintain her faith in existence beyond her own perception. Maybe if she'd had some control over when she could see him, when she could indulge the fantasy that he belonged to her, but they saw each other on his schedule, at his whim. This was reasonable: he had the Meadowlark, he had the wife and child, he had more to juggle and more to lose. She had only her work and him. Piaget argued that infants developed their sense of object permanence via touch, persuading their brains that material reality rested not in the visual, but in the physical. It was only when Strauss was solid in her arms that she believed in him, let herself stop fearing, at least for that moment, how hollow she would feel when he was gone.

He was married. They owed nothing to each other. He would eventually be gone.

Hours alone in her tiny office, hunched over her work, all she could think, worry about was him. It was only when she was with him that she could focus on her work, and when she could, she did so obsessively. The druggy combination of desperation and wild desire she felt for Strauss, she also felt for the fugue project. The two were married in her mind, as if they had enabled each other, as if they now, despite competing viciously for her attention, fed each other, fueled her need for more of both. She spent too much of her time without him miserably sifting through the details of their past encounters and the odds of future ones; she knew an end was inevitable, but for it to arrive without warning, without girding, felt fatal. He urged her to enjoy the infinitesimal present, the perfection sandwiched between beloved past and annihilating future, and when he was with her, she almost could.

She felt, in every way, *awake*. On the rare nights Strauss fell asleep with his arms around her, she stayed up, making feverish lists of new research avenues: How could a woman with no past distinguish between memory and dream? How could she imagine the future if she couldn't imagine the past? How were glucose levels indicative of the participation of the limbic system? How can we know if our choices create or reveal ourselves? She listened to him breathe, nudged him when he began to snore, and let herself fantasize a brilliant future, not just tenure, not just prizes and publications, not even just the MacArthur, but the way it would feel to create a fundamentally new model of human consciousness. How it would feel to discover something profoundly true—to think of something that no one in the history of the planet had thought.

"See? I'm the same as ever," Lizzie told Gwen. "Still planning to take over the world. Stop worrying." She didn't tell Gwen how confusing it was that lust and ambition had tangled; that too often, when she dreamed of triumph now, it wasn't the moment of discovery she longed for. It was the moment she could report it to Strauss, and make him proud. Her work used to be the only thing she cared about; now sometimes she feared she only cared about it as a way of being closer to him. But wasn't that a good thing, she told herself, caring more for a person than for a project? Wasn't that what you were supposed to want?

The night before he left for the Chesapeake Conference, Strauss told his wife he was working late. This was at Lizzie's request, but she was edgy, didn't feel like being touched. He was irritable, would never say, *so what am I doing here*. She worried he was thinking it. This was and was not a relationship; she didn't know how much she was allowed. There was no more discussion of breaking things off. That seemed like a joke to her now, that she'd ever thought she could step away. When they ended, it would be him that ended it, her that endured. She hated finding this in herself, but: she didn't want to ask for too much. She couldn't risk asking for something he refused to give.

Strauss lounged on the leather couch. Lizzie paced, reading the spines on his bookshelves, lifting the items on his desk one by one. Stapler. Post-it pad. Pen. Pen. Best Dad coffee mug.

"Stop fidgeting."

She picked up the Moleskine he used to record strangers' first memories, but did not open it. He had accumulated more than ten of these journals, and she was forbidden access to all of them.

"What's the point?" she said. "All these stories, are you ever going to *do* something with them?"

"Elizabeth, are you angry with me for some reason?"

She sounded angry, she knew that. She shook her head. He took the journal gently from her hands. "Do you want to know why I collect these?"

He gave her a different answer every time she asked.

"It's a reminder." He buried his face in her hair, inhaled deeply, sighed. He loved the smell of her shampoo. She'd given him a bottle to keep in his office. She liked the idea of him inhaling the idea of her. "Each of these memories is a buoy in a sea of forgetting. Why hold on to that moment, when everything before it slipped away? If we create ourselves from our memories, then is that first memory our Big Bang? Does it determine everything to follow?"

Lizzie closed her eyes, inhaled the idea of him.

"The key isn't remembering, Elizabeth. It's forgetting." He turned her around so they were face-to-face. "We are what we remember, yes? Yes. So ask yourself, what if you remembered something else? If our forgetting is nearly infinite, then so must be the alternate versions of ourselves. Other Elizabeths! Other Benjamins! They could exist—they *do* exist, somewhere in our brains. Imagine if you could choose which moments you remembered: it would be godlike. To be reborn as something new, but this time, to be your own creator."

Gwen arrived for their institute lunch date bearing Tastykakes. "Carcinogenic dessert substitute, as requested," she said. The baby dangled in a belly sling like a human kangaroo. "Now, where is he?"

She'd been needling Lizzie for weeks about wanting a tour of the institute, which they both knew was code for wanting to meet the man who ran it. Lizzie was unwilling to risk it. She was less concerned about what Gwen might say—though this was a plausible concern—than what Gwen would hoard in her arsenal for future use. She had no interest in seeing Strauss through anyone's eyes but her own.

"Europe," Lizzie said. "Sorry."

Gwen rolled her eyes, but allowed Lizzie to take her on a tour, and did an impressive job of feigning interest. It wasn't until they sat down to takeout in Lizzie's tiny office that she finally broke. "If he's so great, why are you hiding him from me?"

"Congratulations," Lizzie said. "You sat on that one for almost forty whole minutes."

Gwen unfurled a breast and guided Charlotte's mouth to nipple. This had once been a painstaking procedure that more often than not drove Gwen to tears, but she now did it one-handed and without looking. Lizzie glanced away. There was something about the increasing ease of Gwen's motherhood that made her feel ever less like the Gwen who had belonged to Lizzie.

"That's not an answer," Gwen pointed out.

"Why bother meeting him? You already know you hate him."

"I don't hate him."

Lizzie exchanged a look with baby Charlotte, and the look said, *your mommy's full of shit.*

"Okay, I do hate him. But only because he's making you unhappy."

"How am I unhappy?"

"Let's see, you're *obsessed* with someone who—where is he now? On vacation with his wife and kid? You happy about that?"

"Not that it matters, but he's at a conference," Lizzie said. "Without his wife."

"Wait, is this that Europe conference that one of the fellows got to go to? Weren't you hoping it would be—?"

"It couldn't be me," Lizzie said. "That would have looked . . ."

"So now you're fucking up your career so you can fuck him? Does he have a magic dick?"

"I thought you were trying to curse less in front of the baby."

"Okay, sorry, does he have a magic pee-pee? Because otherwise I have no idea why—"

"How about we talk about something else?"

Gwen spit out a single, bitter laugh. "How about anything else, *please, god*? I know, how about this human being I issued from my uterus that seems to hold no interest for you whatsoever."

"Sorry?" The more accurate adjective was *confused*—Lizzie had thought she was holding back on the subject of Strauss. She'd thought she was downplaying. Which invited another, equally accurate adjective: *humiliated*. Imagine if Gwen knew how much mental real estate she devoted to him, how Strauss was the first thought she had on waking and the last before falling asleep; if Gwen knew how often Lizzie distracted herself wondering what he was doing, whom he was with, whether he was thinking of her, how she would endure if he wasn't. She had admitted to Gwen once, after too much wine, how jittery she felt now when she wasn't with him, like she couldn't quite get comfortable in her skin. With him, she'd told Gwen, there was a perfect stillness, as if she could breathe. She was trying to explain how it felt to need, how this felt like progress, giving herself permission to need someone this much. Gwen said, funny, with Andy it was always the opposite. Being with him finally allowed her to be still, even when he wasn't physically there. With him in her life, she finally felt a cessation of need. Funny, Lizzie said, and resolved to stop trying to explain things to Gwen. "Let's talk about Charlotte," Lizzie said now. "How was baby yoga?"

Gwen talked mothering and Lizzie nodded and asked appropriate follow-up questions and they spent the rest of the lunch break exchanging depressingly polite small talk. When they ran out of safe subjects, they stood, and Lizzie walked Gwen to the parking lot in silence.

"Please don't sulk," Gwen said.

"I'm not sulking. I'm just . . ."

"Refusing to talk about anything that actually matters?"

"I don't understand what you want from me," Lizzie said.

They reached Gwen's car. Gwen hugged her, the baby squeezed between them. Lizzie stiffened; tried not to, couldn't help it. Gwen let go.

"I want you to be happy," she said.

"What if this makes me happy?"

"You're reshaping yourself to suit someone else's needs. How can that make you happy?"

Here was another humiliating answer: Lizzie had spent her whole adult life untethered from obligation, free to suit her own needs. Was it so wrong to want to be tethered for once, to spoon herself around another body? To allow herself to feel incomplete? Gwen had given up plenty of herself for Andy and Charlotte, but they were never supposed to talk about that, how she'd settled down, and in eagerness to do so, maybe simply settled. Gwen had done what she was expected to do, and so Lizzie was expected to accept she was happy.

"He's getting everything he wants out of this situation," Gwen said. "And what are you getting? Whatever he wants to give you."

"Maybe that's enough for me."

"I don't want to be cruel, but you need to hear this. There is no future here. He is not leaving his wife for you."

Lizzie refused to allow this to hurt. She told herself the same thing every day.

"And thank god," Gwen added. "If this is bad, imagine if you were his *wife*."

"What makes you think I want that, marriage, kid, happily ever after? Just because you did?"

"Okay, then. What do you want?"

Lizzie didn't permit herself to ask that. And she could tell Gwen knew it.

"This is not what it looks like to be happy."

"You're the arbiter of feeling now? You know everything because you have a husband and a baby?"

Gwen strapped Charlotte into her car seat with determined calm, the infuriating air of someone refusing to rise to the bait. She didn't have to answer. The first time they'd spoken after Charlotte's birth—before the long, sobbing calls at 3 a.m., Gwen hyperventilating, Gwen admitting she longed to climb out the window, slip into the night, start a new life that wouldn't be beholden, for all eternity, to this alien creature—Gwen had been all awe and wonder. Had said, blissed out, she never knew what love was until now. Life had never had meaning, not really, until now. *It's like I just landed in Oz.* Lizzie told herself then: Gwen did not mean to imply that Lizzie's life was a gray Kansas prairie, that it would remain so until she, too, squeezed a living thing through her vagina. This was relevant: Gwen did not mean to be cruel. And then there was the other issue: for all Lizzie knew, Gwen was right.

"You haven't wanted to fuck your husband in months, and from what I remember you didn't much care for it before Charlotte, either. So maybe don't lecture me about what counts as a good relationship."

Gwen closed the baby into the car gently. Then looked at Lizzie without the anger or hurt Lizzie had expected—had intended. There was nothing on her face but pity. She spoke so quietly Lizzie had to lean forward to hear.

"I had no idea you were so afraid to be alone." Then she climbed into the car and shut the door. She did that quietly, too. Don't want to alarm the baby. Gwen adjusted her side mirrors, checked her rearview, checked and double-checked the baby, did not once check Lizzie, backed cautiously out of the space, and drove what mattered most to her away.

WENDY

A hypothetical

All memory is imperfect, Dr. Strauss reminds me. We all forget things that happened and remember things that did not. I am not special.

All memory is choice and culling, Dr. Strauss says. We cannot control the brain's choice, but we can advise. We can make the effort, in one direction or another.

What he means to say: I have more power than I want to believe.

I am the one who banished myself, and myself can return only on my invitation.

Some nights we play a game. Invite your brain to imagine, he says. What if you were someone else. The brain chooses not to remember. Invite it to invent.

Why, I ask.

He says, to see what will happen. Why else do anything?

So. What if.

What if there was a woman.

Picture her alone. Lonely. Tired. Picture her one night grinding her teeth so hard it almost wakes the man beside her, a man with fetid breath and the ghost of a beard, hair everywhere—chest, knuckles, back, chin—except where it belongs. Balding skull, shiny in the moonlight. Picture her picturing her future with this man, in this house. He tries to be kind. She tries to behave. She tries not to want the things she used to want.

Not memory. Invention. Imagine a woman lying beside a man who could have been a stranger, who thinks one night, what if he was. Who thinks, this house feels like it belongs to someone else—what if it did. What if nothing were familiar again. What if she could leave it behind, let herself be made into someone else. What if instead of grinding teeth and trying so hard to be better, to be the woman he needed her to be, she simply was not.

LIZZIE

The hotel bathroom was even dingier than the bedroom. This was not what Lizzie had pictured. The weekend in Chicago was meant to be compensation for Strauss not bringing her to the conference, but also for the secrecy and the contingency and the wife and all the other ways this relationship fell short of being an actual relationship. Lizzie had imagined rose petals. Champagne. Lush bathrobes, maybe an in-room Jacuzzi. Not an airport hotel, chosen because the wife saw the credit card bills and the wife would raise her eyebrows if he deviated from frugality. Lizzie couldn't afford a hotel room, could barely afford the plane ticket, and the idea of putting it on her credit card, letting him strategize the cash withdrawals required to pay her back, left her feeling seedier than the seedy hotel, so she let it go. They'd ordered room service, shared an overcooked and overpriced steak. The carpet smelled like cigarettes. The bedding was stiff but unstained. There was still the fact of privacy, of two uninterrupted nights together, which under other circumstances would have been enough. She couldn't have known this night would be one that demanded a different kind of privacy. Now she sat on the closed toilet seat, shower running, wondering how long she could stay behind the locked door before he got curious. The test would register blue or pink within five minutes of pee hitting stick. There was time.

She'd done this four other times, and remembered each bathroom: The science center bathroom, redolent with pee. The dorm room bathroom shared with five other girls, milk crates piled against a door that no longer locked. The studio apartment bathroom with the toilet nearly inside the shower. The sea-blue guest bathroom, boyfriend's father slicing Thanksgiving turkey just on the other side of the door. Negative. Positive. Negative negative. It was the kind of truth so easy to know.

She was in no hurry. It almost didn't matter. If this was a false alarm, she could forget it had happened. If this was a problem, she would solve it. She had done so before. What mattered was the man on the other side of the door, waiting for her, and whether she would tell him. What mattered was what he would say.

Not, certainly, marry me.

Not, you should have it. We should have it. Together.

Not, unless he was a liar, whatever happens, you can count on me, you won't be alone.

What mattered was that she had done an excellent job of looking away from reality, but the view from the toilet seat was tunnel vision. She saw it too easily, what he had to offer, and what he did not.

"Why are you being like this?" he said.

"Like what?" she said. "Like who I am?"

"This isn't who you are," he said.

"How would you know?" she said.

"I know you," he said. "Don't suggest I don't know you."

He knew her better than anyone had known her. But he didn't know her at all, not really, because since she'd met him, she had become increasingly alien to herself. Especially now that she'd stopped talking about it to Gwen; stopped talking about much of anything that mattered to Gwen. She lived in a pocket universe and he was its only other living occupant. This version of herself was true, but not complete. This version of herself asked nothing of him, never had, so no wonder he was confused now, the two of them naked on this cheap bed under these used sheets, time stretching endlessly forward, and Lizzie finally, audibly, expressing a need.

"I don't know how to do this," she said. It was as if Gwen had infected her, had shown her a crack she could not unsee. And now, the test, the what-if. Entropy was fundamental; cracks only widened. "I don't know how to be with you halfway."

He put her hand on the hard bulge in his boxers. "There's nothing halfway about this."

The Lizzie he knew would have made herself laugh, and then accepted the unspoken invitation. But tonight she was not being like that. She was being like this.

"I can't count on you," she said.

"For what?"

She could not answer that.

"I don't know how you feel about . . . this or your intentions, and every time I start thinking about the future—"

"Elizabeth." He squeezed her hand, hard. Tweaked her nipple. "The future is an illusion. Just as much as the past. I want to be here, now, with you. That's how I feel about this. I'm fully clear on that. So it seems this is about how *you* feel. What you want."

She sat up. She wasn't allowed to want what she wanted, which she resented. She wasn't allowed to say she wanted it, which she resented even more. A voice in her head, Strauss's voice, and she resented that, too, asked how she knew what she was allowed, and what if her assumptions were wrong. What she might be denying herself by refusing to ask.

"This will end," she said. "I don't know how I'm supposed to—I can't feel this way about you, knowing it will end."

"Everything ends eventually," he said. "You would be so much happier if you gave yourself permission to accept that and move on."

"Bullshit."

"Do you want to leave, Elizabeth? Is that what you're saying?"

She didn't answer.

"You're acting like a child."

"I hate when you say that."

"I hate when you do it."

They were having a fight, for real, a luxury she'd never allowed herself because it didn't seem safe to shake something so fragile. She turned onto her side, away from him. He put an arm across her, gathered her in, tight, his chest warming her back, his need hard against her.

"I bought a pregnancy test at the airport."

She thought if she said it with his arms around her, she would be able to sense his reaction, but there wasn't one.

"Did you take it?" A careful, controlled voice, betraying nothing. Maybe that was betrayal enough.

"Not yet."

Lizzie returned home to find her mother on pink-tipped crutches, left foot encased in plaster.

"What happened?" She was surprised to find herself genuinely distressed. What happened: dark house, late-night craving, forgotten stair.

"Why didn't you call me? I gave you the name of the hotel for emergencies—this didn't seem like an emergency?"

"I knew you were busy."

Too busy to hear about panicked crawl across tile, pain, pain, pain, a "mildly thrilling, wholly embarrassing" ambulance ride, a ride home from the recently dumped Eugene who was a prince through the whole thing until he suggested they get back together and "threw a hissy" when she refused. All this, and no one had thought to call Lizzie.

She spotted an unfamiliar vase of lilies on the entrance table. The card read *All our love, Becca.*

"You called Becca. In Israel. But you couldn't call me."

"Becca called me. Becca calls me every Saturday after havdalah. When she couldn't reach me, she called Crystal—" This was the next-door neighbor, a woman Lizzie had known for thirty years and wouldn't have had the first clue how to contact by phone. "—and tracked me down. I'm feeling much better now, thank you for asking."

Where there should have been an upwelling of tender concern for her mother, there was instead: affront at the assumption she could not be counted on. Dismay at the prospect of a future in which she must be counted on. The nightmare vision of said future, their very own *Grey Gardens*, old maids into eternity—Lizzie helping her mother to the bath and toilet, Lizzie attending her mother's daily pills and callused feet, Lizzie putting life on hold until her mother was dead and thus harboring inevitable impatience for the event. She was a horrible person. Victim only to her own blackened soul.

"I was thinking that when the house sells, I might go stay with your sister for a bit."

"In *Israel*?" Their mother had taken Becca's aliyah as a personal affront. She looked at Lizzie like Lizzie had suggested visiting the moon. "In Albuquerque. She didn't tell you they're moving home?"

"Home is Arizona now?"

"New Mexico, and I'll take what I can get. Mordecai got some kind of job offer. The kids need a grandmother. And that woman—" This was the only way she ever referred to Becca's mother-in-law, who had invited Becca to a Shabbat dinner during her lonely junior year abroad and thus was, by Epstein family calculations, responsible for all that followed. "She's of no use to them whatsoever. Last count she had thirty-two grandchildren. It's indecent."

"So now you like children?"

"I like my children's children." A bold claim; she reconsidered. "Well, we'll see. Anyway. I have something for you. I found a box of photos that never made it into an album—I got this one framed."

It was a picture of the three Epstein women. Becca was twelve, lips screaming pink, left hip jutting out in what Lizzie remembered as her "model" pose. Lizzie was seven, hairsprayed bangs aimed at sky, suspenders holding up pleather miniskirt. Their mother, perched over her girls, was unthinkably young and dressed younger, Hawaiian shirt knotted above her midriff, go-go boots green and knee high. Becca had wanted to enter a modeling contest, she remembered now. They'd spent the day at the mall, spent money they didn't have, staged a photo shoot, told Lizzie's father that they spent the day at the movies. A secret between ladies, her mother had said. One perfect day.

She had forgotten all about it. Her mental picture of the past was streamlined to suit her needs. She remembered her father, loving him. She remembered how it felt to be her father's daughter. She remembered watching TV with her grandmother, and her grandmother slipping away. She remembered her sister leaving, and leaving more, and eventually one day not coming back. She remembered resenting her mother's presence then, more so, her absence. She remembered her family as the family her mother left behind. If Strauss was right, and every mind contained infinite alternate selves, then there was another Lizzie whose remembered family was this family of the picture, their happiness evidenced in goofy grins.

"I can't believe you're just going to . . . leave." They both heard the unspoken *again*.

"You know, in all this time, you've never asked me why," her mother said.

"Why what?"

"Why I left."

This was not a conversation Lizzie was prepared to have with her mother, but the fact that her mother knew this felt like a dare. "Because I know the why. His name was Dick."

Lizzie's mother shook her head. "Dick was, you might say, a dick. He wasn't a reason for anything."

"That's great. It's not that you wanted him, it's that you didn't want us. So glad we're having this conversation."

Usually her mother would have given up. They didn't do open hostility, any more than they did honesty or vulnerability. But her mother did not stop. "There's this idea, when you have a child, that you're supposed to become an entirely different person. That woman you study, what's it called, what she has?"

"Fugue state."

"It's like that," she said. "Or it's supposed to be. You're supposed to stop wanting what you want. You're supposed to want what's good for the child. And I kept waiting for it to happen. To stop wanting things."

"You left because you didn't want me? That's what you're telling me?"

"I'm telling you I wanted you and I wanted more than you, and if I'd been someone else, I probably could have figured out what to do with that. What kind of mother leaves her children? No kind of mother. It was wrong. It was terrible, probably. I did it anyway."

"It's not like you abandoned us," Lizzie said, though it was like that, even if it wasn't technically that. There had been visitation, eventually shared custody, but it had always been there: the fact that her mother wanted less of her.

"It was selfish," her mother said. "You think I don't know that? I'm a selfish person, always have been. I thought that would go away when I had a child."

Lizzie didn't have the nerve to ask what she would have done if she'd known better.

* * *

In the end, Lizzie and Strauss had taken the test together, although she made him stand outside the bathroom door while she peed. She wondered about that, alone in the dank room, trying to force out a sufficient stream, whether you could have a baby with someone you wouldn't let see you pee. She flushed. Set the stick on the sink counter, let him back in, and they waited. She wondered what she would do if he said he wanted the baby, wanted her, that this was the excuse he'd been waiting for. Would it make her want a baby more, if he came as part of the deal? Would it make her want a baby less, if it drove him away, or would she cling to it as his replacement, finally a thing she could love without fear of loss, a thing she could possess and so control? A piece of him she could hold on to forever? Thoughts like this, she thought, were evidence she shouldn't be a mother.

She didn't want to "trap" him. She wasn't interested in that particular cliché. She did not want his child. Nor did she want to be his wife, or whatever she would become if she replaced his wife. Yes, she wanted, with Hobbesian greed, all of him, to consume him, to be with him at all times, to own every piece of him and give every piece of herself away. This was unrelenting desire of body and heart. But brain knew all of him would be too much. Would want too much. She understood this from the unspoken terms of their arrangement, the priority his needs took over hers, and she understood this from the way he spoke of his marriage, the way, though he would never see it himself and she would never tell him, husband had bulldozed over wife, flattened her into nothing. He was not a good father, she could tell. If she did want to have a child, which was unclear, she wouldn't want to have it with a bad father. None of this made her want him less. It simply made her wants diffuse, impossible. She didn't want to take him from Madeline. She wanted to *be* Madeline. She wanted to be a woman other than she was, someone who would be made happy by his husbanding, someone who would want to raise his child. Someone willing to make him her priority, someone who didn't need to be her own. She had never wanted so much to be someone so unlike herself, and she hated him for it.

He watched the clock; she watched the clock. She thought how miraculous the human brain was, that she could allow it to think these things while he was standing right here in front of her, his fingers threaded through hers, and he would never know. No one would ever know—the brain would swallow them, and with any luck, she would someday forget she'd thought them. That was a wonder.

What are you thinking, he said. Nothing, she said. They watched the clock. The stick did not turn pink. There was the predictable hesitant relief, him waiting to make sure relief was an acceptable emotion, her waiting to determine whether relief was what she felt, it seeming very important in that moment to say something true. I'm sorry, she said. That you're not pregnant? he said, nervous. No. Just. For this. That it . . . might have happened. It's not like you managed that on your own, he said, relaxing now, she could tell. She felt so proud, even at a moment like this, that she could read his moods, that they were hers to read. You're exceptional, he said, but as far as I know you're not divine. What if I said I was in love with you, she asked him. Is that what you're saying, he said. She said, I'm just saying, what if. They went home a day earlier than planned, kissed goodbye before getting off the flight, then Lizzie hung back, let him leave first, because sometimes the wife and daughter surprised him at baggage claim. The daughter liked to hold up a home-made sign.

"Did you regret it?" Lizzie asked her mother now. "Leaving? Or, I don't know. Leaving the way you did? Would you do it different, if you could go back?"

"Are you asking because you really want to know?"

Lizzie nodded.

She thought about it for a while, or at least—and given all the years she'd had to consider the question, this seemed more likely—pretended to think about it.

"I'm sorry, but no."

Lizzie tucked the photo safely into her bag and promised her mother she would help get the house ready to sell, get their lives ready to pack, that they would sift through the memories together, even the forgotten ones or the ones better left that way. Maybe, all this cleared air between them, Lizzie could do a better job loving her mother. Maybe, with Becca back on the continent, she could be a better sister. They could all find their way back to some alternate version of the past. Her mother hugged her, and Lizzie allowed herself to hug back. Even with her mother's arms around her, she knew that it would not happen, that Lizzie would absent herself from the house and packing as much as possible, would move gratefully into her own apartment and incrementally more adult life, would offer emptily to visit her mother and Becca in Albuquerque but would not, because her mother had made her choice, and chosen the easier daughter, the one willing to be chosen, and Lizzie could not hold this against her but would anyway. Still, she held on, just a little longer.

ELIZABETH

How old I am now: not too old, I decided, to fuck someone new. There were good reasons. There was the night Alice hit Pause during a commercial for some retiree dating site and asked if I thought I would ever love again; I asked if I looked like a retiree.

There was desire. Desire for him, against which I remained infuriatingly helpless, but also desire to feel desire again. To be desired. I was used to not having, but I was tired of not wanting. I had, of course, fantasized over the years about other men, hands and tongues real and imagined. But the idea now of touching any of them, *anyone*, felt about as viable as fucking the cartoon fox from *Robin Hood* I'd once imagined I would marry. I would have to get over it.

And there was revenge, which I could not take on a dead man, but longed for nonetheless. There was the principle of the thing, turnabout as fair play; there was the fact of the betrayal and what should have been its consequence. Whatever loyalty I'd owed him was gone, as he was.

My husband was dead, and I was not. That was reason, too.

I was too young to know any widows, but I had plenty of friends who'd shed themselves of their husbands; they steered me toward the Internet and its plethora of lust-enabling apps. It seemed simpler, or at least less soul-scraping, to start with a known quantity. How old I am now: not too old to be attractive to another man. I called Sam and invited him to dinner.

"Dinner?" He said it as if I'd forgotten the word for coffee.

"Dinner."

Not too old to be attracted *to* another man, and if Sam hadn't historically fallen into that category, it was only, I decided, because in deference to Benjamin, I'd not given him the chance. Here was a man who believed I was smart, maybe lovable. Here was a man whose heart beat.

Proust was right about the madeleine thing. Benjamin studied memory, and now I study him. My findings: death is a forgetting. First the useless substitution of mental for corporeal, spirit for flesh, then the creeping fade, amnesiac slippage. Death as the struggle to remember the touch of fingers and lips and taste and tongue. Abrasion of texture. Memories polished until their surfaces wear away. Absence of novelty; mess of reality shaped to fit tidy story. It's why the best memory is a madeleine memory, dormant till summoned, its teeth still sharp.

A lemon cough lozenge, and I remembered sweating and shivering under a wool blanket, everything snot and fever and his hand cool on my forehead, giving me permission to sleep. Burned coffee, and I remembered his first effort, so proudly proffered, the man who didn't drink coffee because it was too easy, stymied by his new French press, until finally, like a magician, producing the mug with a flourish—disgusting, watery, grounds swimming like pulp, but I choked it down, for him, because he'd exposed himself to failure for me. Apple pie: our trip to Vienna, the sad search for his father's house—torn down, built over, like every other trace of the Viennese Jews—the pilgrimage to Freud's office, steaming apfelstrudel, in Hitler's favorite café, which shamefully turned out to be ours as well, the irony, he said, Freud's city so good at remembering only what it wants to, then kissing me across the table while old men glared, because Vienna was a place where you did desire in secret. Salted caramel: Paris again, both of us trying too hard to recapture the past, until the concert in St. Chapelle, the *Goldberg Variations* echoing on stained glass, a secret stash of caramels, candy surreptitiously slipped from palm to palm, sugar melting on tongue, strings soaring into impossible steeple, my hand in his hand, home again.

What did a widow wear to a dinner that might or might not be a date? This one wore her tightest bra, shoulder straps jacked up to keep everything in place. Strove for an illusion of firmness. Jeans, so as not to look like I was trying so hard. A slimming black sweater with a semi-indecent V, so he'd know I was trying a bit. My only black heels were the heels I'd worn to the funeral; I wore boots. Lipstick, a smudge of eyeshadow. Hair down, as it never was anymore, lightly tousled, as I remembered some long-ago *Cosmo* had advised, hair that looked like it had just had sex putting men in the mind for more.

I waited for Sam outside the restaurant, a small Italian place on the edge of the city, where he could still feel reputably urban but I could find parking. It was too cold for November. It felt like I was cheating on my husband. Sam kissed me on the cheek, his lips chapped and cold. I let him lead me inside, pull out my chair, hand me a menu, order us a bottle of wine.

Your husband is dead, I reminded myself. Your husband thought you were his trial to endure, and he likely thought it while inside another woman.

When this proved insufficient, I reminded myself of the hair on his back and that year with the Viagra; the sound he made when he ate soup; the weird divot in his left thigh and the splotch of mole on his ass; his insistence on mixing raw onion into the burger patties, forgetting every time for eighteen fucking years that I hated the taste; his annual Father's Day sulk and the obligation to assure him he was a good father, no space left in that day of fathers for the fact that I was, every year, one year longer without one; the lunch dates and doctors' appointments and anniversaries and birthdays he left for me to remember, his brain too clogged with more important matters; the pee on the toilet seat; the lint in the dryer; the gall and shame of it, to find myself a sitcom wife, nagging sitcom husband about the pantry he'd failed to stock and the dishes he'd failed to wash, the fucking when I wasn't in the mood; the hair in the drain and the spotty scalp from which it fled. I thought: remember that.

We dipped breadsticks in olive oil. We sipped chardonnay, joked about the imminence of nuclear war. I tried to remember how dinner became date, who was meant to brush whose hand reaching for the bottle of wine. The candlelight made my ring sparkle. Its tiny diamond flared every time I reached for my glass—a little lighthouse, warning of what waited in the dark.

We talked about entropy. Sam was studying what he called the discovery of time. Through the eighteenth century, he said, nature was assumed constant. Nature was defined by its constancy, and constancy by nature—the eternal heavens, the steady state equilibriums of physics and capitalism, the conservation of energy. Then the nineteenth century discovered progress and decay. They discovered the universe is a paradox, he said, held in place by two opposing forces: the tendency for things to stay as they are and the tendency for things to fall apart. It was the inevitability of decay that unsettled them—so profoundly, Sam argued, you could blame it for the end of the age of empire. The laws of physics were atemporal. It was unacceptable that life should be an arrow aimed forward in time.

" '*It's a poor sort of memory that only works backward*,' " I said, one of Benjamin's favorite lines.

"Lewis Carroll. Exactly." Sam explained Carroll's immersion in nineteenth-century science, his membership in the Society for Psychical Research, his engagement with the limits of enlightenment rationalism as the ground beneath it gave way.

Shameful truth: I liked him best when he was explaining things to me. I always liked them best when they were explaining things to me.

I told him about Alice.

"You really don't mind having her there?"

"You mean, is it cutting into my busy daily schedule of sloth and nudism?"

He blushed.

I waved a breadstick in warning. "Stop imagining whatever it is you're imagining."

He covered his red face with his hands, laughing. I tried to remember if this was how it worked. "I don't know how you do it."

"What?"

"You don't let anything touch you. You just keep going, you *joke*. Like some kind of mythological warrior."

You mean like the Tin Man, I thought. All shine, no heart. I smiled, tightly. "Nevertheless, she persisted."

I beamed mythological will at him: Ask a follow-up. Imagine for one second that not everything that looks easy actually is. Say, Elizabeth, I don't ask you personal questions because it seems like you're afraid to hear them, but how about just this once, you tell me if it hurts, and how much.

See me, I thought, and it was dare and plea together.

"I like your hair down," he said. "You should wear it like that more often."

"I'll take it under consideration."

"It makes you look younger."

"You say that like it's a compliment."

He blushed again. When the bill came, he insisted on paying. He helped me with my coat, put his hand on the small of my back as we threaded through the crowd.

Sam, I knew, went to the gym regularly. He willed his feet up the StairMaster by imagining his mind a nineteenth-century factory owner, his body its steam-driven pistons and pumps, the worker and also the work. I knew he'd had two serious girlfriends since we met, one who'd wanted to get married right up until the day Sam proposed, the other who had tenure in Chicago and was disinclined to give it up. I knew he mildly wanted to have children, and felt, at age forty-three, mildly haunted not by his own biological clock, but by the steady ticking that surrounded him. As if he were Captain Hook, every date's womb a crocodile. There's going to come a point, he'd once said, when even the younger women aren't young enough. Then he'd apologized.

I did not assume he'd been pining for me all these years; I simply thought he might want me if he could have me. I thought I wanted someone to want me, right up until we reached the parking lot and he took my hand.

"Is this okay?"

I nodded.

"I didn't know whether this was supposed to be . . . I mean. This was nice."

We'd reached my car. The widow books all said your life did not end with your marriage. His hand tightened on mine. Want him, I told my body, urged steam against pistons, pumps.

I said, "I feel like I'm in high school."

"You look like someone waiting to be kissed."

I forced a laugh. "I wasn't aware that was a facial expression."

"May I?"

"What?"

"Kiss you."

"Okay."

The strange pointlessness of a kiss. The slurp and smack of wet on wet. The passivity of parted lips, mashed tongue. Hands threaded through hair, knob of groin against thigh. Absurd pantomime of need. I staggered on jellied legs, let myself be supported by the car behind me, his arms around me. It could not be real, his enactment of *felt*, when I felt so much nothing.

"Do you want to get out of here?" he whispered, and there, finally, a feeling, the requisite Joycean depth of desire, yes I said yes I will yes. I want to get out of here very much.

The human nose has 350 olfactory receptors, made up of ten million olfactory neurons—together composing 3 percent of the human genome. This endows us with the capability to detect one trillion smells. Unlike the mechanisms for sight, touch, and hearing, the olfactory bulb is directly connected to the amygdala and hippocampus: emotion and memory. There's a theory that smell triggers emotions more powerful than any other sense. This is known as the Proust phenomenon, and remains unproven.

Still, though, there was a brand of laundry detergent I found intolerable, because it smelled like his sheets had smelled the first night I spent at his house, a night I spent lying awake, unable to think about anything but the wife who had washed them. A whiff of pot behind the Wawa and I was back at the Pixies concert, Benjamin absurd in his souvenir T-shirt, absurdly old but making me feel so mercifully young, pretending, because it was my birthday and because he loved me, that he wasn't in hell. A nameless perfume, floral and expensive—my face buried in a stranger's mink coat, my ball gown shoved up to my waist, Benjamin's tuxedo pants at his ankles, safely swaddled in the wool and fur of the coat check room, furtive groping and thrusting, Benjamin behind and then Benjamin on his knees, Benjamin trying to make it up to me because he'd introduced me as his dilettante wife, because he'd said I was a scientist first and then a writer and then who knows, fireman, tightrope artist, you know what Berlin says about the fox and the hedgehog, as if I was not standing there beside him, smart enough to, yes, know what Berlin says about the fox and the hedgehog. Even coffee sometimes, brewed just strong enough to be the coffee he'd brew for me in the middle of the night, all those adrenaline-fueled nights toward the end of *Augustine*, writing till 3 a.m., till dawn, awake because my brain wouldn't slow enough for sleep, not when she was so close, when I had almost pinned her to the page, and he would pout and sulk and it was the first time I'd ever seen him jealous, and I liked it. He begged: come to bed. I said it would be a shame to sleep now, after you've gone to all the trouble with the coffee. Benjamin longing, needy: I'm not saying we have to sleep.

The problem was my car. Sam shifted the passenger seat back an inch; long legs, longer than Benjamin's. I wrapped my fingers around the gearshift, squeezed, Sam wrapped his around mine, did the same.

Benjamin and I had not, of course, fucked in a car for a very long time. We were too old, or he was, and then I was, and we were married—and cars are not, we'd agreed even when it was necessity, conducive to anything but fetishized fucking.

Sam's fingers crawled up my forearm, shoulder, found neck, tender ticklish spot where hair met flesh and brain stem cerebellum, caressed.

Benjamin, I found out, only after we were married, did not allow people to eat in his car. It was a compliment to me, he once said, that he'd been so open to the dripping and smearing of fluids.

Sam said, I can't believe this is actually happening. He raised my hand to his lips, said, you smell amazing.

In a different parking lot once, I knelt in the back seat well and Benjamin phrenology'd my head, delicate hands feeling for imagined swells and contours as he hmm'd and ahh'd and noted that here was my propensity for criminal behavior, over here was a grand and rapacious wit, and here, he said, a knobby protrusion, indication of sexual deviance. Knobby protrusion, I said, alarmed, and he squeezed himself into the back seat, pants down, knobby protrusion arrowing toward its desired deviance.

Sam turned my face toward his and kissed, said, now I'm the one who feels like we're in high school. I pointed out that with six years between us we wouldn't have overlapped in high school, and he laughed, said, unless I was hot for teacher. The car was a year and a half old, which I remembered because we'd bought it six months before Benjamin's death, driving home all giddy bourgeois until a pothole blew out the left rear tire. We pulled over. We called AAA, because we were, as he called it, helpless intelligentsia. We waited. We listened to classical music. I played *Tetris* on my phone. He said, as I recall we were once better at making use of spare time in a vehicle. I said, we used to be more flexible. He said, I'm just saying, it's tradition for a captain to christen his new ship—and which one of us, I said, is the captain here, and before you answer, consider the consequence of mutiny. Sam sucked on my fingers, one by one. My right hand, not the one with the ring. The first time, with Benjamin, at the train station, knowing, both of us, that it was the worst thing we could do. The car smelled faintly of Indian takeout; Sam tasted of garlic. I knew I was going to throw up and pushed him away, fumbled the door open and gasped in a bolt of cold air, and then I did, half-digested lasagna splashing on concrete, the sour pain of it good, real, deserved. Sam rubbed my back. Said, I'm sorry, I'm so sorry.

Tactile memories are controlled by the haptic system, somehow; it's understudied. Haptic memories decay in seconds, like the mental echo of a loud noise, or an after-image of the sun. The Atkinson-Schiffrin memory model maps the possibility of consolidating sensory register into a long-term store, but most of what we touch, we lose. I touched myself sometimes and tried to imagine the hands were his. Sometimes I stood beneath the skylight on the third-floor landing, waiting for the sun to pass overhead, because the touch of sun on skin was the same as it had been the first day I moved in. The surprise of it, a hole cut straight through the gloom, material evidence that he was willing to remake his life for me—his promise, in glass-framed sky, that if I hated living in the house, dark and old and someone else's, we would leave. Kissing me in the sunbeam, a blizzard of dancing dust. It was all lost, the body's memory of his lips, his fingers, his hair, his tongue, but the sun was constant, and warm.

I got home to find Alice waiting up for me, like a nervous mother. "So?"

It was ridiculous, rehashing a date with a teenager. But I sat down. "Awful."

She made a cringing face.

"Not awful, I mean." Poor Sam, I thought, and wondered if he was still thinking of me, and how. "Perfectly fine. But . . ."

"This is the first date you've gone on in, like, twenty years, right?"

I nodded.

"Not to mention the first date since . . . ?"

I nodded again, and swallowed down whatever was swelling in my throat. I refused to let her, of all people, comfort me.

"Maybe you should give yourself a break? It's kind of a big deal you even tried. It's not like you can just switch it off, right? Missing him?"

It was only hearing it from a teenager, framed as a stupidly naive impossibility, that I understood why the night felt like such a failure. I should have been able to switch it off. I'd stayed up two nights in a row, reading his emails, scouring them for details I didn't want to know, trying to piece together what had happened in the lacunae between messages, what had passed between him and these girls in the flesh. It seemed only fair that rage supplant pain, and maybe what I had felt most as I read, beyond surprise and disappointment, was relief. Here was an excuse not to love him, or at least a reason to love him less. Here, finally, was a cure. It was plainly unacceptable, wanting him. Except I still wanted him.

I couldn't remember the sound of his voice. There was video, of course—speeches, awards ceremonies, mostly, a handful of vacation clips. There were voice mails on my cell phone I couldn't delete. But the way he sounded when it was just us, when we were alone together? That was gone.

I thanked Alice for waiting up. I excused myself, turned down the thermostat to the semifrigid level Benjamin had preferred, and went upstairs. It was easier to sleep beneath the weight of blankets, shivering against the cold. It was good to have concrete reason to shiver. Cold, Sam had explained once, during the dregs of some endless winter, is not a thing. It's an absence, the emptiness left behind when heat leaves. Cold is a nothing we imagine into a something, simply by giving it a name.

ALICE

She was still herself enough to feel guilty for what she'd done. She'd cheated on Daniel, whom she supposedly loved. *Cheated* felt like too trivial a verb, the kind of trespass you'd make in a game of checkers or, worst-case scenario, a calculus class. It wasn't the right word for what she'd done, which was allow someone to love her, then transform herself into someone who couldn't love him back.

After their first kiss, Daniel had pulled away for a moment, whispered, *I can't believe this is actually happening,* and she had thought maybe now everything would be easy.

She avoided him for several days, until she missed him too much not to call. She waited until it was dark, and very late. Alice dialed the number, tucked her blanket over her head. Eighteen hundred miles away, Daniel did the same. He told her about midterms, about missing his little brother's first home run, about the boy in his hall who'd drunkenly mistaken his laundry hamper for a toilet, and she let the words blur into pure sound, the song of Daniel.

She felt so alone.

"Daniel." She missed saying his name.

"What is it?"

She knew he could hear it in her voice, because he knew her, and it had been so long since anyone did. But she couldn't tell him what it was, couldn't tell him about Z and the things A had let him do to her. She couldn't tell him that she couldn't remember why it had seemed like such a good idea to come here, that she'd been so certain she wasn't running away but now she felt like she'd run away and couldn't go home. She couldn't tell him that she hated her mother for leaving and her father for being left. That she wanted her mother.

She couldn't tell him she didn't love him anymore, because she wasn't sure it was true, and she couldn't tell him she'd done something she should never have done if she'd loved him, because then he would leave her, and she wasn't ready to lose him.

They said good night at 1 a.m. At two, still wide awake, she summoned an Uber.

She was already crying by the time she reached Zach's door. He opened it, bleary and boxered and not visibly displeased to see her. He gathered her into his arms, stroked her hair, rubbed her back, let her lie in his lap, wipe her nose on his boxers, performed reassurance and she tried to perform reassured.

"You cry a lot. I may need to become the kind of guy who has tissues."

He thought she was the kind of girl who cried. He guided her to the bed and lay beside her, then adjusted his laptop so they could both see the screen.

"Trust me, this will work." He played them a YouTube video of a baby orangutan watching a man do a magic trick, then played it again. Alice watched it loop, mesmerized, soothed, until eventually she could breathe again. The pillows smelled mildewed. Zach smelled like burgers. The man put an apple into a bucket, made the apple disappear. The orangutan's jaw dropped, the orangutan laughed so hard it toppled over. The man put the apple in the bucket. It disappeared. And again, and again. Somehow, she laughed.

"See? Magic."

Not until later, when they were almost asleep, his body spooned around hers, did he ask if she wanted to tell him. She did want to. "I can't."

"Why?"

She dug a condom from his nightstand. She didn't want to talk. She wanted the absence that entered her whenever he did.

The next day, she wrote Daniel a cowardly email. It said thank you for loving me, it said I'm sorry, it said I can't, it said goodbye. It said nothing about meeting someone else, because real Alice had not.

*   *   *

I am no one, she thought when she was with him. I am whatever stories I choose to tell. Is this what you wanted, she thought, a question for both her mothers, is this what you ran toward?

And it was so easy, like submitting to gravity: he did not expect, he did not demand, he did not need, he did not care. He did not see, or fail to see. To name a thing—Alice dimly remembered from the stories she used to read, all those wizards and wishes and magic—was to define it. And this was why the prudent person kept her name a secret.

Who are you: no need to answer if you could avoid anyone who might bother to ask.

She invented details of her imagined self as needed: the residential motel in Columbus, the seedy apartment complex outside Detroit, her mother's bad boyfriend, her own bad boyfriends. She stole her aunt Debra's story for her own, invented a best friend who'd OD'd in front of her, described the girl's glassy stare, her seizures and drool, told him this was why she'd gotten sober, at least the first time. She conjured herself into Wendy Doe, into her mother before she was a mother, when she was just a girl who hated herself so much she willed it gone. She decided perhaps this was better than chasing nonexistent answers. Instead of finding her mother, Alice would become her.

He still called her Anonymous. She let him photograph her, body part by body part, leg ear hand nipple cunt. She learned to like it, to touch herself under the lens's gaze, to believe what it told her, that from the right angle, she could be beautiful. He agreed never to aim it at her face.

Zach taught her how to use his camera, urged her to take her own pictures, but she always found herself paralyzed once the thing was in her hands. In his hands, the camera captured everything: dying neon, rotting fruit, a woman's thigh, an old man shuffling down a grocery store aisle, brass knuckles in a weedy gutter, mundane made to matter simply because someone aimed a lens and argued it should. Alice had always only taken pictures of people and places she loved, or was publicly trying to. She was a born yearbook editor, a believer in the pixelated past. The story, she'd always thought, was in the photo feed, array, collage, the carefully cultivated selves flattened into their idealized two dimensions. Then her mother vanished, and the photos left behind all felt like lies. Alice felt the same looking at pictures of herself: some girl she didn't know, a stranger pretending otherwise. Zach said photography was as much about the photographer as the subject, each photo a distillation of self, and maybe this was why Alice kept refusing. She didn't want him to know that her distilled self was vapor, that when she looked through the camera there was nothing special to see, because there was no one special to look.

"Tell me what you want," he would say to her in the dark, his body at her service. She could not. She did not know how to say that she wanted him to decide for her, wanted her body forced to his whims, did not know if she was even allowed to want this. He took her silence as evidence she did not want at all, or not as much as she should have, as much as he did, would not say this, knew better than to ask what was wrong with her, but she could track his mounting frustration, came to anticipate the point when he would give up, shove her roughly where he needed her to be. So she got some approximation of what she wanted after all. He had stopped going to AA meetings—you're my meeting, he told her, the only Anonymous I need—and he'd started drinking again, just casually, just occasionally, never "problematically," except that one time she'd met his father and, according to Zach, his father's eyes had prowled hungrily over her skin, his father's hands had not-so-accidentally grazed her ass, her cleavage. His father had done what father does best, psychically marked his claim on her body and was probably even now jerking off to her undressed image. Zach's narration ended prematurely when he rammed his fist through the drywall. She bandaged his hand; he cried; she put him to bed. He said that was his last drink, again. He kissed her fingers, curled his body around her, said, *you're bad for me*, as if she had wrought his destruction, and she felt guilty, as if she had. Also, shamefully, proud, powerful, wholly unlike herself, and that night she'd climbed on top of him in the dark, stayed on top, as she'd never brought herself to do before, swallowed the pain of his grip on her waist, found finger-shaped bruises in the morning, and pressed them, hard, so her body could remember.

Zach wanted her to apply for a job at his coffee shop. You need a job, he said. You can't stay in the old lady's attic forever. He assumed the widow was old, the manse Brontëan decrepit, and she let him. He told her barista was the best kind of job, mindless, that the concept of loving your job was a capitalist scheme to lull the worker into submission. Alice had never imagined loving a job. Her capitalist urges were pure.

Sometimes she would meet him at the café to wait out his shift. She liked sampling the elaborate coffee drinks with whipped cream and flavored syrups. Sometimes he drew her dirty pictures in the foam. That day, he drew a heart. He was getting sweeter, and she found this problematic. It had been easier to lie about herself when he was a stranger, but she couldn't exactly reintroduce herself now that he'd started to care. He was starting to care. She could feel it when he kissed her, when he tucked a strand of hair behind her ears, like he was enacting the playbook he'd learned from a movie: this is how you tenderly handle a woman you love. She couldn't let him love her, not when he barely knew her. She certainly couldn't let herself come to care about him—that was the opposite of the point.

When his shift ended, they walked through the city while he aimed his camera at everything he saw. Buildings, shopkeepers—never homeless people, he said, because that would be tacky—but everything else was fair game. His eye was always roving. She used to resent this, assume he couldn't be listening with his eye pressed to the viewfinder, scanning the world for a more interesting focus, but she'd come to understand what he meant when she first met him, that this was his way of seeing. And he was so strangely determined to see. Sometimes in this city, dirt and rats and bodies, she wished she could walk with her eyes closed.

As they walked, Zach ranted, angry at his mother for putting up with his father, angry at his father for everything. It was his favorite topic. She told him she was sorry, as she always did, and was.

"You're always sorry, never angry," he said.

"What do you mean?"

"When you talk about *your* mother. You make her sound like . . . never mind."

He still thought her mother was a drug-addled mess who had hung herself. She told him to stop hedging.

"You make her sound like total shit, okay? Your father's a ghost. She was all you had, and she abandoned you."

"She died." Alice hated herself for saying it. She could have turned herself into anyone—why had she chosen to be the kind of liar who would make up such a treacherous lie? "It's different."

"Is it? I mean, obviously it is, I'm sorry, I just—if I were you, I'd be fucking angry."

They kept walking. She was looking down, but could tell he'd lowered his camera, was looking at her. She was angry now, at him. The whole point of a him was to allow herself to go unseen.

"I choose not to be angry at her," she said.

"It's that easy? You choose not to be, and you're just . . . not?"

"Why are you pushing this?"

It was the closest they'd come to a fight, and she didn't like it. You didn't fight with people unless you cared about them. You didn't answer uncomfortable questions about your dead parents, even when they were fictional. You didn't start asking yourself forbidden questions just because a stranger dared you to. That's all he was, she reminded herself, a stranger. She only knew the version of him that knew this fake version of Alice, so how could he be anyone else?

"Whenever you talk about her, you just don't seem, I don't know . . . like yourself. It's like you're holding back."

"You know me so well now?"

"I thought I did," he said. "I want to. I tell you about my shit."

"Did I ask you to?"

"Fuck you," he said. Then, "That came out sounding worse than it did in my head."

"Whatever."

"Why are you being this way?" he said.

"What, unlike me?"

"Well, yeah."

"Maybe you have no fucking idea who I am." Alice still wouldn't look at him, but she heard the soft click of his camera's shutter. She felt the urge to rip it from his hands and smash it against the cement. "I have to go."

"What, now? Here? Let me at least—"

"I have to go," she said again, and when she turned and walked off in the opposite direction, she assumed he would not follow her, but she didn't turn around to make sure.

*   *   *

She walked aimlessly. She checked her phone, wondering why Zach hadn't texted her, asking her to come back, asking where she'd gone. When he did text, she ignored it. She wanted to call Daniel, but Daniel was done. Daniel had let a drunk skank sext Alice a shot of Daniel's hands and lips all over drunk skank boob. She did not want to think these words, but they beat their insistent tattoo. *Drunk skank*. Daniel, when Alice called at 3 a.m. to ask what the fuck, had told her not to say those words, defended *drunk skank*, she was his friend, he said, unlike certain skanks who will remain nameless. He was drunk, too—too drunk to have drunk-dialed Alice. Daniel was responsible even in the sloshed depths of irresponsibility. You think I don't get angry, because I don't vent it at you like a fucking child, Daniel said. You think I don't have needs, because I can acknowledge yours? Fuck you, she'd said, and he said, You missed your window of opportunity on that.

She walked, and she missed being known as much as she missed being unknown, and eventually she called her father. She missed her father.

"I miss you, too," he said. She asked how he was, and he told her about the dinner he'd had with the neighbors, the chili he'd cooked. He didn't ask her anything.

When she was younger, still young enough to want to tell the story of her day, her mother was the one she'd told. Her mother would fire back detailed follow-up questions, as if she actually cared who'd cheated herself into an extra turn at four square or whether the clique of girls who referred to themselves proudly as *the clique* had devoured another one of its own. She remembered everyone's name and each of Alice's complaints; she adopted Alice's grudges and, on the rare nights Alice allowed herself to admit weakness, she would promise that while life would never get easier, Alice would get better and better at handling hard. Alice's father was usually absent for these conversations. When he was there, he rarely participated, never remembered the details.

He'd asked her no questions about college, and—other than the general and persistent question of why the hell she wouldn't just forget this whole foray into the past and move on—no questions about her time in Philadelphia. Not that he left any ambiguity about his position.

"I'm worried about you, honey. I don't think it's healthy, you being there."

"I'm not Mom. I'm not going to lose it."

"I didn't say that."

"You didn't have to."

A silence. "Can I ask you something? Something you don't want me to ask?" she said.

"That doesn't sound great."

"I know you don't want to talk about this, but . . . what was Mom like? When she got her memory back and came home. Did she remember anything?"

"I told you, she didn't."

"But did she seem, I don't know, was she happy? Was she upset?"

"She was your mom." Her father sighed. "You want to know how she was when she came back? The same as she was when she left, but more so. The anxiety—it was always bad, I knew that even at the beginning, but this, it was confirmation of everything she feared."

"What do you mean? What was she afraid of?"

"After Ethan, after Debra—when you lose people the way she did, you know how easily things can fall apart."

When you lose. Alice had never noticed before, the judgment embedded in syntax. One sister had—passive voice—been lost. The other sister had lost her.

"Your mom felt like she was the only thing keeping her world together. That if she let down her guard for one second, everything would collapse. She took the fugue as evidence she was right. It's why we wanted to put it behind us. As I *really* wish you would."

"That sucks," Alice said. "But I don't see what it has to do with me being here."

"Alice . . ." He paused. "Do you want to know the story of what happened to your aunt Debra? The whole story?"

"I thought I did."

In the version she had always heard, her mother was sent to Philadelphia to bring her baby sister home. She'd found Debra staying at an artists' squat on South Street, some fire hazard of a warehouse scattered with sleeping bags and blowtorches. There was a party, baby sis had gotten high, gotten screwed. All of this, he confirmed, was true, but it elided some salient details.

"They had a fight. During the party. It was supposed to be a secret that Debra was here. When Debra found out that your mom had told her parents, that your mom was there to drag her home? Well, you know sisters," he said, though Alice did not. He said Debra exploded, called her sister a traitor, a lapdog, happy to do their parents' bidding because she was too frightened to live her own life. Debra called her sister pathetic. She called her embarrassing. "You have to understand, Alice—your mom did *everything* for Debra. Taking care of her, defending her to your grandparents, trying to keep her happy, when by all accounts she was a person determined to be miserable. So when Debra said that . . ."

When Debra said that, her sister lost it. Because you know sisters. A strange man, one of the other squatters, offered Karen a drink, and Karen decided to prove her sister wrong. It wasn't yet a habit, imagining herself into someone new, but she was a natural. She took the drink. She took his hand, let him lead her deeper into the warehouse, away from Debra who could, for once, take care of herself.

"That's when it happened. The OD. By the time your mother came back, it was over."

"I don't understand, who was the guy?"

"Nobody, that's the point. The point is, what happened, it didn't just happen. Your mother let it happen, because she decided she could be reckless, just this once. She blamed herself."

"So which sister am I supposed to be here? The spoiled one who ruined everything because she didn't want to be rescued? Or the responsible one who ruined everything by being irresponsible for the first time in her whole life?"

"That's up to you."

The mistake, Alice thought, wasn't her mother's one bad choice, but the choice she'd made every day after, to impose logical causality on bad luck, to believe in crime and its punishment, to blame herself—and it was her father's choice to let her do so.

"What are you so afraid is going to happen to me here?" Alice asked.

"I'm afraid of everything, Alice. I'm afraid every minute of every day that something will hurt you. That's what it means to really love someone."

She didn't want to be loved like that.

He told her to remember that "Wendy Doe" was a symptom. Her mother was her mother, and nothing she found out here could change that. She told him she loved him, then they hung up.

She walked. She gave herself permission, just for the day, to imagine that her mother had returned again, was hiding in the pedestrian swarm of Rittenhouse Square or passed out on a cardboard flat on Broad Street. She stopped veering around homeless bodies without seeing them. She forced herself to see them. Just the women at first, middle-aged bodies burritoed in sleeping bags or pushing can-heaped carts; then all of them: the emaciated teens shilling for a smoke outside the methadone clinic, the man her father's age whose dog had more teeth than its owner, the women not much older than her, their dirt-faced children. The skyline sparkled; the city asked you to look up. Alice looked down. None of the faces were her mother's. She walked, aimlessly at first, and then with purpose.

It was like walking through the database of unclaimed persons, and Alice knew: if her mother was lost somewhere, it was somewhere like this. If she were a loving daughter, a dutiful daughter who believed in her mother's ongoing existence as much as she claimed, then wouldn't she devote her life to this search, wandering the country block by miserable block, studying faces until she found the one that meant home? The other option: abandon her mother to chance, abandon herself to a forever of not knowing, and when she let herself imagine this, she could understand why her father had expended so much faith on death.

She walked to South Street, site of her mother's supposed original sin. The neighborhood was nothing like she'd imagined. There were no artists' squats, no rebels, no heroin chic, only a cheesy tourist imitation of bohemia—overpriced clothing stores, shiny condo complexes, a coffee shop that sold rock-star-themed cupcakes. It was all a Disney vision of adolescent rebellion, and Alice couldn't help but feel it suited her. She could never be anything more than a fake rebel. She wandered the blocks. Anything grubby and tragic had long since been sandblasted away. The only trace left here of either sister was Alice.

ELIZABETH

I tried to be mindful of other people's suffering. Benjamin's mentor was dying of prostate cancer. My last remaining grad school friend had endured four miscarriages and several endometriosis surgeries before undergoing an emergency hysterectomy; at forty-five, she was trying to adopt. Our dry cleaner's son was in a coma, and according to the sign, she could afford his care only as long as customers kept stuffing crumpled bills into the box. Sam's sister-in-law was a Somalian immigration activist whose Occupy-era arrest record was about to get her deported. My sister's youngest daughter had type 1 diabetes, her oldest son was a recovering heroin addict, our mother had dementia, and Becca cared for them all almost single-handedly, which did not make up for the fact that she'd dragged our non compos mentis mother to the polls and yanked the fascist lever on her behalf, but obligated me to keep my mouth shut. I read my emails and I read the news. Misery abounded: earthquake victims, mudslide victims, wildfire victims. Battered women murdered by their husbands. Young black men murdered by the cops. Children murdered by assault weapons. Refugees rejected, encamped, homeless and starved and dying. Bomb blasts; drone strikes; helicopter crashes; more drone strikes. Famine. Poverty. War. Genocide. There was a wild abundance of suffering, and comparatively, mine didn't even register on the meter. I knew this. I did.

Even in my own house, my suffering was inferior. I knew this, too. Alice's loss was fresh, however determined she was to pretend otherwise. She'd lost interest in asking questions about her mother, had started spending days and often nights out of the house; I deduced a boy, and was pleased for her. Sam, who continued to bring me coffee at the library, the two of us pretending away any change, wanted to know how long she intended to stay, or how long I intended to let her. I knew it would be better for both of us if she left before she got too curious again, but I'd gotten used to having her around. The room was always supposed to belong to someone's daughter—originally Benjamin's, and failing that, I'd briefly imagined, maybe mine. Alice was just giving the house what it wanted.

Things were starting to cohere. A fog was lifting, certain desires revealing themselves: I wanted Alice to stay. I wanted Benjamin alive, so I could hate him. I wanted to look under the next rock, and wanted the will to endure what I found there. I wanted to tell him there was some virtue in endurance after all.

I did not want to write this book.

This was plausible reason for returning to the Meadowlark. At some point my agent would need to be informed, so she could handle the publisher, but Mariana, I told myself, deserved to be the first to know. The book was meant to burnish his legacy, and the Meadowlark was that legacy in glass and concrete, Mariana the designated tender of its flame.

We arrived at the same time. It had been raining since dawn, and I looked it. Mariana, as usual, looked impeccable. Heels clacked, skirt swished. Her umbrella was large and black, wood-handled, expensive. I had no umbrella. Mariana invited me beneath hers. I declined. I wanted to feel it, the cold, the wet. Luscious evidence that I was here in my body, that the present was more real than the past. Mariana shook her head, wondered aloud why I insisted on making things hard on myself. Then she invited me into my husband's office, where she sat me down like a guest and brought me a cup of tea.

I told her I couldn't continue with the book, that digging into my husband's past and prettying it with lush prose had lost its appeal. Then I told her why.

"That seems like a reasonable choice," Mariana said flatly, as if I'd told her I'd opted for sushi over salad the night before.

"I gather, from your utter lack of reaction, that none of this comes as a surprise."

"Is that a question?"

Was it a question? Mariana had been Benjamin's buffer, his amanuensis, the woman he trusted to shore up the bureaucratic walls within which he, hypothetically if ever more infrequently, could pursue knowledge with a purity of heart. I'd been googling the names of his girls, promising students, bright stars of the next generation; none of them had grown up to be scientists. I had drawn the obvious conclusions as to why; Mariana, I assumed, could do more than guess.

Was it a question? There was a difference between suspicion and confirmation, and, like entropy, the movement from one state to another was a one-way trip. Benjamin had dedicated his professional life to the possibility that the brain could be taught to selectively unknow that which it did not want to know. He'd failed.

"It's a question," I said. "Did you know?"

"Is there any point in rehashing this? Especially in this climate, if you want his legacy to—"

"Fuck his legacy."

When she laughed, she looked like a person I'd never met before. "Okay." Mariana tapped a pen on the edge of the Lucite desk. "Okay."

She knew, she admitted. More than that, she'd been the one responsible for smoothing things over.

"He wasn't a groper," she added, like I was to take comfort in this. He wasn't the man who would cradle your hips at the copy machine or materialize in a dark corner, all bulges and tongue.

"So everything . . . at least. Everything was consensual."

"Lizzie." The way she looked at me—a very gentle contempt—was so familiar it made my eyes sting. I wondered if she knew how much she'd absorbed from him. "How would I know who said no, or who wanted to?"

"And when he was done with them, he ruined them."

"Only their careers," she said. "Which you would know about."

It was one thing to suspect she thought it, but another, more brutal thing to hear it out loud.

"I shouldn't have said that. It's not my place to have an opinion about your marriage."

But why else had I come? Not to find out what he was. I needed to know what I was, and she'd been there from the start—she knew who I used to be, and whatever I became. I needed a witness.

"Please. Opine away."

It was like she'd been waiting twenty years for permission. "I was jealous, you have to know that." She must have seen the look on my face then. "Not because I wanted him for myself! God. No. It was—you know he used to compare me to you, right? *If you were more like Elizabeth, if you could only be creative, like Elizabeth.* You know I came here to do stem cell research? You ever wonder how I ended up lobotomizing mice? I think it terrified him, looking back on it. Too risky for conservative funding sources. But he would never say that, not the great Benjamin Strauss, so instead he tells me that kind of work, it's not for people like me. It's for people like you."

All this time I'd thought she worshipped him.

"Then I saw what it meant, him thinking you were 'special.' I felt sorry for you, for a while. Now . . . I don't know. The ones he picked always got screwed. The ones he ignored, well—" She gestured at a stack of cardboard boxes in the corner. "It seems we got screwed, too."

"You're leaving?"

"The board made its choice." She shrugged. "Your husband spent the last decade telling me he was grooming me to take over when he retired. It's why I stayed all this time. Apparently he told the *board* I was a perfect second-in-command. He told them a great scientific institute needs a great scientist at its helm, and that I'm just a bureaucrat. I'm what he made me. This whole year, tying myself in knots to impress them—turns out I didn't have a chance. What a fucking joke."

Mariana never cursed.

"I didn't know, Mariana. I swear."

"They offered me the opportunity to stay on, in my previous position. Suffice to say I declined."

"I don't blame you."

She smiled, too sadly. "I hope not."

She was going to Michigan, she told me—back to real research, back to stem cells, a junior position in a second-rate lab in a city where she knew no one, but all she wanted, she said, after these years on the sidelines looking over the shoulders of the men she'd once wanted to be, was to finally do the work.

"You know the most jealous of you I've ever been?" she said. "It wasn't anything to do with him, or maybe it was—but only because it had nothing to do with him. You started over, writing that Augustine book. You found something that was entirely your own. I want that."

I wanted that, too.

I drove home slowly, wondering if Alice would be there, not sure whether to hope for it or not. I was in a truth-telling mood, an exposure-and-closure kind of mood, and who knew how long it would last. If the house was empty, I thought, if I had absolute privacy to shield me from potential humiliation, maybe I would finally call Gwen and apologize. Tell her, in truth-telling mode, that I'd decided I was the one who owed the apology, I was the one who'd walked away, because it was either let myself be seen by her or be loved by him, and I'd made my choice.

A childhood best friend or someone else's child, I could almost hear Gwen judging me. *Those are your options? Come on.* All these years, all this supposed maturity, and still glomming on to other people's families, hiding from the complications of my own. The Gwen I imagined was always meaner than the real one. That was maybe another apology I owed her, another reason I'd walked away before she could push.

The house was empty. It felt emptier now than it had before Alice had arrived, and I suspected this would not change once she was gone. If I told her everything I knew about her mother, she would leave. This was a stupid reason for discretion, but I had better ones.

Nina had left me a voice mail after we had dinner, apologizing "if I said something to upset you." But she'd been understandably on edge, she said, because of Alice. It seemed like we needed to talk, she'd said, just the two of us, and I must think so, too, she'd said, or why else would I have brought the girl to dinner. She invited me over to her place. Nina lived on the bleeding edge of Germantown, not because her father had grown up there, but because the neighborhood had cycled: undesirable Jews gave way to undesirable African Americans gave way to gentrifying hipsters, postmillennial children seizing cheap rentals and progressive bragging rights. "You people fucked up this city when you ran away," Nina told Benjamin when she announced the move. "We're fixing it." Benjamin, who had more than once lectured me on the politics of white flight, the redlining, the city's Jews' liminal state, white, but not quite white enough, told his daughter he hadn't gone to all this trouble just to let her live in the shtetl. Still, at the end of dinner, for which he paid, he slipped her enough to cover the security deposit and the first two months' rent. I'd never been invited inside.

I did not want to go, certainly not now, maybe not ever. If I was going to have this conversation, I wasn't going to have it on her territory. As I'd deleted the voice mail I had indulged the temptation of never speaking to her again, allowing that dinner to cap a relationship that had never really existed in the first place. Imagine the relief if we laid down our arms and gave each other permission to disappear.

How much more are you going to let him take from you, my internal Gwen wanted to know, *or, better question—how much of yourself are you going to give away?*

ALICE

Alice did not intend to eavesdrop. She'd wandered the city for hours and returned to the widow's house, spent, wanting nothing more than to shut the blinds against sunshine, crawl into bed, pull covers over her head to deepen the darkness, and pretend to be asleep until it was true. The house was empty when she arrived, which had seemed like a gift. By the time the widow came home, Alice had accomplished her mission, was in bed, trying not to hear her father's voice, Zach's voice, her mother's voice playing in her head. She was tired of noise. So when the widow called her name, asked if she was home, Alice stayed silent. There was no harm, she thought, in pretending she wasn't there. She was tired of being anywhere.

But she *was* there, and when the doorbell rang and the widow greeted Nina, their voices trickling up the stairs, it seemed too late for Alice to reveal her presence. She wasn't trying to eavesdrop on their awkward small talk, and couldn't hear much more than the tenor of their voices and the occasional word. It was only when one of those words was *Alice* that she allowed curiosity to overpower etiquette, slipped quietly out of the guest bedroom, and stationed herself on the stairs, a perfect vantage point to learn what was said by women who assumed she wouldn't hear.

"The ears were a dead giveaway," Nina was saying. "Too square? Slightly too big? Tell me you didn't notice."

Alice tugged at her ears, about which she had always been slightly self-conscious.

"Some things have to be beyond the realm of possibility," Elizabeth said.

"If I can do the math, so can you. You're telling me you didn't wonder if it was *possible*?"

Alice willed herself to either advance or retreat. Stop the conversation or stop herself from hearing it. Either way, she advised herself, do not stay. Do not listen.

She didn't move.

"I spent eighteen years hoping she didn't exist," the widow said. "I knew that it was possible. But even when she showed up, I didn't think . . ."

"You did think. You just didn't want to."

"You're right," the widow said. "I didn't."

Alice tugged harder at her ears, the traitors. Alice tried not to draw the logical conclusions. You didn't spend eighteen years hoping someone didn't exist, unless you knew she might.

That morning, before Alice had gone into the city, the widow had asked her about her earliest memory. Alice told the story of the circus—the sticky sweet of cotton candy, the beeps and boops of dancing clowns, her father's hand large and warm around her own, her tiny toddler foot sunk deep in a mountain of elephant poop, tears, tantrum, all of it family lore told so frequently, in such delicious and ever-improved-upon detail, that Alice no longer knew whether she actually remembered or not.

This was not her real first memory. Her first memory: her mother, slumped over the kitchen table, crying. It was a circus-era memory, she thought, maybe three years old, maybe four. Old enough to ask Mommy why she was crying.

I don't know.

Young enough to toddle after Mommy wherever Mommy goes, follow her out of the kitchen, down the hall to the front door, now open, to say, Mommy where are you going, the words like a magic spell that closes the door tight, because no one's going anywhere.

I don't know.

It had shaken something loose in her. That some things could not be known, even by the mother. That the unknowing was maybe cause to weep. What if, Alice wondered now, she'd actually wept because she remembered something, and the something was Alice?

She went down the stairs. "She was pregnant?" Alice said to the widow. Wanted to stab her finger in air, shout and curse, spit venom at this woman who'd stolen her trust. *J'acccuse*, that was what she wanted, but she was Alice, polite, well behaved; she was, within the walls of herself, collapsing. "She was pregnant, and all this time, you *knew*."

The widow was shaking her head, no, definitely not, no, except, "I didn't know. Not for sure. I didn't know anything."

"You knew enough to keep it a secret," Alice said. She turned toward Nina, then thought better of it, turned away, did not want to examine the incriminating contours of her features, eyes, chin, ears.

"I was going to tell you," the widow said, the line as feeble as she suddenly seemed.

Alice wanted her to hurt, the way Alice hurt, the way surely Alice's mother had hurt. Because if Alice was the child of her other mother, the figment, it meant the figment had been fucked by someone.

Someone who is my father, she thought, but pushed the thought away.

"You kept telling me you two were *friends*, that she was so happy and carefree here—and all the while, you knew *this*."

Alice had swallowed her district-mandated dose of sex-ed. She read the news occasionally and feminist-ish sex blogs obsessively; she both lived in the world and had an encyclopedic knowledge of *SVU*'s rape-sodden version of it; she knew about consent—enthusiastic, withdrawn, unvoiced, inebriated, abrogated, and otherwise. She knew a drunk, high, or otherwise impaired woman could not be asking for it, even if she was, slurringly, explicitly asking for it. And if impairment negated consent, Alice did not see how her mother's mind, so screwed up it had erased all record of its own existence, could offer any. *Wendy Doe* might well have satisfied an urge with unmitigated enthusiasm. Karen Clark could only have been violated. Which Karen Clark would have known the moment she discovered she was pregnant. Alice had had enough of these dreams to imagine how this would feel: Alice was her own worst nightmare. So wasn't it safe to assume she was also her mother's?

She felt like an orphan, daughter of someone and someone else, and the someone else could be anyone, but if he were, why would the widow look so afraid.

She felt like causing pain. "You knew your husband was probably a rapist."

Elizabeth did not object, and that was confirmation enough. Nina said Alice's name, approached as if to touch her, and Alice recoiled, her mind in no condition to make any decisions but her body certain of what it needed—and what it needed, immediately, was physical removal from both of these women, so it told the widow to go fuck herself, then walked out the door.

XI

IX

WENDY

It never happened

If I won't remember, it never happened. If I won't remember, it never happened.

XII

XII

LIZZIE

He got her flowers. The card read, *for all the things I should have said*. It was the closest he'd ever come to an apology, which wasn't the same as delivering one, much as offering flowers in exchange for things not said wasn't the same as saying them. Fortunately, the flowers were not hand-delivered, which meant he wasn't there to see her dissolve into tears. This was a phrase she had used before without thinking of its composite words, but now, huddled on the floor of her office, back against the door, legs pulled up tight against her chest, body shaking uncontrollably, she thought about it: the dissolution. That was how it felt, that something in her was dissolving, the wall she'd erected around the things she wanted, the same wall that hid from view all the pieces of herself she'd torn off and given away. She had tried not to want him, and failed. She had tried not to need him, and failed. She had tried not to love him, and this, too, had obviously, piteously failed. And in the process, she had become a woman who made do with less. She had become a woman who lived for a man, a Lizzie who let herself be the Elizabeth he imagined her to be, in exchange for nothing more than the feeling she got when he looked at her and saw something special. She had become a woman who needed someone else to believe she was special.

She got herself together, managed to make it through the rest of the day. She did not go down to his office to thank him for the flowers—but she also did not stray far from her own office. If he wanted to find her, he would know where to look. He did not look. When she left the building that night, she barely made it into the parking lot before the dissolve came again, and with it the tears. She did not want to be this person, weak and needy; she did not recognize this self. It had been a long time since she'd recognized herself.

That night she lay in bed, thought about the flowers, reconsidered their value as apology, as token of love, thought maybe this was a foolishly self-inflicted wound, she could have as much of him as she needed, if not as much as she wanted. She could love him as is.

But she could not call him to tell him this, because she was not allowed to call him. She could not curl her body around his, let his steady breathing steady hers until she fell asleep, because he was asleep beside his wife.

Dissolve: to disintegrate, to break down, to melt away.

The next day: a resolution.

"I think we should take some time out from—" They were safely inside his office, behind the soundproofed door, but it still felt dangerous to say it out loud in the middle of a workday. She gestured toward him, then herself. "—you know. This."

"I don't understand what you think I did," he said.

It was telling, Lizzie thought. That it wouldn't occur to him he had actually done anything, only that she might think he had. She was collecting bricks for a new wall; this would do.

"I just need to think," she said.

"You know I hate when you resort to cliché."

It was a lucky coincidence for him, how so many reactions he didn't like qualified as cliché.

Another brick.

"Maybe I am a cliché, has that occurred to you?"

"If you want to tell me what's really going on, we can have a conversation about it, but if you want to act like a child, maybe you're right, and you need some time. To *think*." He made this sound like a verb she lacked the capacity to enact. Lizzie left. Did not cry until she'd returned to her office. Did not, once she'd started, stop for a very long time.

He was fine. She spent every day trapped inside his brainchild, surrounded by him even as she was trying to avoid him, tortured by proximity and distance at once. He was fine. When they were forced to interact, he treated her like she was anyone, which was to say, no one. He treated her as he'd been treating her ever since they'd started the affair, of course, but before this, she'd understood it to be an act. Unless it was everything else that had been the act. His performance was effortless enough to believe in. He was fine.

She had asked for it, but it still felt like punishment. To be finally *seen* by someone who now looked through her—it made her feel like she did not exist, or did not want to. His absence was a wound; her absence, apparently, was painless. She survived one week. She survived two, then three. She managed to resist telling Gwen—she didn't want approval, nor did she want shame, if she changed her mind. She wasn't even sure she was allowed to change her mind. He wasn't acting like a man who wanted her back.

She wasn't sleeping.

Love should make you stronger, she imagined Gwen saying, and those were the nights she almost picked up the phone, called Gwen, risked the *I told you so*, but she couldn't, because telling Gwen would make it real, would make it even harder to go back to him. Then one night she broke, and did tell Gwen, who was so relieved, so proud. Gwen said she would kill Lizzie if Lizzie ever went back to him. She did not know how she would endure the year unless she went back to him; she did not want to go back to him only because she could not otherwise endure.

She couldn't quite breathe.

Her mood was contagious. Wendy had retreated into a cloud of gloom. And, on a less existential level, she'd retreated into her room, refusing to leave. She was taking a break from tests, she said. No more research. "You tell Dr. Strauss that if he wants to throw me out, he can throw me out," she told Lizzie. Lizzie would not be telling him this.

Their conversations tended toward the monosyllabic, and occasionally, at least until the bottle of whiskey stored under Lizzie's desk ran down, toward the liquid.

"Why are you so miserable?" Lizzie asked her once.

"Why are you?"

There was no reason not to answer somewhat honestly. "When I think about how many days I have to live through before the end of this year, I'm a little tempted to knock myself into a coma."

"Dark."

"Yep."

"If you hate it here so much," Wendy said, "why not just leave? Nothing's stopping you."

Lizzie shook her head. She had teased herself with the possibility. She wasn't a quitter, especially not when quitting would require something so radical as public failure and transcontinental relocation. But if she was really ready to sever herself from Strauss, if she was serious, then shouldn't this be the obvious next step? "You can't walk away from a fellowship like this in the middle, not without a good reason. People would assume I either got kicked out or flamed out, and it amounts to the same thing in the end."

"What's that?"

"The end of my career."

She had no options. Either that or she wanted to believe she had no options, because that would mean the only option was returning to him. She couldn't be sure. And she was afraid to act, one way or another, until she was. "Basically, I'm trapped."

Sometimes, Lizzie thought, Wendy looked at her like she hated her. "You have no fucking idea."

WENDY

Practical considerations

The thing to consider, he says, is that I have nowhere else to go.

It was inappropriate, the thing we did together, and of course it can never happen again. Probably, he says, this should be the last time we discuss it.

The thing we did together, he says, and it's almost like he believes it.

Not that it wasn't meaningful to him, he says. I shouldn't think that. Everyone makes mistakes, he said, but we should agree that this mistake is unrepeatable. There's no shame in misinterpreting things, he says, and of course he is flattered. But we need to respect certain boundaries.

The thing to consider, he says, is what people would think. There would be questions, certainly. An investigation, possibly. He says he'd hate for me to face the skepticism of those who distrust my memory, but it's to be expected, since my memory can't be trusted.

He doesn't say, what do you remember. So I don't know what he would say if I told him I remembered his beery breath, his grasping hands, the fist of hair he tugged so hard it burned, his palm against my mouth, hard, teeth slicing lip, taste of blood, his voice saying be good, behave, saying I see how you look at me, saying you don't have to do anything you don't want to do, you don't even have to stay here, saying if you run away now, feel free to keep running, saying trust me, I know what's good for you, haven't I always done what's good for you.

He would probably say my memory cannot be trusted. This is objective fact.

He says, regardless, if anyone even had suspicions, I would no longer be able to stay at the institute with him.

And where would I go then?

He's only worrying about my future, he says. My safety, my happiness. I have no identity, no way to support myself, nowhere to go but a hell of last resort. A shelter, a sleeping bag on the street. You don't want to rely on the kindness of strangers, he says. The world is not kind to women like you.

If we keep what we did to ourselves, he says, there's nothing to worry about.

You're well cared for here, he says. You're happy here. Why should that change?

And he's right. This body is a prison. As long as I'm trapped inside it, I have nowhere else to go.

LIZZIE

On the final day of the third week since he'd last put his arms around her, Lizzie came to work to discover Wendy Doe was gone. In her place was a woman wearing her face, sitting primly on the bed, shoulders hunched, legs crossed, trying to take up as little space as possible.

"You're her? The research assistant?" she said. She enunciated, as Wendy never had.

Lizzie understood immediately.

The woman stood. She held out her hand. "Karen Clark," she said. Lizzie forced herself to shake it and tried to smile. "I'm sorry, this must seem strange to you—though not as strange as it does to me! They told me you've spent a lot of time with . . . well, me. I wish I could remember it." She laughed, thinly, fakely. "Actually, to tell you the truth? I really don't."

"Your memory came back." Lizzie felt like the woman was miles ahead and she was limping to catch up.

"I woke up in this strange place, and—" She laughed again. This time it sounded even less sincere. "Let's just say I caused quite a fuss. They called the man who runs the place, and he explained the whole thing. It's like something out of a movie."

He hadn't alerted Lizzie. He hadn't even waited for Lizzie in the room, to be here when she found out.

"I'm not a research assistant, I'm a grad student," Lizzie said. "You were—I mean, this, the fugue state, it was my project." Emphasis on *my*, she thought. Or emphasis on *was*.

"Yes, sorry about that," the woman, Karen Clark, said. "They told me you'd probably want to do some tests, but I'd really rather go to my own doctor."

"There's nothing medically—"

"They told me," Karen Clark said abruptly. "But I don't know them. And I don't know you."

Wendy had talked with her hands and her body, flagrantly without care. This woman kept herself still, balled up tight. The part of Lizzie that still imagined herself an objective observer filed this away: body language shaped by memory, the physical inhabitation of one's own body expanded or constrained by the experiences that body has undergone. Proof of a limit on what the body could remember.

"I wanted to thank you before I left."

"You're leaving? When?"

"My husband's flying in from Colorado. He's reserved me a room at a hotel downtown, so as soon as I fill out some paperwork—"

It was happening too fast. Wendy Doe was a subject, Lizzie reminded herself, not a friend. But once she was gone, who would be left?

"Do you need help, packing up? There's clothes, and—"

The woman shook her head. "I'm leaving everything here. You can have it. Or donate it. Or something."

"Oh. Well, I would at least love to talk to you for a bit, before you go. We could sit down and—"

"No tests, I told them."

Lizzie wondered why she sounded afraid. "No tests. Just talking. I'd like to get to know you." It felt treasonous, but she reminded herself these were not two women, they were one. Karen Clark symptomatic, Karen Clark cured. "And maybe you'd like to know how it was for you here. I'd be happy to answer any questions about—"

"I said no. I just want to forget this ever happened." Laughter. Fake. Smile. Fake. "I suppose that's all taken care of!"

Lizzie nodded, pretending she understood. Given the intensity with which she would have liked to pretend the last several months never happened, maybe she did. All too soon, after some perfunctory forms and a few more awkward handshakes, it was time. Strauss never turned up.

"I could give you my number, my email address," Lizzie suggested. "In case later you change your mind about wanting to know more about your time here?"

"Thank you, but no."

"Wait," Lizzie said. She nudged Wendy Doe's dresser out from the wall and extracted the notebook she knew she would find hidden in the crevice. She hesitated before handing it over—it felt, somehow, like a violation of privacy. Even more than it would have for Lizzie to read it herself. Which was a seriously tempting proposition. But the journal belonged to this woman. "If you change your mind, I think you'll probably find some answers in here."

Karen Clark took the journal. Then she carried Wendy's body away.

The photograph of Augustine watched Lizzie from the wall. No one chose madness; no one preferred to be a subject. Remembering was reversion to good working order, and Lizzie should celebrate. Lizzie should be happy. She closed herself in Wendy's small bathroom, which seemed a safer place for the tears. So it was the crying that was to blame for what she found there, discarded in the trash can, the empty box with the familiar logo. Not the test itself, with its incriminating pink plus or lack thereof. Just the box. Just the question.

XIII

XIII

ALICE

Alice's parents believed life began at conception. They held this belief quietly, but not so quietly Alice hadn't had it driven home since puberty, and most especially since the dawn of Daniel and Daniel's fertile sperm. Alice walked to the train station near the widow's house and got on the first train that would take her away; she didn't care where. She thought about her mother, awake to herself, a six-month gap in her mind, a fetus in her body, and wondered whether her mother wanted to rip the thing, the *Alice*, out of her body with a coat hanger. Alice wondered if she had felt all these years like she was raising someone else's child. Maybe Alice had found the answer she thought she wanted, the reason her mother was gone. Her mother had birthed a daughter she never asked for, could not remember conceiving, raised her for the prescribed eighteen years—who wouldn't flee the moment her sentence was up?

Her mother could not have wanted her, she thought as the suburbs streamed by the filthy window.

Her father could not have wanted her, she thought, then thought *which one.*

She called her father, who noted, like he knew it couldn't be good news, this made twice in one day.

"Dad." She swallowed. She didn't want another father, any other father, much less the likely one, under the likely circumstances. She wanted him. Alice tipped her forehead against the glass, closed her eyes. His wife had left him, then his daughter had left him alone. What kind of daughter would do that, if not the kind who was no daughter at all? "When Mom came back from Philadelphia, how long after that did she get pregnant?"

A pause. She tried not to make anything of it.

"Why do you want to know?"

"I just do."

"I told you, it was a few months."

"How many?"

"Alice."

The widow said she didn't know Wendy Doe was pregnant, not for sure. It could have been a mistake, a coincidence, a false conclusion they'd all leapt to, because the dramatic always seemed likelier than the mundane. It could have been true, the story her father had told her, the frantic honeymoon, the miracle baby, the fresh start. If he told the right lie, she might allow herself to believe it.

"She had a miscarriage. Before she disappeared," he said. "A bad one. A late one. And I didn't . . ."

"What?"

"Neither of us handled it very well. But especially me. We were fighting. A lot."

They had never fought, not once that Alice could remember. Sometimes her mother had begged him to have an opinion, make an argument, get angry. He always abstained.

"When she left—I thought she left me, at first, that's why I didn't tell anyone. I was . . . I guess I was ashamed. The things I said to her. But then she came back, and she was—" He stopped.

Alice knew what she was.

"She didn't remember how it happened," he said. "That's what she told me. I told her it was our miracle."

"What did she think it was?" Alice asked.

"I always wanted you," he said. "You have to hear that. I wanted to be your father."

That had not been the question. "What did *she* want?"

"She left because of me—which means whatever happened to her, it was my fault. I wasn't there to protect her. She forgave me, Alice. It was my job to help her forgive herself. She just needed to see it could be something good. Our fresh start."

He sounded desperate. She imagined this was how he'd sounded when he pleaded with her mother: to keep the secret, to keep the baby, to pretend away the past.

Alice's parents almost never engaged in displays of affection, public or, as far as she could tell, otherwise. But her father believed in chivalric acts of care. He unfailingly held the door for his wife, pulled out her chair, helped her with her coat. A younger Alice had studied the two of them in these moments: the gentle graze of his hand on her waist as she stepped into a building, their fingers collaborating on stubborn buttons, her mother's smile when he took her hand, helped her out of a car, the surprised blush, like it still never occurred to her that she was someone worthy of his care. They loved each other, to whatever degree was necessary. Alice had always been sure of that.

"And it was our fresh start," he said. "You were. We were happy. All of us."

"Apparently not."

"You can't blame yourself for that."

"Oh, trust me, I don't." It felt like the kind of line on which she should slam down the phone. But you couldn't slam a cell phone, and Alice couldn't hang up on her father, whether he was her father or not.

"Come home," he said. "Please."

"Is there anything else you're lying about?" she said. "Now's the time."

"Nothing. I swear. Ask me anything."

"Why are you so certain she's dead?"

"I've lived with uncertainty, Alice. I don't want that for you. For either of us. You have to trust me. It's going to be easier for you if you decide she's not coming back."

"Even if it's bullshit."

"Even if."

"I'm hanging up now, Dad."

"You know that I love you, right? You have to know that."

"Okay."

When the train stopped, she got off. She didn't care where she was. She sat on a bench overlooking the platform. She was no closer to understanding Wendy Doe than she'd been when she arrived. But she'd known Karen Clark her entire life. Karen Clark she understood, well enough to picture her after a miscarriage, feeling betrayed by her body, her luck, her husband. Karen Clark depressed. Karen Clark angry. Karen Clark, discovering irreconcilable differences between the woman she'd always been and the woman she wanted to be. Solution: trial separation from herself. No more Karen Clark. Karen Clark, so unnoticed there was no one but her husband to notice her gone.

Then six months later, everything unruined itself, it must have seemed. Wendy fled the body, returned it to Karen, Karen returned herself to her husband, and delivered unto him a daughter. Alice could imagine her father helping his wife to understand. Teaching her the proper way to narrate her own story. He liked things to be tidy, *nice.*

When Alice was ten, her parents had rented an RV for the summer, with the intention of driving to the Pacific. By Utah, they'd endured two flat tires, a minor accident, an unspeakable septic tank crisis, and what even Alice acknowledged was about a hundred hours too many of mother-daughter warfare. They dumped the RV in Salt Lake City and flew home, where her father turned the failed vacation into family lore, a series of entertaining hijinks that he seemed, in defiance of all logic and reality, to remember with genuine fondness. This was his superpower—to uncover and polish the bright side until it occluded all others; to bend reality to his will.

He would have said to her, you lost a baby. You thought you might lose your husband. The strain of it broke you. He would have said, it's important now that you hold tightly to both. So she did, until she couldn't anymore.

Here is the lesson you should learn from the soap, Alice's mother told her, when they first started watching: your past is less important than the way you remember it. You could be an orphan who grew up on the streets, hypnotized into remembering a royal childhood, and *poof*, you were a princess. You could be a dashing hero with a wife and three children, brainwashed into forgetting both love and bravery, and *poof*, you were a nobody, with nothing. Your past, Alice's mother said, is a story you tell yourself. If it doesn't suit, simply invent a new one. Alice often played this game herself, or tried to. Lonely on the fringes of a loud party, shivering outside her camp bunk as a boy told her she was too ugly to kiss, she would promise herself she had only to endure the moment until it was past, then forget it. If you don't remember, it's like it didn't happen. Add it to the list of lies her mother told her, because her mother must have known this was pointless. *Our fresh start.* Easy for him to say. It wasn't his body that had to forget.

*   *   *

She didn't know where she was, and she didn't want to be alone, so she texted Zach a screenshot of the map with the little GPS dot indicating *you are here*, wherever the hell here turned out to be, and asked him to pick her up. She apologized for starting a fight that morning. She told him he had scared her, saying he wanted to know her. She told him she wanted him to know her, for real. But when he came for her, as she hadn't quite believed he would, she wasn't ready to say it.

He'd borrowed his father's car. They drove in silence. He put his hand over hers, and she flinched. He took it away. She didn't want him to touch her. Neither of them had expected that. Just make it back to the apartment, she thought, to his safe room with his door safely closed, and then you can fall apart. But then they were back in his safe room, locked in against the night, two of them on the futon, facing each other, safe space between. And she still did not want to be touched.

"You're scaring me," he said.

She wasn't sure which of the things she needed to say could actually be said.

She needed to say: *My father is a stranger.*

She needed to say: *I may have destroyed my mother.*

She needed to say: *I need you. Or I need someone, and you are here, so, please.*

She could not say any of these things, though, without saying the first thing, that everything about her was a lie. So that was where she began. She told him her story from the beginning, and as she did, she let herself believe she would be forgiven.

"You were just screwing with me? This whole time, I told you every-thing, and you were playing some kind of game? What, find some pathetic drunk to fuck? Do you laugh about me with your friends?"

"No, I told you, I just needed to be someone else."

"So who are you today, other than a liar?"

"I'm sorry."

"What do you want from me?"

"I don't know." This was another lie, because she did know. She wanted to stop feeling like she did not exist.

And then he was on top of her, and it didn't matter that she didn't want to be touched, because here he was, touching her. "Is this what you want?"

"Get off."

He straddled her, heavy, pinned her arms by the wrists, stronger than he looked, and they were both fully clothed, and nothing was happening, she told herself, nothing real was happening, but he was stronger than her and he was not letting go.

"Get *off*!"

"You want to play games? You want to pretend to be someone else? Maybe I'm someone else, too, you think of that? Who knows what I'll do."

She was shaking her head, because this was not happening.

He let go with one hand, long enough to grab her boob, squeeze till it hurt. "Scared?"

She clawed at him. "Fuck you."

"Fucking liar."

She was pushing at him, but it was like pushing a wall, against a roof that had caved in, and under his jeans he was hardening against her and he was telling her to go ahead and cry, she was good at that, she could win an Oscar for that, lying little crying slut, and she was saying in a voice she did not recognize, *please* and *don't* and he shouted *shut up*, and he hit her, hard, across the mouth.

"Shit." He let go. Climbed off.

Climbed off, she told herself, before anything had actually happened. She tasted blood.

"Jesus." He uncapped a bottle, tipped it back, swallowed, swallowed, swallowed. "Shit."

Her lip throbbed. Her boob throbbed. Here was how it felt to be seen. She wondered, what did he see, that he did that? He approached again, tentative, held out the bottle. She took it, swallowed. She didn't know why she was still there.

"You're bleeding."

He gave her a tissue. He'd followed through on his threat, become the kind of guy who owned tissues—for her. She blotted. It didn't hurt, much. It was bearable.

"I'm sorry?" Then, unconvincingly, he laughed. "Look, you got me apologizing to you." As if this were her victory. "I am apologizing, though. Really. I shouldn't have gotten so mad."

Don't, she told herself. But, "I'm sorry, too."

He was standing. She was sitting. He was between her and the door. She only noted that as habit, though, the way her brain noted when she was alone in an empty parking garage or a restaurant bathroom at the end of a long, dark hall.

"What do you want to do?" he said.

"I don't know."

"You want to go?"

She shook her head. She had nowhere to go.

"You want to stay?"

"I don't know."

"Okay." He looked at the door, almost as if he was thinking that maybe he should go. "Would it be okay if I sat down?"

"It's your futon."

He sat down, sort of next to her, sort of not.

"Watch a movie or something?"

"Okay."

They watched *Ghostbusters*, because he had just downloaded it, and that was okay. By the time Egon invented the proton blaster, he'd put his arm around her, and that was okay. When Sigourney Weaver ripped off her clothes and declared herself the Gatekeeper, harbinger of the end of the world, she startled awake, found her head on his lap, his hand stroking her hair, and that was okay, too, so they went to bed. She let him kiss her. She let him run his fingers down her body and creep inside it, and now she knew how it felt to be touched like an apology. What do you want, he asked her, what can I do, and tonight she found herself capable of response. Do it again, she said. Hurt me again. But it was an accident, he said, he would never hurt her deliberately, he said, he was not that kind of man, he said, and she told him he owed her something, and persisted until he grabbed her hair, yanked it hard, slapped her across the face, did precisely those things she instructed him to do, hardened against his own will, rammed himself inside her with such force that she thought she might tear, and she pulled him against her. Wondered if this was power. If this was desire. What this was. What it made her.

She bit his lip until it bled, and before he fell asleep, he kissed her with the taste of blood and asked if this meant they were even. She didn't think she would sleep, but she did, with his arms around her, too tight. She woke up before him, lit by dawn, memorized the look of him, sleeping, smeary. She made it to the bathroom nearly in time, puked twice, once on his toilet and once on his tile. Then she stole his favorite camera and left.

ELIZABETH

I was a woman who had woken up beside a dead body, and the body was my husband. I had slipped my hand into his dead hand. I had endured. My husband on a stretcher, our good navy sheet over his face, and I endured. My husband a thing loaded like freight, driven away from me, and I endured. My husband a body in a box, my husband underground, decomposing, food for ants and maggots and worms, and here I still was, enduring, visiting his dirt, laying a smooth stone on the larger stone that marked the it of his body, leaving him, again, again, behind, alone. If I was the kind of woman who'd done these things, what couldn't I do? I was the kind of woman who loved Benjamin; I was the kind of woman who stole him, married him, lost him, grieved him; I was the kind of woman who'd forgotten to ask the question, what kind of woman, but wasn't that simply maturity, the acceptance of growing up, no longer dithering about what kind of woman would, because whatever it is, I did, and so I am.

I was also the kind of woman who declined to ask the right questions, until it was too late.

It was cold and damp, but once Alice had gone, Nina and I relocated to the front stoop. She pulled a joint and a lighter out of her coat pocket. "You mind? I feel like this is the kind of conversation that . . ."

I indicated I did not mind, and once she'd taken a long draw, I held out my hand. This was the kind of conversation that.

We inhaled.

"So, that went well," she said.

"Nina, we're all making a lot of assumptions here, but there's no evidence your father—well."

There was something about sitting in the dark, both of us facing the deserted street. Like we could pretend we were talking at no one.

"She can take a paternity test. Then we'll know for sure."

"If she wants to." It was hard, under the circumstances, to imagine Alice wanting to do anything I asked of her again. She would have her own reasons for wanting to know, but whether she decided to share that information with us, or use it in some way against us, was up to her. "But even if it was him . . ."

If, then what? There was no explanation that would have made a sexual encounter between researcher and subject appropriate. I didn't just know that, I'd written the book on it. Wendy Doe was under our protection. Wendy, as I remembered her telling me many times, had nowhere else to go. If he'd slept with her, he'd done it when we were together, when he was supposedly torn between me and his wife. Jealousy was not on the list of emotions I was permitted to feel about this prospect, and I finally managed a brief flicker of hatred for him, because even from the grave he'd found a way to make me a stranger to myself, or the woman I wanted to be.

"You really didn't know?"

"It's true, what I said before. I didn't even know for sure she was pregnant. I just knew it was a possibility."

"And she wasn't . . . with anyone? That you know of?"

Nina was the one who'd blown into the house wanting to know why an eighteen-year-old girl whose mother had crossed paths with Benjamin eighteen years and nine months ago had his ears. The fact that she was abruptly backing away from the possibility now persuaded me, more than anything, that it must be true. There were plenty of men around the Meadowlark; plenty of opportunities. I'd seen her with Anderson myself, his arms around her, her tongue in his mouth. At first I'd tried to think it might have been him. Then I let myself stop thinking about it at all.

Now I tried to remember what I might have willfully forgotten, evidence I had chosen not to see, as I had with the students, with the emails. I'd written the book on this, spent years digging through the records of researchers who claimed the bodies of young women under their care;

wrestled, page by page, with the question of victimhood and prey, of consent and complicity. Girls like Augustine had derived power from their helpless personas. They had, some historians argued, molded their bodies to suit the men's needs, because compliance gave them not just fame, but control. On the other hand, *I* had argued, control was context-dependent. To be better off within the walls of the Salpêtrière only meant they were held hostage to its demands. Disobedience meant risking loss of what small freedom they had, as Augustine had discovered, chained in a basement on the grounds she'd once ruled as unofficial queen.

"She was a subject, not a patient." I took the sloppy joint again, sucked deep. It burned. "She was totally mentally competent, even without her memory."

"That's a bullshit distinction, and you know it."

They were close, in a way, Benjamin and Wendy. I remembered catching her hugging him once—and that was how it felt, like I had caught them. She would reference, casually, or seemingly casually, things he had told her, music he had played for her, almost as if she were trying to make me jealous. I had dismissed it at the time, because I was wholly in his thrall but self-aware enough to know it, and understand I was filtering everything through my need for him. I assumed I was projecting it onto her, if not a need for him, then an awareness of him, his mind, his presence. But maybe she had wanted him, too. Or she had not, and that was the best way she could think to say so. She had nowhere else to go.

If he had done something, I had to believe he'd thought the something was welcome. But he would have known better; he would have felt guilty. Was it why he'd been so intent on leaving the country for his sabbatical, why he'd stopped allowing subjects to live on the institute grounds, why instead of discarding his latest mistress, as he'd apparently done without exception before and since, he married her?

He was a man who always wanted to do the right thing. He would eventually have found some way to believe he had.

"It's not like he never slept with anyone he shouldn't have." She breathed a puff of smoke at me. "No offense."

Even if he was a predator, I thought, it did not have to mean I was prey. But the opposite held, too: even if I wasn't prey, it didn't mean he was not a predator. Still. "This is different."

"No kidding."

When she was seventeen, in town to take a tour of the one college that would not only have her but would have her for free, she'd spent the weekend with us. It was the first time in years she'd spent the night in her own house. For a while, Benjamin had kept her room as a shrine, giraffes and elephants galloping across the wall, a nightlight that spattered the ceiling with stars. She hated the college, she hated the city, she did not want me to take her shopping. She mentioned, in passing, a girl-friend—said, when he started in surprise, oh, that's right, I guess I forgot to tell you. It was a cruelly efficient demonstration of exactly how little he mattered. But when she climbed into the taxi without hugging him goodbye, he was undaunted, radiant. September, he said, I'll get her back.

"I'm sorry," I told her.

"For what? You didn't do anything."

"You never really got the chance to know him," I said. When Nina moved east, I stayed away, at his request. She blames me, not you, he promised, but when you're there, it's harder for her to forget. "Maybe if you did, this would be . . ." I didn't know. Less difficult, or maybe more. Impossible to believe, or too obvious to have missed.

"I loved him," she said.

After graduation, we paid her rent, or most of it. When he died, I kept sending checks. She sent the first one back, but not the next. Our wills were identical, all communal assets defaulting to the spouse. He could have designed things differently. I would have, I think, if the daughter had been mine. But maybe he wanted a reason for her to need me.

"It's not like I didn't already know he was . . . I knew a lot. I loved him anyway. He was my dad, you know? But this? What am I supposed to do with this? Assuming there's a this."

"He was your dad," I said, firm. "That's allowed to matter. You're allowed to keep loving him, no matter what."

"What about you? Are you allowed to keep loving him, no matter what?"

"I think that's the wrong question."

"Why?"

I couldn't tell her it was because I simply did love him. That wasn't choice, it was fact, and it wouldn't change just because I wanted it to. The right question was how was I supposed to live with that?

"I know you think I hate you," Nina said.

"No."

When she took my hand, I wondered why. My cheeks were wet, and I wondered at that, too. She squeezed, and I said thank you, and wondered if she had never hated me, what I had always felt for her.

"I hate him, though," Nina said. "I really want to hate him."

She felt like family.

Benjamin's heart did not break. It beat too fast, ventricles quivering. Disordered electrical activity desynchronized chamber contraction. The organ's ability to distribute blood to the rest of the body, its raison d'être, subsequently failed être. Blood flow to brain decreased. Brain function decreased. Autonomic systems stuttered. Lungs failed, kidneys failed, body failed. Heart sparked then stuttered then stopped. Husband slipped from sleep to unconsciousness to unbeing. I slept through it.

That morning I discovered I could not will my own heart to stop. The body wants to live, until it doesn't. The heart wants to beat. A heart once broken, however, has various means of self-destruction. Grief can spur overproduction of calcitonin gene-related peptide, which overcoats the cells designed to seek and destroy infection, which depresses immunity, enabling disease or cancerous mutation and ultimately death. A faster route to the same end, takotsubo cardiomyopathy, occurs when emotional shock spurs a hormonal one, which in turn incapacitates the left ventricle, which in turn removes the widow from her misery. *Widow*, because broken heart syndrome most frequently befalls women. Then there's the French, who until the 1870s thought you could die of nostalgia, the longing for a long-lost life. The French—*quel surprise*—were big believers in the deadliness of a broken heart, *des maladies de la mémoire*. Children died of missing their nannies; soldiers died of missing their home. Nostalgia, of course, is the distortion of the past into an unattainable perfection, and maybe this is the most important point. Misremembering the past can kill you.

ALICE

Alice hid out the day at the movies. It was all she had the energy to want: darkness and transport. She ate a Snickers bar for lunch. She ignored the widow's calls, and she ignored her father's. There was nothing from Zach. She napped through a matinee. She didn't know what she was supposed to do. She missed her mother.

Her lip was swollen and tender. She was bad for him, Zach always told her, and now she wondered. The logic here felt murky: Alice lied to Zach. Zach hit Alice. But: *if A, then Z* suggested Z was inevitable outcome of A, gave A all power over Z and Z none over himself. And maybe, she allowed herself to think, this had been the intent all along, because hadn't she ultimately asked for pain? Maybe she was her mother's daughter, a born victim. She was her father's daughter, too, and maybe she was genetically primed to love a monster.

In the break between movies, she checked her phone again. More texts and voice mails from her father, from the widow. A message from Nina, the girl who might be her sister. All of them family as much as they were not. All of them wanting to know if she was all right.

She was not all right.

Nina's text offered dinner and a place to sleep, if she needed, one or both, on neutral territory. She texted back to say yes. One real dinner. One more night of sleep in a stranger's bed, and in the morning she would wake up knowing what to do next.

Nina's studio was squat and sloppy, oozed cozy. Mismatched wood furniture mosaicked with tile and bottle caps. A wall plastered with Polaroids of household objects in bizarre, extreme close-up. Blankets and throw pillows everywhere. It was an apartment that promised a soft landing; it delivered an ambush. The widow was sitting in wait, ridiculously prim and posed, on Nina's overstuffed armchair.

"Family dinner?" Nina said weakly.

"I'm out of here."

"To go where?"

"What do you care, either of you?"

"Humor me," Nina said, and the widow still said nothing. She looked like a wax dummy of herself. Nina lit a candle at the coffee table, which had been set with woven place mats, pink and purple ramekins of olives and Parmesan cheese. "I made spaghetti. Let's eat. Then talk."

Alice sat down at the coffee table. The wood floor was reassuringly firm beneath her. She put her hands on the table. That was firm, too. Nina sat beside her. The widow lowered herself, carefully and creakily, across. A candle flickered between them. Alice's mother liked candles. She liked to slide her finger through the flame. When Alice was a child, she thought that was magic, that her mother was a witch.

The widow wanted to apologize for lying, wanted to explain, again, that she'd been so uncertain and Alice had seemed so sure—that her father was her father, that her life made sense—it seemed cruel to destabilize her with unfounded suspicion. Then she corrected herself. "And I was afraid to tell you," she said. "I was afraid what it might mean."

Nina wanted her to take a paternity test. "So we can know. You must want to know."

Must she? If she wasn't a match to Benjamin Strauss, it would mean her father could be anyone, any man who'd passed through or near the Meadowlark Institute that month. She would probably never know who had done what with or to her mother. She would probably never find him. Another missing person.

And if she was a match to Benjamin Strauss? She didn't know what that would mean, but whatever it was, she didn't want it.

"My mother didn't want me to know," Alice said. "She didn't even want to know *herself*. Maybe she had good reason."

"You want to follow your mother's lead here, considering what happened—"

"Nina," the widow said sharply. "It's her decision."

"It's okay," Alice said. "I'm not going to break."

"Sorry," Nina said. "Big mouth, as usual. What do you need? You tell us."

"Some space, maybe?" Alice said. "And some garlic bread?"

Nina passed the basket, and Alice took three pieces. She hadn't expected an appetite, any more than she'd expected to be tempted by the idea of a sister. They ate. Spaghetti Bolognese, garlic bread, sautéed asparagus. Alice gobbled it all up. She was cavernous. They chatted about television and politics. The widow laughed at Nina's jokes. Alice did not pretend to smile. She felt no impulse to cry.

They finished dinner, washed the dishes together, and finished that, too. They ran out of tasks. Nina said Alice could stay. The widow said Alice could come home. "Only if you want."

Before she left, Nina folded her into a hug. "One way or another, whatever the DNA says, in a way he made us both. That counts."

The widow, wine sodden, asked Alice to drive. Alice hadn't been behind a wheel since leaving home. She had to concentrate, which was good.

"It might not be him," the widow said into the silence. "And you only have to find out if you want to."

"I can't even find out the things that actually matter, though." What happened, and why. Whether her mother wanted her; whether her mother ran from her. Whether her mother had wanted the man who was her father, or feared him.

Wendy Doe had discovered she was pregnant, then immediately allowed her memories to flood back in, knowing they would erase whatever had come before. Alice didn't know if that was strength or weakness, but either way it seemed like answer enough.

She squinted in the glare of passing high beams. There was perverse pleasure in the blindness that followed the bright. The destructive possibilities of the wheel in her hands, the exhilaration of escape.

"Do you think she wanted to forget?" Alice asked.

"Yes."

"And maybe she didn't entirely. Forget."

"Maybe."

"How could she, when I was there? A reminder. No escape from that."

"People can always find a way not to know something they don't want to know."

Which of us, Alice thought. All of us.

"I'm never going to know, am I," she said. "Not what happened to her here, not why she left this time. Not where she went."

"Maybe not," the widow said.

The thought of knowing anything more was intolerable, because everything she'd come to know just made things worse. But the thought of not knowing, of living every day certain of nothing, that was equally intolerable, and here was the problem—here was the swell of temptation, to bear down on the gas, speed into oncoming lights, easy and ultimate escape, and she was, after all, her mother's daughter. She was her mother's daughter, and she was her father's daughter, and no one could blame her for wanting to be anything but. The road blurred, the speed ticked up, the widow yelped, Alice let the tears run, the snot flow, the road unspool, but could not make herself want it—not escape, not erasure, not transformation. She did not want to trade pain for oblivion. She did not, in the core of her wanting, want to be anyone but Alice, even this Alice, Alice in a nightmare, Alice orphaned and deorphaned, Alice a hybrid of figment and monster, Alice gripping the wheel, tight, tempted, resisting, temptation persistent, but she was not her mother. She was not her mother, fragile and fled into fantasy. She was the daughter her mother had raised to be stronger than the mother. She was not going to break.

XIV

UNFINISHED FUGUE

WENDY

You

Now there are two of us squatting in this body, both of us wonders of science. Baby to be born only a few months after her mother. Call the *National Enquirer*.

I thought I was writing this for her, to force her to remember me, but now I know better. Now, there's you. Now, the three of us are in this together. She is our host; we are her guest. Eventually, both of us will have to leave. This is something you will grow up to understand: sometimes you have no other choice. Sometimes there is nowhere else to go. I can't stay here, with him. I can't both remember him and love you.

I've always assumed she is a coward, but maybe she's no more coward than I am. I hope she has somewhere better to go.

Somewhere cold, I hope. You should have snow.

I remember snow. Cold, like pain, but fresh and sweet. Toes numb, tongue out, sky falling. Remember to wear waterproof boots, please. Gloves, not mittens. Two pairs of socks and a scarf, a hat. I would knit you a scarf, if I had time. I've felt it, for a while now, the end of time. Her need to come home. It will be easier to let her. I won't have to look at you and see him. I won't have to see anything anymore. I won't have to try to forget. I can love you now, while you're still an idea. Let her love you when you're flesh and his blood. It happened, but it didn't happen to her.

She might hate me for leaving her with you. I would hate me. Do hate me. If she does remember—him, it, me—she might still find a way to love you. I would love you. I'm your mother, but I will not lie to you: she might not.

It's not your fault.

LIZZIE

Wendy's window overlooked the parking lot. Lizzie imagined her lying awake, watching headlights dance across the ceiling. She might have seen Lizzie and Strauss knotting themselves together. If she had been a witness, she'd been their only one.

Lizzie watched through the window as Karen Clark paced the parking lot curb, waiting for the taxi that would take her—and her hypothetical fetus—to her hotel. She watched the woman turn back to face the Meadowlark, impassive. She watched the woman take the journal Lizzie had given her, Wendy's journal, and drop it in the trash. The taxi arrived. Karen Clark climbed in, shut the door, drove away.

Lizzie considered retrieving the journal. Pulling answers from the trash was apparently the theme of her day. Surely in that notebook was some indication of what had happened, and with whom. Of whether Karen Clark would be receiving a nasty surprise from her trusted doctor. When she did, if she did, she would want to know, wouldn't she? Lizzie couldn't decide. This was more like the theme of her year.

Enough, she thought. Wendy was gone. Lizzie had no subject, no lover. She had a mother but not a family. Her love, the love she'd given herself up for, had no evidence: no photographs of her and Strauss, no love letters, no witnesses, no past. If she left, it would be as if she'd never been here. She could erase herself from the year and the year from herself, unmake all her mistakes, escape the distortion of this city's present and past, regain her essential shape; she could hit the reset button and revert to the person she meant to be. The body did not have to remember.

Here, she decided, is what she would do. She would remove herself. First from this window, soon from his fortress. She would call Gwen to apologize, because Gwen only wanted to protect her. She would go back to California, nestle herself between mountains and sea. She would luxuriate in sunshine, fresh doughnuts, roads that ribboned and swooped. She would find some way to explain the sudden departure, right the wrong to her résumé; she was a bright young thing, she could forge herself a bright new future. She would propose a new project, find something new she could love without reservation, that would not depend on anyone's participation or approval but her own; she would not do this to prove anything to him. She would live like he wasn't watching. She would be self-contained. She would acquire a home, which she would furnish and in which she would hang posters she bought at museums. She would go to museums. Join a gym. Overcome her fear of waxing. Maybe get a dog; she'd always wanted a dog. She would return to her rats, on which she could rely. She would build her new self as a scientist built a theory, each step deliberate, logically predicated on the one before. She simply needed to take the first step, which was away from this window, from the parking lot where she might eventually spy Strauss in his car, sitting at the wheel, waiting for her to change her mind and join him in the dark. When he discarded that hope, he would drive home to his family, kiss his sleeping daughter, climb into bed with his wife, move on. She would not watch this. She would not be his audience. She would turn away. She would leave him. She just needed to sit here a little longer, to be ready, to be certain. As soon as she was, she would.

Except that when dusk came, she was still sitting by the window, waiting to glimpse Strauss one last time as he left the building, and so when he came looking for her, finally, she was there to find. He stayed in the doorway.

"I'm sorry," he said.

"Don't be sorry, she got her memory back. That's good, right?"

"No, I mean. Yes. I'm sorry if this is upsetting for you. I thought it might be. But that's not it."

It wasn't like him, the halting speech, the uncertainty. The look on his face, as if for once he needed something from her.

"I'm sorry I didn't say this sooner," he said.

"What?"

"May I?" He gestured toward the room, and when she nodded, he came in, sat beside her on the bed. It had been so long since they'd been awkward with each other, since Lizzie had needed to be so aware of the space between.

"I want to be a good person," he said. "I want that very much."

"You are a good person."

"Am I?"

He looked down, kneading his fingers. She couldn't stand it—she stilled them with her own. They held on.

"You are a good person," she said.

"If I were, I would pull some strings, get you a fellowship somewhere else, away from me."

"I don't want a fellowship somewhere else." She had decided. "I don't want to be away from you."

"You make me want to be a better man," he said. "But that shouldn't have to be your job."

He turned toward her, finally, and she felt her lungs expand for the first time in weeks.

"I thought it would be harder for you if I told you the truth," he said. "But the truth is, I love you."

Lizzie breathed.

He kissed her forehead. "I love you." He kissed her nose. "I tried not to." Lips. "But I do." Neck. "I should have said so sooner." Lips.

The door didn't lock. She wedged a chair under the knob. They consummated his confession in Wendy Doe's bed, and she fell asleep in his arms. Lizzie dreamed that he told her he loved her. She woke up in the dark, trapped beneath his weight, numb, tingling. He shifted off of her, kissed her, and it felt like a goodbye. His wife was waiting. "It won't always be like this," he whispered.

"What will it be?"

"Different. Better. I promise."

He kissed her again before he left. He loved her. Maybe it could be enough.

ALICE

Alice took the test, and the test confirmed. Benjamin Strauss was her father. Benjamin Strauss had inserted himself and his genetic material into her mother's body, when her mother was someone else. He had done so with her permission, or he had done so without. He had known she was carrying his baby, or he had not. Alice would have to content herself with the either/or, because fact was out of reach. She did not want a new family, a stepmother, a half sister; she wanted her father back, and her mother. But she was not her mother. She would not refuse a reality simply because it was one she did not want.

Elizabeth had speculated that Alice's mother was trying to protect her—that Wendy Doe had wanted the baby but couldn't find a way to love it. An adoption, of sorts, for the good of the child. Alice thought this sounded like her mother. Not Wendy Doe, but Karen Clark, the mother she had known, who had lied to her, then disappeared. She believed her mother had been trying to protect her. She believed, tried to believe, that her mother had wanted her, but even if this was true, her mother was still gone.

Her father was not her father. Her father was a dead man she would never know and never want to. The man she wanted to be her father had claimed her as his own. He loved her as his own, but that was before she knew she was not. Alice thought it might be harder for him, now that he could no longer pretend. He was a mild man, but he was stubborn in defense of what he believed to be right. He had once hit a deer, then sat on the side of the road beside its bloody wreckage until it died, because no one should have to die alone.

Her mother was still gone.

She left Philadelphia. She watched clouds swallow the skyline, reclined her seat, stretched out in the extra legroom she'd acquired on Elizabeth's pity dime. She didn't tell her father she was coming home and she wasn't yet, exactly. She used her stolen camera to take pictures of the mountains as they came into view, then left it behind on the seat when she got off the plane. No one noticed. No one was watching. This no longer felt like a threat. She was almost ready to go home, to face her father, to begin again as a family of two. She was almost ready to find out who she was going to be without her mother. But not yet. First she went to the cemetery, where she had never been. It was time to visit her mother.

She'd expected to feel something, standing over the grave. Here was her mother's name, carved into marble. Here were dates, her first and last. No body, but that didn't matter; wherever the body was, Alice knew, her mother was no longer in it. In another kind of story, her mother would be lurking in the graveyard shadows, haunting her faked death, and upon Alice's arrival would finally succumb to temptation and reveal herself. This was Alice's story: her mother was not coming back.

Alice knew this, too: her mother's life was not defined by its end, any more than Alice's life was defined by its beginning. The eighteen years in between, eighteen years of care and caretaking—these were not stories or suppositions, these were facts. The fact that her mother eventually left couldn't invalidate the eighteen years that she'd stayed.

She'd chosen a stone from the woods behind the Meadowlark. It was the color of a burnt sienna crayon, smoothed to a shine. Alice rubbed a thumb over its surface, then set it on the gravestone. Elizabeth had said this was how Jews mourned their dead. She felt a little silly and a little sacred.

"So? You tell me. What am I supposed to do now?"

She wondered if she should wait for a sign, something to prove her mother was watching. She searched herself for the faith that her mother, that anyone, was watching, came up empty, and found that she did not mind. The sky was clear, and so much bigger here. She'd forgotten that. She'd forgotten also the smell of the columbine, the cool, clean comfort of peaks on the horizon, proof the world was more than traffic and plastic and pain. She'd forgotten the sharp taste of cold, the way snow made everything new. The way her mother would always button Alice's jacket up to the top, wrap a wool scarf tight around her nose and mouth, insist on a second pair of socks, gauge carefully her daughter's readiness to battle a cold world, then kiss her forehead in benediction, say okay, you're ready to go. Now, she remembered.

ELIZABETH

Gwen looked old. Unlike herself, but still familiar—like her mother, I realized, and felt lighter imagining the look on her face if I said so. Except this was a new Gwen, who might by now have deemed her mother beautiful. It sat heavy again: she was a stranger.

The Wok, on the other hand, looked precisely the same. Low-lit and grimy, air thick with fried delight. The strip mall was located precisely between our two childhood homes, just close enough that once we were allowed to roam semifree, we could rendezvous there, lock bikes to lamppost, pool babysitting spoils for a steaming plate of beef lo mein and an extra-large wonton soup. We didn't actually like the food there; no one actually liked the food at the Wok, but the price was right, the ritual comforting, and Gwen's parents loathed it just enough to make each visit a small rebellion. Small was the only kind of rebellion either of us ever dared.

I'd saved every fortune, pasting each strip into an album expressly for that purpose. It gave Gwen a reliable opportunity to mock, another Wok perk. It's not like they'll give you your money back if it doesn't come true, she would say, and I wouldn't explain that I wasn't preserving the future, I was preserving us. If I had, she would have shrugged. The past wasn't real for Gwen; I was its designated keeper, while she was charged with dragging me, clingy and reluctant, one day at a time into the future.

I ordered the lo mein and she ordered the soup, as ever. We shared.

"I was glad you called," she said. "I've been wanting to reach out, but . . . it didn't seem like my place."

I thanked her for coming to the funeral, and for the card she'd sent in its wake. She asked polite questions about the house, the Meadowlark, my mother; I asked about Charlotte's plans for after college and Andy's new business. It was polite and it was excruciating.

Then she made a noise between groan and shriek that I remembered from her tennis days, the agony of missing a serve. "I'm fucking sorry, Lizzie."

"For what?"

"For being an asshole twenty years ago. For letting twenty years go by. For not, I don't know. *Doing* anything after he died."

"What were you supposed do?"

"How about fucking *something*?" Gwen said, and I knew then how little we had both changed.

I told her that if she'd caught me a month before, I would have eagerly accepted the apology and presumed it deserved. But that after all these years of thinking she was indeed shitty—that I was the flattened roadkill, she the one at the wheel—I'd recently been reminded the past came in different versions, and I no longer had much faith in the infallibility of mine.

"Midlife crisis therapy? You, too?"

"More like, catastrophe?"

"God, I'm so sorry, again, losing him, I just can't imagine—"

"No, not that. I don't want . . . I want to talk about us. What happened back then with us. Will you tell me? Your side of the story?"

"Lizzie, it's forever ago. Can't we just agree we're both sorry and get on with it?"

"Please."

She told me our story. In her version, I was not the protagonist. Her story was the story of a young mother trying to keep a baby and marriage alive. Back pain, breast pain. Never alone, because always the baby, grabbing, feeding, shitting, crying, wanting; always alone. Also, in love, swamped by inchoate joy, unable to speak of it, unable to speak of anything else. Finding time to shower: a gift. To sit on a toilet uninterrupted: a rare and miraculous blessing. Her husband pawing at her in bed, impatient, as if she could ever again fathom inviting friction and rub, the pleasure of pain. She knows her body differently now. It is fortress; it is food; it is earth mother goddess warrior queen; it is nothing that belongs to him. He stops pawing. She lies awake in the dark, imagining fires and car crashes and rape-murders and nuclear holocausts, all the ways her child will die. She touches herself gently, tries to carry herself to sleep. While all the while, the best friend, the one person definitionally supposed to understand, won't even try to understand. Talks endlessly about the sex she is or is not having. Is having said sex with a man who no longer desires his wife, now that his wife is a mother. Occasionally remembers to ask about the baby, about whom she plainly gives no shits. Keeps secrets. Exactly like the husband: rebuffed once too often, reciprocates by pill bugging into a tight ball; if you don't need me, I don't need you. No one sees how much the mother does need, or would, if she had the energy to do so. "I was just worried about you, and it felt like you were punishing me."

"I was an asshole." Then I was crying, in the middle of the Wok. It wouldn't be the first time.

"Well, then I basically told you I hated the guy you were going to marry. We might be even?"

I let it stand, but we were not even. I could see it now: I'd walked away from her because I was too weak to walk away from him. Without her to witness it, I could pretend I was strong.

I told her everything about Alice and her parents, the real ones. I told her about Alice leaving, and how quiet the house was with her gone. I'd dreaded her saying, after all these years, I told you so—but I couldn't have blamed her. Gwen had told me so. Gwen was the only one who knew that a different future had been possible, and I'd willingly picked this one.

"You regret it? Marrying him?"

"Can you regret your whole life?"

She told me she and Andy were separated. Nothing dramatic, nothing traitorous, just too much quiet between them with Charlotte gone. "So if it makes you feel better, my whole life is a cliché, too."

"I'm sorry. Am I sorry?"

"I don't know yet. I don't know . . . well, basically, anything, really."

"In that case, you're welcome."

"For what?"

"For living proof that there's someone's life more fucked up than yours."

"I can always count on you."

When we cracked open our fortune cookies, mine said *You are talented in many ways* and hers said *The object you desire will come to you*. Gwen handed it to me without asking. I tucked both into my wallet, because this was what we did. Does this mean we're friends again, she asked, before we drove home to our separate empty houses. We're something, I said, which seemed like progress.

Modernity is fracture. One century ago, we remade the world, broken. Tore apart the map of Europe. Portioned the brain into neurons, the stream of consciousness into discrete, synaptic spark. Monet and Seurat pestled beauty into blots of color; Flaubert and Rimbaud splintered the language of daily life. Cantor and Frege split infinity; Einstein and Bohr quantized light, time, space. Life divided itself into genetic material. Photography sliced memory into moment. This was the Western world into which hysteria and fugue were born. Women broke from their bodies; men broke from themselves; no one was surprised. Everything was falling apart. Nature's primal law: everything is always falling apart.

On an island off the coast of Maine, there is a house with no locks. There are neighbors made invisible by trees. There is the smell of the sea. There is a farmers' market in a shed, payment on the honor system. There is a lighthouse in the distance, keeping watch. There are no memories here for me.

Gwen and her husband bought the house years ago, when the island was a secret and the property cheap. In winters, it stands empty. Take it, she told me. As long as you need.

I wanted a place that would not feel like going backward. This place, this house and its rocky shore, has no past or future. Everything is sense and body—the reek of the mudflats, the freshness of pine, the weight of dark. Nina thought I was running away. I tried to explain that it was the opposite. Running to, rooting down—trading dissolution for reabsorption, in a place that refused boundaries, where I could be alone and remember how not to be lonely. Where I would stay as long as I needed, then no longer. She didn't understand, and this was fine; there's a luxury, I've discovered, in no longer having to explain myself.

In this house there is a pine desk, and I keep nothing on it but Benjamin's collection of first memories, which I now read, a little each day, like one might read the Bible. Interspersed with the first memories of everyone he knew are all the versions of his own, written, rewritten, its edges sanded and sharpened then blurred again. The scar on his father's lip that whitened with a smile. His hiding space beneath the dining table, bare knees raw against carpet. The taste of challah. The clatter of his mother in the kitchen. Sometimes he remembered the smell of soup, sometimes it was brisket. The memories chasing one another. His father's head bobbing with the music, his father's tears, his father's eyes closing as he willed himself back to a murdered past. Always the scientist, Benjamin noted the circumstances of each version of the memory, what had happened that day to spark the emergence of some new detail, how he was feeling about his career, his daughter, his life, his wife. There was no mention of Wendy Doe; there were no names, no confessions. But he wrote, *today I am feeling guilty, more than usual.* He wrote, *today I am wondering if I can ever be a better man.* He wrote, *today I remembered how to love her.*

It was a different flavor of grief, mourning the man I thought I'd loved. Finding a way to forgive myself for having loved him. Sometimes I read the memories aloud, like poetry. Sometimes I play his Bach. Sometimes I stream old episodes of the soap, which they say will be canceled soon, though I doubt it. This is the bedrock principle of the genre, the reason it is secretly the art most true to life: it continues. One day at a time, through love and betrayal, divorce and death, forgetting, transforming. There are no happy endings, no tragic ones. There is only what comes next.

Things fall apart, this is nature's law—but not its only one, Sam would remind me. Entropy breaks, conservation preserves. Continuity via radical transformation, the fluidity between states—matter that can change is never wholly lost.

On the island, there is one store. They call it The Store. There are men who make their living on summer lobster boats and spend winters in The Pub, telling and retelling the same beery fish tales. There is an infinite sea. Old women walk large dogs. On the island, everyone knows your name, or wants to. Everyone knows where you live, and who used to live there. No one wants to know too much. There is one hill. The beaches are made of rock, sea-smoothed boulders slick with algae and small, round stones. I collect sea glass. I imagine shipping our glass here—the wineglasses we gifted ourselves for our wedding, the grass-green dessert plates from a long-ago anniversary, the handblown menorah from Paris—and smashing it on the rocks, one by one by one. Broken pieces of us rubbed smooth by time and tide. On the island, children still ride in the back of pickup trucks. Groceries and mail arrive by ferry. It refuses to settle in my mind, that this is how people live. That here I am, living.

The ferry docks at three every afternoon, and most days I walk down to meet it. I wait through the unloading and the loading, the blast of the horn, and wave it goodbye when it goes. There is pleasure, there is power, in the choosing to be left, again, again, again. When the ferry's out of sight, I pick my way down the gravel path that opens to the sea, where I wait for the sun to fall. I still have too much of the suburbs in me; I'm still afraid of the dark. Less so, every night. I'm getting used to the stars. I breathe, listen to the lap of the tide, remind myself there is no danger here. That it is my choice, moment by moment, to be afraid. Moment by moment, I make myself endure, and some nights I'm still there, huddled on the shore, when the sky sings its inevitable dawn.

I was a scientist for a while, and picked things apart; I was a historian, in a fashion, and pieced things together; Benjamin thought I was a dilettante, and I believed him, but now I wonder. If the self and the past are both stories we tell ourselves, malleable and iterated, then maybe I've been working the same job all this time. Maybe I want more, and better, than I let myself imagine.

I want, finally, to write again—not about Benjamin or his Meadowlark, but about the building as it was before, and the women who haunt it. Women whose stories were mutated or erased by men who thought they knew better, women who were disappeared from their own lives. I have the asylum archives, along with the institute's files. Mariana saw to that on her way out—patient and personnel records, all the names of all the women in Benjamin's domain, and maybe I'll tell that story, their stories, too; maybe there's only the one.

I remember, more every day, how it felt to give myself to something so wholly—not a person, but a question—and every day, I think less about him, and more about the women, ghosts waiting for someone to hear them. I scour the files, I highlight, I note. I think, *find something here to love*, I think, yes, I will, I have.

ACKNOWLEDGMENTS

Writing a book always feels improbable, but this one often felt impossible—
and would have been without the wisdom and support of:

My literary agent, Meredith Kaffel Simonoff, whose determination
that this book belonged in the world persuaded me to prove her right.

My editor, Kathryn Belden, who helped me tease out a version of the
story I hadn't imagined possible before she got her hands on it.

The tireless teams at Scribner, CAA, and DeFiore and Company,
including: Michelle Weiner, Colin Farstad, Jacey Mitziga, Ashley Gilliam,
Nan Graham, Sally Howe, Jaya Miceli, Abigail Novak, and Kathleen
Rizzo.

Miranda Beverly-Whittemore, Holly Black, Sarah Rees Brennan,
Brendan Duffy, Kelly Link, Lydia Peelle, Anica Rissi, Lynn Strong, and
Lynn Weingarten, who read versions of the book, helped me navigate
plot labyrinths, and offered the kind of friendship and occasional sanity
checks no writer can do without.

Leslie Jamison and Adam Wilson, who read multiple drafts, talked
me through several revisions—not to mention off several ledges—and
have been more generous with their time and advice than seems possible.
They never stopped pushing me to make this book better, and it's largely
because of them that I found the confidence to try.

In an effort to make both the history and science in this book as accurate
as possible, I devoured more books and journal articles than I can list
here, but my understanding of fugue states and hysteria were especially
shaped by Ian Hacking's *Mad Travelers*, Elaine Showalter's *Hystories*, and

Asti Hustvedt's *Medical Muses*. The latter is a beautiful and unsettling biography of Charcot's three most famous subjects: Blanche, Geneviève, and, of course, Augustine. It was Douwe Draaisma, in *Forgetting: Myths, Perils, Compensations*, who introduced me to the idea of studying memory by studying forgetting—and who noted that the English language lacks a noun for the thing forgotten. William Everdell, in *The First Moderns*, originated the theory that modernity is fracture.

I'm very grateful to the historian Anne Harrington for her course on "Madness and Medicine," which I took twenty years ago and haven't stopped thinking about since. The spark for this book was lit in that lecture hall. I'm grateful also to Emily Goldman, who talked me through the mechanics and philosophy of musical fugues; to my graduate school adviser, M. Norton Wise, whose "hinge of temporality" theory I borrowed for my fictional historian of science—and finally, to Natalie Roher, for the rats.

ABOUT THE AUTHOR

Robin Wasserman is the author of *Girls on Fire*, an NPR and *BuzzFeed* best book of the year. She is a graduate of Harvard College with a master's in the history of science from UCLA. She lives in Los Angeles and teaches on the faculty of the Mountainview Low-Residency MFA Program.

BOOK CLUB FAVORITES
READER'S GUIDE

MOTHER DAUGHTER WIDOW WIFE

ROBIN WASSERMAN

This reading group guide for Mother Daughter Widow Wife includes an introduction, discussion questions, and ideas for enhancing your book club. The suggested questions are intended to help your reading group find new and interesting angles and topics for your discussion. We hope that these ideas will enrich your conversation and increase your enjoyment of the book.

INTRODUCTION

Exploring the intricacies of identity and memory, *Mother Daughter Widow Wife* is a powerful investigation of who, and what, a woman can become. A vivid examination of the iconic roles of mother, daughter, widow, and wife, this unforgettable novel traces the journey of a woman with no memory of her past—Wendy Doe, subject of experimental observation at the Meadlowlark Institute for Memory Research—the daughter she left behind, and the research assistant who becomes fascinated with her plight. A jaw-dropping, multivoiced journey of discovery, reckoning, and reclamation, *Mother Daughter Widow Wife* is an ambitious inquiry into selfhood by an expert and enthralling storyteller.

TOPICS & QUESTIONS FOR DISCUSSION

1. After dinner with her mother, Lizzie reflects on "how inessential she'd discovered herself to be" (17). What makes her feel inessential in this moment? Her mother, her childhood home? Leaving Los Angeles and her boyfriend? The thought of Wendy Doe?

2. Why does Alice decide to retrace her mother's steps?

3. Why does Elizabeth invite Alice to stay? What is she looking for, in Alice?

4. Describe the purpose of the chapters written from Wendy's point of view. Usually short on plot, what do they add to the story?

5. After an important conversation with Wendy, Lizzie theorizes that autobiographical memory forms the self. Do you agree or disagree?

6. Why does Wendy say she's not interested in discovering who she was before the fugue state? Do you believe her?

7. Describe the story of Augustine, as told by Elizabeth. Can you draw a connection between her life and Wendy's? Lizzie's?

8. Elizabeth says, "*History, like writing, is an exercise in decision making*" (104). What does she mean by this? How does this truism play out in her life?

9. The Meadowlark Institute occupies a great deal of space in this novel, serving as home and workplace to varying degrees for the women in its orbit. What's the relevance of the institute's history? Of its layout and location?

10. Why does Alice seek out Zach? What does she get from their encounters? How does his betrayal affect her?

11. Wendy is fascinated by people who can't stop remembering—twelve-step groups, survivor groups, PTSD support groups. Dr. Strauss calls her capacity to forget her "superpower." Do you think this is accurate? What does he mean by that?

12. Describe the beginning of Lizzie and Dr. Strauss's sexual relationship. Who initiates it? What changes between them? What stays the same?

13. Alice's father calls Wendy Doe a "symptom . . . Her mother was her mother" (260). How do you believe Wendy Doe fits into Karen Clark?

14. What are the dimensions of Mariana's relationship with Dr. Strauss? What did she do for him? What did she mean to him, and him to her?

15. How does the secret of Alice's parentage change your understanding of the characters, particularly Dr. Strauss?

16. How would you describe the relationship between Lizzie and Wendy? When Karen recovers her memory, what happens to that relationship?

17. Do you think Karen remembered any part of Wendy's experience? What's the role of baby Alice in this process?

18. At the end of the novel, what does Elizabeth decide? Does she move forward through remembrance or forgetting?

ENHANCE YOUR BOOK CLUB

1. Read Robin Wasserman's debut adult novel, *Girls on Fire*.

2. To learn more about Robin Wasserman and *Mother Daughter Widow Wife*, visit www.robinwasserman.com/.